By

NICK J SHINGLETON

MAPLE
PUBLISHERS

Godless

Author: Nick J Shingleton

Copyright © Nick J Shingleton (2021)

The right of Nick J Shingleton to be identified as author of this work has been asserted by the author in accordance with section 77 and 78 of the Copyright, Designs and Patents Act 1988.

First Published in 2021

ISBN 978-1-915164-08-7 (Paperback)
 978-1-915164-09-4 (Ebook)

Book cover design and Book layout by:
 White Magic Studios
 www.whitemagicstudios.co.uk

Published by:
 Maple Publishers
 1 Brunel Way,
 Slough,
 SL1 1FQ, UK
 www.maplepublishers.com

A CIP catalogue record for this title is available from the British Library.

All rights reserved. No part of this book may be reproduced or translated by any form or by any means, electronic or mechanical, including photocopying, recording or by any information storage and retrieval system without written permission from the author.

The views expressed in this work are solely those of the author and do not necessarily reflect the views of the publisher, and the publisher hereby disclaims any responsibility for them.

CONTENTS

Chapter One
Deman Circe, Kent, England

'Fornicator.'
'Thief.'
'Non-believer.'

One word scratched onto the forehead of each convict. The bodies limp from their own weight, as knees cracked and clothes ripped. The Marshal had tied two men and one woman to three crosses the previous morning, and they stood at the mouth of the sea defences, between the village of Deman Circe and the long sandy beach. In the moonlit night, their cries for 'Water,' or 'Food,' blended with the wind, and every day they moved a little closer to death. Birds had pecked their eyes out as flies buzzed around their wounds, attracted by the blood. And if the offenders survived this torture, the scars etched into their skin made their lawlessness public knowledge.

Winnie Harper gazed upon the prisoners in the light of the first quarter moon, as the easterly wind hissed and the crosses groaned. She stepped away from them, and perhaps, a couple of her own imagined wrongdoings.

Standing near to her little sister, Regan, as the ten-year-old girl played in the sand, singing.

The desolate beaches of Deman Circe stretched for miles. And between the scarecrows grew immense human totems, standing fifteen feet tall, with arms stuck out as if pleading for mercy. The grey pallid torsos, rotting legs, and hands - of men, women, and children - all tied to a great pole rose toward the sky, their faces contorted in a perverse mask of pain. Fresh bodies placed at the top pressed own the mushy middle section, and they crushed the rotten skeletons at the bottom. Crumbling the bones and scattering them to the prevailing winds. Any flesh was black and rotted, half-eaten by scavengers, who scurried over the cadavers, picking for food. And hands bore the distinctive M branded on their left palm. Malefactor. *Lawbreaker.*

It was no wonder outsiders rarely visited. They'd complain The Marsh was a sparsely populated area of wetland, with free-folk, who purchased bodies from the county gaol in Canteria and dotted them along the low sea walls. A mythology created to appease The Sinners, who had roamed the South-East coastline since the Guardians took power, and the first Guardian banished these phantoms to the seas.

Superstitious stories, Winnie thought. The Sinners did not exist, it was folklore told around the fire at night or in the pub, and parents would whisper tales of children being taken if their own misbehaved. Of boys or girls, who were stolen at the shoreline by these unseen spectres, and made to walk the beaches looking for the living to feed off. A half-baked legend, but Winnie kept away from the demonic structures, afraid a hand, half flesh, half bone, might reach out and grab her.

Winnie sighed as a thin layer of sand stuck to her face, and her ponytail thrashed around in the wind. She picked up her lamp, longing to go home and sit by the fire. To take off her heavy boots, and dry the scraggy old shawl, which gave her no protection from the drizzly rain. And most of all, Winnie wanted Regan, to stop singing.

'Misty mist here to stay

built so high, to save us all.

To keep death out, they cut us off,

and Britain will live whilst France will fall.

We have survived it, all because of that wall.'

Regan sang a nursery rhyme that was about the thick liquid barricade that The Guardians had constructed six years earlier blocking France from Britain. Winnie was familiar with the impenetrable barrier, as was every person who lived on the South coast. On a clear night, before they built the Barricade, Winnie could see the distant lights of France and imagined the lives of the people there. She'd pretend there was a handsome Frenchman looking out to the English shore, maybe looking for her. The Red Plague had reached its peak by the time it hit France, but the Guardians still built their wall, and Winnie's memories of those lights had died, probably like the people in the French villages.

The seagrass continued whistling as the wind blew them in every direction. Winnie stomped her feet, wishing they would stop. The Legend said the seagrass spoke to The Sinners, telling the ghostly apparitions that people were on the beach collecting washed-up barrel jellyfish.

Regan stopped singing. 'I can't see Mummy or Calum.'

Winnie stepped forward. Regan was right, the light from their lamp was gone. 'Mother, Nell!' she cried out, sending the seagulls squawking into the charcoal sky.

'Winnie,' her mother's voice shrilled out of the dark.

'What's wrong?' Regan frowned. She shivered, the drizzle soaking her.

'Take this and keep it high.' Winnie thrust the lamp into Regan's hand. The wind blew sand and she squinted, seeing only a blur.

The woman staggered into sight. Winnie reached Nell, her mother, as she dropped to the sand, with Calum, Winnie's nine-year-old brother, lifeless in her arms. Winnie grabbed the boy and checked for a pulse. It was faint but there. She struggled, picking the boy up and turned toward Regan, who swung the lamp.

Winnie ran, aware it might be too late, but she had to get home. Her boots boomed on the wooden planks that led up to the road, crushing the scattered scallop shells.

'Stay with me, Calum,' Winnie muttered, rushing past the broken down cottages and the decrepit pub, toward their home, at the end of the alley. Winnie almost dropped Calum as she tried but failed to open the door. Nell and Regan caught up, flinging the door open. Winnie plonked her brother onto the hard wooden table, and heaved, catching her breath. She stepped back, eyes wide, looking at Calum's arm. It was turning grey, creeping up from his fingertips and into his forearm. The Sinners were real. Soon the grey would cover his body. And the stories Winnie eagerly dismissed as lies would now kill her little brother.

'Where's Da?' Regan whispered, standing by the door.

'In the pub, with Uncle Landers,' Winnie snapped, scrabbling around in the dark, looking for candles, with only the kitchen fire to guide her. She found them and struck the matches. So much for coming home.

'He got lost, I called for him....' Nell wiped her runny nose, '... I didn't think they were real. You always said they were just stories, *Winnie*... but I heard them, The Sinners... they'd already... touched him.' Nell burst into tears, sinking to her knees.

'Did they touch you?' Winnie asked.

'What?'

'Did they touch you?'

'We need Uncle Landers.' Nell looked to Regan.

'We don't need him. The priest can't do anything, might as well stay in the pub with Da,' snapped Winnie.

Regan ignored her sister. She ran out into the night, leaving the door wide open. Winnie closed the door and stared at the wood, gazing at the cracks because she didn't want to admit, her brother was dying.

Winnie turned, facing Nell. 'Ma, there's nothing we can do. We need to prepare him for his journey into the Farscape.'

'We wait for Landers –'

'No. We have to do it.' Winnie scraped a chair across the stone floor, ordering Nell to sit with Calum.

She searched around the sparse kitchen, looking for the Clannen dolls. Calum enjoyed playing with the small religious figures, but he could have hidden them anywhere in the cramped two-storey cottage. Winnie opened the cupboards, throwing pots and pans on the floor, as she hunted for the dolls. Even the two dead rabbits strung up at the window did not escape Winnie's gaze. Where would he have put them? She paused, and only her mother's sobbing broke the silence.

The dolls would be all together, somewhere in the cottage. Somebody whispered in her ear. It told her the dolls were in the bedroom. Winnie shook her head, ignoring the voice, but it carried on.

She relented, and clambered up the small staircase, heavy boots banging. They wouldn't be under the bed he shared with Regan, because he liked to squirrel away his few belongings under Winnie's bed, so she looked under her own. Calum would hide under Winnie's bed, especially if Da had threatened him with the belt. The dolls were in their bag, and Winnie grabbed them, rushing back.

Winnie took five candles, placing them at each corner of the table, before lighting them. She asked Nell to move because she couldn't be in the square once the final candle was lit.

Winnie placed two dolls near Calum's shoulders, one at his feet and the third she held. She shouldn't be doing this. It went against the law of the Guardians, to have a woman use the Clannen Dolls, but Calum was grey, and once it infected his face, it would be too late. Calum would become a Sinner, stealing the living to feed.

Winnie sweated. She felt the moisture down her back, as her hands trembled. She kneeled at the bottom of the table, clasping the doll. 'Mother, Father, I speak for this child, protect him from the darkness coming for him. I've no right to ask, but *please* protect my little brother. Let him walk with you in the light.' Not the words spoken by a priest, but they sounded right.

The doll shook inside her hand. It rattled and Winnie wanted to set it free, but a priest never did this, and she kept her hands tight. A light sparked out of her fingers, Winnie kneeled at the bottom of the table. Nell's raised eyebrow said, *'You shouldn't be doing that.'*

The cottage walls closed in on Winnie, and her pulse quickened. The voice inside her head spoke. Was it the dolls talking or her inner whispers? It told Winnie to approach Calum and lay her hand on his leg.

'Touch the boy, if you want to save him.' She resisted, and the light inside her hands became brighter, as if angry, and Winnie shuffled to the table.

'What are you doing?' Nell backed away.

'I don't know,' she whispered.

The voice repeated that she must touch Calum, and Winnie's heart thumped. She was scared that if she did so, she would join her brother and become a Sinner. Or save him and take his place instead. And her hand lingered over his leg.

The whispering gathered pace, demanding her touch. Winnie looked at her mother. Would Nell stop her? Winnie grabbed his tiny legs, wrapping her fingers around his trousers.

A boom shook the tiny cottage as Winnie connected with Calum and an extraordinary light burst from his body. Nell shielded her eyes, screaming, but Winnie held onto Calum's legs. The grey seeped out of Calum and into Winnie. Her body juddered, and she was outside of herself, watching the strange event. The grey crawled up her fingertips and into her arms.

'Let go,' Winnie yelled to herself, but her body ignored her. The light exploded, and the spiritual rope connecting her to her physical body sprang back. The force knocked her off her feet and into the wall. A sound cracked in her neck and she fell to the ground. The last thing Winnie saw was Regan running through the door with her father and the priest, and then she heard her little brother speak.

'Mummy,' the little boy croaked.

***

Stickiness covered Winnie, gluing her to the ground. The sensation sucked into her body. Her skin prickled, as the watery feeling seeped into her muscle, down to her core. It tickled her bones, like a delicate finger caressing her skeleton.

Winnie's eye sockets itched. It moved through her face, reaching down inside her. It twisted and knotted around her bones, burrowing its way into her marrow, to wake her and make her understand.

She coughed, opening her eyes. All Winnie saw was black. She scrabbled about, and the air suffocated as if it was cocooning her. 'Mummy,' Winnie whimpered. She might be a girl, a woman, of twenty-three seasons, but right now she wanted to hear her mother's voice.

'Winnifred,' a small voice whispered.

A flame burst into life and she sat up. She was not at home, and she did not recognise the voice. 'Who's there?' Her eyes darted around the darkness. Something was different. Everything was damp as if her movement changed the atmosphere.

The voice said, 'We've been calling, and you came.'

'I... I don't understand.'

Something touched her hair. She jumped as it placed its hand onto her shoulder, breathing into her ear. 'Let me show you,' the voice whispered.

Chapter Two
Bononia-Sur-Mer, Northern France

Helena's new buck teeth gleamed. They contrasted the old stained ones in her mouth, reminding Bee of a decaying rabbit. Bee waited behind the bar for Helena to order her ale, but the woman said nothing, and Bee rubbed her forehead as the creeping headache she'd had since last night wasn't getting any better. The pain stabbed behind her eyes. Bee knew it wasn't a headache, it was something else, something she'd buried long ago. And now it was waking up.

Tapping her fingers on the dirty bar, Bee glanced around the old tavern and out of the window, ignoring the eight patrons who sat drinking. The early evening sun shone through, revealing the threadbare carpets and grime which covered the glass and most of The Raven, no matter how much Bee had cleaned the place.

'There's something different about you,' Bee said, mesmerised by the white teeth that took her mind off the pain inside her head.

Helena wiped the palm of her hands on the pleats of her full dress. She hissed, 'Fuck off Anglo, and give me a beer.' Her well-spoken French accent laced inside every English word, and she slurred, having already consumed three beers. She slammed two coins on the bar, lighting her cigarillo, blowing the smoke in Bee's direction.

The new hiss to Helena's acid tones amused Bee. She grabbed a jug, opened the tap and poured the brown hoppy liquid into the tankard, sloshing it onto the bar. Helena dropped her cigarillo onto the threadbare floor, stomping on it. Gulping the beer, she wiped her mouth with her sleeve, demanding another.

Helena Berger was a survivor of the Red Plague, which had claimed more than half of the world's population. The woman was a grubby figure, but Bee remembered her as a beautiful young woman, well-spoken, who did not drink. She had lost her husband and children to the virus and started drinking. Helena spent most of her time with the little money she had, in the taverns.

She was younger than Bee, but Bee couldn't tell anymore. The thick brown hair was dirty, the face pitted, and the epidermis around her neck was being eaten by the last traces of the virus, giving her the appearance of being half dead. Helena covered it with skin bought from the apothecary and she'd sewn it unevenly into her flesh.

'Are those teeth whiter than the rest?' Bee asked.

Helena smiled, running her tongue over the false teeth. 'A new batch came from over the Channel. Any part you might need.' More coins dropped onto the bar, and Helena licked her teeth. 'The plague spared you, didn't it? Bagged yourself a grieving widower, and Malick got an English *lady* to warm his bed.'

Bee gritted her teeth, and the pain inside spread. 'The apothecary must be thriving.'

'They might even have enough skin to cover that Chelchith Smile of yours. Make the whore pretty for her husband.' Helena slurped her beer, snorting.

Bee curled her fists, ignoring Helena's remark. She was familiar with the nasty comments. They were the same every time Helena came into the alehouse. 'You're more than welcome to drink elsewhere, Helena.' She pulled at the buckle of her black cuff bracelet, pinching it to calm her. Bee's headache was crippling, and she wanted to reach over the bar and strangle the woman, but killing customers wasn't good for business.

Helena scratched an open wound on her cheek and sniffed her fingers. 'This place suits me, just fine.'

Bee raised her eyebrows. The bar was a filthy hovel, with faded paintings hanging from the stained walls, tables pilfered from places left empty after the plague. The place did remind Bee of Helena.

Bee's husband, Malick Rose, had acquired 'The Raven' over five seasons ago. One of six alehouses in Bononia, Bee had tried making the place pleasant, using old thick curtains, but she soon learned the locals didn't care about the décor. They just wanted somewhere to drink.

'Besides, I enjoy the conversation here, even if a trollop is behind the bar,' Helena carried on.

Bee kept quiet, pouring the third beer. She slammed the jug onto the bar, ignoring Helena's cackles of 'Witch' under her breath. Bee put her hand out for payment, snatching the money from Helena.

The woman shuffled into the corner. The tatty red dress dragged along and Helena's moth-eaten shawl fell down, exposing freshly sewn skin attached into her shoulder. She sat with Rolfe and Bernard, two survivors, both equally scabby. They gossiped, chattering in French. The English rulers had outlawed French more than a hundred years ago, but since the wall cut them off, those who remembered how to speak it blatantly used it.

Bee pinched the bridge of her nose. She inhaled, hoping she could control what was about to come. She'd meditated before arriving at the tavern, but that only held it off, it was going to explode. It was pushing Bee, whispering, that the time was now.

She wiped down the bar, fuming. The locals had called her witch and other things, since the day she arrived. Bee, as far as everybody thought, caused the blockade between France and England.

The trouble was, they were right. Bee was a part of the reason for The Barricade. She had accepted Malick Rose's hand in marriage, two months after his wife, Nadine, died from the plague. He'd offered protection in wedlock, and she took it. Malick was a gentle man who rarely raised his voice, took care of his family and didn't mind the strange, unsettling smile Bee's scars created. Having rinsed the beakers, Bee placed them on the drainer, as a wave of nausea swept over her.

The door burst open and Aimee bounced in, loosening her cloak before placing it on a wall hook beside the bar. Her tight brown dress showed off her figure. Gerald, her husband, followed, carrying three heavy bags. He walked around behind the bar, pushing back the thick curtain and disappeared. Aimee and Gerald boarded in the tavern, they had free lodgings and it meant Malick always had somebody on the property.

'Sorry I'm late, Bee. Gerald ended up buying me the most wonderful shoes.' Aimee came behind the bar, kissing Bee on both cheeks. 'How are you, have I missed anything?' Her French accent was much weaker than Helena's.

Bee glanced over to the table, spying her customers watching her. 'Somebody has new teeth, and she's drunk again.'

Aimee looked over. 'Well, they're just lovely.' She stifled a giggle, pushing Bee to the other side of the bar.

'Three more beers, witch!' Helena shouted from her table, and Rolfe and Bernard smiled.

Aimee poured and lined them up on the bar, she spotted Bee stick her fingers into the three beers, and grabbed Bee's wrist. 'Just ignore her, Bedelia.'

Bee's head banged, like fists beating against her skull. It was coming, and there was nothing she could do to stop it. Gingerly, Bee nodded, and then slopped the beers onto the table. Neither Rolfe nor Bernard looked, avoiding Bee, as she held out her hand for payment.

Helena placed the money on the table. 'There we go, trollop.'

Bee bit her lip, and the headache split her skull. Sliding the money off the table, she said coldly, 'Call me trollop all you want, Helena, but I wasn't the cunt *fucking* Malick until Nadine was three months pregnant, was I?'

Bernard and Rolfe coughed on their beers, and froth went over the table. The entire pub was silent, all looking toward the pair. Bee stared as the pieces of Helena's surviving skin turned red, and the woman said nothing.

Malick had been honest with Bee when they first got married, about his liaisons during his marriage to Nadine.

She saw the guilt in his face and thought nothing more of it because it didn't affect her. Bee had listened to Helena's taunts for years, and she'd had enough, as the banging inside her head got louder. She walked away from Helena, knowing all three of them sat, dumbstruck.

'You'd better go. You know Mr Rose doesn't want you walking home in the dark.' Aimee kept her eyes to the ground, embarrassed. She'd never heard Bee swear.

'Thank you, Aimee.' Bee fetched her black leather coat from the hook. She pulled it on, the leather reaching down to her shins. Then, her abdomen erupted, like a knife stabbing inside. She buckled, crying, and held the bar to keep standing.

'Bedelia,' Aimee squealed. 'Are you unwell?'

Bee's head swam in distinctive reds and blacks. Her body got hotter, her hands shook. Powers Bee had buried wanted to resurface. She pushed them deep down inside. It was like she had overeaten and was forcing more down. Bee closed her eyes, trying to bury it. And then it was gone.

'Shall I send for Mr Rose?' Aimee looked at the patrons. They wouldn't help. Instead, she called for Gerald.

'No,' Bee hissed, heading outside. The colours dissipated, leaving her mind cloudy. This wasn't right, her abilities shouldn't be returning.

***

The walk home hadn't cleared Bee's head, and she forgot about Helena because Bee had more pressing worries. She'd squashed her abilities back inside and little beads of sweat ran down her forehead, as Bee bit her nails wondering what might come next.

The gate creaked as she swung it open, and Bee looked at the sizable four-bedroom house. During her six-year marriage to Malick, she'd watched the climbing vines inch up the walls of the house, circling first the ground-floor windows, but now they reached high enough to start at the top bedroom.

The front of the house was dark, as everybody would be in the kitchen. The broken shutters all pulled and secured, and every night, Esther closed them, because even on a lovely September evening, there was always a draft in the house. Bee didn't know if the cause was the few missing roof slates, but they couldn't afford to fix it, and she didn't care. This house was a palace, and Bee loved it.

Letting out a sigh, a name sprang to her mind, Oren. Bee hadn't thought about him or his family in a long time. She'd blocked them out, relieved never to see them again now she lived in France. She'd lived periodically with him and his wife, Leena, when Bee was twenty-two and placed in Lunden Tower. She shuddered, thinking about the man. Bee leaned against the front door, breathing heavily, trying to stop the bile rising in her throat.

And then she thought about Luther.

Theirs was a relationship born in fury. She'd known Luther since she was eight years old, and they knew every inch each other, coexisting. Sometimes it was if they were one person, and while Bee blocked out Oren and Leena, she could never block out Luther. That bond was indestructible, and Bee never wanted it to break. What she wanted was to have him here in France, but it was too painful for Bee to think about, and she kept Luther a secret.

Once inside the house, Bee pushed Oren and Leena from her mind. Glad to be home, she hung the coat on its hook and Tristan rushed down the dim hallway to hug her legs.

'Mamma,' Tristan cried, holding his arms up.

Bee picked up the boy, and sat on the bottom of the stairs, her arms wrapped around him, ruffling his long blonde hair. It needed a good cut, but Malick liked it long, and Tristan chattered, telling Bee about his day with Aunty Esther.

'Have you grown today?' Bee asked.

'No, Mamma,' he giggled.

She played with his hair. 'I think you will be tall like your father.' And his face lit up as Bee spoke about Malick. 'And when you're seven, you might be as tall as me,' she tickled his tummy. His laughter sent little shivers of pleasure down her spine.

'I'm sorry, Bedelia, I thought he was still in the garden.' Malick's niece, Esther, rushed from the kitchen, shooing Tristan back. 'Uncle Malick's in his study. He has guests.' Esther was one of the lucky few who did not contract the virus. She was twenty-one, with healthy skin and thick brown hair. She took out her matchbox and lit the candles.

'What about Viola?' Bee asked, taking the matches out of Esther's hand. 'I'll do that.'

'Asleep. Tristan tired her out,' Esther said, heading back into the kitchen.

Bee paused. She wanted to see Malick but knew better not to interrupt when he had company. She headed into the dark corridor, toward his study, her boots quiet on the carpet, and she lit the first and second candle, then Bee struck a new match.

20

Something, a flash of a face in the dim, burst before her, so fleeting, so quick, she dropped the match, gasping at what she thought she'd seen. Bee peered down the corridor, but there was nobody there. Leaning against the wall, eyes closed, she wanted to forget that face, not wanting it, or any of them here. Bee's mind sprang back, hearing Malick's strong French accent through the door.

'...the Juna's a legitimate business ship, you ruined it when you got involved with Omega.'

'Look,' snapped Somer. 'We've had this conversation before, we can't back out.'

Another voice joined in. This was Teppo. 'It's good money, Malick, and those Skin Traders gave us no choice. You know what Omega will do if you back out.'

Bee recognised Somer Peron's harsh voice. Malick's best friend and his twin, Teppo, were always together. They were the brothers of Malick's first wife, Nadine, and Bee leaned against the wall, remembering how ill Nadine had become before she passed away.

Bee had come from the general store and found Nadine collapsed in the kitchen. She complained of a headache and had a rash around her neck. This was the first sign of infection. Bee took her to bed, and Nadine insisted on going to the spare servants' quarters, next to Bee's room. Bee recognised the fear, and held Nadine's hand, promising she would look after her.

Eight days later, Malick was on the verge of selling the Juna to pay for Nadine's medicines when Bee found him in his study. A gas lamp lit up the room, and the ledgers were opened at his desk. He stared at the wall fiddling with Nadine's Clannen Dolls.

Bee placed a cup of tea on the desk as Malick asked after Nadine. Bee stayed in the shadows, watching Malick study the tiny figures, his face red and puffy from where he'd been crying, and he waited for an answer.

'Do not sell your boat, Mr Rose,' she whispered. 'You and Esther need to prepare yourselves that Madame Rose doesn't have long.'

Malick crumpled in his chair, saying, 'Then I'll sell the Juna, I can get more medicines for –'

'It won't make any difference, sir.'

'Come into the light, Bedelia, let me see your face when you tell me why I shouldn't sell my boat.' He beckoned her.

Bee stepped before the desk. She explained, 'Your boat is worthless, nobody is sailing and you'll make pittance by scrapping it. No medicines have worked, and if you buy more, Nadine will still die.'

Malick's eyes glistened, a tear rolled down his cheek. 'I have to save her.'

'Think about your son, and Esther, Mr Rose. You need an income to support them when the plague goes, and if you sell that boat, you have nothing.'

Malick shook his head, looking down at the Clannen dolls. 'I've been a terrible husband. I'd have thought the Guardians would've protected somebody like her. She's the believer, not me. Perhaps Priest Felix is right,' he continued solemnly. 'Perhaps this curse has come from the Guardians themselves. Maybe we angered them.'

Bee stepped closer. 'Your priest spreads lies, telling people to pray, to repent, and it may save them from the Red Plague. This plague was not sent by the Guardians. Those European Guardians weren't immune. Only Eldric and those in the Upper countries have survived.

'And what did they do? They put a Barricade up, stopping the virus entering their lands, leaving people to die. So don't, Mr Rose, put your faith in those trinkets because they won't help.'

Malick clenched his jaw, and then he shouted, 'I can't just let her die, Bedelia.'

Bee said bluntly, 'Mr Rose, Nadine's internal organs are failing. Her skin is being eaten, and she throws up the black blood. She doesn't have long, and no medicine or money will stop that.'

He slouched back into his chair, and Bee's heart raced, worried she'd spoken too plainly. The pain etched into Malick's face, was a look that he'd worn since Nadine had first become ill. She stepped back into the shadows, preparing to leave the study.

'Sir, I don't know what kind of husband you are, but you should make amends before it is too late,' she said.

'Bedelia, you are brutal in your honesty, have you lost somebody to it?' he asked.

Bee remained hidden in the darkness. She paused, and then said, 'No, sir, I have not.'

Malick huffed, 'Then what makes you an expert?'

Bee gripped hold of the door handle, and she said gently, 'Because I know death, Mr Rose.' And Bee left the study. Nadine passed away the next evening and Bee remained in the shadows.

'We're not bloody Flesh Finders.' Malick sounded angry, and his voice brought Bee back. 'For fuck's sake, they're murdering people. Don't you see anything wrong with that?'

Malick rarely sailed now, leaving it to Teppo and Somer to run the daily business of import and export, and as Bee listened, she understood the twins were smuggling people through the Crack.

'You helped us offload those people,' Somer carried on.

'You gave me no choice,' Malick snapped.

'Baptiste has made it perfectly clear what he'll do to us, including Bee and the children if we don't carry on,' Somer reminded him. 'You don't want to fuck with these Skin Traders.'

Skin Traders were a recent addition to the bandits, robbers and highwaymen now roaming France. Customers kept quiet when Bee was behind the bar, but there were whispers of them being some kind of slave traders. Straining to overhear the conversation, she held a match ready to light if the door opened.

'Better them than us,' Somer argued.

Teppo said, 'We've made more money in the last five months than we did all of last year. Omega's deal is simple. We carry on... or...'

There was silence, and then Malick said, 'fucking hell.'

Bee's hands shook as she lit the remaining candles. There was Crack? Had Malick got involved in something dangerous? He'd been quiet over the last couple of months, brooding alone in his study, and when she'd asked questions, he'd say everything was fine. Bee considered what Skin Traders were, nobody talked about it in front of her, but Bee had a good idea what it meant.

Heading to the kitchen, the aromas hit Bee. Garlic, rosemary and thyme filtered up through two blackened pots. The fireplace dominated the kitchen, and Esther stood over one of them, stirring. Kitchen tools hung around the fire and surrounding walls, Malick had driven in hooks for the cook when Nadine was alive, and hidden to the side was a small metal door, for the bread oven.

Bee didn't notice the oak table set for six people, as she watched Tristan through the window. He tried to manoeuvre the chickens back into their pens, and they clucked, scattering, as Tristan chased one. It was one chore his father had given him, to teach responsibilities. Bee counted to ten, watching the mayhem outside, but she needed the distraction.

Viola grumbled in her cot. It woke Bee from her daydream and she checked on her daughter. Bee tingled inside, smiling, as Viola grasped her finger, and the baby carried on sleeping through Esther's clanking of the pots.

Bee desperately wanted to hold Viola, smell her, but she busied herself around the kitchen by doing nothing. She settled on staring out of the window, scratching her scars, and watching Tristan.

'Have you had a good day, Bee?'

She didn't hear, focused on Tristan, grabbing the last chicken and putting it in the coop. He stopped and waved, and Bee did the same. Thinking, why was The Barricade cracking? It wouldn't bring anything good.

Esther watched Bee touch her face. 'I asked how your day was.'

'Sorry, I was miles away,' she lied. 'What's for supper?'

'Boiled lamb, and we've guests tonight.' Malick's gruff French voice boomed from the hall. Behind him came Somer and Teppo Peron. Both big bulky men, with tied-back brown hair, in their late-thirties, a few years older than Malick, and both had survived the plague.

Bee's heart sank, but she asked the men to take a seat, getting a bottle of wine out of the pantry, and plonking it before Malick with five glasses for him to serve. She gave Malick a kiss and a sympathetic smile. There was a heaviness in his expression, and Bee wished they were alone.

'Are you okay, Malick?' She brushed his dark hair out of his face.

Malick nodded, 'And you?'

'Yes, yes, I'm fine.' She scratched her cheek scar, and Malick's half-smile darkened, but he said nothing, pouring the wine. His hawkish eyes bored into her. She always knew when he was watching, and Bee kept her back to the group, putting dirty utensils into the sink.

'Dinner's ready.' Esther had already dished up the meat into mismatched bowls and placed the first two before the guests. They thanked her and sat waiting for everybody to join them at the table.

Bee checked her window reflection and didn't like it. She smartened her shirt up, and turned back to Malick, giving him a terse smile. He nodded, pointing for Bee to take the seat at the other end. Tristan sat on one side of Bee, and Somer opposite Tristan. Esther finished serving and sat near Malick, opposite Teppo.

'Shall we give Thanks to the Guardians?' Esther held her hands to Malick and Somer. Everybody held hands, except Bee. She never gave Thanks, and the people at the table knew better than to ask.

Malick held his niece's hand, but he said nothing. Bee and Malick watched each other, as both kept their secrets.

Bee wanted the evening to be over, wanting the twins out of the house, so she could speak with Malick. Esther finished the Thanks, and the family began dishing up various foods onto their plates.

'Was it busy at the tavern?' asked Malick, and taking his knife and fork, he started eating.

'Not really.' Bee didn't want to talk, but the group focused on her. Taking her cutlery, she said, 'the usual customers, Helena being polite as ever.'

Malick was about to ask her something else when Tristan asked Bee to help him cut up his lamb, as Teppo and Somer started chatting, and Esther joined in.

Bee concentrated on Tristan. She listened to the conversation and chipped in politely, but her mind swelled. This differed from the tavern. A feeling Bee knew well, a childhood memory, of when They came and taught her how to hide these abilities, making it trickle like an underground stream, and that she controlled the powers and not the other way around.

These Spectres returned before Bee left for the Tower, revealing the devastation she could cause because she had never been shackled. She didn't think they'd find her in France. She thought she'd escaped, and everything became a little clogged up, as the Spectres now invaded her home. A woozy nostalgia began in her stomach, creeping up, and Bee was alone in the kitchen, as everybody, including Malick, carried on their conversations, unaware of the presence.

Breathing in, Bee watched, hearing snippets of words, and taking hold of her knife and fork, she cut into the lamb. Slow and concentrated, that was all she could do. The Spectres surrounded the table, three of them dressed in clothing unknown to Bee. One stood behind Malick, the other two on either side. She kept her head down, eating, ignoring the laughter and the chat, pretending the Spectres were not in the kitchen.

'Bee, I asked if you were okay?'

Malick's voice cut through Bee's inner fog. She sprang to attention, up from the carrots and meat, as everybody at the table stared. Giving a meek smile, Bee nodded, but the Spectres still stood in the room.

Teppo asked Tristan a cheeky question, the boy giggled, and the table resumed chatting. Bee rounded her shoulders, a coldness developed around her, Malick talked with Teppo and Esther, but periodically she caught him watching, while he ate.

The Spectres on either side moved toward her. Bee sat up straight, and they drew closer. Silently she asked them to leave, but they whispered they couldn't, and Bee closed her eyes, clutching her knife and fork. Inside, her heart pounded, she choked, wanting it all to stop.

'Please, you're not supposed to be here,' she said, looking over Somer's head to the Spectre behind.

'Sorry, Bee, what did you say?' Somer asked, with his mouth full of lamb.

The Spectres crept through her, up her bones, and Bee clenched her cutlery, eyes closed, trying to force them away. 'Please,' she croaked, 'please, get out of my house.'

'Malick,' Somer turned to him. 'There's something wrong with–'

Bee slammed her fists on the table, seeing the faint outline of a man, standing in front of her. She shouted, 'Get out of my house, you can't be here. You're not fucking supposed to be here!'

Everybody at the table stopped eating. Bee didn't see the surprise in their faces as she stared up at the Spectre, the thing only she could see. And then it touched her forearm.

Bee sprang back, screaming, knocking the chair over. Her heart flushed blood around her body fast. Bee panted, holding her arm, thinking she'd been burned, but there was nothing there.

'Bedelia?' Malick was already up. He seemed so far away, rather than just at the end of the table. There was panic in his eyes. She wheezed, needing air, but her lungs didn't want to fill, and everything became raspy and harsh. Bee saw the bewildered looks on everybody's faces. Forks still half in the air, eyes wide.

'Shit,' she gasped, backing away.

Sharp intakes came from the table. Viola woke, angry wails, and Esther rushed over to pick the baby up, soothing her.

Malick gripped her arms, asking, 'Bee, what's wrong with you?'

She shook her head. The words stuck, and they stared at each other.

At the table, Tristan innocently asked, 'Papa, what does fu –'

'Tristan.' he cut the boy off.

Sweat dripped down Bee's cheek, she couldn't focus, and she jolted, hearing Tristan's name. She looked to Malick, reaching up, Bee's hands shook. Caressing his face, she said, 'It feels like danger to be so in love with you.'

Then Bee fainted.

Chapter Three
Deman Circe, Kent, England

A voice spoke and Winnie's eyes sprung open. She tilted her head, listening to the muffled sound. Uncle Landers was saying something, something about her. Winnie struggled to hear, but she couldn't move. Somebody had crossed her hands over her chest. She was laid flat in a confined space.

She remembered the burrowing, something twisting around her bones, revealing secrets and histories. There were screams – her screams – and a black form swamped her body. Then a scintillating light ripped through her skin, pulling her apart and rebuilding her into somebody new.

Above was driftwood, and she was encased in it. Winnie scraped the wood with her nails until daylight sneaked through the cracks. She fidgeted, panicking. She was in a coffin.

Did they really think she was dead? Would they burn her? She smelled smoke. The service had taken place.

The coffin was on top of the funeral pyre. *This couldn't be happening!* And Winnie thumped both fists on the lid.

'Help, please,' she cried out, but Landers droned on. 'Get me out!' she yelled, kicking, and the pyre crackled as the heat rose. She coughed, choking on the burnt evening primrose used at funerals. Winnie kicked again and screamed. Something creaked, and Winnie stopped. *Had the wood dislodged underneath?* The box moved, thrown from side to side, and Winnie hit her head on the wood.

Somebody shouted, 'Winnie!' It was her mother's voice.

She clawed at the lid, as the coffin crashed to the ground, splintering. Sunlight blinded her, and fresh air rushed to her lungs. Winnie's legs and arms flailed like a doll, as she scrambled on the sand. She wriggled back, hearing the questions. 'Why was she alive?' And the frightened villagers closed in on Winnie.

She rose off the sand, backing away. Nell, Virgil, Calum, and Regan stood in their Sunday best, wide-eyed. Winnie smiled, seeing Calum. She'd saved him, but there was fear in his eyes, and he hid behind Nell, grabbing her cloak. Feargal stood next to her family, opened-mouthed, and the other familiar faces stared as the funeral pyre burned.

'Calum?' she smiled.

Landers pointed his finger. 'Witch.'

He'd called her a 'Witch'. That couldn't be right. The flames in the pyre grew, and the heat scorched one side of Winnie's body. She should be in there, her body burning. And the word 'Witch' was repeated.

'I'm not a witch,' she panted. She turned, unsure where to go, wanting to get away, and then she ran.

'Winnie,' Nell shouted.

***

Lunden Tower, Lunden, England

Lord Guardian Eldric clutched his chest. Staring up at the red canopy of the four-poster bed, Eldric's eyes glazed over as a tear ran down his cheek. He wondered if his heart was about to give out, and his blood rippled. This spasm, the jarring inside his body, told him a new Guardian was cementing themselves to him, and he groaned.

He'd not experienced anything like this since his eldest daughter arrived in Lunden Tower aged twenty-two, and by twenty-six, she was dead. This sensation meant only one thing.

Throwing the blankets off, Eldric eased up. His sixty-year-old body got stiffer each day. Rupert, his valet, came to the bed, helping the naked man onto the cold stone floor. Eldric arched his shoulders and shuddered. The open wounds in his back were getting worse. A layer of dried blood had formed around the tears, and streaks of light pushed through. This body wouldn't last much longer.

He thought of Verda, his Spanish consort, who'd smuggled two babies out of her prison, and like a fool, when the servants told him the babies were dead, he'd believed them. He'd even attended the funeral of his second daughter, born several years after the first girl. He allowed Verda out of her confinement and watched as she cried over the casket. The bitch had played Eldric and played him well.

Rupert placed slippers at Eldric's feet and held out Eldric's housecoat, not looking him in the eye. Eldric noticed the man twitched his nose.

'Is it worse, Rupert?' Eldric asked.

Rupert escorted Eldric to his bedroom dining table, pulled out the chair and seated The Guardian. 'Yes, my lord, it is.'

Eldric grumbled under his breath. His back was breaking up, and he understood why.

Rupert set the meal before him, and every day was the same, steak and eggs. Gable, his young wife, told him he wouldn't live long enough to produce a male heir if he carried on eating so much food, but Eldric dismissed her comments as madness.

The fire burned. It was always cold in the tower, and above the fireplace, banners hung, showing the royal badge of a single man leaving a lake. Eldric looked at the image of the lake, known as The Farscape. It represented when Alfred, the first Guardian, took power in Britain and spread his bloodline throughout Europe. The man in the banner was Eldric. That was his first body, and he'd had many faces over the years, but without a male heir, this body he lived in now could be his last.

A knock interrupted Eldric's thoughts, and he crammed more food into his mouth as Rupert went to the door. The servant explained the Guardian was having his afternoon meal. The intruder carried on, and Rupert returned, repeating the man's request for an audience. Eldric nodded and carried on eating.

Claude Ramas, an advisor, entered and bowed. 'Lord Guardian,' he smiled.

Eldric scowled, gazing at the handsome young man, wishing he was thirty again, and not living in the shell of an old man with wrinkled skin and greying hair. A distinguished man, Eldric liked to think, but still old.

'What is it, Claude?' He ripped into the steak, piling it into his mouth. Lips smacking as he chewed.

'Reports from Dai Castle, Sire. The Barricade has a crack, just off Krallar.'

'How long?'

'Not sure, but they suspect it's been there about a year,' Claude stated.

Eldric slammed his fist on his plate, and it flew, crashing to the floor. 'What have those brainless idiots been doing for the last year?'

'Reports suggest it's just been found. Somebody hid it.'

Eldric turned to his servant. 'Rupert, how long have you served me?'

'Forty years, Lord-Guardian,' Rupert said.

'Do you remember the servants who attended Verda?' He looked at the ruined food.

Rupert shook his head. 'No, Sire, I don't.'

'Find out what happened to them.'

The servant nodded, scraping the food off the floor. He shuffled to the dining table and prepared another plate.

'Who is Verda?' Claude asked.

'Verda was the mother of my eldest daughter.' Eldric snatched the cutlery out of Rupert's hand. 'You remember Bedelia?'

34

Claude's lips curled, nodding.

Eldric paused, seeing the smile. Six years ago, he'd ordered Bedelia's assassination, once she'd assisted with the completion of The Barricade. And Claude complied. Eldric never asked for details, and Claude never revealed his method.

'Verda had two girls, said both were stillborn. She lied about both.'

'I see, my Lord,' Claude whispered.

Eldric gulped some wine. 'There's another one alive. Verda hid her as well. Find that girl, Claude. I sense she is near that crack. She must be brought to me.'

'And The Crack?'

'Go with Oren to Dai, have him close it.' Eldric stabbed the meat, forcing it into his mouth. 'Rupert, send me the Scribe, tell him, I'm writing a Royal Decree.' He watched the old man scuttle out of the room. He returned his attention back to Claude. 'Who is your finest inquisitor?'

'That would be Daniel Cooper.'

'Send him to me now, as I've a list of staff I want him to question.' He took another mouthful, knowing Claude's inquisitors bordered on torture. 'And he's to report only to me.'

'And then?' Claude asked.

'You, find that bloody girl. I'll have Oren fuck her like he did the other one because I will have an heir.'

'Consider it done, Sire.'

***

Deman Circe, Kent, England

Winnie leaned against the wall of the crumbling tower. A broken circular building, covered in moss and flora, and the roots of wild red valerian forced its way through the brickwork. A flower with a pungent scent which attracted butterflies and bees.

Winnie sat in the only dark place she could find, with arms wrapped around her knees. She rocked, mumbling as her left eye twitched. Winnie had been dead. Something or somebody showed her things. Things Winnie didn't understand and her whole body shook.

Somebody, they'd told her, was coming from the other side of The Barricade. Winnie was to break it open and then her work would be completed. She let out a hysterical giggle, covering her mouth, at the absurd idea she could breach the massive structure.

Winnie stroked her long hair, clawing her fingers through it. Her eyes widened, pulling at it. The fiery red had gone, there was only white hair, and she clawed the strands, muttering faster.

Something attached itself to Winnie's soul. She wheezed, eyelids flickering, heart palpitating as they fastened themselves, becoming a part of her, and then two more people attached. Winnie wanted to vomit, and she attempted to wriggle free, but they dug into her, syphoning off Winnie's energy and then it flowed back. In the distance as her eyes blurred she could see figures, The Sinners as she knew them to be, observed.

Winnie scratched, wanting to get rid of them, but it didn't work. The more Winnie pawed, the more agitated she became. Gasping, as the three strangers engulfed her because she couldn't fight them and their essence mixed together. The Sinners, hid, watching as the three new energies stabbed into Winnie's being. They let Winnie connect and did nothing to stop them. Her mind splintered and Winnie screamed.

A creak from the rickety steps outside the tower sounded. Winnie jumped, not wanting to be found, least of all by Priest Landers. He'd called her a witch when she broke free of the coffin, and Winnie guessed, he'd have her sitting in the chair, shouting sermons from the Holy Writ, the bible of the Guardians, said to be written by Alfred, the first Guardian, and have the Clannen dolls surround her. He'd be in his element, frightening Virgil and Nell into believing their daughter was a witch.

Winnie paled thinking about what she'd done. Taking those dolls and using them had saved Calum's life, but most likely at the cost of her own. Winnie presumed she was going to end up dead because she was unnatural. People were not supposed to return from the dead.

'Winnie?' The broken wooden door opened slowly. Virgil, her father, stood in the frame, his silhouette basked in the red evening sun. Winnie slinked further into the darkness, guessing Landers and Reece Tanner, the village Marshal, were outside.

Virgil repeated her name, and Winnie said nothing, hoping he'd go away and look for her elsewhere, but he took a step inside. 'I know you're here, love,' he whispered.

'Go away, Da,' she muttered.

'Winnifred, let me take you home.' Virgil closed the door.

'I keep hearing them, Da, they keep telling me things,' her voice trembled.

'Who do you hear?'

Winnie's fingers crept along the moss-covered walls and then she came into the light. Quickly she shuffled back into the dark, seeing Virgil's surprised expression.

'What's happened to your hair, sweetheart?' He didn't come any closer.

She moved half her body back into the light, her fingers tapping the wall, and she covered her face with her hair. 'They keep telling me things,' Winnie repeated.

'Who do?' Virgil asked.

'The Sinners, Da, they told me to pick up the dolls, that I could save Calum. I think they lied to me.' Winnie's voice spiked, her nerves fraying.

'I'll take you home.'

'What, with Landers and the Marshal?' she sniffed a grin.

'They're concerned. You broke your neck. You were dead.'

Winnie wrapped her hair around her fingers. 'What about Calum?' she asked.

Virgil nodded. 'The boy is well enough, he doesn't remember much, it's like he slept through it all. What frightened him and Regan more, was seeing you rise from that bloody pyre.'

'He remembers nothing?' Winnie thought she might cry. 'Didn't he say anything about the voices?'

Virgil edged closer. 'What are these voices?'

'When I was... when I was...' She didn't want to say the word 'dead'. 'I heard a voice, telling me they'd been waiting for me.'

Virgil looked back at the door and whispered, 'What did it say?'

Winnie looked over Virgil's shoulder; behind the door, Landers would be listening. 'Says I've got to open The Barricade, I've got to let the one that has no God in.'

'Who has no God?'

She backed herself into the dark, it was safer in there. 'I don't know, Da. I keep hearing them, many voices. I don't know if it's me talking or somebody else.'

Virgil nodded, but he did not comfort his daughter.

'Landers called me a witch, Da,' she whispered, changing the subject.

'But...'

'Landers doesn't know shit.'

Virgil's eyes widened. Pulling out his hipflask, he took a gulp. 'Don't say that, Winnifred. He's the voice of the Guardians.'

Winnie laughed. 'I don't think Eldric will have a voice for long,' she uttered, her voice still rising as if she were afraid.

'Speak like that and I can't protect you,' Virgil said. 'You're my daughter. I want to help you.'

Winnie jumped out of the shadow. Standing before Virgil, she said, 'But I'm not your daughter, am I?'

Virgil paled, hearing her utter a secret truth. 'How... how did you find that out?'

She heaved, wishing it wasn't true. 'The Sinners, those voices told me; told me, I didn't belong to you.'

'That's untrue,' Virgil shook his head, taking her hand. 'You're my daughter, I brought you up, and I love you.'

Winnie's eye twitched, something she'd started doing since returning. She couldn't control it, and as she became more scared, the more her left eye and head twitched.

'I'm scared, Da,' she said. 'I'm scared the priest is going to hurt me.'

'Landers… he's a good man. He's your uncle, he doesn't want to hurt you.' He pulled his hand, as Winnie, tightened the grip.

'He tells us what we should hear, Da,' Winnie wiped a tear from her cheek.

The old door flew open, and Landers stormed inside, face red with anger. 'That's enough blasphemous talk. She needs a few hours in the chair.' He grabbed Winnie's wrist, dragging her toward the door.

Virgil shoved Landers back. 'Don't even think about using the chair.'

'She's a witch, Virgil. The Guardians teach us to be careful of these creatures,' the Priest hissed. 'The Marshal has sent word to Dai. We'll take Winnie there, the priests there can help.'

'Da,' Winnie cried, 'I said he'd hurt me.'

***

Lunden Tower, Lunden, England

Lunden Tower courtyard was busy, and Rupert hurried across it, weaving through people. He'd already sent the Scribe to Eldric's chambers, now he had to find Will, and he headed to the Great Kitchen.

The distinctive caw of ravens sounded, and he stopped to look up at the high stone wall that surrounded the Tower, and three ravens sat, calling down, mocking him. A sign, Rupert thought, a message sent to warn him that he was going to die. Superstitious nonsense, but Rupert couldn't shake the feeling.

For an old man he could keep pace when needed, and now it was needed. The tower was busy with servants, courtiers, coming and going at the request of the three Guardians left in the fortress. Rupert greeted any passing staff with a smile, and stopped twice, to make polite conversation about Eldric, because the Tower was a place that thrived on gossip.

Once inside the hot Kitchen, Rupert watched and looked. This place was no respite for the poor souls indentured there. The meat cleavers whacked into large carcasses, and different spices lingered in the air. The cooks shouted at their vassals, wanting things done as a matter of urgency. Rupert paid no attention; he was only interested in finding Will.

Rupert spotted the scruffy elderly man hunched over a table in the corner, shelling peas. The cook gave Will simple tasks, rather than see him out on the streets.

'Will, do you remember Verda?' Rupert sat down next to him.

'Lady Verd –'

'Hush.' Rupert grabbed the man's sleeve.

Will pulled the pod string, running dirty fingernails down the centre. A pea jumped onto the table, and Will popped it into his mouth, checking the cook didn't see. 'What about her?'

'Can you leave here?' Rupert looked around. Nobody watched them, but he couldn't be sure.

Will looked at his hands, wrinkled with black spots, and his clothes ragged. 'I ain't got anywhere else to go.'

'Remember those problems we helped her with?' Rupert whispered.

Will was silent.

'I thought that Wise Crone of yours bound them completely?' He played with a peapod, pointing to Will to carry on. People might notice the old man had stopped shelling the peas.

'She did.'

Rupert wiped his brow. The heat of the kitchen made him sweat. 'Well, the second one has woken. Your Crone didn't do a good job. Now, Eldric's looking to put heads on spikes.'

'Some things can't be locked up.' Will popped a pea, smiling.

What Rupert didn't see was a young man, about twenty-six, short blond hair, wearing nothing but black, walk around the kitchen. The man picked up a carrot and started munching on it, as he watched Rupert talk furtively with a scruffy old man.

Rupert rose from the table. 'Be careful.' He walked out, not looking back as the young man approached the table and sat by Will.

Chapter Four
Bononia-Sur-Mer, Northern France

The window shutters of the house remained closed. The early morning sun broke through the shafts as Viola suckled on Bee's breast. Now eighteen months old, Viola rarely took her mother's milk, but when she did, Bee enjoyed the moments.

Bee slept most of the night, unsure how many hours she'd drifted in and out of consciousness, but the changes came. They assembled, locking with Bee, crystallising as they restored her, the ability to make things happen through will alone, nailed itself to her soul. Bee blocked it as best she could, but it sank into her, becoming more powerful than she'd ever experienced and soon Bee wouldn't be able to fight the changes. For now, she resisted, the best she could.

During the night Malick watched over her. Bee must have had a fever, because he placed a cold cloth over her forehead and when Viola woke, he got up, tending to the baby. She remembered a knocking at the door late in the night, voices, but Bee didn't stir, unable to move from the battle within.

Looking up, Bee saw more peeling red paint in the corner, as another new patch appeared in this old half-empty house. The only furniture left was the locked gun cabinet, one old grey provincial sofa and a wooden display cabinet, empty except for the ticking clock. Most houses in Bononia were like this, but Bee didn't care, she'd grown up without any material possessions, and these few things made the house feel like a home.

Malick thundered down the stairs, boots banging on the uncarpeted runs. He headed toward the kitchen, to get his morning coffee. Bee rocked Viola, her chair creaking and she listened as he came back towards the parlour, and then the questions started.

'Are you feeling better?' Malick asked in a strong French accent.

Bee watched Malick blow into the coffee cup, leaning against the doorframe. A striking man, rugged, at over six foot, with black hair, and intense green eyes, unshaven, and he waited for an answer. His breeches were loosely tied, his shirt not tucked in, and his black waistcoat hung from his big frame. It was the usual dishevelled appearance Bee associated with her husband.

Viola grumbled as Bee stopped feeding her. 'Yes, thank you.'

He stood over her checking her forehead. 'You're still hot, and you were mumbling in your sleep. Don't go to the tavern, Aimee will cover.'

She scratched her cheek, saying, 'I wasn't feeling well last night. I'm fine now.'

'Don't lie. You swore in front of everybody at the table, including Tristan,' Malick reminded her.

Bee settled Viola, answering back, 'It's nothing Somer and Teppo haven't said.'

'And what happened at the tavern?' he asked. 'Gerald and Aimee came by after I'd put you to bed. Aimee's never heard you speak like that before, and she's concerned because you nearly collapsed. You should've told me you were unwell, I would have sent the twins home.'

'I didn't want to ruin the evening, and I'll speak to Aimee later,' Bee said, making smiley faces at Viola, enjoying having her daughter at her breast.

'Perhaps it would be wise to spend a few days at home.' He carried on sipping his coffee.

Baffled, Bee asked, 'Did I embarrass you?'

He paused, as if unsure why Bee asked him this question. He then said, 'I wasn't a good husband to Nadine, and you know that, but airing it in public the way you did, would have embarrassed Nadine.'

Bee frowned, saying, 'I don't think Nadine gives a shit, Malick, she's dead.'

His eyes flared. 'That's exactly what I'm talking about, Bedelia. I've spoken to you several times about swearing. You're a respectable married woman, not a vassal anymore, so behave like one, and besides, I've got bigger things to worry about.'

She cooed Viola, and said, 'What, like being a Flesh Finder?'

Malick coughed into his coffee. 'Where did you hear that?'

'I overheard you with Somer and Teppo.'

He didn't answer and headed down the hall toward the kitchen. Bee followed, cradling Viola as Esther walked down the stairs. She handed Esther the baby, and buttoned up her nightdress, telling the girl to go into the parlour and Viola cried, upset her food source had gone.

Bee closed the kitchen door. 'Smuggling people is quite different from tobacco or beer.'

'It's business, Bedelia. Somer and Teppo have been using the Juna, and they've got us into trouble. I'm not sure how we can get out of it.'

'And if there's a crack, I've got a right to know.' She stood in front of him, hands on hips.

'And what are you going to do, go back, take Viola?' Malick asked.

'Is that what you think?' Bee gasped, hurt. 'I don't want to go back, but I'd like to see my children and my father.'

'Maybe one day you'll go back and see your boys,' he said.

'You're making those people into vassals,' Bee shouted. 'You're making them into somebody like me.' Bee breathed fast. Her stomach churned, imagining the horror those people were going through. She'd known nothing else, and now these people were going somewhere terrifying.

'Bee, I didn't know,' he stressed. 'This Omega forced Teppo and Somer. It started with beer, and then it became people. She threatened that, well...'

'Who's Omega?' Bee asked.

'She's the woman who runs the black markets out of DulPenne. She'll kill the twins if they back out.'

'You need to make the twins stop,' Bee carried on.

'I can't do that. They're family.'

Bee guessed this would be the response, and said, 'You paid that debt when you married their sister. They are not your family when they put this one at risk,' Bee whispered, lukewarm.

'Omega threatened *all* of us.'

Bee's face tightened. 'What do you mean all of us?'

Malick saw the change of expression. 'Us. You, me, Viola, Tristan, Esther, all of us, do you understand?' He didn't look at her.

'Perhaps you could –'

'No, Bee, there's nothing we can do.' And he sank onto the table, deflated.

Bee edged closer, taking his hands, she pulled Malick up and wrapped her arms around his frame. Looking up, she kissed him. Bee then smelled a familiar aroma on Malick. It was something that hid in the bones of a person. A hint of burned wood and sweet vanilla lingered on him. It was Bee's smell, a part of her make-up, and the essence was faint on Malick.

A diluted fragrance from generations of breeding watered down until only the few can detect. Malick had been around somebody who had traces of her kind of blood running through them. He must have assisted the twins recently with the kidnapped people, as The Crack was awakening her senses.

Bee asked, 'How do you get these people?'

'They sail through The Crack, a small boat meets them with the cargo,' he told her. 'And then the traders collect them.'

She whispered, 'Helena's got new teeth. Fresh, spotless, they could have come from a living person. She suggested getting skin for my scars, and cover them up.'

'At first, I thought they were selling the people as slaves. That's what Somer told me. About five months ago, I heard a whisper, a Skin Factoria in DulPenne and I guessed what they were doing.' He blew the words out as if he was glad to have finally shared it.

Bee wriggled free of Malick. 'And what do they do?'

Malick stared at her for a long time. 'It's too horrible, Bee, and I don't think a woman should hear–'

'You tell me,' she uttered.

Malick waited several seconds. 'They starve them for three days and then kill them.'

'And what happens next?' Bee knew the answer but needed to hear it said.

He shook his head, looking at the floor. 'I can't say it.'

She asked coolly, 'Do they dismember the bodies?'

Malick looked dismayed, as Bee said those words in such a matter-of-fact manner. 'Every viable piece,' he whispered.

Bee's eyes widened, secrets came flashing back, she pushed them away, muttering, 'And I thought I was bad.'

Malick whispered, 'I'm sorry, Bee.'

'I thought the apothecary was selling dead peoples' teeth,' Bee erupted.

Malick went to touch Bee, but she stepped back. 'I didn't know, not until...'

'Don't touch me,' she gasped.

'What do you mean about being bad?' he frowned.

'I was... I was...' Bee stopped. Her secrets didn't want to come out. Sweat trickled down her back. Bee's insides almost broke, crushed under the weight of learning her husband was a Human smuggler. The kitchen shrank. Backing away, Bee headed toward the kitchen door, storming outside.

***

Malick slammed his office door. Bee refused to speak after she'd walked out, so he left and came to The Raven. The walk through the streets of the town hadn't lightened his mood. He greeted a few newcomers on his way to the tavern. They lived in boarded-up houses, all wanting a fresh start, and The Crack that Bee was angry about, provided that opportunity.

Malick sank into the leather chair, pulling a bottle of cognac from the desk drawer. He stared at the green bottle, and then the tired office. He was as guilty as the newcomers, having stolen the furniture for The Raven from those empty houses, and most of it came from people who had been friends.

He tapped his fingers on the bottle, far too early for a drink, but Malick pulled the cork, knocking it back. This is what he'd been afraid of, that Bee would want to go back to Britain, once The Barricade was open.

Malick hoped she would forgive him, but it was the horror in Bee's face, he couldn't shake. He took another gulp, remembering the strange comment she made about being bad, and he wondered what she meant.

They had found Bee on the beach, dying, the day after The Great Storm. That morning The Barricade had risen like a smoky black Goliath out of the Channel, separating

France and mainland Europe from Britain. It was a night of dangerous rain, violent winds, illuminating lightning and thunderous roars that shattered the glass windows of every Bononian house. Fishermen's cottages flattened, their boats smashed, planks, masts, sails destroyed. The monstrous structure, so vast, stretching South to West, standing high into the clouds.

Debris once lost, lay churned up, littered along the sand-swept beach. Broken boats, crushed men, their bodies shredded and twisted, and terror locked into their death stares. Fish, seaweed, mixed with the vacant eyes of dead children, as the fishing tackle, dead birds, and fish tangled into the shattered bloodied bodies of men and women, were strewn along the shoreline. Their clothing torn with their limbs battered, and severed. Many things, once hidden within the ripples of the currents lay spewed up. The sea's secrets became tangled with the living and it took those French souls as payment for The Barricade.

Nadine was four months pregnant. They spent the night, huddling together in the pantry, as it was the only room without windows. Malick held his wife, as she whimpered at every sound, and he prayed they would survive the night.

The next day, Nadine wanted to be brave, and Malick took her to the beach. The devastation went on for miles, and he remembered the heat of the sun and lack of a breeze. They heard the tears of their friends, and the people they knew as they staggered along the sand. Malick's heart pounded, Nadine almost fainted, and he was about to take her home, when they found Bee.

A man nearby lay dead, dressed in breeches and blue shirt, blood-soaked and a deep cut to his neck. Bee's throat was slit, leg broken and lips ripped apart. The practice of the Chelchith Smile was something once common in England, but hardly seen in France. She lay in the sand, choking on her blood. Bee's dress was shredded and she clung to her black cuff bracelet, and even now, she refused to take it off.

Malick gathered Bee into his arms, and they ran back to their home, taking Bee to the servants' room in the attic. Nadine and Malick cut her out of the bloody clothes, and they both stepped back, looking at the stranger in the bed. There were scars all over her upper body, and dark, tiny potted marks around Bee's right eye, then Malick noticed what he thought was a bullet scar in the right shoulder. Nadine covered Bee, and both Malick and Esther helped tend the wounds. Nadine sewed her up as best she could, saying there was little point in wasting money on doctors as the woman would die, and Bee clasped Malick's hand staring only at him.

During the initial days of Bee's arrival, they all took turns watching over her, and sometimes Bee would mutter deliriously because of her fever, the name, Luther. Nadine and Malick concluded he must be the man who'd died on the beach and only once Bee had recovered would they tell her of his death, and they cremated him at the local Temple. Yet she never asked about the man.

Bee's broken body healed fast, and only the scars around her mouth showed she'd been attacked as Bee hid her neck wound, and then they had a new houseguest. Bee stayed in the attic and was told she could wear any of the clothes left in the room. The maid and stable lad were dead, so Bee mainly wore the stable hand's clothes.

She was quiet and completed any chores required, rarely leaving the house, and keeping only to the garden. She watched any visitors, sizing them up and she called Malick, 'Sir' and Nadine, 'Madame.'

Malick watched Bee, noticing she didn't conform to polite society, as Nadine called it. She rode a horse like a man and got dirty from with hard work. She taught Esther to care for the horses, and Bee spent hours alone in her room. *'The woman kneels, staring at the wall,'* Nadine told him.

One evening, Bee joined them in the parlour, saying very little, and she focused on the crackling fire, still wearing breeches, rather than changing into a dress for the evening. Nadine presented her with a cross-stitch and Bee looked at the material, dangling it between her fingers, inspecting the circular disc, touching the stitching.

'What's this?' she frowned.

Nadine explained, adding, 'It's what ladies enjoy of an evening, passes the time.'

'This is enjoyment?' Bee questioned slowly. 'Thank you, Madame Rose, but no...' And she vanished out of the parlour, leaving Nadine opened mouthed.

Nadine turned to Malick. 'There's something not right with her.'

Trying not to laugh, he went after Bee and found her in the backyard chopping wood. The whacking echoed in the night, and Malick followed the sounds to the small shed. Watching Bee swing the axe in a relaxed expert manner, woke something up, a stirring he'd not felt with Nadine.

'Bedelia, come inside, you're still recovering.' He was enjoying watching. She'd tied her auburn hair off her face, and Bee's features shone in the moonlight.

She stopped, wiping her forehead, Bee said, 'It's better than sewing.'

A good observation, Malick thought as a warm sensation swam through him, and he continued watching her. 'I...I think you should come in, it's dangerous at night, even here in the yard, and I don't want you getting scared.'

Bee smiled, 'Go back to your wife's cross-stitch, Mr Rose. I'm not afraid of the dark.' And she picked up another log, placed it on the stump, bringing the axe down.

Bee's facial injuries healed completely, giving her a slightly deranged smile, and Malick questioned Bee about the wounds and scars on her body. They worried she might bring trouble by having her in the house, but Bee said, she'd never put his family in danger.

It was three months before Malick and Nadine took her to the temple. Bee wore breeches, as they took her outside of the house for the first time. The women sat either side of Malick as the small carriage trundled along the broken roads.

Nadine covered her nose and mouth with a scarf, choking on the stench. The wind carried the sickly sweetness of the open air cremations through the streets, but Bee didn't bother with a mask. Malick had grown used to the smell, having helped with the body removals, and a series of cremations.

'The smell doesn't bother you, Bedelia?' Malick asked as the horses bumped along the road.

Bee kept her eyes front. 'No,' she answered.

'Some say because these people died too soon they come back, feeding off the blood of the living,' Nadine commented as the buggy bounced along.

Bee said quietly, 'No, Madame Rose, vampires don't exist. Once somebody is dead, they're dead.'

Surprised, he stared, but Bee kept facing forward. There was a sadness he hadn't heard before, and Malick wanted to comfort her.

They rode along the lanes, the many boarded up houses, acknowledging the haggard faces of the few people walking in the muddy paths. Malick drew the carriage to a stop, outside a redbrick building with a bell, and Bee took a sharp breath as she looked at the stained glass windows.

'Why have you brought me here?' she asked.

Malick helped Nadine disembark, and then held out his hand to Bee. 'Nadine thought you'd like to visit.'

Bee screwed up her face, still sitting in the carriage. 'I'd rather not.' She didn't budge.

He held out his hand. 'Please, Bee, do it for me.'

She looked at his hand and climbed out without any assistance. Bee remained by the horse, spooked about entering the Temple grounds.

Nadine, then seven months pregnant, slipped her arm through Bee's, pulling her through the gate into the cemetery. She dragged Bee up the path to a small wooden plaque and flower. The graveyard itself was full of tiny plaques like the one Bee stood before. There were hundreds dotted in the grass surrounding the gravestones. Each piece of wood represented somebody who'd died during the height of the virus, and though it was still present in the town, fewer people were dying. Malick stood behind, as Nadine and Bee looked at a sign, the name read 'Luther'. Nothing else.

'We thought you'd like to visit Luther. We cremated him after we found you because of the virus.' Nadine gave a little smile and tapped her hand on Bee's.

Bee nodded, she smoothed out the creases of her breeches. 'Thank you for your kindness, Madame Rose, but this isn't Luther.'

Nadine's voice rose, asking fast, 'Then who was he?'

Bee shrugged, 'I don't know. I never asked his name.' She bolted back through the gate and into the carriage. She didn't speak on the way home and went straight to her bedroom. Refusing to talk about the man who had died without a name.

She chopped her auburn hair off, cutting it close to her head, much to everybody's horror, and Malick found Bee a beguiling woman. He kept away, knowing that a married man who was about to be a father shouldn't have these thoughts. He was intrigued by the scars, her sleek movement, because Bee was a puzzle, he secretly wanted to solve.

Malick became distant from Nadine, brooding over his fascination for Bee. He'd never experienced these emotions for his wife, nor any of the other women he had liaisons with during his ten-year marriage. He only realised Nadine had guessed his secret when she demanded Bee leave, and Malick refused.

He'd watch Bee groom the horses, catching her whispering secrets into their ears, thinking nobody else was around. The name Luther popped up and she'd tell the horse that she would wait for Luther, always, and soon they'd be out of the dark. Bee caught him on a couple of occasions, and she'd fluster, apologising, stepping around Malick, vanishing. And he became more enthralled by Bee.

Nadine gave birth to Tristan. She didn't want Bee present, but there was no choice as the birth became complicated. Bee ordered Esther to run to the general store, giving her a list of herbs and medicines and by the time the girl returned, Bee had cut the baby out, and he held his new born son. Malick watched both frightened and in awe as Bee sewed Nadine back up, placing particular herbs over the incision. The methodical way Bee behaved reminded Malick of a soldier who tended wounded comrades, whispering words of comfort and love. Bee stayed with Nadine until she was well enough to look after Tristan.

Nine weeks after Tristan was born, Nadine contracted the Red Plague as she'd weakened due to the difficult birth. Malick sold most of their belongings to pay the doctors but nothing worked as the virus ravaged her skin, exposing the muscle and bones, and then it ate into Nadine's internal organs.

Malick wanted to sell his schooner, The Juna. Bee reminded him that he needed an income to bring up Tristan once the plague receded because Nadine would not survive. Bee was frank in her advice, but she was right. Nadine died, and Bee faded into the background as Malick, Somer and Teppo cremated her.

He was now a widower with a new-born son.

Some evenings he'd sit in the kitchen or parlour, and asked Bee to join him, and it surprised Malick that she did. There were nights he sat watching Bee as she sat stoically in her secret world. He couldn't take his eyes off her, and Malick was consumed by guilt because he'd never loved Nadine.

Other nights, he talked. Only then Malick understood he was being studied as if she was trying to figure out who he was, and what she was. She was a strange creature, giving a little but not enough, and Malick wanted to kiss her. Bee smiled and laughed as he taught her French, and how to play Backgammon because she'd never played board games before, and Malick fell more in love with the woman with a Chelchith Smile.

Teppo, Somer and occasionally his friend Philip would join Malick for an evening drink in the kitchen. The first visits overwhelmed Bee, her hands tremored if the men's voices got too loud. She'd wring her hands, gripping her black bracelet as she sat beside Malick at the kitchen table. He prayed Bee might open up, because he wanted Bee to be comfortable with him, but she was always quiet.

Tristan and Bee bonded immediately, and she was the first to hold him if he cried or if he needed feeding. She'd get up in the middle of the night, change him and sing, rocking him back to sleep, and Malick would listen by the door, hearing her talk to Tristan.

A month after Nadine's death Malick opened The Raven. He'd broken into a vacant bar and redecorated it. People wanted ale, and after a few false starts, the pub reopened.

The locals still blamed Bee for the rising of The Barricade, calling her a witch, and then the names like whore and trollop started because she was still living under his roof. Malick knew Bee was involved, and he wanted to protect her from the name-calling, so two months later he asked her to marry him.

Bee flatly refused to be married in the Temple, and the local magistrate married them. She'd stuttered over the vows, over her surname, saying McKay, after some consideration. She allowed Malick to kiss her on the cheek, and he believed Bee had the same feeling for him.

The wedding night had been a frightening experience. He wanted to kiss Bee, but he ended up flat on the floor with his face in the carpet. She twisted Malick's arm around his back, pinned him to the ground, choking him. A piece of Bee's timid ladylike veneer broke, and her good manners gave way to profanities he'd only ever heard sailors use.

She whispered into his ear, *'I ain't no cheap cunt you can fuck, just because I've taken your name. Touch me again, and I'll cut your heart out.'* Bee let Malick go because he promised he'd never try it again. He'd have sworn anything to stop her breaking his arm.

A week later, Bee frightened Helena Berger at the general store. He questioned Bee, expecting an argument, but she opened up a little and allowed Malick to kiss her for the first time.

That same night Malick rode home around midnight and stabled the horse. He was twenty foot away from the front door when two masked figures stepped out of the darkness, cocking their guns. Malick went for his weapon, but the larger of the two men punched him in the stomach, and he went to the ground.

'Gives us the money,' the larger Frenchman growled, 'We know you got it.'

The second man hit him twice in the face, and the blood poured. Malick was on his knees, dazed, as they kept punching, going through his long coat, hunting for the money bag.

The front door opened, Bee strode out in her breeches, holding two revolvers. She walked up and without uttering a word, blasted the gun into the kneecap of one man. He fell to the ground, blood and bone everywhere. The crack of the bullet echoed, and sleeping birds took flight, squawking, panicked. And his screams punctured the night.

'That English bitch shot my knee,' the attacker screamed, repeatedly thumping his hand into the gravel path, crying.

Malick scrambled back, dizzy from the hit. He sweated, heart pounding, and everything became mixed. The second attacker dived toward the dropped revolver. He gripped it, as Bee crushed his fingers into the gravel, bones cracking under the weight of her heavy boot.

She aimed one revolver at the wounded man's head, and the second man looked down the barrel of the other gun. Malick heard her say icily, 'Unless you want your brains blown out, I suggest you both leave.'

'Shoot her,' the wounded man cried, as the second attacker yelled in pain.

'My son is upstairs asleep. I don't want to wake him by killing you.' She looked at the second man. 'You've got one chance to take your friend.' Then she pressed the gun against his temple.

'But – but his knee...'

'Pick him up then,' Bee growled. She leaned in close to the men, whispering.

Malick's head spun, but he heard snippets, words like, 'come' 'family' and 'last'. The second man stumbled, dragging his friend, and he thought the wounded man said, 'Oh-my-god,' as they vanished into the night.

Malick took another swig, remembering that night, as the gate between him and Bee opened. The strange connection he had with her wasn't always there, but today it was a flood of anger and isolation. It crawled around inside him as if something dangerous was about to escape. A dark side of Bee, he ignored, because she kept a room of secrets and she refused to share. He wanted it to stop and took another drink.

Growling, he threw the bottle against the wall, smashing it. The liquid exploded as the glass shattered, falling to the floor. The old wooden panels soaked in the cognac, and he stewed, grabbing another bottle off the shelf. Malick pulled the cork, knocking it back. Once again, Bee had turned the conversation around from her and back to him.

A knock at the door interrupted his thoughts. 'Go away,' he shouted.

Aimee walked in, closing the door. 'Philip is here. He's with a bald man, mean-looking. Baptiste, I think Philip called him.'

The men entered, wearing long heavy coats, and battered wide-rim hats. Baptiste had a dagger and both carried revolvers. Aimee scurried out of the office, closing the door.

'Philip, Baptiste, why are you here?' He got up, welcoming Baptiste first. A sliver of a man, with gapped false teeth and long greasy hair, Malick knew better than to offend him. He kissed him on each cheek and nodded, and then repeated the same to Philip.

'Good to see you,' Philip said, and he held onto Malick, sniffing him.

Malick heard the sniff. It was unsettling, and he distanced himself, as Philip clung to him, just a little too long.

'Bit early for a drink?' Philip glanced at the cognac. 'Is everything all right?' his accent as strong as Malick's.

Malick shrugged, 'Sometimes...' He sat back at his desk. 'What can I do for you?' He pushed all thoughts of Bee away. His stomach churning; was it having Baptiste in his office, or was it drinking so early?

'The twins have impressed Omega. She will invest some of her men into your ship.' Baptiste grabbed a chair, sitting down. He took the cognac and swigged from the bottle, before lighting a cigarillo.

Philip circled the room and then leaned against the wall. 'They got quite a crop last trip.'

Malick ran his hands through his hair. 'That wasn't part of the deal. They are using the Juna to pay off their debt, and then it's completed.'

Philip smiled, 'Omega won't like that.'

Baptiste flicked ash to the floor. 'You'll be sailing across in the morning.'

'But–'

Baptiste placed his gun on the desk. 'We spoke with Teppo, and he's preparing the ship.'

'You spoke with the twins?'

'Keen to help,' Philip grinned.

Malick nodded, eyes on the weapon. 'Tomorrow it is.'

Philip then asked, 'How's my Godchild?'

'Tristan is growing fast. Probably getting underneath Bee's feet at the moment.' Malick gave a smile.

Baptiste rose from the chair, grabbing his gun, he smiled, baring new white teeth. 'High tide is midday.'

The door closed behind Baptiste and Philip, and Malick took another drink.

Chapter Five
Bononia-Sur-Mer, Northern France

Philip wrapped his coat around him. The sun was hot, but something spooked him. He closed the tavern door, but didn't move. Breathing out gradually, he couldn't shake the sensation he'd experienced when he'd embraced Malick. He peered up and down the street, but everything was out of focus, from the houses and few shops to the few people who walked by.

Colours flashed around inside his mind. He stumbled as he followed Baptiste along the crumbling path. His feet tripped up, and his insides felt woozy. This was something new.

'I think Malick's been in contact with a Guardian. A full-blooded one.' Philip tried getting on his horse, but the drunken sensation made it difficult, and the horse neighed, stepping away.

'I didn't think there were any left, 'cept for...?' Baptiste lit another cigarillo, watching Philip struggle, as he mounted his horse.

'This one doesn't feel like Omega. There's a destructiveness they've been hiding... I don't know...' Philip gripped the reins, steadying the animal.

'Does Malick know what happens to the people?' Baptiste asked.

Philip's dizziness eased. 'Don't think so, Somer told him they were bringing slaves, and he wasn't happy with that. I've warned him not to back out... well, threatened him.'

'Would he hide one?' Inhaling the smoke, Baptiste waited.

'He's not a guardsman. Besides, I've been there when they offloaded the cargo, there's been no full-blooded Guardians.' Philip finally mounted the horse.

'Malick married that Briton? The one found after the Barricade came up?' Baptiste's eyes glinted with interest.

Philip settled himself into the saddle. 'That's right, but I've spent evenings with Malick and Bee. She's a little odd at times –'

'How so?' Baptiste threw the butt of his cigarillo to the ground.

Philip shrugged his shoulders. 'Bee went to Temple a few times after they married, and she refused to drink from the Guardian's goblet. I'd been up to the priest. Bee cradled Tristan, and Malick pinned her into the pew, suggesting she drink from the goblet.'

'What did she say?' Baptiste asked.

'She said, *'Be grateful I'm listening to that bullshit the priest peddles, but I'm not drinking out of some rotting cup to honour some fictitious god.'* She stopped shortly after they married. Malick goes because he has to take Esther.'

Baptiste remained quiet, considering what he'd been told. 'She actually said 'bullshit', and called the Guardians 'fictitious'?'

Philip grinned, nodding. Most women didn't swear, and Philip laughed. It clicked with Philip what Baptiste was thinking. He rode up next to him, forcing the man to stop. 'I've felt nothing from her or their daughter.'

'They have a daughter too.' Baptiste steered the horse along the path, 'Mrs Rose sounds like an interesting lady. We'll pay her a visit for morning tea.'

***

Bee sat at the table, dressed in her old breeches and shirt. She stared at the wall, as if she were daydreaming. Next to her was a lukewarm cup of tea and a chopping board. The bread knife stood upright on its own, spinning. Bee played with it, reconnecting to the power, and the point burrowed into the board, going around and around.

She'd spent an hour whispering her mantras, but the abilities refused to listen, and in the end, Bee gave up, letting them flow. The worst of it happened during the night, now the last embers attached themselves to Bee, making sure they bonded to every bone.

The energy crept through her body. The knife turned as her blood rippled, and the sensation knitted itself back into Bee's bones. She'd wanted to forget these powers, as they were a reminder of Britain and her bondage, but as Bee flexed them, they already felt like they were a part of her again.

Bee's body juddered. Something else was fastening itself to her. Two distinctive branches of the same bloodline connected, and that meant two more siblings were alive, but one of these children had only half her blood. Bee cut them off, blocking them out. That life no longer existed.

She looked around, this wasn't her kitchen. Everything was here before she turned up. The pots, the pans, even the tea set, belonged to Malick's life before he married her. Bee felt like an outsider again, looking at somebody else's home.

The knife dropped, and it banged on the board. Bee would apologise tonight and hoped Malick wouldn't ask too many questions, and she would refrain from asking about the people smuggling. She'd ask when things settled down. Bee decided she'd have to wear a dress for dinner to try and make an effort. She'd wear the green one, Malick's favourite.

Esther's singing drifted from the parlour with the children as Tristan chirped to a song about counting. Esther had asked questions about their fight, but Bee lied, saying it was over money. Bee's stomach bubbled and twisted as two heavy thuds sounded at the front door. Bee sat looking toward the hallway. Whoever was behind that door was coming for her.

'I'll get it,' called Esther.

Bee ran through the hallway, as Esther reached for the handle. Bee slammed her hand on the door. 'Take Tristan and Viola to the Raven, tell Malick, I need him here. You stay there,' she whispered.

'But–'

'Go out the back.'

Esther nodded, gathering up Viola. She took Tristan by his arms, and the boy kicked at being handled.

'Tristan.' Bee grabbed the boy, pinching his arms, and he whimpered. 'Don't kick your aunt. You need to go to your father, you'll be safe there.'

Esther dragged him down the hall, as Philip called through the door. 'Mrs Rose.'

Bee's body tingled. She opened the door, and Philip stood there.

'Philip?' Bee could smell he was a Guardsman. She'd never noticed it before because she'd blocked her abilities. He was not a full-blooded Guardian, but could recognise people who had the blood flowing through them.

'Mrs Rose, Bee.'

'Malick isn't here. He's at the Raven.' She tried closing the door.

Philip pushed his way inside. 'I want to talk to you.'

'There's nothing I can do for you, Philip,' Bee stammered.

He shut the door, gripping her arm, dragging her to the kitchen. 'My friend, Baptiste, would like a word.'

Bee's face paled. A greasy looking man in a duster coat with crooked white false teeth held a revolver to Esther and Viola. She heard Esther's heart beating fast as her abilities tuned themselves to her surroundings. The man signalled with his pistol for Bee to sit at the table, and he pushed Esther to Philip.

'Where's the boy?' Philip asked, grabbing Esther.

'He ran,' Esther muttered.

Baptiste put his gun on the table, kneeling before Bee. He rubbed his hands over her leg. 'Is she?' He looked at Philip, and the man nodded. Baptiste licked his lips, whispering, 'Your daughter, she must have her mother's blood running through her. Omega, she'll get a good price for you, and little Viola.'

Bee said nothing, gazing at the greasy man, and then she head-butted Baptiste, sending him flying. Blood poured from his nose, and Esther screamed, covering Viola, backing into a corner. Bee picked up the chair, swinging it around, and crashed it into Baptiste's body. He fell to the ground, groaning.

Philip's mouth dropped. He lunged at Bee, grabbing her by the shoulders. She held onto him and jumped, with a kick to his stomach. Philip flew into the stove and Bee went over the table, while the kitchen knife and pistol fell to the floor.

'Get out, Esther.' Bee scrambled up as Baptiste grasped her leg, pulling her toward him. She cried out, stomping his fingers till he let go. Rising from the fall, Bee picked up the knife, running at Philip.

Philip swung a punch. She ducked, elbowing him in the head. Baptiste leapt up, clasping his arms around Bee. She dropped the knife and ran backwards with Baptiste into the sink. Pans and cutlery crashed to the floor, and Baptiste's bones cracked. The man whined, releasing her.

Baptiste punched Bee in the face, and she tumbled back. He pulled a blade from his pocket and Bee recognised the knife. A three-bladed twisting spiral knife and the butt was carved with a rose. Bee stared at the knife, it was her knife, a blade made for killing and nothing else. She'd last seen it on the day she closed The Barricade, when she handed it to the chaperone.

Philip pulled his own dagger out and held it to her neck. 'Bee, stop.'

Bee counted, and everything slowed down. She grasped Philip's wrist, twisting it. He screamed, dropping the dagger. The knife fell into Bee's free hand, and she forced Philip's hand onto the table, sticking the blade through his hand and the wood underneath.

Blood spurted into her face as Philip screamed and fell to his knees. Bee gripped his neck, and, in one movement, she brought the weight of her body on top of him. She squeezed, twisting Philip's head, and the bones in his neck crunched and broke. Bee casually dropped Philip, looking at Baptiste.

She spat blood, cricking her neck, stepping over Philip. 'Go, Esther.' And she watched Esther, holding Viola, run out of the door. Bee rolled her shoulders, studying Baptiste. 'Where'd you get that knife?' she asked.

The blade glistened, and Baptiste smirked, 'Off a dead Englishman.'

She pulled the blade out of the table, and Philip's hand fell. The coppery bloody odour was intoxicating. It reminded Bee of her own history. The ease of killing, and every kill she'd committed. Baptiste ran, and both headed for the door. He opened it as Bee slammed her body into him, shattering the windowpanes as the door crashed into its frame.

Baptiste dropped the twisting knife. Bee dived, picking up the blade. She punched Baptiste, raising the knife, about to plunge it into the man's head.

'Bedelia!'

Malick's gripped her hands. Bee choked, she was ready to kill, and his voice shook her. She was too slow as Baptiste grabbed his pistol running out of the door. Bee blinked, blood and sweat trickling down her face. She stuttered, and Malick pulled the blade out of her hand.

***

Philip's body lay slumped under the table. Malick stood by the sink, staring at the spiral knife on the drainer. He replayed the image of Bee with her arms raised high, standing over Baptiste. The room was a mess, chairs everywhere, some broken, pots and pans, all over the floor, and the door on its hinges.

Bee sat at the kitchen table. Clothes ripped, soaking in blood, and the bruising on her face was spreading. Malick had put a bowl of water and towel out before Bee, suggesting she should clean up, but she hadn't moved. It had been more than half an hour since Malick walked into what? He didn't know, and Bee remained quiet.

Smashed crockery lay on the floor. He picked up the handle of an old and finely painted tea cup. It had been part of a wedding set from Nadine's parents. He'd wanted to give it to Tristan when the boy came of age.

'Why is Philip dead on my kitchen floor?' Malick inspected the handle, and a minute went by. 'Explain why you were about to kill Baptiste?'

Bee rubbed her fingers over her cheeks. 'Something about a payment not being honoured.'

He caught her action. 'The truth, please.'

Silence.

'Bedelia.' He thumped the drainer, and the knife jumped.

Bee chewed her lip. 'You'll hate me when I tell you.'

'I won't hate you, Bee, but you can't kill Philip and expect me not to want to know why?'

She cleared her throat. 'I am a full-blooded Guardian.'

Malick frowned. 'Is this a joke?' He threw the pieces of crockery into the sink. 'For fuck's sake, Bee, this is serious.'

'Philip somehow realised. He and that man wanted to take me to your Omega,' Bee snapped.

Malick shook his head, saying, 'You…you can't be a Guardian, because Guardians are Gods.'

'They're not Gods, Malick,' she said.

'Philip's known you since you arrived, wouldn't he have detected something straight away?'

'You knew he was a Guardsman?' she asked.

He said nothing, choosing not to explain it was Philip who'd boarded the Juna and singled out the people with Guardian blood. He was the one who decided who went to Omega's abattoir.

Tristan had burst through the tavern's door, red-faced, teary-eyed, and babbling incoherently. He'd left Tristan with Aimee, running home to find Esther coming toward him in the street, clinging to Viola, only just managing to get out that Bee had broken Philip's neck, and then attacked Baptiste. Malick ran, frightened, wanting Esther to be wrong. He didn't believe Esther, and it was only because he'd witnessed Bee about to plunge a knife into Baptiste's head, did he realise Esther was telling the truth.

Bee then said, 'I masked my abilities, but they've come back.'

'And so you killed him because he thought you were a Guardian?'

'I wasn't planning on it, Malick.' Bee made eye contact for the first time.

'Why should I believe you?'

'I'm not lying,' she whispered, 'I thought I was protecting all of us, by burying my abilities.'

'How did you bury them?' he queried.

She let out some air, about to reveal something. 'I meditate. I've done it every day since I came here. You asked me once why I did it, I said it was something I learned at school...' and then Bee looked at the knife.

He followed her gaze to the three-spiralled blade, the perfect killing weapon. 'This knife... do you recognise it?'

Bee kept silent and Malick repeated the question again.

'Yes,' she murmured.

'What about this knife?' He picked it up. 'And remember you're riding the line here, Bedelia.'

She kept quiet, and he wasn't sure what her expression told him. Different emotions crawled across her face, sadness, honour, pain. Bee was going into the secret place, where she never took Malick, and he felt snippets of isolation and loneliness rise up, as she prepared to enter.

The kitchen clock ticked, and Bee's breathing got faster, and the clock kept ticking. His heart raced, watching her rub the nape of her neck, and her body trembled as she unfolded that secret something. Bee looked like she would choke on her words, and Malick thought she might faint again. He walked to her, crouching, slipping her hand into his, and she squeezed it.

'Bee, you've always been a little upside down.' He stroked her face. 'I don't know another woman like you. That's why I love you, so I need to know.'

Bee gave him a sad smile. 'Promise me, Malick,' she whispered, 'you'll remember that when I tell you?'

'Always.' He squeezed her hand.

She took a deep breath, saying, 'It's my knife because I'm a Reaper.'

He blinked, unsure if he'd heard right. The words went around, becoming jumbled and then reformed into the same sentence. Bee was a Reaper? A State-sanctioned killer? His hand slipped, and he backed away. Malick had been in love with Bee since before he'd married her. She had given him a beautiful daughter and claimed Tristan as her own son, and now Bee was telling him, she was a highly trained assassin, loyal to their Overlord, and always the Guardian.

He whispered, 'A Reaper, please tell me you're making this up?'

'It's the truth.'

He stood over her. 'No, it can't be true.'

'Remember, you promised,' she said.

Bee breathed, and he stood listening, and it seemed as if she were the loudest sound in the kitchen. He remembered the night, the night he was attacked by the robbers, and the way Bee strode out of the house, so confident in her manner.

'What did you say to those robbers that night?' he asked.

Bee rubbed her cheek scars, he could see her hands trembling. They jittered between her nose and lips, and she looked at the floor, uttering, 'Perhaps it's better I don't tell–'

'Say it,' he yelled.

Bee took a breath. 'That I'd find them.' she paused and then the confession spilled out, with each word becoming colder and tough. 'Tie up their family, their wives would hang first. I'd slit the men's throat, and their children would be last. Those children would die, knowing it was their fathers who got them killed if ever they came back.'

Malick staggered back. Bee's admission was calculated, so different from the woman who'd been quiet moments before. Nausea bubbled through him, and he ran his fingers through his hair. Malick blinked, shaking his head. It couldn't be right. 'Who was your Overlord?'

'Fredrick Kendal, Overlord of Rolfen, till I was sent to the Tower.'

'The Butcher of the River?'

There were only a few English Overlords heard of in France, but Fredrick Kendal was a notorious figure in both countries, known for issuing warrants of executions, for even minor offences. He'd owned lands in the Normandie Region before the Barricade came, and governed the lands along the Medaway River.

'How many people have you murdered?' he asked.

'Executed,' she corrected.

'Is there a difference?'

'Yes.'

'How many?' he repeated.

'Forty-five executed. Five prisoners, four Reapers and two priests in self-defence.'

Malick clenched his fists. 'Fifty-six people!'

'But – but four of them were Reapers...I was...I was training...they'd have killed me otherwise,' Bee defended herself.

'You were twenty-seven when I married you, Bedelia. You'd already killed more than most Reapers that age,' he roared, turning away from her.

'Yes, but Lord Kendal enjoyed terrorising his –'

'Have you murdered children?' he questioned. Her silence meant only one thing. She had. Malick kicked a chair, splintering it into the wall. 'You're Tristan's mother, I left you with Esther, *and* I let you into my bed!'

'You told me that your father was hung by Reapers, I was scared.'

'Scared?' Malick raged, 'I scared you?'

'I didn't want you looking at me, the way you are now.'

'You didn't trust me, Bee.' He remembered something. 'You said you were a vassal. What's the truth? You can't be all three.'

'I am all three.'

'How?'

'I grew up a vassal. I was eight when I started training as a Reaper. Twenty-two when Eldric learned I was a Guardian, and by twenty-five, I had three children,' she said.

'And why would a man even sleep with a dirty Reaper?' he asked. 'Who fathered those children?'

'I don't want –'

'Is it this English Luther you whisper about in your sleep?' he demanded, his French accent becoming broader, the angrier he got. 'The one you refuse to tell me anything about?'

The question silenced Bee. 'No,' she eventually answered. 'Luther is my friend, my Unseen.'

Malick carried on, not registering Bee's last words. 'Reapers aren't allowed to have children, why are you different? Who fathered them?'

'Eldric's my real father, he signed a Royal Decree,' she muttered. 'Lord Oren and I –'

Malick closed his eyes, Bee sounded broken. He ignored it, shouting, 'Eldric? He's your father? And you had sex with your cousin?'

'It's not what you think, Malick!'

He grabbed her chin, pawing her scars. 'Bedelia, you really are a 'cheap cunt,' after all?' he squeezed her arms, and something rose inside him - anger, but it came from within Bee, and then it exploded. He was thrown across the room, his body smashing into the cabinet and then the floor. Crockery crashed around him.

Bee rushed, falling to her knees, touching him. 'Oh god.'

'Stay away.' He pushed her, scrabbling up. Bee looked visibly shaken, but Malick didn't recognise this woman, he didn't know who she was.

Bee stood up, her eyes narrowed. 'And what about you, Malick?' she asked icily, stepping closer. 'What about those people from Britain, how many did you send to die? Were some of them children? Are those children now pieces of flesh sewn into the likes of Helena?'

'What?' he gasped.

Bee had changed from the quiet tones of a wife to the chilling accent of a Reaper. 'You're like me, a baby-killer.

You may not have pulled the trigger, but you murdered them, all the same.'

He slapped Bee across the face. 'I'm nothing like you because you're just a heartless fucking Reaper.' He wanted her to say something, anything, but Bee kept silent. Malick looked down at his hand, he'd never hit a woman before and backed away.

'At least I know what I am,' she uttered.

What she said was the truth, though he couldn't admit it. 'You made me love you, Bee. I wanted you. I've only ever wanted you.' Malick's eyes glistened. 'And our whole marriage is a lie, Bedelia. Everything is a lie. You need to go, get out.'

'And where am I supposed to go?' she demanded.

'Anywhere away from me.'

'Please –'

'Je ne te veux pas, Bedelia.' He turned to Bee and saw her face pale. She knew French well enough to understand.

'Then say it in English.'

He looked directly at her. 'I don't want you, Bedelia.'

Chapter Six
Bononia-Sur-Mer, Northern France

The kitchen was a wreck. Bee looked at the many broken things and then Philip's body. His glassy eyes stared as if asking Bee why she'd killed him and flies crawled over his face and eyes, as they'd caught the scent of the dead.

This man was one of the first people in Bononia who was friendly to the English stranger. She considered Philip a good friend, and she'd killed him. And she'd do it again if she had to.

After Malick shouted he didn't want her, Bee clammed up, sewing her emotions shut and the silence inside Bee's head, drowned out Malick. Bee retreated into her quiet world, and hardened her mind. Malick told Bee he was going to check on Esther and the children, and when he returned, she had to be gone.

Everything was broken, chairs, blood, crockery, glass everywhere. Malick shouted at Bee to bury the body, saying, *'Tristan shouldn't have to see what his mother did.'* Instead, she walked past Philip into the hallway.

Up in the bedroom, she changed into clean breeches and grabbed two carpetbags out of the wardrobe. Clothes were shoved into one bag and there, hanging in the closet was the green dress Malick bought her. Touching it, Bee smiled, and her heart ached because she only wore it in front of him. It tied around her body, with an elegant drop from the bodice to the ankle, and Malick always said she looked exquisite in it.

Bee closed the door on the dress.

She'd seen nothing wrong in marrying Malick two months after Nadine died, but Bee didn't know she'd have to sign a contract. It wanted a surname, and she didn't have one. Bee remembered telling Malick her surname was McKay, Rufus's name, she'd used that.

The wedding night frightened Bee. Malick wanted to kiss her, and though Bee wanted the same, she'd threatened him. Malick stayed away, watching Bee like he always did.

The marriage wasn't even a week old when Bee learned what the town thought. The store was a ten-minute walk. With Tristan in a homemade sling and Esther carrying a basket, they headed to the few open shops.

Bee hadn't witnessed the panic-buying. The scrabbling over one another like frenzied animals for the last egg, or piece of meat before they locked themselves in, praying the Red Plague wouldn't come to their doors, and though the peak had been reached more than a year before Bee was found on the beach, people were still dying.

The general store had a few shoppers at the counters. Most of them did their own shopping as the maids were dead or gone. The women dressed as presentably as they could, but most of their clothing had seen better days, as they tried to run their homes or tend to the sick.

They wore long dresses, coats, hats, and gloves, as Bee carried Tristan wearing breeches, shirt and heavy boots. The women sniggered, muttering as Esther followed Bee inside.

The store was big, and on one side, the apothecary counter stood, the shelves decimated, with jars either empty or half full. A few herbs lined the shelves behind, and a young man, dressed in shirt and a tie rang up the till. It clanked as he put the money through for an exhausted looking woman.

At the back hung coloured materials and opposite were the staples, butter, eggs, and flour. They joined the small queue, as rationing had been introduced and every shopper had a list, which they had to stick with. Mr Allard, the owner, holstered a gun, and Esther told Bee, he'd shot several people during the peak of the plague. The place smelled of fresh bread and sweet stuff, Bee didn't know what, she'd never really had much sweet stuff.

Then the whispering started. Bee was taking everything in about the store, the fine decorated barrels, the pens and paper for sales, and the baskets hanging overhead. In Britain, she never visited these stores, and every time she came to the shop, Bee spotted something new to look at.

'Hello, Mr Allard,' Bee smiled, as it was their turn at the counter, and she gave him their list.

Mr Allard, a middle-aged, moustached, and well-groomed gentleman, greeted her with a smile and took the list. 'How are you today, ladies? And how is young Tristan?' and he peered inside the sling, seeing the boy asleep.

'Fine, thank you,' Bee answered, watching as Mr Allard filled the basket Esther handed over.

'She's fine, the English trollop is fine,' a woman whispered behind her back. Bee recognised the voice belonging to a Mrs Helena Berger.

There was embarrassment in Mr Allard's face, and Bee nodded for him to carry on. Esther shifted in her boots, as Bee placed her hand over the girl's shoulder, telling her not to worry.

'... Nadine's not even dead three months, and that mutilated whore is warming Malick's bed,' Mrs Berger carried on. 'At least she isn't alive to see this, may the Guardians protect Nadine.'

Another woman joined in, 'Malick must be desperate to marry that lowborn English rose.' And all the women gave a haughty laugh.

'Malick should take the belt to her, teach the harlot how to dress properly, dressing up like that,' Mrs Berger sniped. 'He'll treat her like he did Nadine. Chase other women, once he's had enough of that butchered face.'

'And you should know, Helena, your liaisons only stopped when she turned up,' another woman said, and the women all giggled.

Then one woman whispered, 'Malick just never loved Nadine,' followed by mutters of *'Poor Nadine.'*

'Nadine said once she has scars all over her body,' another woman said.

'Ladies,' Mr Allard called over the counter. 'That's enough.' And he handed the basket back to Esther as Bee paid.

'Thank you, Mr Allard,' Bee nodded. She turned and looked at the small group of five women. All of them wearing shabby outfits, and Bee did look different, and she always would.

Bee straightened her back as she held Tristan in his sling, and stepped into the group. A familiar coldness rushed through Bee, and she spoke in a disquieting manner as if she were hiding behind her Reaper uniform.

'So, there's a problem here,' Bee stated, and the women gasped, pretending to look at a counter. Bee nodded to a young woman, 'You,' her voice hard, 'your name is Mrs Helena Berger? Your husband is friends with Malick?'

The woman stuttered, 'Yes, that's correct.'

'You think Malick should take the belt to me because I don't wear a dress?' Bee got up close, and in the woman's face.

Mrs Berger's jaw dropped. 'I didn't...mean anything by it...' She looked to her friends, but nobody said anything.

'Tell me,' Bee uttered, 'has your skin caught fire by the lashes of a belt?'

The woman paled, hand to mouth, staggering back. 'No, Mrs Rose.'

Bee spotted the guilt in the woman's face. 'Be thankful for that, Mrs Berger.' She looked at the other women, who were all too scared to move. Bee remained close to Helena. 'My husband is a good man. I do not see why Malick screwing his new wife is any of your business.'

The women gasped, and one woman started, 'That's because –'

'Do not finish that sentence,' Bee interrupted.

Turning, she nodded to Mr Allard, thanking him for his service, before ushering Esther out of the store.

On the walk home, Esther was excited, finding it funny at the way Bee spoke with the ladies. Once at home, Bee advised she'd talk to Malick about the incident, as she didn't want the girl to worry her uncle.

An hour later Bee was upstairs in the nursery feeding Tristan, cradling him in her arms. She sat in the rocking chair with a bottle to the boy's mouth. The front door slammed, and then came muffled voices as Malick's boots thumped up the threadbare carpets, and he came into the nursery.

'Mr Allard came by and explained what happened.' He stood, arms folded, over Bee. 'Would you have told me?'

Bee carried on feeding. 'Yes, I would have told you.'

'You frightened Mrs Berger, do I need to apologise for your –'

Bee's raised her eyebrows. 'Why do you need to apologise?' she rocked Tristan.

'And did you say I was screwing you?' His French accent becoming more noticeable, but he didn't raise his voice.

Tristan grumbled, and Bee soothed him. 'I did.'

'Look, you've obviously had a tough upbringing, but it doesn't mean you can be rude to my friend's wives,' he snapped. 'This street language people aren't used to. You're a contradiction, Bedelia. You speak like a lady, other times more like a sailor.'

'Good thing I didn't say we were fucking, otherwise, Mr Allard might've had to get the smelling salts out,' Bee sniped.

'There's no need to be sarcastic, Bedelia.'

'But it's acceptable they call me 'tramp' suggesting you use the belt on me? And politely tell me you were sleeping with Helena while Nadine carried your son,' she retaliated. 'But that's okay because I'm a mutilated whore.'

He rubbed his jaw, crouching by the chair, saying, 'Bedelia, I'm sorry they called you those names, but I'm going to spell it out bluntly that I'm in love with you and have been since before Nadine died.'

Bee's heart jumped, muddling. 'They...they said you were desperate,' she whispered. 'And you only want me to warm your bed.'

'And they were right. I *was* desperate to marry you, because I want to build a life with you.' Still on his knees, Malick got closer. 'And I thought you accepted because you felt the same.'

'And I do,' Bee gasped, surprised that she'd said it. 'But I thought you'd you have Teppo and Somer hold me – and that you'd force – and I didn't want that.' She stopped for a second, then added, voice trembling. 'Malick, I don't get this world...it makes no sense...it makes no sense that I can't stand the thought of not being with you, and I don't understand why.' Her heart slammed against her chest, wanting to tell the whole truth, but it was too painful. She couldn't reveal she was a Guardian, let alone a Reaper. Malick wouldn't want her after that. Nobody wanted a Reaper.

He grinned, touching Bee's cheek. 'You're a little back to front, but Nadine never made me feel this way.'

Bee shook her head, eyes on Tristan. She hated admitting her feelings. Something a Reaper never did and Bee panicked, 'No, I shouldn't have said anything.'

'Look at me, Bedelia,' Malick whispered, and she trembled, looking at him. 'You're allowed to have these feelings.'

'But–'

'Nothing bad is going to happen by having them. I promise I'll keep you safe, always.' He squeezed her hand, as somebody knocked at the front door, and then Esther called up, saying Somer was waiting.

He shouted down, and then turned to Bee, 'We'll talk properly tonight, and can I ask something, may I kiss you?'

Holding Tristan in her arm, she nodded, and Malick remained on his knees. He leaned in close, and kissed her tenderly. Bee wanted to explode, as she kept kissing him, and something inside Bee unlocked, things she'd kept trapped sneaked out, and they clawed their way toward Malick.

'See,' he whispered, brushing Bee's short fringe. 'That wasn't so bad.'

That night Bee watched, heart in her mouth, from the parlour window, as two robbers threw Malick to the ground. He had a gun but wasn't quick enough. Bee stared at the cabinet. She'd have to explain herself once she'd rescued Malick, but it was better than having him dead. She'd owe him an explanation, and Bee decided some truth would be better than all of it.

Taking the key from the vase, opening the cabinet, she grabbed two revolvers, loading them. Bee closed her eyes. 'I remain in the darkness and wait until it is my time to die,' she whispered, taking comfort from these words. Bee marched out of the door, heading straight to Malick's attackers.

Bee closed her thoughts about Malick as she caught her bruised reflection in the wardrobe mirror, her face black and eyes swollen. It had been many years since Bee had seen this, but it was a familiar face. It told Bee she'd survived.

The bag packed, Bee sat on the bed, touching the linen. She'd purchased it after moving into the marital bedroom as Bee wanted something of her own when nothing inside the house belonged to her. Bee cringed, thinking about the argument, as she'd been cruel calling Malick a 'Baby-killer.' A name she'd heard many times, and she saw the hurt in Malick's face when she used it, but Bee couldn't take it back.

The voices whispered again. Somewhere in the distance of herself, they called, begging her to return and if she did, Bee would be free. Rubbing her scars, those intrusive feelings grew, telling Bee to finish what she started. And in the silence, she decided.

Opening the chest of drawers, Bee rummaged until she found the porcelain silhouette she kept hidden amongst her underwear. Touching the face, Bee smiled at the image, as it was the only thing she could take to remind her of Tristan, and she slipped it into her pocket.

Down in the parlour stood the gun cabinet. She went to the garden and fetched the axe. Bee held it high. Was she going to do this? Was Bee really going to steal his weapons? She could pick the lock, but Bee smashed the axe into the wood. After several whacks, the door crashed to the ground, and she filled the second carpet bag with revolvers, pistols, bullets and cartridges, leaving two guns for Malick. Bee loaded a pistol before tucking it into the back of her breeches. Everything had changed in a matter of hours. Bee had no family, no home and no husband. To Malick, she was a monster.

Heading into the kitchen, Bee hunted through the kitchen drawers, taking any knife that could be used as a weapon. On the drainer was the three-spiralled blade, and Bee picked it up, caressing the butt, and smoothing her hand over the sharp edges. This was something her Father, Rufus, had given Bee once she'd completed the apprenticeship. Bee flicked it around in her hand, pleased to have it back. Then she slipped off her wedding ring, placing it on the table near Philip's body.

Bee pulled on her leather coat and tied the belt, placed her wide-brimmed hat on and closed the front door without looking back. The horse waited as Bee hung the bags on either side of the saddle before mounting. Sighing, she looked at her black bracelet. Bee was alone, about to leave everybody she loved, behind. And about to embark on something which could get her killed.

***

People pushed and shoved, men, women and children worked and shouted, weaving around each other, carrying great boxes of fish, kegs of beer, or vegetables, all wanting to get somewhere fast. Bononia Port was busy for a half-dead town. The salt in the air could clog the lungs when the sea was rough, but today it was a beautiful clear day.

Schooners, clippers, and brigs moored at the quayside. The fishwives cried out, their shrieks cutting into the noise as they sold their husband's daily catch. Voices from all directions came from the boats, and slavers hustled four chained people down planks. They jeered and poked the new property, as the raggedy men with rotting flesh prodded their loot. If one of these people turned out to have guardian blood, the sailors would have extra money.

Seagulls screamed, looking for food, and they dived at the barrels of fish, while the salty air mixed with spicy food stalls. Shanty houses had sprung up, serving as shops or workshops. Grubby men with bent hats and old coats sat in old barrels, their gnarled hands feverishly mending the mountains of nets.

And Malick's two-mast tall ship, the Juna-Ray was ready to sail.

The twins, Teppo, and Somer Peron were on board. Teppo dozed on the deck with a beer, and Somer was in the captain's cabin, completing paperwork. The clanking of wood against wood as somebody ran up the plank, and then a splash, woke Teppo. Cursing, he went to investigate.

The figure, dressed in a long black coat, boarded, carrying two bags, and their wide hat hid their face, but Teppo recognised Bee's jacket. Teppo's chest tightened, the person's movements were wrong as if they were lurking in a half-world. One foot here and the other foot somewhere dangerous.

He'd only seen this movement once when he was a child and Reapers hung Malick's father. Nothing was known about Reapers after the Barricade went up, and now one was heading towards him.

The Reaper discarded the bags, pulled something out of their back and started running along the 120-foot ship toward Teppo. The person stared up at him, and Teppo dropped his beer, smashing the bottle onto the deck. His eyes widened, looking at Bee raising her gun, and Teppo's heart pounded. His pistol, it was on the bench, and he dashed toward it. Bee slid along to stop him, firing a warning shot over his head.

'Don't make me shoot you, Teppo.' Bee stood, extending her arm, aiming the weapon at him.

'Bee, Malick isn't here,' Teppo garbled, shaking, and he saw Bee's bruises. 'And what happened to your face? Did he hit you after last night?'

'Don't be stupid, Malick wouldn't do this,' Bee snapped.

'Then who did?' he asked.

A door swung open, and Somer sprang out, brandishing a revolver, ready to fire. Bee palm punched him in the face, sending him onto the deck as Bee grabbed his weapon, aiming the guns at each brother.

'Can you get me through The Crack?'

'Bee?' Somer frowned.

Seagulls squawked, and the quayside voices chatted in the background, filling Teppo with outside noise, as he stood, staring at Bee, confused.

Somer coughed, wiping his nose, looking at the blood on his fingers. 'Give me the pistol, Bee. We don't want you hurting yourself.'

'Don't patronise me, Somer, I'm a better shot than either of you.' Bee leered down at Somer. 'And don't try anything or I'll shoot you and gut your brother. Now can you get me to The Crack?'

'Look, Bee, whatever's gone on between you and Malick, I'm sure you can–' Teppo began.

No, he's made it clear.' Bee kept the guns on each brother.

Teppo noticed a small crowd gathered on the quayside, but nobody was coming to their rescue. The splash he'd heard was the boarding plank Bee had dropped into the waters below.

'I'm sure it's just a misunderstanding.' Teppo tensed, praying that Bee wouldn't really shoot him.

Bee shook her head. 'A misunderstanding?' she said coldly. 'You know what I am, I can see it. Tell me, how would you feel?'

Somer cut in. 'What's she talking about, Teppo?' He was still on the ground, but his twin didn't answer.

Teppo paused. Though he didn't know what had gone on, he'd probably feel the same as Malick. 'And if we don't help?' he asked.

'I'll kill you both now,' Bee told them. 'And even if you are both dead, I'll make you sail this boat.'

'That's impossible,' Teppo gasped.

Bee smiled, 'Would you like to find out?'

'What's she *talking* about, Teppo?' Somer got louder, shaky, and he looked up toward his brother.

Bee placed the pistol at Somer's head, saying calmly, looking at Teppo. 'I understand twins have a special bond.' She cocked the pistol, pressing the barrel into Somer's forehead. 'If I shoot Somer, and leave you alive, will a piece of you be missing for the rest of your life?'

Teppo's heart raced, hearing the threat as Somer raised his hands. 'We can get you through, but we've not enough men.' The words rushed out, afraid for his twin.

'Get the Juna out of the harbour, and I'll deal with that.' She withdrew the pistol, walking away from Somer.

'What the fuck?' Somer uttered.

Teppo rushed over to Somer, helping him stand. He said, 'Bee is a Reaper.'

Chapter Seven
Bononia-Sur-Mer, Northern France

Malick saw the smashed gun cabinet. Every weapon gone, except two revolvers. The same guns Bee had used when she rescued him, and he cursed. He headed to the bedroom, calling out Bedelia's name, but there was no response. Everything in the room looked the same, except his wife was missing. He opened Bee's wardrobe. It was empty, only the green dress remained.

He pulled it out, sitting on the bed. He'd been angry upon learning Bee was a Guardian, but learning she was a Reaper frightened Malick. He remembered being an eight-year-old boy, watching his father swing from the noose, with two Reapers standing in their black uniforms on the gallows platform. Malick sometimes threatened Tristan with Reapers when the boy misbehaved, and Bee asked him to stop. Now he knew why.

Malick had continued yelling after he'd said he didn't want her, and Bee stood in the kitchen, withdrawing right before him into her secret world. He shivered, remembering the chilly sensation he got from Bee, that connection he always had with her then hardened and he'd caused that.

Bee was Reaper, Guardian and vassal, and he'd been too quick, ignoring that she loved him. Instead he'd called her 'A dirty Reaper,' and Malick wanted Bee back, whatever she was. Ashamed, because he'd forgotten his promise so fast.

Putting the dress down, he was about to leave, when Malick remembered the Porcelain silhouette. Ransacking the drawers, pulling them out, throwing them on the bed, he couldn't find it. Sighing, Malick headed down through the house to the kitchen. Opening the door, he found Philip staring up, and then he spotted it.

Malick walked up to the table, eyes fixed on the wedding ring, and his world crumbled. Bee's presence, the ripple which connected him to her swept over him, and the same desolation lingered. She was letting something out. He didn't know what it was, but it was ferocious.

Picking up the ring, he rubbed it. The ring was a plain silver band because when they married, he couldn't have afforded anything more. Bee had never complained about its simplicity, and he remembered the night of the robbery.

She'd shot one robber, and chased them away. Bee dragged Malick up, taking him back to the house, and she dumped him on the stairs, before bolting the door. Once the weapons were back secured in the gun case, she pulled at his face, checking for bleeding.

'Your nose isn't broken, but you'll need stitches,' she commented as Esther came halfway down the stairs, pulling on her dressing gown. Bee asked Esther to prepare his bedroom, but the young girl stayed, watching.

Malick slapped Bee's hands away, getting off the stairs, backing away. He sweated, panting, and stared at Bee, not quite grasping everything as Bee looked relaxed, considering she'd kneecapped a man.

'Shit, Bedelia, what the hell have you done?' he snapped.

Confused, she said, 'Just saved your life.'

'What, by shooting the man? And my guns, they're locked.' He winced, ribs aching from the punches.

'But they'd have killed you.'

Malick got up close. He was much bigger than Bee, towering over her, but she didn't move. 'I was dealing with it, Bedelia,' he raged.

Bee stood her ground. 'You were making a piss-poor effort of dealing with it from where I was standing.'

Affronted, Malick yelled, 'You've really overstepped the mark, and they'll come back. You've made us targets, putting Esther and Tristan in danger.'

Bee said calmly, 'They won't come back.'

Malick frowned, 'And how would you know?'

'Because I know men like that,' she answered.

Malick glared at Bee. He'd been looking forward to coming home, being able to sit with Bee and have a conversation; instead, he'd been attacked, and she'd shot somebody. 'I don't need you to save me,' he sneered.

Her eyes tightened. 'Fine, next time they can shoot you.' And Bee started towards the kitchen, shouting to his niece, 'Don't fucking bother, Esther, he can sort his *fucking* self out.'

Malick grabbed her arm, squeezing it. Bee yelped as he yanked her back. 'Don't swear at Esther, she's fifteen years old.'

'And she's just lost her aunt, Malick. Esther's parents are dead, her friends are dead. Half the town is dead, I did it so she didn't have to see you dead,' Bee hissed.

Malick was silenced.

'I did what I thought was right, so fuck you, Malick.' She wrenched her arm free. 'Fuck you,' she whispered, slamming the door on his face.

He stood in the hall, stumped by Bee's outburst as he hadn't considered Esther. Malick shouted because he was angry that he hadn't been able to defend himself. After all, Bee had risked her own life to save him, and she'd been better at it than he ever could be.

'Uncle Malick, say sorry,' Esther said, heading back up the stairs.

'How come it's now my fault?' he bellowed into the empty hallway, but Esther was right, he needed to apologise.

Malick hesitated, and then he went into the kitchen. Bee sat at the head of the table, in the dark, with an oil lamp lighting up the room. 'Bedelia, I shouldn't have shouted.'

'I'm sorry I swore at Esther,' then she added, 'and for swearing at you.'

His ribs hurt. 'Well, your choice of language is certainly something.'

'Every night since you've opened The Raven I've sat waiting.' She drank her tea. 'The militia is useless. They won't help you.'

'You still shouldn't have done it,' he said.

Bee sat Malick in the chair and then headed into the pantry. 'I didn't do it just for Esther, my feelings haven't changed from this afternoon.' Clanking sounds came from inside the pantry as things were moved. Then there was a long silence. She returned with a bowl, a glass, whiskey, clean cloth, and Esther's sewing basket, setting them out on the table, not able to meet Malick's gaze. 'You teach me French, and are polite about my burnt biscuits, even though they look like something the cat's puked up, probably tastes like it too.'

'They're not that bad,' Malick commented, noticing her embarrassment, and he was confused. That afternoon she'd struggled to explain herself and now Bee was different, more confident.

Bee gave him a little smile, 'I only go to that bloody Temple, as it gives me a chance to sit with you. I wouldn't go otherwise.'

Malick replayed her last sentence, *'A chance to sit with you.'* Then he said, 'And I thought you were a believer.' Knowing full well Bee didn't believe in the words of Priest Felix. She'd hold Tristan, and sit in her secret world.

'You don't believe it either, but you take Esther because she wants to go.' She inspected the wound again.

'If we didn't go, we'd be the talk of the town.'

Baffled, Bee said, 'We are the talk of the town, Malick.'

'People gossip,' he told her, 'and I don't want you getting hurt, more than you already have been.'

'Your friends already think you married a whore, they'll call me heathen soon enough. I won't faint at a few women trying to hurt my feelings. I'm used to being insulted.' She paused, then said, 'Your way of life is very different from mine.'

'You said you know men like those robbers, how?'

Bee pulled a face. She chewed the side of her lips thinking about it, and he noticed her expression changed. It darkened, giving Bee a dangerous look, and then it was gone.

She answered, 'I've encountered men like that before. I'm not property, nor human, but there is always a time to fight, and a time to protect somebody.'

Malick thought about what she said, 'What does not property or human mean?'

'I'm a Passive Being, no feelings, no intellect and my body belonged to the master. Even my death did.' She got some water and soaked the wound, before filling the glass with whiskey. Malick picked it up, but she snatched it back placing the needle into it.

'You're a vassal?'

'They didn't call it that.' Bee cut the thread and washed her hands in the whiskey. She cleansed the wound in the alcohol before threading the needle. Bee inhaled and said, 'I have three children. Hamish was two when I last saw him, and Oliver, six months old. My...we... did our duty and produced children.'

'I didn't know –ouch,' he cried. Bee wasn't gentle, pushing the needle into his skin, and it surprised him that Bee was speaking so freely.

'Why would you know?' Bee pulled the thread, repeating the action. 'I didn't know them, but I miss them.'

He asked, deflated. 'Luther, is that their father?' wincing as she pinched his skin.

'Luther isn't the father... he's my...' Bee bumbled, '... he's my... oh never mind.'

'Did you love their father?' he asked, understanding most vassals didn't marry.

She looked puzzled, saying, 'Love? No, that's something for free people.' Bee tied the thread off, agitated. 'I produced children with my master, and his uncle got the heirs he wanted,' Bee whispered, checking the stitching. 'None of us had any choice in the matter.'

And Malick remembered the unfinished sentence Bee had said earlier in the day. 'You were forced to have children?' A single chill travelled down his spine, imagining the horrors, and now he understood why Bee defended herself on their wedding night.

'His wife couldn't give him the children that his–' she paused, scratching her scars. 'His wife couldn't have children.'

'You said you had three children?' Malick asked softly. The kitchen clock ticked as he waited for her to speak.

'Oliver and my daughter are twins.' Bee laid her hand on his shoulder.

Her answer left a gap in the conversation, and then Malick asked, 'What did you call her?'

Bee looked away. 'I didn't give her a name, and I've never seen her. The uncle said she was incomplete, sending her away before I was even allowed to look at her. I don't know where she is.'

'What would you have called her?' he whispered.

Bee smiled wistfully. 'I'd have called her Edith.'

Malick wanted to reach out, touch her, but he clasped his hands together, asking, changing the subject sharply. 'And where did you get your shooting skills from?'

Bee blinked, pulling away. 'From my father, Rufus, I was his vassal as a child. I did everything he ordered, and in exchange, he beat me.'

'He's family?'

'Not by blood, he took me in as a baby. When I was eight, everything changed. He taught me to read, write and shoot, beating me if I didn't get it right. I then had a new master at twenty-two.'

'Your father doesn't sound like a good man,' Malick uttered.

'Rufus is a tough, mean old cunt, and he didn't give me much affection. I think he loved me, but he taught me I had to be hard.' She wiped her hands on her breeches several times, hands trembling.

'Did he teach you to swear as well?'

'Amongst other things.'

Malick stared, they were going to talk when he got home, and he wondered would she have revealed less if the robbers hadn't been at his door. She was coming at him like an avalanche.

'Why are you telling me this now?' he asked.

'Because after what happened outside, I wasn't sure I'd get the chance. You make me feel safe and wanted.' Bee pulled at her black bracelet, and then said, 'and... and I do owe you an apology because I was wrong.'

Warmth spread through Malick. 'An apology for what?'

'Because... I've never felt like this before... because I'm in love with you, but I'm scared, that's why I nearly broke your arm,' she whispered, going slightly red.

'Bedelia, I–'

She kissed him and then withdrew eyes wide. 'I'm sorry, I shouldn't have – you're hurt – and I, I –'

He kissed her back. Malick's heart beat faster. He ignored the pain in his ribs, holding Bee, afraid to let go because if he did, she might reject him. Malick picked her up and pushed her onto the table, tugging at Bee's clothes as she fumbled with his shirt. His blood raced as her hand slipped around his neck, kissing him.

He pulled Bee's top off, and for the first time, touched Bee's skin and her scars. Malick didn't want to stop. His hands were inside her trousers, pulling them down as he moved Bee up the table, discarding them onto the floor. Quickly he unbuttoned his breeches, climbing on top of her.

'Sorry if I do something wrong,' she whispered.

Malick heard her voice shake. He stroked her hair, asking, 'Do what wrong?' he looked at her, and she stared back, her breathing shallow.

'I don't know.'

He smiled, 'You love me, Bedelia Rose, that's enough.' Malick kissed her. Those words excited him because he'd wanted to hear them, and the sex became a combination of fear, hunger, and want. It was hot, animalistic and fast. Now they'd found each other, and Malick lay breathless on the table, holding Bedelia, never wanting to let go.

'Sorry I took so long to say...' She whispered, 'I thought – and my scars –'

'Your scars are beautiful,' he said, kissing her cheek. And Malick then made love to his wife for the first time. This was an extraordinary tactile moment. He'd slept with Nadine and other women, but making love to Bee was different.

It was slow and hypnotic. Bee entwined herself around him. A seductive, but fearsome sensation he'd never experienced before. He opened himself up, letting her creep around, marking him. She washed through him, a sexual fluidity embracing every piece of him, settling deep inside. And he accepted she was choosing him, but for what, Malick didn't know. It left him sensually haunted because his wife willingly placed herself inside him, fusing herself into Malick, and only him.

A knock at the front door brought Malick back to the present. Opening it, he saw a sweaty young boy, panting, at the door. The Harbourmaster's son wiped his forehead, trying to catch his breath.

'Mr Rose,' the boy said, 'my father sent me.'

'Yes, Artie?'

'Somebody boarded your ship. It sailed out of the dock about a half-hour ago.'

He frowned at the boy. Did he hear right? Malick closed the door, saying nothing to the boy. His boat gone, but who would have taken it? And why? Malick sighed, heading back through the kitchen and into the garden. He grabbed the shovel and passed the vegetable patch, down to the muddy overgrowth, and he dug. Every throw of mud more forceful, as the hole got bigger. Malick fumed.

Bee had stolen his bloody ship.

Chapter Eight
DulPenne, Spanish Netherlands

Marisol dismounted her horse, and the accompanying rider took the animal and tethered it. Marisol, better known as Omega, breathed in the stink of urine as the hot sun increased the stench while workers coated the skins in the alkaline-lime mix. The whole tanning process lasted for several weeks, beginning with the carcasses being boned. This tannery was separated from the town's abattoir and heavily guarded. Men stood watch, armed with pistols and rifles, and only authorised workers had access.

The townsfolk knew what happened there, but they pretended they didn't. They preferred to think of DulPenne as simply a market town, where people could buy human cargo from Omega's traders in the square. Once a month, the market expanded, making room for the new commodity to be sold, and the sounds of chains, cries and the lashing of whips would echo through the dirty narrow streets. Businessmen, farmers, anybody who needed people would come to the town in the hope of securing new property to work their lands. The residents adopted a culture of blindness when it came to the murdering and of dismembering humans. It was easier not to talk about, and that kept the locals alive.

Marisol entered the courtyard through a small door inside a massive wooden gate. Inside, six pieces of hide were stretched out. The workers had un-haired, degreased and unsalted the product, and then it was soaked in water. They'd stretched out the eighteen feet of skin, and shortly it would be immersed in vats of tannin.

Once the process was completed, the workers would cut the skins, and sell them to the apothecaries. This turning of human skin into leather strips, and selling to plague survivors didn't turn Marisol's stomach. To her, it was another form of commerce.

Marisol stumbled, and the rider caught her arm. 'Omega?' he frowned.

She pushed him away. Marisol had woken up feeling this way, her abilities whispered that she had two Guardian siblings. One was on this side of The Barricade, but the other was in Britain, and two full-blooded Guardians could bring her a lot of money.

She'd arrived in DulPenne several years before they set up The Barricade. And those two children, she'd forgotten about. Thoughts flashed, and Marisol remembered Verda, her mother, pushing babies out of her body and the servants vanishing with them. She never knew what happened to the first girl, and when the second child was born several years later, Marisol was told she was dead. However, these sensations told her that both were alive. Verda did not survive Britain, but she died knowing

Marisol had escaped, and Eldric couldn't hurt her, not in the way he had Verda.

She had survived by being cold-blooded. When she'd landed, she had been merely Marisol, a young girl, no more than thirteen. But when she and her men had seized control of the town, she'd become Omega though not yet in name. Over the years she had grown ruthless; a business that had started in selling beer then became human trafficking.

The Guardians were as susceptible to the Red Plague as their subjects, and most perished. Marisol then slaughtered the surviving few, and the locals gave her the title 'Omega' because she was the last Guardian in the region.

And once The Crack was discovered, Marisol sent ships through. They smuggled tobacco, materials or whiskey, but then Baptiste kidnapped children. Easy pickings, he told her. People needed workers to tend the land, and for breeding. There wasn't enough healthy local population left. And Marisol started selling slaves.

A close advisor pointed out many people were of Guardian descent. He separated them, explaining more profit could be made in selling body parts for medicinal purposes, and Marisol saw the potential. And it wasn't only skin the survivors wanted.

Human bodies had value, and Marisol built a small empire out of human skin, masks, bones, teeth, and blood. Whether people wanted human fat-based soaps or tinctures laced with Guardian blood, if people believed enough in their healing properties, she would sell it.

Verda would be ashamed of what she had become. Marisol blinked. She hadn't thought about her mother in a long time, and the spark of these two sisters brought those memories back.

Marisol felt as if she were back inside those tower walls. A little girl, seeing things she wasn't supposed to see. She'd hear every grunt as Eldric climbed onto her mother. The Guardian was obsessed with having a male heir, and he showed no interest when he learned of the two baby girls. There were whispers that Eldric wanted a boy because he was the source of the Guardian abilities. Marisol listened but never discovered the truth.

'Omega, we've new cattle.' Stephen, a young man, in his twenties, approached.

'Let me see,' Marisol said, pulling her hair back. It was shaved on either side, and she tied it into a tail. She wore old breeches and boots, clothes that were suited to a place like this.

'Twelve this time. The Guardsman says one is heavy with Guardian blood.' He walked beside her, out of the private courtyard into an ugly white building, with its windows blacked out.

They entered, and the smell was the first thing that hit Marisol. Shit and piss. The cattle relieved themselves in buckets, and the workers used it in the tanning process. Straw covered other raw human waste, and men surrounded the pens, watching the cattle starve for three days before being slaughtered.

'Is it getting difficult?' Marisol asked, walking up a well-trodden mud ramp, and looked over the captives.

'We think the English know about the Crack, but we're going further west now. A Finder in Almer tells us people are noticing,' Stephen explained.

'Kill them, we need their skin,' she growled, as her head banged. The new presence of another Guardian was affecting her.

'But that'll damage the product.'

Marisol stopped, grabbing his shirt. 'Our buyers don't care.'

'Yes, Omega,' Stephen said, looking at her hand.

A group of twelve had been placed inside one pen. They were bedraggled and greasy, keeping their faces to the ground, frightened. There were five beaten men, with their breeches and shirts bloody, and four women in ripped dresses, and behind the group, three children hid. She gazed down on the group, four of them looked scrawny, not like the other eight who had plenty of meat on them.

'Not one of our best herds,' Marisol commented, standing over the fence, and the whimpering tears of the women annoyed her. 'Pay the Finders more, if they go into the towns.'

'But the town's soldiers and Reapers–'

'They'll do it for more money,' Marisol snapped. She looked at the group, as one large dirty man faced her. There was always one. Usually, they turned and cowered after a minute, but this man carried on. He stepped closer, and the guards aimed their rifles.

He raised his hands. 'Please, we've done nothing wrong.'

Marisol gestured to the men to lower their rifles. What this man said, she had heard many times. They would beg for freedom, promises of telling nobody, and if that failed they would ask for their children's lives to be spared. Once they understood they were not leaving, the men would become aggressive, making demands and empty threats. She'd heard them all, and never once released a person.

'Don't waste your time begging,' Marisol said.

'But you can let us go. We won't say anything,' the man pleaded.

She bared her teeth. 'It's too late.'

The man rushed towards the gap in the fence, grabbing her ankle, trying to pull Marisol into the pen. The gunfire started, and it mixed with the women's screaming. The guards fired, aiming at his feet, avoiding his body, and the man cried, falling into the old straw.

'Omega!' Stephen shouted.

She jumped inside the pen and stood over the man, who scurried back on all fours toward the group. She lurched forward, grabbing him and forcing him to his knees.

'You will pick two, a woman and a child.' Marisol's head hurt. The blood connection was fastening itself to her, and the odour of faeces was nauseating. She punched the man to the ground, ordering him to pick. The man trembled, tears rolled down his cheeks as he pointed to a woman and a young boy. None of the group helped as four armed men entered the pen and took the two victims.

Marisol leaned over the man, whispering. 'This is your fault. *You* will hear every scream as their skin is taken.'

The man whispered, 'Please...'

'Set them in the sun.' She punched the man in the face again.

'But it will damage the skin, Omega,' Stephen said.

'Do it!' Marisol shouted, 'unless you want to be next.'

The remaining cattle backed themselves into a corner. Marisol's thoughts swam and she left the building. Everything moved so fast, and she thumped her hand against the wall causing it to crack.

Stephen took the prisoners outside. The woman fought, thrashing out as the men stripped her naked, and the boy struggled, but neither could defend themselves. Their legs and arms were chained, stretched out on the dusty ground, and left to lie in the baking sun.

'Start tonight,' Stephen ordered, not looking at the men.

Marisol ground her teeth, heading toward the gates, and Stephen followed her to the courtyard, as the rider gave her the horse. And in the distance, a horse kicked up dust, galloping up toward the tannery.

Baptiste slowed his horse down, tipping his hat to Marisol. She pulled the reins, as the animal panted, frothing at the bit as Marisol led it to water. Baptiste dismounted and took a mouthful of water from the same bucket as the horse.

'Where's Philip?' she demanded.

'Dead.'

'How?' Marisol frowned.

'Malick Rose's wife turned on Philip – almost killed me.' He gulped more water. 'Fucking bitch broke his neck. Philip said he thought he detected Guardian on Malick, that's why we went there. Turns out she's a full-blooded Guardian.'

Marisol's face tightened. The woman had masked her abilities, which was unusual as Guardians couldn't do that, they were all interconnected. She'd somehow kept them hidden, and that meant Bedelia Rose was a much more powerful Guardian than her. She must be the daughter of Eldric.

'They have a daughter,' Baptiste said. 'A half-breed.'

Marisol mulled over the information, but she needed to lie down, as her head was blackening with pain. 'I need to rest.' And she almost stumbled over her own feet. Baptiste caught her.

'Omega, are you okay?' he asked.

'Take me to the Fort.' She gripped his sleeve. With shallow breaths, she said, 'I need to rest. This Bedelia woman is affecting me.'

'Is there anything you want me to do?' Baptiste asked.

The first rider assembled a small cart for Marisol to journey in. She climbed in and looked down at Baptiste.

'Get the men ready. When I've rested, we'll get this little Bee,' she whispered.

***

The Channel

The Juna sailed towards The Crack, as the waters crashed around them. They'd left Bononia two hours ago with sails at full masts. The brothers watched wide-eyed as each sail shot up, knots tied and the winds blew. Bee made it happen, neither understood how, but it was like watching unseen hands were making the ship sailable.

Teppo stood on the deck, the sea sprayed over, and the gulls flew overhead. He looked down at Bee, noticing her stature. Watching Bee made him shiver. He wrestled with the surreal experience he and Somer had been through, that Bee had overpowered two men, and stolen a boat.

She sat on the deck fiddling with the weapons inside her bag, and he recognised all of Malick's guns. She closed the bag, taking it into the ship's cabin, and returned heading toward them. Teppo backed away next to his brother.

Teppo raised his hands. 'That's close enough.' Bee might have been unarmed, but he didn't want her near.

Bee nodded. 'Sorry I threatened you both, but I didn't know what else to do.'

Somer kept control of the wheel. 'Would you have done it?' he asked.

'I killed Philip.'

Nobody spoke, and the waves crashed against the sides of the boat.

'By age fourteen... by fourteen,' Bee stammered, 'I'd killed four apprentice Reapers. I have killed fifty-six people... and I am good at killing. I married Malick, and I was somebody different. Philip threatened Viola and me, and I broke his neck. So yes, Somer, I'd have killed you.'

'Fucking bitch,' Somer muttered disdainfully, spinning the wheel.

'Is Malick still alive?' Teppo chilled, asking the question. 'Did you hurt Tristan or Viola?' and Bee looked hurt by the question.

She gasped, 'I love Malick, I wouldn't hurt him, and I wouldn't hurt my children.'

Teppo mumbled his apologies, hoping to calm the situation. He'd only seen Reapers kill, and heard the stories. The Bee he knew wasn't like that, she loved her children, Esther, and Malick, and it was hard to imagine Bee as a killer.

'You're not just a Reaper, what else are you?' Teppo asked.

She shook her head. 'I'm a Guardian, and I did help build The Barricade.'

'Fuck!' Teppo gasped, 'Bedelia, why didn't you tell Malick any of this?'

'Because I thought keeping quiet would keep us all safe,' Bee flared.

'And look how that's turned out,' Somer interrupted, still steering the ship. 'You've killed Philip, stolen this boat, kidnapped us, left two children motherless, and lied to Malick for the past six years.'

Teppo held his hand up, stopping Bee answering. 'If you really want to go to Britain, we'll take you, but we can't get to The Crack alone.'

Bee approached. 'Do you promise not to be afraid?'

'Why? What are you going to do?'

She spread her fingers out over his forehead, to his cheek and chin. Teppo blinked, conscious of Bee's touch. He watched her take a deep breath, and then he felt her.

His blood flushed. A crackle came from Bee. She jolted, and Teppo felt violated as she walked inside him. He saw snippets of Bee's childhood, her as a little girl cleaning a blood-soaked courtyard, throwing limbs onto a fire. Then she was older, training to be a Reaper, impaling straw dummies with knives and stabbing prisoners, and Teppo saw Bee get shot.

Then Bee became a Reaper, and he witnessed the killings. She was partnered with a man called Luther, and they would perform executions together, when required. Another man appeared. He was frightened of Bee, and Teppo cringed as Bee fell pregnant by this man.

Luther returned, and he lay next to Bee, his arms wrapped around her swollen belly, and they whispered deadly secrets, as Bee cocooned herself in his body. Teppo shuddered as the spooky bond between two Reapers erupted into him. They were two solitary people carving out a quiet love, only found between killers, because to the outside world they were spectres for the living.

And then Teppo watched Bee hold two young boys, and she was proud because she was something else, not just a killer. He gasped, as her love for Malick consumed everything, and he witnessed Bee cementing herself into Malick and him accepting her. Now Teppo felt like an intruder. He saw the fight as Bee killed Philip, the way she defended herself, protecting Viola, protecting her family, and Teppo choked on the devastation when Malick told Bee he didn't want her.

And out of these images grew something dangerous, and its long winding tentacles moved like a snake toward Teppo. He tried to free itself as it bit into him, seeking something from him, and then it recoiled, juddering as if Teppo were poison and his heart pounded.

Bee struggled, unable to hide the images, but the sense of annoyance descended into him, as Teppo wasn't the one they sought. Bee blocked him, and Teppo cried, his body getting hotter as Bee pulled at his memories, piecing together fragments of people, sailors Teppo once knew. Shapes formed on the deck, thin at first, transparent people, but slowly they became solid.

Teppo pulled away, panting, sweat running down his cheek, unable to shake the sorrow that was Bedelia Rose, and he reached out, touching her face. 'I wish things had been different for you.'

Bee blinked, her face ashen. 'You have your men,' she whispered.

The sailors, men and boys dressed in breeches and long shirts were all people the twins once knew. Friends long forgotten, and Somer stepped away from the wheel, open-mouthed, staring at the spectacle.

'Take the Juna west,' Bee ordered.

'There's nothing there.' Teppo frowned.

'Yes, there is.'

Teppo barked orders at his sailors, and the men scurried around the deck. Somer steered the ship west, and it veered dangerously off its original course. The side of the boat battled the sea, but Somer forced it into the waves. He held the wheel, determined not to let go as the sun vanished, and the sea became rough. The boat was at full sail, and Bee guided the winds, as the ship danced on the waves. The swells grew and the Juna kept close to the Barricade. Teppo watched Bee stand at the bow, and he was in awe.

'What about Viola?' Teppo approached Bee, standing by her, hearing her crackle.

'For now, she's safer with Malick.' She shrugged, looking at her boots. 'He thinks I made him love me, that I used him... the truth is, he made me love him.'

Teppo nudged her, giving her a little smile. 'It's no wonder Malick's angry, I would be too.'

Bee smiled, 'If I stay away, everyone is safe.'

'Why?'

'I'm going to kill Eldric,' she said.

His jaw dropped. 'That's crazy, and what about the boys and little girl, the ones in England?'

Bee paled. 'Did Malick tell you? The girl, well...' she shrugged her shoulders. 'Oren's their father, they live with him.'

'*Lord Oren* is the father? Does Malick know?'

Bee nodded, 'I'm sorry you saw–'

Even though Bee still crackled, Teppo slipped his hand into hers, squeezing it. 'Bedelia, you love Malick, and he loves you. You need to explain everything to him, and you can't kill Eldric, you'll end up dead.'

Bee shook her head. 'That's why I ended up on the beach, Teppo. I'm finishing what I started.'

Teppo rubbed his chin, unsure how he could convince Bee to turn back to France. 'What did Malick tell you about his father's death?' he asked.

'Only Reapers hung him, not much else.'

'He was eight. They forced the whole family and town to watch. The Reapers allowed Andre to play, *'Rite of Word and Life.'* Do you know the game?' He waited for a reaction, but Bee gave nothing away. 'He lost, and the Reaper didn't set the rope right. It was a prolonged horrible death. My brother was there for Malick. If you want to know how an eight-year-old coped with seeing his father hung, ask Somer about Malick's nightmares.'

Bee's gaze drifted out to sea, and then she whispered, 'I murdered my first Reaper aged eight.' She looked up at The Barricade. The black liquid mixed itself into the waters, getting angry. 'Somer,' she shouted, 'turn the boat into The Barricade now.'

Teppo rushed across the deck, shouting at the ghostly shipmates. He slipped, rushing up the ladders to the wheel. It would need all their strength to steer the boat.

'Did she just say–' Somer started.

'Yes. Do it,' Teppo shouted.

Both men clambered, holding the wheel, using all their strength as the rain came lashing down. Teppo and Somer forced the Juna into a breakneck turn. Angry waves hit the boat, the sea spraying up onto the decks, soaking everything and the twins held the wheel. The Juna bobbed and crashed through the giant waves, heading straight for The Barricade.

Thunderclaps sounded, and Bee shouted, 'Get her through.'

The sailors scurried about, pulling ropes, running along the deck. Waves or rain affected not one. It lashed through them, and the schooner turned dangerously fast, and the Barricade was now head-on.

The lightning struck, and energy blasted into the sea. The black liquid wall became thick, as the boat sailed toward the perilous place in the nothing between the two countries. The sea roared, outraged that a boat was heading towards the black mass. The waves ripped over the sides, soaking everything in its path, and the Juna plunged and rose as Bee remained at the bow.

'Whatever she's going to do, she'd better do it fast.' Somer struggled to hold the wheel, as Teppo grabbed it.

Bee stepped up. She held her hands up to The Barricade and the lightning struck.

***

Deman Circe, Kent, England

The rain hit the windows and Winnie's heart raced. The time was getting closer. The voices were whispering, telling her that soon she'd have to do it, but Winnie didn't understand what *it* was. All she knew was that they wanted her to break The Barricade down somehow.

Sitting in the temple pew, her eyes darted around the familiar building. The stained-glass windows displayed images she'd never understood. A man hung on a cross with two empty crosses behind it. A religion before the arrival of the Guardians, and all Winnie knew about it came from the glasswork. She'd never given it much thought, but as she sat behind Landers, and her parents, who each held a Clannen doll, praying frantically for her redemption, she wondered if her fate might end up much like the man in the window, and Winnie's left eye twitched at the thought. The voices rushed into her mind. All of them speaking at once, confusing her.

'–Go now–' one voice whispered.

Another said, 'The one without God is here.'

'Break that Barricade,' another screeched.

And each voice became entwined with each other. Winnie wanted to scream, to tell them to shut up. She didn't think she could control herself for much longer as she tried to ignore their demands. Scratching her arms, Winnie hoped the mild pain she inflicted on herself would make her concentrate on something else, but the whispers kept repeating that she must go.

She tapped her fingers furiously against the wooden pews. Landers turned, glaring at her, and Winnie carried on, unable to stop, preferring the sound to the shrill of the voices inside her mind.

The stale scent of primrose filled the temple. Winnie gagged, gazing at the dishes of flowers which lined the square cavities in the walls. The dying scent reminded her she'd been here a few hours earlier, but stuffed in a box.

Her brain juddered as the whispers continued. The lightning struck in the distance, and she looked up at the window. Tomorrow, she'd been told, Landers would take her to Dai, where there would be a doctor who could help her. Winnie doubted that. She rose from her pew, swaying, as the voices became unbearable. She rubbed her forehead as a lone voice told her to go.

'She's coming,' Winnie whispered. The temple door smashed open, and the rain and wind banged the wood against the stone wall. And she was gone.

Winnie ran into the rain, the thunder, and lightning. The road had turned into muddy streams, and her boots got stuck as Winnie pulled at her shoes, desperate to get to the beach.

Down onto the dunes, she passed the totems and the scarecrows. The voices propelled her forward, and she needed them to stop. Winnie hoped that if she did whatever it was that they wanted it might silence them.

Behind her Landers, Nell and Virgil yelled. The wind drowned out their shouts. She kept running until she was at the beach, her clothes sticking to her body. She gasped, unsure why she was standing there, but this was where the Sinners wanted Winnie.

The vast shoreline heralded frothy waters, all charging towards her. Threatening to engulf Winnie and pull her out to sea. The waves dragged back and rushed forward, clawing the sand, and vomiting it back. The thunder roared, so loud, Winnie stumbled into the water as the lightning came.

It hit one point along The Barricade, and the white forks spread along the wall. Each streak scuttled like a spider, running for miles, and the noise was deafening. The villagers left their homes, having heard the thunder, and they stood in the rain, holding lamps, watching The Barricade light up.

Winnie moved into the shallows. The thunderclaps came, and the lightning struck. It got closer every time, and she stretched her arms out, waiting. And it hit her. She became a rod between her and The Barricade. Nell screamed, but Winnie couldn't hear her as she stood in the waters, lighting up.

The lightning reverberated up and down the Barricade. The great divide shook, splintering the black mass, and Winnie's body burst, her lightning striking the wall. Powers surged through her. It streamed into The Barricade, opening it up. She was thrown back into the water. Nell and Virgil dragged her back to the beach, as the lightning continued.

'She's here,' Winnie whispered. Her face, half charred.

'Who is?' Nell kept hold of her daughter, tears streaming down her cheeks.

'See.' Winnie pointed.

Everybody looked, and the villagers stepped into the shallows, unsure if they really saw it. The Barricade broke into two. And through the break came a ship.

Chapter Nine
Dai Castle, Dai, Kent

Overlord Gilbert Evans stared out from the tower turrets, watching the lightning travel up and down The Barricade. The thunder was so loud, the portly man ducked, frightened he'd be hit, instead, he got wet, his beard sodden with water as the rain lashed down.

The howling wind bit his ravaged face, and he wrapped his regulation military long winter coat around him. Even his hat wasn't keeping him dry, and considering it was late September, Gilbert mused, he shouldn't even be wearing the heavy coat and hat.

Dai Castle was a corner of the world where the wind always blew. The great stone structure had stood for a thousand years, guarding Britain from its clifftop vantage point.

This fortified monster, the largest in Britain, had kept the country safe with its inner and outer bailey, high ramparts and deep moat that protected the country from foreign invaders. No outside force had ever penetrated the thick stone walls. The castle was known as the *'Key to England'* because if an invader took Dai Castle, they'd take England.

That was a long time ago, But Eldric still considered it an important strategic place, and on a howling wild night, as Gilbert stood, freezing, watching the lightning spark along The Barricade, he wondered who they were guarding against.

His soldiers and personal servants stood like him, wrapped in their leathers, but their coats gave them no protection, and they watched the spectacular scene. Their jaws dropped, they held onto the stone walls, watching and muttering. The noise was too loud for Gilbert to hear what they said, but the grimaces, the nudges and looks they gave each other told Gilbert they were afraid.

And he was too.

A messenger pigeon from the village of Deman Circe had arrived earlier in the day. A confusing message about a girl rising from the dead. Gilbert dismissed it as the ramblings of a superstitious Marshal, but now as the lightning struck, he wasn't so sure.

He'd ordered Captain Peirson to bring up some maps. They'd found the location of Deman Circe, because he couldn't remember where it was or what it traded in, and found it was a small fishing village, some miles down from the town of Foulksten.

He knew very little about the place or its inhabitants, except they were free-folk who paid their taxes on time. Several sheep farms surrounded it, owned by Lords who kept vassals, other than that, the information was sparse.

The maps were old, and Gilbert saw the names of two villages, one called Lille Sten and Fangehul, and he rubbed his chin, remembering these places because they'd been wiped off the map. A year before The Barricade was set, Eldric banned all trade with Europe to stop the Red Plague entering Britain. A number of coastal villages ignored this decree and Gilbert was ordered to send a high number of Reapers into the villages.

They rounded up every villager – men, women and children – with the aid of the population register, which included the whereabouts of every person in the area, whether free or vassal. They shot them all, burning the village to the ground. The massacre in both villages reverberated throughout the British coastline and nobody disobeyed the Decree after that but Eldric still built The Barricade.

Gilbert pulled his collar up, and the rain kept coming, with no sign of easing. It was getting hard to see, and his hair stuck to his hat. Nothing was dry. Huffing, he'd already sent a pigeon to Lord Guardian Eldric about the discovery of a Crack in The Barricade, just off Krallar, another derelict village. Gilbert guessed he would send another one, not only about this girl, if it proved to be accurate, but also about the lightning.

He peered over the turret, squinting, as the rain blinded him. The townspeople were on the pebbled beach watching, any frightened screams and shouts, drowned out by the thunderous noise. Lanterns lit up the shoreline, the crowds gathered, and people jostled on the beach. He'd sent soldiers into the town to calm people and ordered them to return to their homes, but judging by the crowds at the beach, nobody had listened.

There had been lightning like this only once before. Gilbert recalled the night nearly seven years ago as he gripped hold of the stone. The Guardians of Britain and the upper countries created the same conditions when The Barricade first formed, and it rose out of the sea, like an enraged leviathan, polluting the channel with an impregnable black smoky wall.

Gilbert's legs almost gave way. Somebody was breaking through that Barricade. A person powerful enough to light up the night's sky in all directions, who could bring fear into the hearts of the population. Somebody who could churn up the seas, create giant waves that roared in vengeance at the wall as the crashing waters swelled and thrashed against it. And Gilbert backed away, letting the rain soak him.

A Guardian was breaking through.

'Sir, don't you think you should come inside now?' a valet stood shivering.

A young messenger boy appeared in the tower doorway, gasping, having run up the spiral stairs. He paused, catching his breath, and pushed his way through the guards, calling out Overlord Gilbert's name.

'Sir, a message came from Guardian Eldric.' He bowed, handing his lord the message.

Gilbert grabbed the piece of paper. He read it and then re-read it. He barked orders, folding the paper. 'Get the royal chambers ready, Lord Oren is coming.'

People scurried towards the door, a few headed back down the stairs and Gilbert leaned against the wall, watching the lightning. At least it wasn't Eldric coming.

He and Oren had been friends since childhood. And under other circumstances, he would be glad to have him in the Castle, but Oren would be here officially, meaning it was not good news for Gilbert.

***

The road from Lunden to Dai

Lord Oren Wraithcliffe stared out of the stagecoach window, but all he saw were trees, bushes and mud, and the night was drawing in, bringing the new sounds of the forest after dark. Opposite, inside the cramped coach, sat Claude Ramas, an Advisor Eldric trusted. It surprised Oren to find Claude sitting in the coach, waiting.

He suspected Eldric was sending Claude to Dai, because of the ripples that had started earlier in the day. Oren knew it meant there was another Guardian in Britain, and he'd heard the servants whispering, it was another girl. He wondered if this new Guardian was like Bedelia and put into slavery.

This girl would be the only reason Eldric would send Claude down to Dai, and he guessed inside Claude's pocket would be a Royal Decree. Oren shrank from the window, growing tired of seeing the endless trees and bushes. He'd hoped he'd never have to put another woman through what Bedelia had gone through, and now as the stagecoach bumped its way towards the fishing town of Dai, Oren didn't know what he was going to do.

The Crack in Krallar was another matter. Oren didn't think he alone could seal it. The Barricade wasn't built to last, but Eldric now liked being shut off from the outside world, enjoying the power and control over his subjects.

Oren fidgeted, his mind wandered between Claude, the girl, The Barricade and his own family. He'd not said goodbye to Leena or his three girls, Eldric ordered him onto the coach, and his trunks were already on the roof. The girls were not full-blooded Guardians, so Eldric did not consider them family. The Lord Guardian often looked at the children with distaste, refusing to allow Oren to marry Leena because one day he'd marry a full-blooded Guardian. Still, for now, Eldric allowed a concubine, and Oren called Leena, wife.

Oren had often wondered where this new Guardian might come from. Most of the Guardians in Europe were probably dead because of the Red Plague, and the few female Guardians in the upper Northern hemisphere were married. Now he worried, because he would either have to marry her, or have sex with her, the way he had with Bedelia.

They'd been on the road for hours. The night had closed in quickly, and Oren huffed. They had another a day's ride before they reached the outskirts of Dai, and Oren wondered if he could handle spending that much time with the man, but Oren had little choice and he'd always suspected Claude murdered Bedelia.

Bedelia, the Reaper, was dead. That was the only information he received, once The Barricade was sealed. She died and not to ask questions. Oren asked because she was the mother of his two boys. He found out she died on the French coast.

Bee arrived in the Tower with another Reaper called Luther. She was twenty-two, and Oren had been told she'd already killed over thirty Malefactors. A higher number than most Reapers of her age, but Bee had also murdered four of her fellow students.

Eldric was pleased to learn of Bee's existence, but he didn't show her off at court. He left her a Reaper. Oren never worked out how she hid her abilities growing up, and he never asked.

Eldric issued Oren a Royal Decree. Ordered to have sex with Bee, and produce children, preferably males. He hadn't wanted to go through with it, and it was Leena who persuaded Oren. Telling him that it would be safer all round if he did what his uncle wanted.

Bee arrived at Oren's apartments at the stated time. She greeted them with a nod and sat at the dining table as the servants brought in a tray of tea. She was a young woman, with auburn hair, tied into a French plait, wearing a killer's uniform. The black thin silvery leather uniform, with a high collar, and a tunic top, skinny black breeches, and knee-high fighting boots, fitted Bee's slender body. Around her hand, Bee wore a bracelet, a huge cuff bangle and Oren had to stop looking at it because he knew what it was.

Most women Bee's age would have commented on the décor of their apartment, asking questions about what upholsterer had made the beautiful velvet sofas or asked questions about the paintings, but Bee looked straight at him and ignored Leena. It was apparent she had no interest in such pointless things.

Both he and Leena were nervous, Leena's hand shook as she poured out the tea. She'd ordered the servants out of the room, stating she would attend to the Reaper, and on the table was a piece of paper with the Royal Seal.

Leena looked at Oren, her cup trembling in her hand. 'Bedelia, do you understand what a Royal Decree is?'

'It is the Guardian's order, and it must be completed,' Bee said. She did not drink her tea.

'Do you know what would happen if you did not comply with the Decree?' Leena asked.

'They will execute me.'

'And Oren,' Leena sipped her tea. 'You are aware as a full-blooded Guardian you are obliged to continue the bloodline.'

Bee said coldly, 'I am a Reaper, I am not permitted –' she paused, as if thinking of the correct word to use, '–to fornicate.'

Leena shook her head. 'I'm sorry, as the daughter of Lord Guardian Eldric, you and Oren are to commence a physical relationship, to produce children.'

Bee did not flinch.

'This is hard, believe me, because you have to sleep with my husband.' Leena handed Bee the document and told her to open it.

Bee opened it, and read it. She placed it on the table and looked solely at Leena. 'When are we expected to start?' her voice was cold.

Leena leaned back into her chair. She closed her eyes, waiting, and then she said, 'It would be advisable to try now.'

Bee nodded.

'Bedelia,' Oren said, 'have you had sex before?'

'No, my lord, I have not.'

He paled, not only was he about to sleep with a Reaper, but he was about to take her virginity. 'Your first time might be painful. Leena will be outside the room, and she will be there for you afterwards. We want to make sure you feel safe.' Oren couldn't look at Bee. He was ashamed that Leena had to take part in this, but Leena had been right, it was the only way the three of them would live.

"I do not need to feel safe.' Bee rose from her chair. 'The Lord Guardian has ordered this. I cannot refuse.'

Oren blinked, her voice was chilling, and he rose timidly, afraid to be alone with her. 'This way, we have a room set up.'

Leena ushered Bee through another door and into a bedroom. The bed freshly made, with two Reapers either side and there was little else in the room, and Bee stepped inside.

'You need to undress, Bedelia,' Leena told her.

Bee undid each button of her uniform, peeling the black armour off, and folded it over a chair. She did the same with her trousers and stood naked, unfazed. Oren did his best not to recoil as he'd never seen a body with so many scars. He was unable to take his eyes off the huge scar surrounded by lumpy skin on her right shoulder, and his breathing became shallow. Oren gripped hold of Leena's hand, afraid he was about to have a panic attack. He coughed nervously, giving Leena a sideways glance, and he spotted her weak smile. Oren asked Bee to sit on the bed, and she did.

'You've never had sex, but have you ever kissed anybody before?'

'No,' Bee answered.

'A kiss has meaning. I only want to kiss Leena, I will do what Eldric says, but I won't kiss you. Do you understand?'

'No,' Bee said.

Leena stood at the door. 'I'll be outside, Oren, I won't leave.'

Oren watched Leena sit down in the tiny hall. He didn't want to shut the door. He didn't want to be left alone with a killer. Oren closed the door, and his hand trembled. He ordered Bee onto the bed, and the Reapers held her arms.

Oren remembered Leena worrying he might not come out alive, he feared he couldn't perform and Bee appeared unaware of the dangerous situation they were all in.

Once Bee fell pregnant, she still completed warrants and executed several subjects until her fourth month. She partnered with a Reaper called Luther, and sometimes she would sneak him into her room. Oren told nobody.

She lived in their apartment, and a baby boy was born. Oren called him Hamish, and Bee nursed the infant, and he continued to have sex with the Reaper. He got a dangerous thrill out of sleeping with Bee because she could kill him, and Bee didn't understand what he was doing to her.

It was odd seeing a Reaper, a killer, holding a small baby, and Bee was a little rough, holding Hamish like a sack, but Leena showed Bee how to look after him, and Bee formed an attachment to the child.

Bee's only visitor was Luther, but when Hamish was two months old, Oren overheard a heated discussion. It was a man, telling Bee that she hadn't been sent to the Tower to make babies. Bee's voice had a chilled tone as she rejected this, stating she could not go against the Lord Guardian's orders as he well knew.

'Eldric's treating you like a prize sow, Bedelia, having you mate with his nephew, giving him male heirs. You're nothing but a cheap cunt to Eldric.'

Oren heard a scuffle, and somebody thudded against the wall. He couldn't see what was going on, but he heard Bee whisper. 'I ain't no cheap cunt, Father, and if you don't like it, I'll gut you right here.'

'Bee, I'm trying to protect you. You're my daughter, not his.'

'I know what I'm doing, father,' she whispered.

The man snapped, 'Oren fucked you to keep his head and, Leena, the poor cow, accepted it. He makes fun of raping you at court, he–'

There was a hush, Bee mumbled something. He couldn't hear what Bee said.

'Father, please, I'll know when the time is right,' Bee hissed.

Oren heard a slap, Bee cried out, but he didn't intervene. Instead, he crept away.

Eldric ordered Bee to go through the Purge, so she could fasten herself to Eldric. She refused, and Oren witnessed Bee's violent nature when she approached the Temple, and she never went through the Purge.

After the events at the temple, he was afraid of Bedelia, and he repeated the conversation he'd overheard with Leena. He then resumed the physical relationship with Bee, and she quickly fell pregnant with twins. A boy and girl were born.

Bee's face lit up when Oren suggested she choose a name for the boy, calling him Oliver, and was surprised when she picked such a simple name. They sent the girl away, Eldric tested her and found she possessed no Guardian abilities, and being of no use, discarded the child. Four months later, Bedelia died in France, and the coach hit a bump, pulling Oren from his memories.

Claude grinned, saying, 'The rain will probably get worse, Lord Oren.'

And in the distance, there came a crack of thunder. Oren shouldn't have heard it, being so far away from Dai, but it rumbled across the skyline. It began at the coast and travelled up to them. A message that something was coming.

It sounded different. Oren banged on the roof, ordering the driver to stop. He stepped out of the coach and looked toward the sky. There was nothing but trees.

'You're right, Claude,' he said as the man poked his head out of the coach. 'Things will get worse.'

His blood crackled, and Oren rolled his shoulder. The power flushed through him, and the thunder and lightning carried, even though they were nowhere near the coast. Standing there in the dark, Oren listened.

He ignored Claude, who got out, stretching his legs. Oren closed his eyes, and his blood rippled through him, in a way he'd never felt it before. Oren cried out, hunching as she clawed at him, making herself known. Little spikes pierced into him, making Oren shudder. She was flexing herself inside him, daring him to touch her, daring Oren to acknowledge her and then she was gone.

Bedelia, he thought.

***

Bononia, Sur-Mer, Northern France

The lightning hit The Barricade. Malick sat in the dark, watching the rain pelt against the parlour windows. Viola had trapped him on the sofa, lying sprawled out across his lap, asleep. He'd lost track of how long she'd cried, begging for her mother. Viola wanted only Bee to comfort her, and there was little he could do except let his daughter cry herself to sleep. Malick wished he could start the day all over again because between them, they'd destroyed everything, and both were to blame.

The black sky outside lit up as the lightning continued hitting The Barricade. Bee was creating the extreme weather, and his heart banged with every strike of lightning. That connection, the one he'd never understood, vibrated through him.

Malick wiped away the crusted tears from Viola's eyes, and she wriggled. Sitting in the dark was better than having to look down at her red puffy face. He'd been so angry, so momentarily frightened of Bee, that she'd run from him, her children, and back to Britain. Only now as Malick sat in the dark, he considered how scared Bee must have been for all those years, hiding her secret.

The front door blew open, Tristan giggled as Esther struggled to shut the door. She sat him on the stairs, his waterproofs sopping wet. She pulled his arms out of the coat and then unlaced his wellies.

Malick heard Tristan ask, 'Where's Mamma?' and Esther lied.

The boy ran into the parlour. Malick watched as Tristan stuck his nose against the windowpane, fingers glued to the glass, excited by the impressive display.

'Come away from the window, Tristan,' Malick uttered, but the boy continued watching, and Malick recalled when Bee flatly refused to attend Tristan's Purge. She tried to convince him not to do it, but it was what Nadine had wanted, and it didn't matter if Bee was now his mother, Malick followed Nadine's wishes.

Tristan was dressed in his Sunday best. Grey knee-high breeches with socks, well-polished boots, and jacket. The boy was excited, he was about to go through the Purge with his Father. Malick wanted Bee there, but she refused, and he instructed her that she had to explain to Tristan, to her son, why she wouldn't be there. He stood, listening to Bee as she sat in parlour with the boy on her lap, and he knew then he would never get Bedelia to change her mind, not even for Tristan.

Bee brushed Tristan's blond hair out of his eyes. 'Today you are going to the Temple, your Father is taking you through the Purge, but I'm not coming. Esther will be with you.'

'Why?' the four-year-old asked.

She whispered, 'I don't belong there, baby.'

'Have you been bad?' Tristan pondered.

Bee set him to stand in front of her, and she tremored, 'There's different reasons why people don't go through the Purge. Some are vassals...' Bee took in a breath, '...and some are Reapers. They are considered unclean by the Guardians, and I'm a vassal.'

The boy looked confused. 'Are you clean now?'

Bee sat, letting out a puff of air. She looked to Malick and then back to Tristan. 'I don't want to be, Tristan. When I was eight, I did something. My father punished me because he'd lost two valuable items, and that meant I'd never go through the Purge, even if a vassal were allowed.'

'What did you do?' Tristan asked.

'I saved a boy's life,' she explained.

Tristan went off in another direction. No longer listening to Bee. 'Priest Felix says people stay in the dark if they don't go through the Purge. Are you scared?'

'No.' Bee gave him a kiss. 'I know what's in the dark.'

That night, after the ceremony, as Bee laid curled up next to him in bed, Malick asked her what happened to the boy, she didn't say much, and she whispered, 'We both went into the dark.' Her voice was quiet as she held onto Malick.

The thunder cracked, and Malick was back watching his son gaze out of the parlour window, staring at the lightening show. Esther dragged Tristan away from the window, slapping him on the bottom, ordering him to get ready for bed, and she'd be up soon. She waited for Tristan to vanish up the stairs.

Standing at the window, watching the lightning, Esther said, 'After Bee had Viola, I asked how she knew she was in love with you.' Esther paused, but Malick said nothing. 'She said she'd never kissed a man until you. You were the first man she wanted to kiss.'

Malick huffed.

Esther gave him a look, 'I thought it was odd because she has three children. She said that –'

'Esther,' he interrupted.

'–said that she'd be hung, if she didn't have children. This man only wanted to kiss his wife.' Esther paused, waiting for a response and then said, 'Bee didn't understand, because she'd not kissed anybody before, let alone have sex.'

'Esther, let's not have this discussion,' he snapped, and Viola moved, trying to stay comfortable.

'No, Uncle Malick we should,' Esther snapped back. 'Bee made me promise not to tell, because she didn't want you to have a wife who only had children to keep herself alive.'

Trapped under Viola, Malick thought this was not how it should be. Esther was twenty-one, far too young to understand the finer details of a marriage, but somehow

Esther had got Bee to open up a little about her life before him. He'd asked about her children and the father, but she'd clammed up. He thought Bee might burst into tears if she'd answered, but she gave him a little smile, with a distant look, saying, *'Behind the Barricade is suffering. It is better to lock it away.'* Malick stopped asking because he hated seeing that lonely expression.

'When Bee kissed you, she understood what this man meant.'

'This isn't helping,' he grumbled.

'Uncle Malick, I've lived with you since I was thirteen. You never kissed Aunt Nadine in the way I see you kiss Bee. Just because she is a Reaper does not mean you can't love her.'

'I know that, Esther,'

'Look, she isn't perfect, but...'

He gathered Viola up, and he stood by the window, with Esther. Looking down at Viola, he said, 'She's murdered fifty-six people, 'perfect' is not the word I'd use.'

'I don't know much about Reapers, but you need to bring her home.'

Malick said nothing.

'I guessed what Somer and Teppo had got you into,' she whispered, 'I never told Bee, because I didn't want to upset her, and I know what happens to those people. Uncle Malick, I don't see the difference.'

He shifted as Esther uttered the reality, he'd only admitted when Bee was gone. When Malick learned about the deal with Omega, he ordered the twins to stop, but Baptiste threatened him and Philip advised Omega would kill his entire family, leaving him no choice but to carry on. And like Bee, he'd kept secrets.

'I can't get her without my boat,' Malick said. 'And I will have to deal with Omega first.' He guessed Omega was now aware of Bee. He'd never encountered the woman but imagined it wouldn't be long before he did.

Malick rocked Viola, as both he and Esther stood watching the last of the lightning show. Malick let Bee ripple through him, and he desperately wanted to keep hold of it. The flashes in the sky dwindled and only the rain pelted against the windows, and the strange, intense connection slowly evaporated. Malick knew that even without this conversation with Esther, he was going to Britain to get his wife back. He'd already decided when he took Bee's wedding ring from the table.

Chapter Ten
Deman Circe, Kent

The rowing boat ducked and weaved on the sea. The waves splashed over its edges, bringing more water into the bottom of the boat. Somer sweated, heaving, as the oars crashed into the lapping sea and Bee sat watching the coastline get closer and closer. The figures stood in the early morning light, swinging their lanterns, signalling they were nearing the shore, and Bee's heart pounded. She was going to meet the person who'd helped her return to Britain.

Six years, Bee thought. Six years she'd been free of this country, and now she was about to set foot on English soil, and she shuddered. Her heart pounded so hard, she wondered if it might burst out of her body and she folded her arms because Bee didn't want to see her trembling fingers.

She hadn't lived in Britain. She'd existed. The abilities running through her were bound into Bee as soon as they ripped her out of her mother's womb. Given to a weapons master, Rufus McKay at Rolfen Castle, he fed her, and she called him father.

Rufus had a temper and Bee learned to hide, when he was angry. At age four, Bee started earning her keep at the castle. A great building on the outside, and hell on the inside. Bee was vassal to the Reapers, the place apprentices of the Medaway trained, and she witnessed broken bones, faces, blood, and wounds no person could come back from.

The trainers had apprentices learn at first with straw-stuffed dummies, and once they mastered the weapons, the apprentices moved onto convicts, repeatedly wounding them, learning to sew up the wounds and then hurt them again, until they killed the prisoner. There were times when the students were turned on each other and only the strongest survived. Bee had to clean the yard of severed limbs, lost eyeballs, heads, arms, fingers and toes and throw them into the furnace which burned, giving off a coppery smell, which choked the throat.

Bee was eight when she killed two Reapers, severing the head of one and she held it up to her father. Bee was imprisoned for three months and then sentenced to become a Reaper.

Rufus changed. She became his pupil and he spent hours training Bee, along with other apprentices. He taught her to read and write, and forced Bee to learn her weapons.

They taught all Reapers how to meditate, to calm the mind after an execution. Rufus made Bee spend hours staring at the wall. Whispering that she had to be strong enough to hide what was inside her. She didn't always understand, and Rufus would take the belt to her.

One day Bee told him about The Spectres, and Rufus whispered that she needed to listen and learn, but keep them hidden. They would come for her, but for now, she had to learn from them.

Bee clung to the boat. These memories she'd entombed in her secret place, were now breaking free from their locked vault as Somer rowed nearer the English shore. Bee wanted to shout, to turn the boat around. She couldn't go back, but it was too late.

Eldric appeared, and his rage pulsated into her, followed by Oren and Gable, their abilities syncing with Bee, and she cut them off. Bee was the outsider. The Guardians' abilities flowed in and out of Eldric. He consumed their powers, making him the most powerful of all the Guardians. Her abilities circled theirs and Bee felt like a shark, circling its prey.

And The Spectres came, still unable to touch her, but they were there.

Bee didn't go through the Purge, though Eldric had tried. She'd heard the priest when she'd gone to the Temple with Malick saying this connection allowed them to enter the Farscape, when they go into the next world. It allowed the parishioners to become closer with the living Gods, giving people Clannen dolls to transfer their energies. This was untrue. It allowed the Guardians to feed off the people, making them stronger, but even priests can only tell people what they are told is the truth. The Purge secured Eldric to everybody, and it gave him control. The flutter of her abilities appearing and then vanishing was enough to make Eldric, Oren and Gable understand she had returned.

Yet Hamish and Oliver were missing.

The sea splashed, the salty taste got into Bee's mouth, as she searched. She sent out her rhythms, seeking that connection, that blood correlation between her and her children, but nothing came back. Bee understood what it meant, and she stared at the crashing waves. Her eyes focused on the shoreline ahead. She blocked all thoughts of Hamish and Oliver out of her mind, building a wall around the pain because Bee refused to admit the truth.

'They're coming.' Somer pointed as the men ran towards the small boat. Several hands gripped hold of its wood. Faces stared at the newcomers, all of them with questions and fear. They heaved the boat into the shallows and onto the sand, letting it drop, and Bee stumbled out onto dry land.

The questions started, 'Where did you come from?' 'Are you French?' 'How did you break down The Barricade?' 'Are you like Winnie?' 'Are you a witch?' the frightened people kept their distance, but the questions continued.

'Go back to the Juna,' she told Somer.

'Can't do that,' he shouted over the questions. 'Teppo's already sailing back.'

Bee turned. In the distance, the stern of the ship faded, heading back toward The Crack.

'I don't want to be here, not with you, but Teppo forced me,' Somer uttered.

Bee grabbed the two bags as a small group gathered around her. Men, women and children, all dressed in old shabby clothing, many with long leather coats and sun-baked faces. This was a quiet place with poor people.

'Where is she?' she asked, 'where is the one who opened The Crack?'

The villagers muttered, shaking their heads, backing away from Bee and Somer, afraid that if they said anything they might get into trouble. Bee had seen this many times. This happened when people were frightened.

And she remembered standing there, in a village much like this one. The houses were broken and ramshackle, no road, just mud and they'd sent her to execute the local Marshal. She'd slipped into his house, ordered him to his knees and by Due Process of the Law, she'd shot him in the back of the head. She never knew what the crime was because it did not matter to a Reaper.

'The priest took her, said she's a witch.' A young man pushed forward with a crying woman. Bee inhaled everything about them. Both were close to the Guardian, but neither were blood relatives, and this new Guardian's markers were everywhere on the man.

'Please, she's my daughter,' the woman cried, 'Winnie's done nothing like this before.'

Bee watched the woman sob. 'What's your name?'

'Nell... Nell Harper.' She recoiled, seeing Bee's bruised face.

'Mrs Harper, I need you to go home and wait,' Bee ordered. She turned to the man. 'Are you Winnie's husband?'

The young man shook his head. "Not yet, but she's not a witch."

'Landers won't let you see her,' a second man interrupted. 'He's put her in the vault, said he's going to take her to Dai castle.'

'Who are you?' Bee asked the man.

'Virgil, her father, I tried stopping him, but Landers… but he just kept calling her a witch.' Virgil wiped his wrinkled sun-baked face.

'She's not a bloody Witch.' Bee pointed to the young man. 'You, take me to them.'

Somer took Bee's bag. 'I hope you know what you are doing, Bee?'

She looked back at the endless beach. The morning birdcalls sounded, the day was beautiful, crisp clouds filled the blue sky. The Barricade still stood, and it hid any evidence that they'd sailed through it only a few hours earlier.

Bee turned toward the dunes, and there were the crumbling towers, which were famous along the coasts of Kent, Sussex and Suffolk. They stood like a beacon, built of brick and thirteen-foot thick. Built to defend the shores from invaders, but no outsiders ever came, and it was the Guardians of Britain who invaded countries such as France. She spotted two figures in the distance, sitting on their horses and they did nothing but watch.

The man started walking, almost running, telling Bee his name was Feargal Drake, and Winnifred had died that morning. He was saying everything so fast, and Bee had trouble understanding, as they walked away from the beach.

Toward the totems and scarecrows, they walked. Bee realised Somer wasn't behind her. He was staring at the totems. He kept blinking, and she remained silent, letting him process the macabre statue. The decaying bodies stared out, and the sickly-sweet odour filled their nostrils. Bee took no notice of the smell, but Somer gagged and she gripped his arm, pulling him up past the corpses, telling him not to look.

'Are they real?' Somer whispered.

'This way,' Feargal shouted.

They were in the village. Faces peeked out of the windows of a few dilapidated cottages, curtains twitching, and grim expressions. There was no need to ask if they were afraid, they would be, because a ghostly ship had sailed through The Barricade and strangers had landed on their beach. This meant that soldiers might come, and even worse, Reapers.

At the other end of the village was the Temple. It was a stone building, with picture-glass windows and an old bell. The roof had seen better days, with a few slates missing. This poor community, Bee guessed, was superstitious, and that was why the priest thought Winnie was a witch. The temple door was left open.

'She isn't here.' Bee didn't enter. She'd never set foot in an English Temple and did not plan on doing so.

'Why do you say that?' Somer asked.

'He'd never have left the door open.' She retraced her footsteps, 'Do you have a Marshal?'

Feargal nodded, pointing to the house opposite. Bee banged on the door. She tried the handle, and the door opened. Calling out, Bee got no response.

Entering the house, she found it was immaculate. A small building, one living area downstairs and upstairs was where they slept, like most in the village. The Marshal's life was simple, and he had minimal possessions. A chair by the fire, the kitchen spotless and by the staircase was a black cabinet.

Bee touched it, stroking the finely crafted wood. Inside, were things she wanted. She backed away, asking, 'How old is this Marshal?'

Feargal shrugged. 'Probably in his fifties, I've known him all my life.'

'What kind of Marshal was he?'

'Marshal Tanner tried not to involve the law, would rather bring us children back to our parents for punishment, than make it official.'

She carried on looking at the cabinet. 'Ever call Reapers in?'

Feargal scoffed. 'He'd do anything not to have them bastards here, why?'

'No reason.' She headed out of the door. Walking around the side of the house, Feargal followed Bee. There were a couple of horses stabled, and the livery was full of the usual animal tackle and feed.

'Does your Marshal have a prison wagon?' Bee asked as Somer joined them in the courtyard.

The man laughed, and then it faded, realising what was happening. 'Tanner hasn't used it for years.'

'Well, it's gone,' Bee said.

***

Lunden Tower, Lunden

Sometimes Gable felt like a prisoner. She walked the Great Tower stone walls, followed by two maids. The sun pushed its way through the white clouds, and considering the early hour, it was bright, and she'd left Eldric asleep in her bed.

He visited most nights, spending less than fifteen minutes with her. He'd climb into her bed, didn't bother with any foreplay, and had sex. Gable didn't call it sex, she considered him more like a pathetic ageing bear, which needed to mate because they desired off-spring. Eldric always wanted sex, and she was yet to produce a child. He usually returned to his chambers, but last night, after Eldric rolled off her, he started snoring, and Gable found the noise insufferable.

She'd bathed, soaking her skin in rose petal warm water and her maids washed her down, cleaning away the smell of Eldric. Gable then dressed quickly, wrapping a thick cape around her and she escaped onto the ramparts. Outside, she didn't need the cape as the sun warmed her face, and Gable peeled it off, throwing it at one of her maids, and she basked in the sun.

Last night something had been different about Eldric. He'd ordered her onto the bed, did his business grumpily, and then went to sleep. He didn't talk or look at her, and it dented Gable's pride. She'd always considered herself worthy of conversation, but last night Eldric didn't even make eye contact and that hurt.

It was the new Guardian. It couldn't be anything else. She'd felt the blood ripples inside her, but Eldric hadn't said a thing when they'd had spent the evening in the Royal court being entertained by the musicians.

In fact, if Gable hadn't experienced the strange sensation herself, she would never have been the wiser. This Guardian felt weak, and confused, as if it had just woken from a long comfortable sleep, and didn't understand what was happening.

Instead, Claude came to her. They'd spent an hour together before he had to leave for Dai, but it was enough time for her to lift her dress and have him. She'd asked about the new Guardian and what it meant for them. Claude buttoned his breeches up, explaining Eldric had ordered a Royal Decree like he'd done with Bedelia, and Claude was instructed to give it to Oren once they found the girl.

Gable didn't like it, she didn't like it one bit. Eldric hadn't told her it was another woman, and now she was worried. What would it mean for her? What might it mean if she could not produce a male heir for the Lord Guardian?

Already she heard the voices below the Tower, and she peered over the high walls, watching the townsfolk scurry around their little hovels. The day was beginning, and voices rose as people woke up.

She smelled the bakeries as they lit up their ovens. It was the same process every day, and soon the warming smell of baking bread would rise into the air, covering the stench of the bodily functions thrown out during the late evenings.

Lunden was a dirty place, and Gable enjoyed watching her subjects bustling down below, but she loathed venturing into the city in a carriage, and if she made trips outside of the Tower, she preferred to sail down the Themes. Today though, she was hemmed inside these walls.

Claude was gone, meaning it was the women of the Court, she had, to entertain her, and many were only interested in currying favour to further their careers. Gable huffed and continued her morning walk.

And then she choked. Her legs almost buckled and her maids rushed to Gable, grabbing her, as she collapsed into their arms. Her breathing was raspy, and all she heard was *'My lady, this –'* or *'My lady, that –'* Gable's heart raced, but if she shouted for her maids to go, Eldric would question her, demanding why she'd ordered them away.

That sensation, the blood ripple cascaded into a profound message of dread. Eldric would have felt it, and it was like an angry bumblebee buzzing inside her. Bedelia wasn't dead.

Gable didn't understand. Claude told her he'd killed her, and he'd been graphic in his description. She'd enjoyed hearing it because the Reaper had caused her many problems and the main two were that Bee had given birth to two male children.

Eldric spoiled those children once Bedelia was officially dead. He'd taken them out of Oren's household and provided nannies, wet nurses, and different servants to serve their every need. And Gable became resentful. Jealous because those children were not hers, and because she believed that if she had a male child, Eldric might still pick one of Bee's children as heir to the throne over hers. And then Leena had come to her, full of hate for those boys, and Gable persuaded Claude to kill the children.

The plan formed over time, and then Claude struck. Eldric had been away on one of his hunting weekends, taking Oren with him. Claude made it look like an accident, that the nanny had been drunk, she'd locked the door, knocked over a candle and the nursery went up in flames, killing everybody inside.

Gable never asked how he did it. She didn't care as long as the children were dead. She believed she would have a baby by now, but no matter how many times Eldric visited her, she couldn't fall pregnant.

As she was catching her breath, the two maids helped her stand. Gable imagined her face paled as she felt queasy. She needed to lie down and hoped that Eldric had left her chambers. He must have already felt the pull of Bedelia, and Gable hoped he'd be too busy and leave her alone.

'Prepare my chambers, I need to lie down, I need a few minutes without you all suffocating me. Lucy, stay with me,' Gable snapped. Thoughts ran through her, she needed to get a message to Claude without any of her ladies-in-waiting knowing. The women left, leaving only Lucy, Gable's most faithful of ladies, as the woman knew all of Gable's secrets, including Claude.

'Lucy, I need to send a message to Claude, tell him Bedelia is back,' she whispered, taking Lucy's wrinkled hand.

'Bedelia, how is that possible?' Lucy's surprise wasn't hidden.

'Will you do it for me?'

Lucy nodded.

Gable added, 'Then send a message to Leena, I wish to take tea, and I will arrive when I'm suitably ready.'

***

Godless

Deman Circe, Kent, England

The rumbling wheels of the prison wagon trundled along the uneven road out of Deman Circe toward the next town. Inside the cage, Winnie bounced as the cart bumped over stones. Winnie rubbed her eyes staring at the sea, praying she hadn't made a mistake letting in the stranger from behind The Barricade.

Dried-in blood and piss stained the wood base, and straw was strewn across it because Tanner allowed the villagers to use the wagon if they wanted to go to market, and the cage stank of old goats and pigs.

Winnie took comfort in the sea's stillness. It was a beautiful millpond, but today no boats were sailing. No voices or whispers spoke inside Winnie's head, and she sat in the back of the wagon, enjoying the peace. She wasn't sure what had happened, but the power and the energy she'd spawned had been truly terrifying, and now she was empty of it.

There had been lightning shooting out of her body. It hit The Barricade and blasted her back. Every time it punched, she hit back, until a crack appeared and a ship sailed through. Her body ached, but Winnie was glad it was over.

The Guardian from France was here. The woman connected with her and Winnie shuddered, sensing a movement in her blood. This was the same experience she'd had after she had woken up in the coffin. Winnie was a Guardian, but her part was over, the Sinners told her, because she'd brought back the one who is without a God.

Winnie didn't know if the Sinners were telling the truth about her being a Guardian. She didn't care as long as the voices stopped, and the fleeting sensation and the French woman vanished.

Winnie touched her cheek, wincing. The lightning strikes had charred her face. The burns were sore, but Landers refused to give her any herbs, saying it was the Will of the Guardians and she could suffer because she'd opened The Barricade. Winnie cursed Landers under her breath, but the pain gave her something else to think about, instead of wondering what might happen next.

Reece Tanner, the Marshal, and uncle Landers sat up top. Landers argued with Tanner, telling him to ride faster, but the Marshal refused, explaining the horses were old and walking was the safest speed.

They were heading to Dai Castle, but they hadn't got far from Deman Circe. Winnie had never seen Dai Castle, she'd only heard how magnificent it looked on the clifftop, and Winnie wished she were going for different reasons.

'Hey!' she thumped her hand on the wooden back. 'I need to pee. Can we stop?'

'Shut up, Winnie,' Landers shouted, and the wagon rumbled on.

In the distance, six riders appeared. They rode fast toward the wagon, all dressed in long duster coats, wide-brimmed hats, and carrying revolvers. All aimed toward the prison wagon.

The horses neighed, and Winnie bounced around as the wagon stopped. The Marshal said something. There was a bang, and the few trees shook, as birds flew out in all directions, their terrified screeches masking the sound of the bullet. Winnie cried out, and she clambered into the corner of the cage, her heart beating fast. Tanner's body thumped to the ground; she whimpered, not having seen a man killed before. Winnie couldn't take her eyes off him, as he lay there gurgling. A tear rolled down Winnie's cheek. The Marshal had always been kind to her, and now he was dying.

The men with guns surrounded the wagon. They peered from under their hats, some unshaven, some smoking, and all of them had a glint about them. Winnie swayed as weight moved from the top of the cab. Landers jumped from the wagon to the ground and walked around to the door.

'You got my money?' Landers asked, holding out his hand to the man on the horse.

The rough looking man spat from his horse, and it landed between Landers' feet, but he handed the priest a small leather pouch, in exchange for the keys. 'You always were a selfish bastard, selling your own niece.'

'They'll be expecting her at Dai,' Landers face lit up, hearing the sounds of the coins.

The rider nodded, 'We'll take her to Arena Porta. I've a friend who owes me.'

'Uncle Landers,' she gasped, reaching out and grabbing him. 'Please.' But Landers shook her off.

The man laughed, 'Your life for his life.'

Winnie popped her head through the bars. 'Uncle Landers?'

'Shut up.' The man banged the wagon, and Winnie scuttled back.

Landers didn't look at Winnie as he mounted the animal and then rode back toward Deman Circe, without uttering another word to his niece.

The man peered into the cage, but he couldn't sustain eye contact for long. 'You don't look like a Guardian!'

'What does a Guardian look like?' She jumped up, hands clinging to the bars.

The man almost fell off his horse, not expecting her to move so quick and he pulled his horse away. Winnie swayed again as another man took over the reins of the wagon, and they started moving. She slid to the back of the wagon, with riders on either side of her and the wagon moved.

'Shoot the priest,' the man said.

A rider stopped his horse, pulled out a rifle, cocked it and aimed. The trees remained motionless as the birds too afraid to return, but the gulls that had returned to the beach, burst into the air, squawking, telling each other it was safer in the air.

Winnie gaped, her uncle fell off his horse, and she bundled herself into the back of the cage. Closing her eyes, Winnie counted to ten, and she rushed to the bars. Landers was still on the ground, and a rider approached.

She watched the man dismount, go through Landers pockets, and then shoot her uncle in the head. Just to make sure he was dead.

Chapter Eleven
Bononia-Sur-Mer, Northern France

Tristan sat with his arms crossed, slumped in the chair at the kitchen table. Malick watched the boy screw up his face, refusing to eat his egg on toast. He'd had a tantrum because Bee hadn't made them. Malick plonked Tristan on the chair at the table, growling that Tristan had to eat all his breakfast or sit there all day.

Malick cringed. He'd been reduced to shouting at his son over an egg. He was not a man who shouted, especially at his children, and he watched guiltily as Tristan kicked the table leg.

Esther fed Viola, with most of it ending up on the table. Malick sighed, looking at the kitchen, there wasn't much left in the way of dishes, but, between him and Esther, they cleaned it, making it resemble the family kitchen. Malick wanted to keep things as normal as he could for Tristan and Viola, but that wasn't working.

'Uncle Malick?' Esther nodded to the garden.

Through the windowpane, he watched a woman approach. Behind her were Baptiste and three men. This was it; he now had to deal with Omega. The hairs on his neck stood up. Could he do this? Could Malick protect everybody he loved and still get Bee back?

Omega allowed Baptiste to enter the kitchen first. She said nothing, circling the room, looking at the mess and at Malick, ignoring both Esther and Tristan. Omega positioned herself in the centre, hands on hips, with three riders behind her.

He'd never seen or spoken to Omega, but he knew her name was Marisol and it was reported that her mother was Spanish. She darkened the place with her presence. The woman's head was shaved, except for the mane running down the middle. Her eyes were blackened with thick make-up, and her leather coat hung down to her knees. Malick wondered if it was cow or human hide she wore.

'So, you're the fool who married a Guardian and didn't even know.' She shoved Tristan off his chair and sat down to eat his breakfast.

'Hey!' Malick lurched forward but stopped as the men aimed their pistols at him.

Esther grabbed Tristan before he started crying and whispered something in his ear. He didn't make a sound.

Malick said, 'Bee stole the Juna and went back to England. She isn't here.'

Omega lit up a cigarillo, watching Malick. 'This little Bee has left you in the shit, Mr Rose.'

'What do you want?' He observed Omega, noticing the resemblance between her and Bee.

Omega smiled. 'I'll trade your Bedelia, for Viola. And perhaps I'll let the rest of your family live.' She licked her lips, looking at Esther.

'But she's gone.'

She leaned into the chair, smiling. 'You will help me.'

'And if I don't?'

Omega raised her eyebrows, getting up from the chair, telling Stephen to stay with Esther and the baby. 'Come with me, Mr Rose. Baptiste, bring the boy.'

Baptiste grabbed Tristan, as Omega pointed a gun at Malick, nudging him out of the door. She grabbed the spade and threw it at him.

'Take me to Philip.'

Malick looked at the shovel and then his son. He clenched the spade, wanting to hit Omega with it. Malick walked down the path. They stood in the overgrown patch before the newly disturbed ground.

'Dig him up,' Omega instructed. 'Philip was valuable alive, and I can still make money out of him dead.' She tapped her foot on the mound.

'Please, not in front of my son.'

Omega took hold of Tristan's hand. She bent down and smiled. 'Now Tristan, I understand Philip was your Godfather?'

His eyes lit up. 'Uncle Philip?'

'That's right.' Her eyes focused on Malick and then back to Tristan. 'Now your Mamma killed Uncle Philip, and he's here, in your back garden. Your father will dig him up. You must watch. If I catch you closing your eyes, your father will end up in the ditch. Do you understand?'

Tristan looked at his father. He nodded, whimpering.

Omega kept hold of Tristan's hand. 'Go ahead, Malick, because if you don't *all* of you will end up like Philip.' And she motioned him to start.

The shovel hit the dirt and Malick threw the soil into a pile. He kept his eye on the boy, watching Tristan. The fear in Tristan's eyes grew, and all Malick could do was dig.

Philip's hands appeared first, and then his pale face, with his teeth showing. Malick coughed, trying not to throw up.

'You must be quite something, Mr Rose?' Omega laughed.

He stopped digging. 'And what does that mean?'

'Well, you're handsome enough, I guess.' She stepped closer. 'But Guardians don't marry commoners. They fuck them, but they certainly don't marry them. Your little wife must really love you.'

'Obviously not enough, otherwise she wouldn't have left.'

Omega grinned. 'Yes, well, if I have you and the boy, I'm sure your little Bee will fly back.'

Deman Circe, Kent

Bee watched Nell fuss over the fire. The woman's face was all puffy, and Bee guessed she had probably been crying since Winnie had died. Nell's hands shook, prodding the wood to warm the place, even though the sun was warming up outside. Somer sat in the corner as Feargal moved Nell to a chair, and Virgil sat at the table, his hands clasped around a bottle of whiskey, and the way he guarded it, suggested he needed it.

'Feargal said something about your son, Calum. Something you call, Sinners, touched him,' Bee said.

Nell glared at Feargal. 'That's right.'

'I need to talk to your son.'

'No,' Nell refused.

Virgil rose from his chair. His boots banged on the wooden stairs, and a few minutes later, he came down holding Calum's hand. The boy yawned, still wearing his bedclothes, rubbing his eyes, looking at the strangers in his home. Virgil sat him on the chair opposite Bee, and she knelt before him.

The horror in Calum's eyes made her remember the bruises, and Bee touched her face, ashamed to look at the boy. 'It doesn't hurt if that's what you're wondering,' she whispered.

Calum looked at her, and then he said, 'They said you'd come.'

'Who did?' Bee asked.

Calum kept looking at his parents, unsure, and Virgil nodded. The boy stroked Bee's bruised face. 'I'm to tell you, your children are dead.'

Everybody in the room gasped. Bee did not take her eyes off the boy, because she needed to keep control. 'Yes, I know,' she whispered and then Calum clasped his hands around her face.

'They said the one without a God can return the land to its people,' he muttered.

'I don't understand.' Bee faced the boy. The people in the kitchen faded, becoming a blur. She could hear their heartbeats, but they were awash of colours, and the atmosphere had a nervous electric streak running through it. Then it became just her and Calum.

'Let me show you,' he said.

The boy tightened his hands around her face. Bee cried out, but he held fast and then she saw black.

There was nothing at first. Bee blinked and only the black surrounded her. Then the flashes of colour came, images sparked, things she didn't understand hit her, impacting her. There was a man in a cave. He stood at the mouth of a waterfall, and it was beautiful. Colours changed, shimmering, greens, reds and yellows. They became rainbows, spectrums bouncing off the rocks, and the waters were as if oil had mixed with it.

Those ethereal colours called to Bee. She reached in to touch the pool, and her heart sank when the image evaporated around her. Then she saw the same man leaning over the water's edge, and he drank from the well.

The man looked like a miner, his clothes raggedy. A filthy creature with blasted sand masking his face, but Bee could see. The face so familiar, she saw a man with features similar to Eldric's.

And he exploded, lighting up the cave, and the waters erupted. The painful screams echoed, they echoed from this man, down the generations and they burst inside Bee. He was reformed, piece by piece, the light encased within a body, imprisoning the power within the construct of a man. And the name Alfred came to mind.

She heard a voice –Somer– he was yelling, telling her to stop. His hands were all over her, trying to pull her free of the boy's clutches, but the boy would not let go. She saw the man imbued with this new power. He hid the well, closing it up with his strange new abilities. Boulders fell, hiding its secret place, and he left three men to die inside the cave.

This man, this Alfred, went into the world, infecting it with his powers. He destroyed the old society, forcing Britain first, and later other countries to come under his control. He spread throughout, becoming stronger, dominating everything, and Bee understood why Eldric needed a male heir.

She gasped and fell onto her backside. Her body jarred, bile rose in her throat, everybody was still a blur. Sweat matted Bee's short hair. She panted, staring at the boy as he sat in the chair watching her. Calum had shared his secret.

Bee's legs wobbled, as she pulled herself up from the floor. She snatched the whiskey out of Virgil's hand, gulping it down. The woody liquid burned her throat and Bee heaved, feeling sick. And then she took another long gulp.

'You need to kill the beast,' Calum whispered.

Wiping drips of whiskey from her lip, she kneeled back in front of Calum. 'What about Winnie?'

'Winnie's work is complete,' his little voice said, afraid that he might say something wrong.

'Thank you, Calum.'

And Bee suggested he returned to bed. She said nothing, waiting for him to go back upstairs. She took a final gulp and handed the half-empty whiskey bottle back to Virgil.

'Mrs Harper, Winnie's not yours, is she?'

Nell shook her head. 'We thought we couldn't have children, we… we bought her from a baby farmer.'

'Were you told anything?' Bee asked.

Virgil swigged from the bottle. 'No, she was an old woman, probably dead by now.' Followed by another gulp. 'What's going on with Winnie?'

'Winnie is –' a knock at the cottage door stopped Bee. She asked, 'Are both your children upstairs?'

'Yes, why?' Nell whispered.

'Feargal, Somer, go upstairs and make sure those children don't come down.' She ushered them up the stairs. The men outside would already know how many people were in the house, but Bee wanted to keep the children safe.

Bee directed her to open the door. 'Mrs Harper, be natural.'

Two men stood there. They varied in ages, with stained teeth, old breeches, dirty boots, long leather coats and greasy hair. One of them smoked, and they pushed inside the cottage looking at Bee.

'Virgil?' The smoking man nodded. 'Where's Winnie?'

'Landers took her,' Virgil said.

'Never seen her do that before,' he continued, walking up to Bee, eyeing her up. He concentrated on the scars across her lips, and he licked his own, walking away.

'There's something wrong with her, that's why Landers took her to Dai... to see if they can find out what's wrong,' Virgil stammered.

The man removed his bent-up hat and sat at the kitchen table. He sighed, 'Virgil, Virgil, Virgil, your daughter is a Guardian, that's why we've come.'

'What?' Virgil uttered.

'Omega will give you a good price for your daughter,' he hissed, flicking ash on the kitchen floor, as he dropped a bag of coins onto the kitchen table.

'I'm not selling my daughter,' Virgil snapped.

Bee watched the second man blocking the door. It didn't matter as neither man would get out, and she played with the knives she'd hidden in her pocket during the voyage over.

Nell wailed, 'She's not a Guardian.'

Bee moved, striking the smoking man's throat, and grabbing the back of his head, she sliced the carotid artery, deep and fast. The man gurgled as blood poured down his clothing. The man at the door stared, and Bee threw a second knife into his neck. He grasped it, choking, collapsing to the ground.

Nell screamed, and Virgil grabbed her, backing away. Somer and Feargal thundered down the stairs. Somer stopped at the bottom run, and Feargal almost pushed him off.

Bee shouted, 'Feargal keep those children upstairs. Somer, with me.'

'Fucking hell, Bee, what have you done?' Somer stood opened mouthed, over the bodies.

'They're Flesh Finders.' Bee pulled the blade out of one man's neck and then out of the second. Nell cried out, horrified. 'Shut her up!' Bee shouted, rolling the bodies together, but Nell carried on. She grabbed the woman, plonking Nell on a chair. Bee pointed her bloody knife at the woman's eye. 'You be quiet unless you want Reapers to come.'

Bee saw that spark. Something she hadn't seen in a long time. She'd seen it in the eyes of the people she'd been about to kill. A message, a secret transferring between killer and victim, and it said, *'Please'.* Bee blinked, and stepped away from the woman.

Nell's tears rolled down her cheeks, blubbering. 'But... she isn't a Guardian...'

Bee exhaled, looking at the woman, and Nell shut up. Nell's blotchy face worsened, she snivelled, wiping her nose on her long sleeve, repeating that Winnie wasn't a Guardian.

Bee's tone became softer, 'Mrs Harper, Winnie is a Guardian, and those men would have sold her, and there will be other men like that.' She wiped the knives on her coat, and turned to Somer. 'We need to get these bodies out of here.'

He snapped, 'It's your mess, you sort it out.'

Bee ignored him, 'We'll take them to the Temple.'

Virgil stepped towards Bee, 'if you go out the back, there's a path, nobody will see you.'

'Thank you, Mr Harper.' And Bee slipped the knife away.

***

Bononia-Sur-Mur, Northern France

Malick stood alone in a red landscape, and his heart beat faster, as he looked around. The scattered trees looked lifeless but flames swirled inside their great trunks. Even the red ground had fluidity to it, and Malick crept through.

This was somewhere he wasn't supposed to be. Fear gripped him and he wanted to go home, but Bee's presence stabbed at him; this was somewhere she belonged.

Three figures emerged from the red mist. They surrounded Malick, and he stood at the edge of the precipice, and the rock beneath crumbled. The three figures lunged, gripping him, as he toppled over the edge, falling into the darkness, taking them with him.

Malick gasped, spitting out water. Eyes wide open, and he was still in the kitchen and in the bath tub Esther had filled, as Teppo looked down at him, grinning.

Teppo laughed, 'Malick, you've got one seriously fucked up situation on your hands.' He headed into the pantry, brought back two beers, and took a seat. On the table were Malick's fresh clothes, Teppo threw them next to the bath. 'Put them on and tell me what's going on.'

'It's a long story,' Malick snapped, splashing out of the bath, drying himself off.

Teppo gulped his beer. 'What? That you married one scary woman?'

Malick pulled on his shirt, and then his long breeches, giving Teppo a brief outline of why Bee had left. He sat with Teppo, drinking his beer. 'I married a Reaper, and Guardian, who was too frightened to tell me the truth, and I proved her right.'

Teppo took a second gulp. 'You always knew something was a little off about Bee.'

Malick glared. 'Well, I ruined everything, and now she's gone.'

Teppo leaned in close. 'Bee did something to me, she grew people out of my memories, that's how we sailed the Juna. I saw bits of her life, and your telling her to go devastated Bee.'

'I know that,' he muttered.

'Bee fell in love with you because you saw a person. You didn't want anything except her love, and you destroyed all that with three words, Malick.' Teppo tapped his index finger sharply on the table. 'She loves you, probably a lot more than she should.'

Malick slumped into his chair. 'I hit her, Teppo, I hit her, and Bee had this nonchalant look as if to say, *'Is that it?'* and it frightened me.' He drank his beer, remembering the argument. 'And the things I called her, it's no wonder she ran away.'

Teppo got more beers from the pantry. Placing them on the table, he said, 'Well, I guess me and Somer are as much to blame. We forced you into people smuggling, by the time you knew what was going on, it was too late. I'm sorry, Malick.'

Malick drank his beer.

'You're going after her, aren't you? Look –'

'Of course, I'm going after her, Teppo,' Malick snapped. 'Do you honestly think I'll let the only woman I've *ever* loved go, even if she is a bloody Reaper?' He finished his beer, with a twinge of guilt about Nadine and then opened the second bottle. 'I've just got to figure out how to keep Tristan safe. Omega has him, and we sail in three hours.'

Teppo turned to Malick, eyebrows raised. 'Omega?'

'She wants to trade my family for Bee, and if I don't go with her, she'll take Viola.'

Teppo whistled. 'Well, just to make things worse, Bee plans to kill Eldric.'

Malick looked up, rolling his eyes. 'Did she say why?'

Teppo sipped his beer. 'Apparently, that's what she was going to do before arriving in France. Your wife is on a suicide mission.'

Malick's heart sank. Not that he had any real plans for how he'd find Bee, and convince her that he loved and wanted her, and everything he'd that said in the argument was wrong. Malick wasn't even sure how he'd escape Omega, but now with Teppo telling him she intended to murder the Lord Guardian, any thoughts of Bee coming home safely were fading.

'Where's Somer?' Malick asked, looking around. Those two were always together.

'In Deman Circe. He stayed with Bee.' Teppo shrugged. 'As the older brother, I suggested he stay. He wasn't happy because Bee put a gun to his head.'

Malick didn't ask for details.

'I didn't sail back to port, I hid the Juna, and those things are still on board.' Teppo drained his bottle. 'I don't know how she did it, but I've never sailed the Juna so fast, there or back.'

'If I can get Bee back, will you come for us?' Malick asked.

Teppo frowned. 'How am I going to know?'

'I'll have to figure that bit out.'

Teppo sighed wistfully. 'Bee as a Reaper is quite something and I've seen this man. They'd kill together, they have what I can only describe as a demented love for each other,' he paused, and then added, 'they'll die for one another, Malick.'

Bee never spoke about Luther, and Malick's stomach hardened, thinking about this man, who she kept a secret. Bee said he was a vassal, and until now Malick didn't suspect otherwise. He knew enough about Reapers to realise they had killing partners, and this Luther had been Bee's. Malick guessed she would try and find him.

Teppo sipped his beer. 'And there's something else.' Quietly Teppo told him his experience about the tentacles which came out of the darkness. He whispered, about the way they attached themselves to him, inserting themselves and then pulled away.

'It's strange.' Teppo took another sip. 'It was like they were looking for someone.'

Malick said nothing, looking at Teppo. He gulped his beer, remembering the red landscape and the figures and then he asked, 'Who were they looking for?'

'They were looking for you, Malick. They were looking for you,' Teppo whispered.

Chapter Twelve
Deman Circe, Kent

Bee straddled her horse. She'd shared Malick's weapons with Somer, but kept most of the revolvers and knives herself. It would be a long ride, and she wanted to get to Lunden, but first Bee had to find Winnie, and if the priest was taking her to Dai, then Bee wanted to go there.

Winnie confused Bee. Like Bee, she had been taken from their mother and given away. Bee always knew she was a Guardian, and she'd learned to hide her abilities. Winnie went to a loving family and had gone through The Purge, but somehow her abilities never appeared. Bee wondered, had these Sinners not touched Calum would Winnie's abilities ever have emerged?

Feargal helped Bee get the bodies to the Temple. Somer refused, but he stole the horses, the saddles, the bags and anything of use out of the Marshal's stable, taking them to the Harpers. She waited for Somer to leave with the horses, and then she hunted for an axe, before dealing with the bodies.

She entered Reece Tanner's home, calling out, wanting to be sure she was alone. Inside, she washed her hands and face in the sink, watching the blood run down the plughole. She took off her leather coat and wiped any remaining blood from it and tidied herself up.

Bee stood before the cabinet. She'd recognised it straight away. When she lived in the grounds of Lunden Tower, she had an identical one, and Bee caressed the wood. It was smooth and well kept.

Searching the kitchen for something sharp, Bee found a large pin. She fiddled with the lock, forcing it open, another skill she'd learned as a Reaper, as it was how the assassin could gain entry to the Malefactor's home. The collections of weapons inside were like hers. Touching each object, she held a knife, remembering each execution she'd performed. And she remembered the deadly wounds Claude inflicted; she'd done similar but where he'd failed, Bee never had.

Inside were revolvers, pistols, shotguns, cartridges, cuff bracelets, a bullwhip, many blades and butterfly knives, and two metal belts. Rare for a Reaper to have two, and Bee took both. The second one meant something to this Marshal. She flung her arms out, releasing the swords, both polished and well maintained, and Bee returned both to the belt form, putting them around her waist. She took all the guns and pulled out two holsters. Loaded the revolvers and buckled them around her waist. In the corner was an old sack, and Bee emptied the guns and bullets into it.

There were gloves, they looked harmless, and Bee put them on, spreading out her fingers, and the needles sprung forward covering her hands like pointed talons, then she retracted them. The Marshal had several throwing stars, all of them clean and they went into the sack, along with the knives and machetes. And then she spotted the uniform.

Taking it out, Bee held the clothing. It was made from a unique stretchy material and soft leather. A delicate piece of clothing that may not stop a bullet, but it would slow it down. Bee held it against her chest. The softness flushed memories through her because she had always felt safe inside her own uniform.

A separate box hid in the corner. Bee's hand trembled, caressing the smooth varnish. She opened it, staring, and inside lay the Reaper's mask and helmet. Featureless in every way, only the contours of a face were seen, slit sockets, a nose and lip shape, nothing else.

Bee took it, and climbed the stairs to the upper level. The bedroom was sparse, with a bed, wardrobe, but not much more. Opening the wardrobe door, Bee looked at the mirror.

The swelling in her face hadn't receded, and Bee pawed at the bruises, as they turned into purple covering most of her face. She let out a breath, as all masks were the same until the wearer put them on.

Slipping the silver metal frame over her head, Bee watched it come to life. The eye holes sunk into her face. The lips opened slightly, as spikes crisscrossed, allowing her to breathe, and the pattern, the teeth across her metal mouth, appeared.

Bee's heart pounded. This helmet represented life before she married Malick. Backing away from the mirror, Bee became light-headed, her blood rippled, making her cold inside. It hadn't completed its transformation, and she clawed, pulling it from her head, gasping for air. She took the mask, along with Tanner's other weapons, and uniform.

Now back at the Harpers' cottage, Bee raised her eyebrows at the state of the horses. They weren't lame, but they were past their prime. Somer had saddled the animals, and he'd thrown two saddlebags over one horse, containing ropes, blankets and the camping equipment he'd found. Feargal stood holding the horses, patting them, waiting.

The village was a sparse place, with broken cottages, their roofs thatched by reeds, many one-storey buildings with fish tackle piled up at the front of the houses. It reminded Bee of the only placed she'd ever called home, and her heart ached.

Bee mounted the horse, she peered down at Feargal. 'If Reapers or anybody comes, just tell the truth. Don't get people hurt, as we can take care of ourselves.'

'What about Winnie?' he asked.

'I'll do my best to bring her home.'

The horse plodded, crushing the shells under its hooves and Bee did not turn to give a final nod to Feargal. The Harpers remained inside as she'd frightened the woman enough and it was best to stay away.

Somer rode up beside her. 'Do you have a plan, Reaper?'

She looked ahead. 'Not getting us killed.'

The blackbirds had resettled as Bee and Somer rode to the outskirts of the village. The village was waking up, and people peered through their windows as the strangers passed. Then Bee and Somer came to the Temple.

Bee carried on, but Somer stopped and stared at the sight. Turning the horse, she studied his horrified expression, and the silence was enough to ensure what she'd done would have the desired effect.

The bodies were dismembered, and each pallid head was stuck on a spike, as the dead men's eyes stared out, with pieces of flesh dangling from the necks. The arms were tied to either end of the cross, and the torsos were tied, with both legs at the bottom. Underneath, a sign read, 'Flesh Finders'.

Somer couldn't take his eyes off the heads. 'Why?'

'It creates fear.' Bee admired her creations. 'Omega is coming, and we may have Reapers to deal with. It won't work on them, but it might on Omega's men.'

'And you just cut them up?' He couldn't draw his eyes from the nightmarish scene.

She nodded.

'You really are a sadistic–'

She grabbed the reins of his horse. 'I'm trying to keep us alive, keep you alive.'

'I'm here because of Teppo,' he snarled. 'No other reason.'

'You got me to Deman Circe, go back.' She played with her cuff bracelet, twisting the buckle. Even with all the weapons she now had, Bee was glad of her bracelet. 'Go back, Somer. I don't need you. I don't need anyone, I never have.'

'No, but you needed Malick to hide behind,' he growled.

Bee rode off. The ash trees dotted the paths and the cottages vanished, as Bee left Deman Circe. The sound of the horse relaxed Bee. Somer followed, keeping quiet. The treeline disappeared, developing into the low-line walls as the pebble beach came into sight. In silence, Bee followed the path along the beach. They passed the totems piled high with bodies, and the human scarecrows.

The sickly stench didn't bother Bee. A childhood memory flashed, of her spreading straw over a bloody courtyard, and Bee shook it off. She waited for Somer to catch up and he looked green.

'Are you going to throw up?' She offered him a water bottle.

He gulped the water. 'No.'

'There weren't so many totems when I left.'

'We never had them in France.' Somer still looked pale.

'France was lucky. I'm surprised though, Somer.' She took a sip of water. 'What the villagers do with the dead is the same as what you do with the living.'

'What?'

'These people are dead, but you and your brother kidnapped living people, sold them, and Omega made them into something else.' Her horse trotted on. 'You and I are more alike than you realise.'

He rode next to her, face screwed up. 'Don't think for one minute I'm anything like you, Reaper. I've never killed anybody.'

Bee retorted, 'No, you let other people do the killing, and you took the money.'

Both rode in silence as the waves swished, lapping against the pebbles. Bee's body swayed in time with the trotting of the horse, and she enjoyed having the sun on her face. There had been a time when Bee wouldn't have taken in such things. She would have ridden, focused on one thing.

The execution of a young woman and her eight-year-old son sprang to mind. Bee received the warrant, rode to the house and stepped inside. Once completed, she returned to her barrack inside the Tower, removed the mask and uniform, kneeled and meditated. A requirement after each warrant was completed, to centre the Reaper back into the living world.

There had been a knock at the door, and Luther explained she was moving to Oren's apartments. By that evening, Bee was holding baby Hamish in her arms, breastfeeding him and Bee thought nothing more of the family she'd killed. This would not be her last execution during her time at the Tower.

Bee squinted at something in the distance. She rode up and dismounted as the horse chomped on its bit. The body of a man lay in a puddle of his own blood. He wore breeches, a long black cloak, and had been shot twice. Once in the back, and once in the head. Brain and bone glistened in the blood. Bee flicked away the flies. Bending down, she inspected the body, and further down the road lay another person. Somer didn't get off his horse, he remained mounted, heaving.

Bee struggled, turning the body over. This man was large, and there wasn't much left of his face. Somer groaned as some flesh fell back into the blood, and Bee spotted the dead man's ring. She grasped the hand, studying the sovereign gold ring, engraved with an image of the Farscape; a tree and lake, embossed in Jet, a stone that was only found in the North. This was the ring of a priest, and Bee dropped the hand immediately, guessing this was the man called Landers, Feargal had spoken of. The man was still warm, shot less than an hour ago.

'Somer, help me get this man off the road.'

He didn't move. 'I'm not touching him, moved enough during the plague, including my sister.'

Bee stiffened. 'Then moving one more isn't going to make much of a difference, is it?' Rage burned inside Somer's face, and Bee expected him to jump from the horse and lash out, but he turned his horse, trotting away.

Grabbing hold of the deadweight, Bee slowly dragged Landers off the road, his boots scraping along as she reached the roadside, and she rolled him down into a ditch. Without knowing who'd killed the priest, she couldn't risk him being discovered. Clambering down, Bee hid the body and clawed her way back up. She did her best kicking up the dust on the road to hide the blood.

Somer was already off his horse and looking down at the second man on the road. This, Bee figured, was Marshal Tanner, as he wore the long regulation coat, and he was still alive. He lay in the middle of the broken road, his insides shot, and blood soaked into his clothes.

'Landers...' the man choked, 'Landers...'

Bee bent down and took his hand. Looking around, she saw there was no sign of the prison wagon, but there were lots of hoof prints in the dust. Bee guessed at least six riders had come along and stolen it.

'He's not dead,' Somer muttered.

'Not yet.' Bee slipped her arms under Tanner, dragging the man off the road, and Somer then gathered the man up, heading over a small mound, where they could hide.

Bee followed. She didn't know why Somer was helping this man, but she watched as he placed him at the base of a tree, leant up against the trunk. Bee tied the horses out of sight, but she could still see the road and the sea opposite. Taking a blanket, Bee placed it under Tanner's head. The man was dying, and there was nothing Bee could do, but she was not prepared to let the Reaper die alone.

'I'll build a fire.' Somer headed deeper into the woodland, gathering pieces of wood.

Bee sat with Tanner. Every so often, the man gasped and Bee gave him a little water. They might be here for minutes or hours. A gunshot to the stomach could be a slow way to die.

Tanner opened his eyes, coughing up blood. Bee wiped his mouth as he looked at her bracelet. 'You're... you're a Reaper?'

Bee nodded.

'Are you... going to... kill me?'

Bee shook her head. 'Not unless you want me to?'

The man gurgled a laugh, and blood bubbles popped from his mouth. It was common that if a Reaper was fatally wounded, their partner would cut their life short to save them suffering.

'Not yet,' he whispered.

Chapter Thirteen
Lunden Tower, Lunden

Gable stood by the window in Leena's plush apartments, admiring the beautiful red curtains and newly upholstered furniture. Leena rushed into the sitting room, surprised to see Gable. She moved a few toys out of the way after the maid took the children into another room.

Something was happening. Eldric had called a meeting in the Grand Throne Room. People scurried about, hands flapping, and shouting came in through the open window. Gable thought this activity was due to Bedelia's return and the discovery of a new Guardian, but this was something else. When Gable tried to speak to Eldric about Bedelia, he'd growled at her, but then she'd noticed the valet, Rupert, wasn't with him. The old man was always with Eldric, and she'd asked after him, only for Eldric to erupt, shouting and cursing, and Gable left Eldric in the Throne Room, festering on whatever caused his anger.

'Apologies, Lady Gable,' Leena said, as another maid entered behind her with a tray of tea.

'Leena, please, no need for formalities.' Gable turned from the window. She gave Leena a welcoming kiss, and both stared out of the window. 'Your dress looks lovely.' Gable noticed Leena's long flowing blue dress, light and delicate.

'What brings you here, Gable? I'm sure it's not to admire my dress,' Leena asked, offering Gable a seat as the maid poured two teas.

Gable waited to hear the door close. Now they were alone, she could speak freely. 'They've discovered a crack in The Barricade, and a new Guardian has been found.' She watched Leena's face pale as she placed the cup shakily back on the table.

'Are you certain?' Leena grasped her necklace.

Gable nodded. 'And we understand what that will mean.'

Leena rose from the sofa, scratching her hair. 'I can't go through that again.'

Gable approached, understanding what Leena was referring to. She guided the woman back to the sofa, sitting her down. 'There is more; I felt Bedelia return. I don't know how, but the woman is back.'

Leena inhaled; her eyes glistened. 'You said Claude killed her.'

Gable took hold of Leena's hand. 'We've nothing to worry about.'

'But if she finds out what we –'

'I've sent him a message.' Gable stroked her friend's face, giving her a tiny smile. 'He'll kill her again before she ever finds out.'

'And if Oren finds out it was me who told about Bee's–'

She scolded, 'Why would he find out?'

Leena got up, stomping around the lounge. She headed to the window, looked out and then turned her attention back to Gable. 'Eldric will hang us for what we did.'

Gable sighed. Eldric would have something more frightening than the noose. Both women would suffer a slow, painful process before death arrived. Her heart pulsed faster, thinking about the endless possibilities. The plan had taken shape over a few months, as both women grew closer after the birth of the second boy. They'd become jealous of Bee, wanting her and the children dead.

Claude killed Bedelia, and then a few months later, he lit the match in Hamish and Oliver's nursery, setting it alight, locking the door, so there was no escape.

The nanny, Eldric was informed, got drunk and started the fire. Nobody told him the door had been locked on the outside, nobody in that room would have been rescued. And it cost the lives of the nanny's entire family. Something Gable couldn't think about now. She needed to make sure Leena didn't lose her nerve; otherwise, she'd lose her life.

***

Daniel Cooper stood in front of Lord Guardian Eldric, who sat reading the parchment Daniel had scribed during his investigation. The inquisitor had smartened himself up before entering, putting on a clean pair of breeches and shirt. He didn't want the Lord Guardian to see any blood stain on his clothing. Never having set foot in the Grand Throne Room, it took him a lot of self-control to stop from staring up at the amazing ceiling and high walls.

The ceiling was covered with row upon row of wooden death masks. They took the casts of the traitors' faces just after their executions, and then carved the faces into wood and placed them above, so every visitor could see what their fate might be.

Daniel dreamed about seeing the death masks, and now he stood in the centre of the Throne Room with Rupert kneeling beside him. He was beaten and broken, hands mangled, a few teeth pulled out, with dried-in blood across his body. His ears bled, and one eye had swollen shut. Daniel stood proud. He'd discovered the information from an old man called Will that he and Rupert had smuggled Verda's two girls out after she'd given birth.

Getting the information had proved to be a painstaking exercise. Not for Daniel, but for Will. The old vassal spent over two hours with Daniel before he couldn't take the pain anymore and let slip that Rupert played a part in the children's supposed deaths.

Daniel had gripped Will while he was popping peas in the great kitchen. He'd slipped his hand under the old man's arm and hoisted him out of the chair seconds after Rupert left. Daniel figured he was worth talking too. Nobody noticed the old man vanish from the kitchen .

The old man smelled terrible, a mixture of the earthly smell brought on by sleeping with livestock. Cabbage, Daniel had thought, that's what the old man reminded him of, but he couldn't work out why he thought of cabbage. After two hours with Will, the man soon stank of blood, piss and shit. A smell the torturer knew well in his line of work.

Daniel's chambers were dark, dank and full of frightening instruments from the Judas Chair to simple whips. The sunlight barely shone through a small barred window, and the walls that were covered in moss, leaked stale water. Every day Daniel threw straw over the blood-covered floor. It hid anything from vomit and bile to human remains and the smells were pungent. Sometimes he'd even leave decaying bodies on the racks when he had a new prisoner to question. A message, that if they didn't confess, they might end up there.

He possessed every kind of implement possible to extract information from people, and Daniel prided himself on being good at his job. Claude, his overseer, requested that anybody connected to the Lord Guardian was questioned, and Daniel patted himself on the back for following Rupert straight away. He'd not considered that a man who'd served Eldric for many years would betray him, but Rupert for whatever reason, was in the thick of it.

Daniel had enjoyed torturing Will. He'd begun by whipping the old vassal. The whip cracked, lashing into the paper-thin skin. Will cried, screamed, puked up, and passed out, then Daniel rubbed salt into the whip's tails to make it worse. The old man stank of piss, and he'd soiled his breeches. The dungeon was a rancid place at the best of times, but Will made it worse.

Yet the old man said nothing.

Will sat in the chair for ten minutes before he finally gave up anything he knew. The modified chair comprising of retractable spikes impaled Will's flesh, and Daniel repeated the questions Claude had issued until the man confessed. Two girls, born years apart, were taken from a woman called Verda. She'd pretended they were dead, and the man who took them was Rupert.

These girls were given to a baby seller in Kent, who sold them. After that, he didn't know. The baby seller was dead, she'd been dead ten years, and Daniel believed Will. The old man died shortly after his confession, but Daniel didn't consider Will to be necessary. Rupert was.

The Room was full of official banners. A draft came from somewhere as they swayed against the stone wall, and soldiers stood, all wearing clean and pressed grey uniforms, with shiny boots, and each man held a rifle, standing to attention.

Three councillors stood at the bottom of the grand podium. Niall Cameron, a short man in his sixties, Una, his wife, a woman in her fifties, and Torin Welby, a young councillor, and new to the position.

Eldric's hands tightened around the parchment, ripping the paper; he glowered, and the torturer stayed quiet. Daniel sweated, hands shaking, so he held them together. Puffed up with the information he'd learned, but unsure if he might not end up in the stocks or worse because of the betrayal he'd discovered.

'Is this true, Rupert?' Eldric asked. His voice was loud, with slivers of anger inside every word.

Rupert didn't move, and Daniel nudged him to say something.

The valet remained quiet.

***

Eldric threw the ripped parchments to the floor and scowled at his three councillors. They stood quietly, waiting to hear what Rupert had done. They had no idea

Eldric had kept Verda a prisoner, and he'd forced himself on her, to give him a male heir.

And now they were about to find out.

'Do you understand what you've done, Rupert?' Eldric asked.

The man said nothing, and the torturer nudged him.

'Sire,' Niall spoke, 'may I ask why we have been gathered here?'

'Treason,' Eldric said, 'Rupert took my two daughters, claiming they were dead, so they would not know me.'

The throne room fell into silence again. People, even the soldiers, exhaled, hearing the confession of their Lord. The three councillors muttered, their expressions paled, and Eldric guessed the next question, so answered it before one of them could ask.

'I kept Verda prisoner after my wife died.'

'Who is Verda?' Torin Welby asked.

Eldric remained quiet. Instead, Niall spoke, 'She was the younger sister of Isabella, married, with a daughter called Marisol.' Then he directed his question to Eldric. 'You said Verda and her daughter drowned on their return voyage to Spain, you showed me the report, Lord Eldric… what did you do?'

Eldric sank into his great peacock throne. He picked the brilliant blue hand rest and tapped his fingers on the oak varnished wood, while the three councillors waited, as did everybody else in the room.

'The night we put my beloved Isabella into the ground, I forced myself onto Verda… she reminded me so much of Isabella, that I told the Spanish, they both drowned at sea.'

Una asked, 'What does this have to do with your valet?'

Rupert prepared everything when Eldric wanted to have sex with Verda. In the morning of the chosen day, Rupert and two maids entered the chambers. The chambers consisted of three rooms, a bedroom, a small living area, where Verda and her daughter, Marisol, spent most of their time, eating and reading, and a final small bedroom for Marisol.

Verda's private chambers were made up of red. Red velvet curtains, rose-red carpets and a soft red four-poster bed, even the drapes were red. The day would begin with Verda being presented with a magnificent breakfast, of bananas with honey, watermelon, eggs, bacon, truffles, pumpkin seeds, freshly baked bread, figs, oysters, dates, with ginseng tea. She'd grazed on whatever she wanted, and Marisol would join her.

The maids then bathed Verda in rose petal water, and she was thoroughly cleaned and douched, then dressed in a simple black sheer robe. Enough to cover her modesty, and enough for Eldric to see through it, and she would then have to lie on top of the bed, waiting.

Rupert would light the cinnamon-scented candles, plump fresh pillows, place fresh roses around Verda, and scatter the petals on the floor. They weren't allowed to speak, and then Eldric came in and spent the night with Verda, as Rupert sat in the corner, listening to the Lord Guardian's grunts. In the morning, Eldric would leave, and Rupert always followed him. Eldric didn't understand how they'd got to know each other, and become friendly.

'Bedelia was your eldest daughter –' Torin started.

'Is my daughter, and she's alive,' Eldric interrupted, and there was another pause in the room.

Una asked, 'She's alive?'

Eldric glared at his councillors. He shouldn't have to answer for his actions, least of all to these three, but he nodded and said no more.

Torin started, his question shaky, 'Do you know where this other daughter is?'

The Guardian sat up, recomposing himself. 'Yes, she is on the Southeast coast.'

Sitting on his throne, he wished he'd done things differently. He should have married Verda, she would have given him more children, and he might have even loved Bedelia and this other girl. Instead, he'd been desperate, and now Bedelia had returned, and she would try again to kill him.

Bedelia's plot had been uncovered, and she'd died because of it. The inquisitors questioned everybody Bee had been in contact with at the Tower, including, Oren, Leena and Luther. None of them had new information other than what had already been passed onto Eldric, that Bedelia was overheard talking to a man about killing Eldric. It wasn't much, but it was enough to assassinate her.

Now Bedelia was back.

She would come for him. He didn't understand why his daughter wanted to kill him. If he'd known about Bedelia, had known the girls lived, they would have been brought up within the Tower. He would have given them everything.

'Rupert!' he bellowed and smiled as the old man jumped, hearing his voice. 'Why did you take my girls from me?'

The old man looked up, his eyes peering through the swollen slits. He couldn't speak and mumbled something. Daniel leaned close to Rupert and listened, as the old man muttered, spitting blood into Daniel's face.

'What did he say?' Eldric asked.

Daniel quivered, 'Something about you stealing from the Farscape, something that doesn't belong to you.

Rupert heaved, managing to say, 'You're not what you appear. You're not a different man, you are the...same beast, transferred into the bodies of...your...offspring. You stole from the Farscape, and we've been...punished, ever since.'

Eldric burned. The man knew his secret. If Rupert knew, then others did. Was this the reason why Bedelia wanted him dead? Had she discovered, he was the reason the world was unbalanced because he'd stolen the soul of a young man, taken it for his own and in doing so, the Guardian had drunk off the energies of his subjects.

'You're not... God, Eldric, that's why Bedelia came... and she'll come...again.' Rupert wheezed.

'My lord –' Torin started.

'Silence.' Eldric rose from his throne, setting slowly down the three steps towards his servant. 'Daniel, do you have a mobile gibbet?'

The torturer nodded.

'Bring it now.'

The man scuttled out, and Eldric paced the room. Everybody stared at him, but all were too frightened to speak. They'd all learned that the body in which Eldric stood in was nothing more than a vessel. He'd killed his own blood to survive, and this was the only reason Eldric needed a male heir. He could not live inside the body of a woman, because he needed them to feed off while they incubated the next mould, in which the Lord Guardian could be housed.

Daniel returned. The gibbet clanked as the metal cage swung and Daniel held it, forcing it to stop rotating. He spun a wheel, lowering the gibbet to the ground, and he opened the door.

'Put him inside,' Eldric ordered.

Daniel grabbed the old man, and Rupert yelped, but he didn't beg. The torturer whispered to Rupert what to do. Eldric noted the man, who was crusted in dried blood with clothes torn, had a serene look on his face, and this angered Eldric even more.

'Bring his head up to mine.'

Daniel requested the help of a soldier, and both men reeled in the metal chains. Each turn made the distinctive clanking of metal against metal, and Rupert, all broken and bloody, stood with his feet on the frame. Eldric chewed his lips, and they both glared at each other.

'You will come with me to Dai Castle, Rupert.' Eldric bared his teeth.

Una stepped forward. 'Is that wise, Sire?'

Eldric swished his robes behind him. 'Yes, ready my people, and make sure Gable is prepared, she is accompanying me.'

Una nodded. She left the throne room, and Eldric turned his attention back to Rupert.

'I've something special for you.' Eldric looked into the eyes of his servant, he chewed his lip. 'You will endure the fires. You will not die, and you will burn for one year and a day. Each day you will burn anew. Every night your body will recover, only to burn again.'

Eldric grabbed Rupert's head. Closing his eyes, Eldric breathed, a rush travelled through his blood, it built up, and then it crashed out of him into Rupert. Eldric's eyelids flickered, as the energy pulsed through him.

Rupert's head burst into flames. The scream echoed throughout the chamber, a painful, sorrowful noise, as the flesh quickly melted, and at first everybody recoiled at the sound of Rupert's pain, but then they smelled the burning. It was an assault on the senses as if a fatty piece of pork was being burnt on a spit. Rupert's face sloughed off Eldric as the skin melted into muscle.

'And you.' He turned to Daniel. 'You are bringing him to Dai with me. Make an example of him.'

Chapter Fourteen
Deman Circe, Kent

Marisol stepped onto English soil for the first time in over twenty years. She'd brought over a hundred riders, all with the sole purpose of finding Bedelia and the second Guardian.

The day was warm, no clouds in the sky, and only a breeze drifted along the shore, and the miles of sandy beach stretched and curved around the land. At the low sea walls were the totems and scarecrows she'd heard about from her sailors, and behind them were a few old cottages. Nobody from the village came down, and Omega's riders gathered on the sandy beach.

Eldric's essence had bit the moment her ship, The Angel, crossed into the English Channel, but the one connection she couldn't find was Bedelia's. She'd lost it the moment Bee broke through The Barricade and now it was gone.

Bee had disconnected herself from Marisol, and she couldn't understand how the woman had managed it. She felt Eldric, his nephew Oren, and another female

Guardian fasten themselves to her, and she also felt the new Guardian. This one was slightly different.

But no Bedelia.

The riders were still landing, dragging up their boats onto the sand. Malick picked Tristan out of the boat and placed him on the beach. Bringing the boy had been reckless, but Marisol wanted all the bargaining tools she could get, and perhaps Tristan might make Bee surrender.

Malick was a different matter. On the sailing over, he revealed Bee only got married because he was a widower, who needed a mother for his son, and she made it clear she would never love him. He claimed Bedelia had intended to take only their daughter back to Britain, now she knew about the Crack, and Marisol didn't know if Malick was lying. The fact was, Bee murdered Philip and almost killed Baptiste, and she'd need everything to get this woman, and if it meant bringing along her husband, she'd do it.

Marisol continued studying Malick with his son. Their daughter, Viola, was only eighteen months old, and if, as Malick claimed, Bee didn't love him, then why did the Guardian have a child with the man? Somebody was lying, and Marisol figured it was Malick because she knew nothing of Bee.

Marisol wrapped her leather coat around her, trudging up the beach, and she stopped between the totems and heard the pathetic groans coming from the human scarecrows. The flies buzzed around both, the living and dead. These were the things she remembered when she left Britain. Apart from the cliffs, her parting memory was how Eldric treated his subjects.

Baptiste stepped up, bald head hidden under his hat. 'They want to eat.'

She ordered the riders to head into the village. There would be a pub, as there was always a pub. She stood back as the men and women headed up the walkways and through the paths. All of them wore long breeches, boots, hats, and duster coats, and all of them carried pistols, revolvers or knives. They'd have to protect themselves when they encountered soldiers or Reapers. What was going to happen next was anybody's guess, and she'd lose good people. The Flesh Finders here would help. They generally did, when given the right payment.

'You with me.' She stepped up to Malick and Tristan. 'I don't want you out of my sight.'

Malick said nothing, holding Tristan's hand.

'Baptiste, find whoever's in charge here, and start getting some horses,' she ordered. 'And have a Guardsman go to each house. I want to know why a Guardian is in this shithole.'

He shouted at three men, and they headed off into the village.

Marisol took Tristan's hand, pulling him away from Malick. She dragged him up the ramp and onto the scallop-covered road. The boy stopped to look at the totems, and Marisol pulled his arms, forcing Tristan to keep up.

'Malick, are you not going to ask how Bee and I are related?' Marisol asked. He was about to answer, but she carried on. 'Eldric kept my mother prisoner. His first wife died, she was my aunt, and so he used my mother instead. Verda, that was her name, she had two girls, your wife came first and then this one, who has lived in some shitty old village for the last twenty years.'

'Bee said Eldric learned she was a Guardian only when she was twenty-two.' Malick concentrated on his son.

'How did he not know?'

'Bee hid them.'

'What happened after Eldric found out?' Marisol turned, waiting for Malick to answer. She listened, still holding onto Tristan as he explained about the Royal Decree and the birth of her three children.

Marisol closed her eyes. Breathing in, she searched for the strands of the two boys, letting her own abilities flow out across the land, and she felt Eldric, Gable and Oren engage with her. But there was no Bedelia, nor were there any children.

'Those boys are dead, I don't know about the girl,' she said, wanting to see Malick's reaction, but he only nodded. 'Your wife hides her abilities, but everybody is connected with Eldric, even you. When you go through the Purge, you give a little of yourselves to him.' Marisol's eyes widened, realising. 'Why didn't Bedelia go through the Purge?'

'She's a vassal.'

Marisol laughed sarcastically. 'Little Bee really has had a shit life, and then she married you. Can't get any lower for a Guardian.' She turned from Malick and tightened her hand around Tristan's wrist, making the boy cry out.

The leading village houses stood in a row, and they were old. Broken roofs, crumbling brickwork, and already many of the shutters were closed. They'd seen a new ship and wanted nothing to do with it.

'Omega.' A young woman, with long black hair, and wearing old breeches approached. 'There's something you need to see.'

Marisol pursed her lips. 'What is it?'

The finder looked nervous. 'It's better you see it.'

Marisol clasped Tristan's hand, pulling him roughly along with Malick behind. Walking through the village towards the outskirts, her boots crunched the shell road. Marisol glanced, and a few faces poked out of their windows. Those who were brave enough to look, backed away as she passed.

She stopped at the temple.

The riders allowed Marisol through the small crowd, and the display before her was astounding. She'd seen nothing so grotesque before. Marisol's fingers twitched, as her mind processed the two mutilated bodies tied to the crosses. She tightened her grip on Tristan until he cried and she let go.

She stared. Almost buckling at the horrific sight, but she managed to keep standing. Marisol knew all the terrible things she had done to the people she'd kidnapped from Britain, but she had not expected to be greeted by this hideous display, and she noticed the worried look in the men and women who surrounded her.

Behind her, she heard Malick whispering to Tristan that he wasn't to look, and Malick stood next to her. Looking at his face, Marisol saw the same frightened expression on his face as her riders had. Both she and Malick stood, eyes wide, at the two bodies displayed, and Marisol read the inscription.

Sweat ran down Marisol's back. Nobody had done this to Flesh Finders before, and though she'd met neither of these men, Marisol considered them to be a part of her because they risked much to hunt down people, and ship them to the Spanish Netherlands.

One rider dragged a man into the circle, forcing him to kneel in front of Marisol. She looked down, and his eyes remained to the ground.

'He smells of Guardian,' the finder said, 'name's Feargal.'

She circled him, saying nothing, and then Marisol crept up behind him and whispered into his ear, 'Can you tell me who did this?'

Feargal looked at the heads. He stuttered, spitting, 'A man and a woman came through the break... they... they came for Winnie... I don't know which one of them did this.'

'Winnie?' She clasped his chin, making Feargal look at her. 'Is she the new Guardian?'

He nodded, his body shaking. 'The priest took her to Dai Castle.'

'This man and woman, when did they leave?'

'This morning, they took horses and left.' Feargal shook.

Marisol grunted, pushing Feargal into the ground. Turning away from the crosses, she watched Malick. His eyes were transfixed to the body parts. He was trying to work something out, but his brain had refused to understand what he was seeing.

'The Peron brothers don't strike me as the kind to chop people up. Your wife broke Philip's neck – came quite naturally, were Baptiste's words – is there anything I need to know about your Bedelia?'

Malick stared at the figures. Tristan was still in his arms, head over his shoulder. Eventually, Malick pulled his eyes from the macabre sight and said, 'No, there isn't.'

***

The Deman Circe Road, Kent

They hadn't moved all day. Tanner lay by the roots of the tree, his head behind the blanket. Bee kept the fire going, and Somer watched the road. Tanner lay there, bleeding out and he still hadn't asked Bee for her help.

The skyline was changing from bright blue into fiery reds as the sun began to dip. Bee pulled her leather coat around her as she sat by Tanner. He'd been falling in and out of consciousness for most of the day, and Bee didn't think he'd last much longer.

'What's...what's your name...Reaper?' he coughed.

'Bedelia.' She wiped the blood from his lips, giving him a sip of water.

The man's eyes widened. 'The same Bedelia who went to France... and... ended up dead?'

Surprised, Bee said, 'I guess.'

He motioned for her to sit him up. Bee struggled, and he cried out in pain, but he managed to sit up against the stump. 'You... you got away... why did you come back?'

'To kill Eldric,' her voice was low. She turned to see where Somer was, unsure if she wanted him to hear whatever it was Tanner was going to say.

The man hissed a little laugh and his breathing became raspy. He smiled. 'Good. Do you... did you have a companion, an Unseen?'

'Yes.' Luther came to the forefront of Bee's mind. He had always been her partner when two Reapers were required to execute a significant warrant. She'd killed two older Apprentice Reapers protecting Luther because they were torturing him, and then a secret bond and bloody friendship grew. Bee never admitted to anybody why she'd killed the two apprentices. If she had, Luther would have been hung.

She put the water bag to Tanner's lips and stroked his face as he sipped from it.

'I'm ready,' he whispered, patting her hand. 'I am not alone as I walk out of the darkness with you by my side.'

'And I remain in the darkness and wait for you until it is my time to die.' Bee responded, as Tanner closed his eyes. She kissed him on the cheek, pulling him to sit with her, his body leaning into her, and she slipped her hands around his neck, twisting it fast. The sound of bones snapping came. It was like Philip all over again.

He slumped into her arms, and she held him. Bee had uttered the secret words passed down between Reapers, a message they were not alone. She kissed his forehead and pulled herself out from under Tanner.

She kept silent and dragged him up against the stump again. She had nothing to bury him with. Turning around, she saw Somer was nearby. 'How long have you been there?' she asked.

'I heard it all.'

She walked by, and he grabbed her arm, 'Are you going to kill everybody we meet?' he asked scornfully.

Bee shook his hand off, heading toward the horses.

'What do those words mean?' he asked.

'Nothing to you, Somer.'

She checked over the horse, patting it, to keep herself calm. She'd never uttered those words before, and she took a long breath. It was strange whispering the secret words, and it gave her a chill, but she hoped Tanner took comfort in knowing he hadn't died alone.

Bee choked, grasping hold of the saddle. The horse stomped, and she hushed it. Malick was here in Britain, and he'd tangled himself inside Bee. Light-headed, she held onto the saddle, yet she bathed in the pleasure of feeling him. Malick wasn't supposed to be here, he was meant to be safe in France, and the horror hit.

Then she heard the sound of hooves cantering along the road. Quietly, she pulled the horses further into the woods, and she looked at the fire. It had long gone out. Signalling to Somer, she crept back through the trees with him, hiding in the bushes.

On the road, a group of fifty riders stood. Bee watched, hearing the French accents. The leader, a woman, had stopped. This was Omega, her stature, the hair tied back revealing her shaved head, the arrogant way she stood over the pool of blood, and leather coat flapping around her told Bee this woman was in charge.

And then Bee saw Malick. Sitting in front of him was Tristan, and for a second she didn't understand what she was seeing. Why was Tristan here? Bee's eyes widened, concentrating only on Malick and the boy. She sank back into the overgrowth.

'Why are they here?'

Somer continued watching. 'If I know Omega, she's brought them as leverage.'

'But I thought if I'd left –'

'You're a Reaper, would you give up?'

There were conversations, Bee heard the name of a pub mentioned, 'The Fortune,' and Baptiste rode on, followed by the others.

'I'll get them back, but I need your help, Somer.' She carried on watching the horses kick up the dust in the road. The echoing hooves became more distant, until she couldn't hear them.

'I'm not helping you kill anybody, Reaper.' He got up and walked back to the tiny camp.

Bee ignored the way Somer referred to her as 'Reaper' and how every time he said it, he spat it out. Malick's brother-in-law hated her, and Bee felt nothing. She'd heard the venom in people's voices often enough when she'd worn the uniform.

'If you want Malick back, help me.'

'On one condition,' he whispered.

'And what's that?' Bee looked up at him, reading his expression; guessing what he was going to ask.

'You promise to go. Make Malick understand you used him. Get them out and leave. He's better off without you.'

Bee held her breath, not wanting to agree, but the hatred seeping out of Somer was building up, and she whispered, 'Agreed.'

Chapter Fifteen
The road to Dai

O ren shifted in the stagecoach. It was cramped, and he wanted to stretch his legs. They were nearing the outskirts of Dai, but he was sick of looking at Claude's face. The caravan of riders continued along the path, and the coach kept swaying. Oren looked out of the window again, and he saw the same tree line. He felt they were not moving, even though they were.

Oren flung the door open, jumping from the coach, forcing it to stop. They'd been on the road for hours, but even the fresh air, couldn't stifle the ripples running through him.

'What's wrong?' Claude asked, stepping out of the coach.

'I need some air,' Oren snapped.

The stagecoach, seven Reapers and ten soldiers, stopped. The horses stomped their hooves into the muddy path, surprised but glad of the rest.

Oren didn't feel Bee anymore. It was like the burst of lightning had brought her up, made her shine and ripple, and then she vanished. Bee hid away from him. This was something Guardians couldn't do as they were all connected to each other. It made them more powerful to have a different Guardian's essence running through them, but Bee was nowhere to be found.

He recalled how when she had lived with him in the apartments, her power was always faint, like a trickle of water seeping out of her. She somehow held it back, and he wondered what might happen once the dam she'd built broke. He'd witnessed a surge in Bee only once, and it had been more potent than anything Oren had experienced, and once it flashed up, it quickly subsided.

Now though, Oren suspected she knew what she was doing. Bee always claimed she couldn't control her abilities, but not being able to feel her, for her to build a wall, took great skill and knowledge.

Bee hadn't gone through the Purge. Hamish was going to complete the ceremony with Bee, and Eldric had put on a grand celebration. Even the servants were allowed to celebrate, and the whole Tower had a party atmosphere. Banners, flowers, different foods and guests from the noble houses, all came to celebrate the birth of Eldric's first grandchild and heir to the throne.

The day started naturally enough, Leena wore a plain gown, and Oren had found Leena and Bee sitting in his bed chambers. Bee wasn't dressed, still wearing her nightgown.

'Bee refuses to go through the Purge,' Leena explained.

Oren approached. 'You have to for Hamish, for your son.'

Bee's face darkened. 'I do not. You fucked me because Eldric needed an heir, as his wife is proving barren. I've given him an heir, and you're still *fucking* me because Eldric wants more. However, it doesn't mean I'll go through the Purge.'

Oren winced, not used to hearing a woman swear and he noticed Leena play with her necklace, becoming nervous. He didn't think anything could defuse Bee's anger.

'It's better to just do what Eldric wants,' Oren stated, 'he will execute you otherwise.'

Bee rose from the bed. During the months she'd lived with them, she'd started to lose some of the hardness of being a Reaper, but as she glared at Oren, the awakening of love he'd seen in Bee dissolved, and the cold-hearted Reaper stood opposite him, challenging him.

'Bee, this is not –'

She said flatly, 'I am not fastening to that cunt.'

Leena gasped, and he started to say 'Bedelia,' but he got no further, as her hand was at his throat, and she smashed him into the wall behind. He struggled, his hands scratching at hers, the life being forced out of his body, and the air thinned within him, but Bee did not let go. His legs kicked out. Leena pulled at Bee's arm, and Bee pushed Leena to the ground, still holding onto Oren, as his face turned red. Her expression, empty, her face said nothing, there was no emotion and then she released Oren, stepping back.

Oren dropped to his knees, gasping for air. He inhaled, needing the oxygen to enter his body. He sweated, pulling loose his cravat and Leena rushed to him, checking his face, whimpering.

'Go to your room, Bedelia,' Leena shouted, still holding Oren. 'I will speak to you shortly.' The coldness in Leena's voice matched Bee's, and Oren watched as the Reaper did as she was told.

Sometime later, Leena spoke with Bedelia, and then she was ready for the Temple. Guardian Eldric, Gable and the few Guardians were already inside. Music was being played, there was laughter, shrieks, the sounds of a celebration and Bee walked beside Oren, with Leena behind, because she was not crucial, like Bedelia. He held baby Hamish, who was grizzling, but Bee never did enter the Temple.

Two priests waited at the great oak door. They stood beside Bee and took hold of her arms. Something changed, she punched one priest in the face, and kicked the second priest, sending both flying, but they were up and grappling with Bee. She was fast, too fast, she gripped hold of the first priest's neck, and Oren smelled the smoke instantly, Bee burned him from the inside out. The priest's flesh started to bubble as she boiled his blood. The second priest froze. Her touch was so quick, Oren backed away because he was witnessing something he'd never seen before, a power that he did not know could exist.

The priest turned white, he screamed as the white started in his legs and headed up to his head. Bee kicked the frozen priest, shattering him into a thousand pieces. A third priest came running. Bee pulled a dagger, Oren never knew where the knife came from, and she stabbed the priest several times in the leg. He dropped to the ground, howling, and his cries echoed throughout the Tower.

Bee fell to her knees and waited.

Six soldiers approached. All aiming their rifles at Bee, but she did not move. Oren looked at the dead priests and held tightly onto Hamish. He was sure Bee would be hung.

'Oren, you need to complete the Purge.' Leena pushed him toward the door.

He was dumbfounded, and watched as the Reaper, Luther, came forward, cuffed Bedelia, pulling her roughly from the ground and dragged her away.

The Temple doors opened, and Oren completed the Purge by walking on hot coals. He thought everybody heard the screams of the priests, but the music played so loud, it drowned all other noise out. Eldric was furious, learning what Bee had done. Oren thought it would be a matter of hours before Bee was hung, and he did not go to his uncle in her defence.

Only Eldric's desperation for male children saved Bee's life. He left her languishing for a week in the dungeon, and then sent her back to Oren's apartment with orders to continue the second Royal Decree, he'd already issued.

Oren didn't want to sleep with Bee. Before the attack on the priests, he'd been having sex with Bee without the presence of Reapers, now Oren made sure the Reapers had secured her arms with metal bracelets, and a Reaper stood on either side. Oren tried and failed, fear made his performance useless, and he would climb on top of her, sweating and shaking.

'I scared you, Lord Oren,' she said after another failed attempt. Bee sat naked on her bed. The small room had nothing but a bed, a side table and wardrobe, it was a place to mate with Bee, nothing more. Oren never used his own chambers, not wanting to soil his and Leena's private space with a Reaper.

'You almost killed me.' He stood in the corner of the bedroom, near the door. He hadn't undressed, instead he'd ordered Bee to strip, and the Reapers strapped her down. Oren undid his breeches, climbed onto her, and then nothing. The Reapers released Bee from the restraints and stood quietly in the room.

'Do you think I enjoy being penetrated by you?' Bee stood up, naked. She stepped in front of him, her face inches away from his. She leaned in, whispering, 'having you touch me, having you insert yourself into me?'

He kept silent. Bee's words were loaded with misery. His heart raced and sweat poured down his cheek. Bee, the woman was gone, and he feared what she might do. He looked to the Reapers, but they did not move.

'You don't see,' she carried on, 'because you boast about having sex with a monster, regale in the stories of how you impregnated a Reaper.'

Oren blinked, and he shivered. He'd used Bee to ensure his own survival. She was to produce male children and then be discarded. Reapers, he believed, lacked empathy. They did not love, and they feared nothing, and he'd often repeated stories about having sex with her. The court wanted to know the details. Did Bedelia enjoy sex with him? Was she any good? And Oren shared the experiences to boost his own standing in the whole squalid matter.

Oren was proud of the boy Bee had given birth to. Pleased he'd finally achieved something in the eyes of his uncle, but in the eyes of Leena, she saw a baby boy who was more critical to Oren than any child she could have with him.

Oren, for the first time, saw Bedelia as a person, and he saw the hurt he caused another human. Since birth, he had had everything without ever thinking about anybody else, and yet a Reaper had revealed something he never thought about, and it left a sour taste in his mouth.

He sweated, needing to get away from Bee. He ran out of the room, down the corridor, and knocking over a maid, who was watering some roses. Oren slammed the door to his own chambers, breathing heavily, blood pumping around him, and he couldn't shake the gloom in Bee's voice. He slipped down the door, held his head in his hands and burst into tears.

After that, Bee learned she was expecting again; she was already pregnant before they'd taken her to the Temple. Eldric was overjoyed and confined Bee to the apartment and some parts of the Tower's garden.

Oren kept Bee as far away from his uncle as possible, sending daily reports to Rupert, who informed the Guardian, and only when Oliver and the girl were born, did Eldric take an interest. Luther became Oren's personal Reaper. He'd learned they'd grown up and come to the Tower together, and Oren did this out of guilt.

A month before Bee went to France, Oren broke down, and Leena held him, as they lay in bed. He confessed to believing the boys were more important than his own children, and he'd overheard Bee making secret plans to murder Eldric, but he never told her how. He admitted neglecting Leena and the girls, and all she did was kiss Oren and let him cry in her arms.

Bee's sister, Oren considered, was different from Bee. She would have gone through The Purge because she was a free subject. Bee had not because she was a vassal and Reaper, but for reasons unclear, Eldric had not felt the presence of this girl until now.

Somebody, a soldier, laughed. The gruff laughter brought Oren back into the forest, and he thought about the new Guardian, as this girl had fastened herself to Oren straight away. She did not have the same strength as Bee, but there were other forces with her, different energies. They lingered near her but not close enough to attach themselves, and it was as if they were waiting for something, but he couldn't figure out what.

Oren looked at the trees, listening to the bird song. 'Tell me about the girl.' Taking a water bag from a Reaper, he waited.

Claude grinned. 'She's Bedelia's sister, and Eldric expects you to fuck her like you did Bee.' Licking his lips, he said, 'well, you enjoyed Bedelia, you might like this one as well.'

'What did you do to Bee?' Oren walked away from their caravan of riders. The trees in front were full of fantastic green foliage. Oren was tempted to run into it, run away from whatever crisis was about to happen.

'Bee's abilities were spent,' he whispered. 'The Barricade was nearly set. I killed the soldier with her, and then her.' Claude relived the moment, 'I cut her lips and broke her leg. And as she screamed, her lips ripped. I climbed onto her, and well...'

'And then?'

'I slit her throat. She lay there in the sands, and I left. She was dead.'

Oren nodded, telling Claude he needed to pee. He shouted to his Reaper that he was taking a walk. The man walked behind him, and Oren waited until he was a safe distance from the coach before relieving himself.

'Luther, do you remember Bedelia?' Oren asked.

The Reaper said, 'Yes, she was a good Reaper.'

'Were you friendly with her?'

'No.'

Oren raised his eyebrows at this response. 'Once we're back on the road, I'd like you to go hunting.' Stepping closer, he kept his voice low, not wanting to be overheard.

Luther's brows furrowed. 'What am I hunting?'

'Bee… Bedelia, when that lightning struck, I felt Bee. I want you to find her and bring her to me.'

'Yes, my lord.'

'You'll take her to my lodge, in the Barren lands.'

'And if she refuses?'

'Make her listen, Luther.'

'Yes, my lord.'

Oren walked back through the long grass and stepped into the coach. He'd mistreated Bedelia when she lived with him, and there were times Oren had forced himself on Bee when it had not been required because he enjoyed the danger. Oren forgot that Bee had feelings, and now as they headed down towards Dai Castle, he realised he was going to have to make up to Bee for the hurt he caused or he was going to have to kill her.

Claude was already inside, eyes closed, preparing for another doze.

'Claude,' Oren sat back in the seat, making himself comfortable. 'The lightning show last night was Bedelia returning.' And he watched as Claude's eyes sprang open.

***

Arena Porta, Kent

The walls seeped dirty water. Small growths of moss pushed its way through the cracks, splintering much of the dark stone walls. Winnie breathed in the mouldy odours. A jittery shiver started in her heart, bewildered at being thrown into a small prison cell.

The ever-present voices were gone, leaving a quiet silence, and Winnie filled it with despair. She choked on the putrid smell of sweat coming from the guard, who was wrapped up in an old black duster coat, with dirty breeches, and a red paisley banner wrapped around his head. On his lap rested a pistol, and the ground-in stench of piss couldn't hide his musty smell.

Winnie looked up to the small barred window. Eventide was drawing in, and the descending red sun would vanish shortly, leaving only the dark. Winnie didn't know how many hours she'd been in the cell, but her stomach grumbled. The soft swishes of the sea outside sang, and the gulls screeched, like her, wanting food, and all they'd given Winnie was a cup of water.

Her left eye twitched. She suspected she was in the cells of Arena Porta Castle because that was the nearest prison block to Deman Circe, and there were rumours about Flesh Finders using it. The castle itself wasn't magnificent like Dai castle, but a large circular tower, like the old tower in Deman Circe. The structures were dotted along the Kent and Essex coastline. The riders who'd killed Landers and Marshal Tanner had brought her here. The owner, an Edmond Harris, hadn't been happy, but the threat of being killed soon changed his mind. And now a rider, who was supposed to be guarding her, snored in the corner of the prison, grumbling and grinding his teeth, as Winnie backed into the corner of her dirty cell, far away from the man.

Those voices, they were to blame for her incarceration. Winnie thought, if she hadn't listened to them, Calum would be dead, but then she wouldn't be trapped in a cell, and that made Winnie twitch even more.

The terrified expression on her mother and father's faces when she sprang out of the coffin was etched into Winnie's memory. She recoiled; remembering the way Calum and Regan vanished behind the skirt of Nell, too frightened to approach their reborn sister. Priest Landers took advantage of the situation to make money, and Winnie wondered if, when they shot him, he understood she wasn't worth it.

Winnie played with her new white hair. The auburn was gone. Calum and Regan's hair was dark brown, and Winnie never suspected Virgil and Nell were not her natural parents. They never treated her differently, and there were times they seemed to love her more. Making sure she went to the local Temple, and every year the family made a pilgrimage to Canteria, to the holiest of Temples, and they stood within the grounds in awe of the old stone structure.

Huffing, Winnie imagined the stained-glass windows in the giant temple. Vibrant reds, golds and blues, sparkling as the sun shone through the twenty-four separate images, all dazzling, for the faithful to look at.

Like the Temple in Deman Circe, these images belonged to another religion. The first Guardians took this place, crushing the beliefs, and used the building as its own Mother Temple for the new ways of Britain. Winnie heard stories of other religions before the Guardians, they prayed in structures called Mosques and Synagogues, and the Guardians consumed those into the faith.

She'd visit and go through a Cleansing, connecting herself deeper to the Lord Guardian, giving a little of her life to him. And now, as Winnie sat in the old cell, she let the Guardian run through her. Something Winnie had never experienced before. The quiet gave Winnie a chance to welcome him. She sensed Gable and Lord Oren, the last two surviving English Guardians, and they all rippled through her. This power Winnie possessed, connected them in a way she didn't understand.

When she broke The Barricade, Winnie linked with the one on the other side. Something sparked and Winnie had felt a threat coming from this woman, not for her but for somebody else. The newcomer shut Winnie out. This woman differed from the English Guardians. Winnie thought about the voices, the Sinners, and how they used her.

'We never used you, Winnifred,' the voices, an echo of three, whispered inside her mind. 'You served your purpose, to bring back the one without a God.'

'The one without God?' she muttered, 'What is she here to do?'

'She will kill the beast.'

Winnie frowned. It made no sense. Who was the beast? And then it sank in. The woman from The Crack was here to kill Eldric. 'I shouldn't have listened,' she jittered. 'I need to go back, close the gap. Stop her coming.'

'It's too late, she's already here.'

And Winnie's eyes widened.

***

Dai Castle, Dai, Kent

The Constable's Gateway opened, and Oren stared up at the high stone walls. The early evening was quiet, even the town below didn't seem to have its usual animated sounds. Occasional shouts rang out as the market traders tried to sell the last of their wares at rock-bottom prices.

The clipping of the horses' hooves echoed, and the coach rolled through the gate into the castle. The driver hadn't stopped, and Oren was out of the tiny confined space, followed by Claude. Gilbert stood at the bottom of the Keep's stone steps chewing his fingernails.

Oren extended his hand to Gilbert. 'It's good to see you.' He hugged Gilbert, relieved to be out of the stagecoach, and a few feet away from Claude. He breathed in the fresh air, relaxing his shoulders.

'Oren,' Gilbert smiled.

'You know Lord Ramas?' Oren introduced Claude to Gilbert, and they shook hands.

'Yes, yes, we've met several times.' Gilbert called for a valet, and a small boy ran over. 'Take Lord Ramas to his chambers, get him settled with whatever he needs. Apologies, but I'd like a word with Oren.'

Claude thanked him for his hospitality and followed the young boy up the steps as two trunks crashed into the muddy ground from the stagecoach and Gilbert shouted at his vassals for their mistake.

Oren slipped on his warm leather coat, pulling the collar up. It was always windy around Dai Castle, and now the sun was setting, the wind had a little more bite.

'Still bloody windy here, Gilbert,' Oren commented, buttoning his coat.

Gilbert laughed as the pair headed toward the curtain wall, taking the great steps until they reached the wall itself and looked out across the town of Dai. The seafaring town had a dishevelled appearance. Chimneys smoked and the houses were worn. Boats and ships drifted in the shallows of the Channel, and both men watched as people clambered in and out of the sea, trying to salvage what boats they could.

If the fishermen knew of the lightning, they would have moored or tethered their ships securely. The storm would only bring them hardship, because they needed to fix their boats to make any money.

Gilbert looked over the high stone wall. 'We sent ships out looking for The Crack, most of them haven't returned after that lightning last night.'

'Any idea how long it's been there?'

'No, and we've had reports of people going missing, that's been going on for about twelve months.'

'People are missing?'

'People are superstitious. I thought they'd made them up to frighten children about boats coming in and sweeping people up.'

'Did you report this to Eldric?'

Gilbert gave him a sharp look. 'What do you think? And then last night, we had the lightning and thunder.' He greeted his soldiers with a nod, as he and Oren continued walking the Curtain wall.

'It was wild, both frightening and beautiful. The people went down to the beaches and, I daresay everybody - both French and English - along The Barricade saw it.'

'What do you know about it?'

'It must have come from a village called Deman Circe, further down the coast.' He pointed in its direction.

'Not from the original Crack?' Oren peered over the curtain, gazing down at the dried up moat below.

'That village reported a girl rising from the dead,' he said. 'I'm guessing it's connected.'

Oren raised his eyebrows. 'How's that possible?'

'You tell me?'

'Do you remember Bedelia?' Oren asked. 'If this dead girl opened a crack here, I think Bedelia did it on the other side. They combined their abilities,' he muttered thoughtfully.

'But she's dead,' Gilbert frowned.

Oren shook his head. 'I felt her when the lightning kept striking. Bee connected with me, and then she was gone.'

'That can't be good,' Gilbert mused.

'Trouble is I felt a third Guardian come through. We've now three new full-blooded Guardians running around Britain.'

'Bee's father is on loan from Rolfen, he's in the Armoury,' Gilbert suggested.

'I'd like to speak with him about Bee.'

Gilbert ushered Oren back down the steps and through the courtyard. The day traders were being replaced by the night sellers, those who sold more ale, and even themselves to make money. This was a quiet time, only becoming riotous later in the evening if a man had drunk too much and refused to pay for a lady's time.

They headed into the Armoury, and Gilbert stopped Oren. 'Mind yourself with Rufus. He's a tough old bastard.'

Oren nodded.

'Rufus,' Gilbert shouted.

A mean-looking, big man, short with grey hair and short beard, with scars across his wrinkled-pitted face, came out. He wore breeches, a grime-covered shirt, dotted with finger marks, and he wiped his hands on his dirty apron, glaring at Gilbert.

'Lord Oren would like a word.' And then Gilbert left.

Oren looked around the Armoury. The place was full of pistols, revolvers, rifles, cartridges, and knives. He'd never seen so much in one room, and then the smells of burnt wood, grease, oils and candles filled the space, but then he'd never visited the Armoury at the Tower.

'You're Bedelia's father?' Oren asked, intimidated by the large man.

'I am.'

Oren recognised the voice, he'd only heard it once in his apartments, but he knew it. 'She's come back,' Oren said.

'Told she was dead.' The man sniffed, wiping his hand again over his leather apron. He sweated, looking back into the distance, wanting to get back to work.

'I felt her, during the storm, only briefly, but enough to know that it was her,' Oren explained.

'Well then, she must be back.'

'You don't seem surprised,' Oren said.

Rufus's eyes narrowed. 'Nothing that girl does surprises me.'

'When Bee lived with us, you came to my apartments, do you remember?' Oren kept his voice low. 'Is she going to kill Eldric?'

Rufus chewed his lips, smirking. 'Don't know what you're talking about.'

Oren sighed. 'Look, I care about Bedelia –'

'Don't lie, Lord Oren. If you cared, you wouldn't have ridden her like a prize horse and then boasted about it,' Rufus sneered, edging closer to Oren.

Oren's jaw dropped. 'What did you say?'

'She knows the lies the Guardians spout, remember that, Lord Oren.' Rufus gave him a little smile. 'Bee had the education she needed–'

'She's an executioner, Rufus, you made her that,' Oren retorted angrily.

'Reapers are made by the likes of *you*,' the old man sneered. 'Bee's been dead for six years, and any plans were her own.' He headed back further into the armoury.

'You were cruel, making her a Reaper,' Oren stated, following behind.

Rufus turned, saying, 'I kept her safe, away from Eldric.' Rufus invaded Oren's space, making him step back. 'Tell me, when did it dawn on you, that you were repeatedly raping my daughter?'

Oren froze. A chill ran down his back. He'd believed Bee had only been in contact with Rufus once while she lived in the apartments. He realised Bee had never lost touch with him.

'How... how did Bee learn to control her abilities?' Oren stuttered, not so confident.

The weapon maker let out a gruff laugh. He walked back into the workshop, picked up a blade, sharpening it on a stone. 'Reapers, like vassals, don't go through the Purge, too much blood on their hands to enter the Guardian's Farscape, but they meditate. They have mantras helping them get through the killing. It helps with focus, and it cleanses their soul.

'When she was a vassal, picking up body parts, she'd hear the Reapers, and she learned. Bee had her own way to keep those abilities secret, and then when she became a Reaper, she entwined them.'

'He'll defeat her.' Oren refused to believe Bee could kill Eldric. 'He's connected to all of us.'

Rufus grinned, 'Bee's abilities are hers alone, perhaps she is more powerful.'

'Do you think that?'

Rufus stopped sharpening the blade. 'Tell me, why did you never tell Eldric it was me you overheard that day?'

'How did you...' Oren sighed, deciding not to pursue the question. 'I'd already wronged Bedelia. I don't know who reported her, but I thought when she came back, at least she had you and Luther. I never thought Eldric would kill her. After Bedelia died, it didn't seem important.'

Rufus chewed his lips. 'Take care, Lord Oren, don't get in Bee's way.'

Oren didn't ask questions anymore, and he left the Armoury worried. Bee was an exceptional Reaper, stationed at Rolfen until Eldric requested all Reapers with over twenty kills to be sent to the Tower. He wanted the best present in the Tower, but Fredrick Kendal did not want to part with Bee because she was loyal. Kendal offered Eldric Luther instead, and Eldric refused taking both Reapers. Pulling up the Collar of his coat, Oren strode across the courtyard, as the day turned to dusk.

Could Bee really kill Eldric?

***

Rufus blew out some air, watching as Oren strode through the quietened courtyard as the night vendors, the alehouses, and whores started their nightly sales. He lost sight of the Guardian weaving in-between the half-shut stalls.

Bedelia was back and sounded more powerful than Rufus imagined. He'd heard rumours about a girl in Deman Circe coming back from the dead. And now, his daughter had returned from France.

Grabbing his coat, he locked the Armoury and headed back to the two rooms Gilbert provided for him. Rufus's pigeons cooed, seeing him return, and he took a small bowl of feed from the mantle, pouring it into each bird's cage.

'Eat up, eat up,' he muttered.

Inside the room stood a small stove, a bed, and candles, and not much more. Rufus rarely ate here, but it was somewhere to rest his head. He lit a candle, placed it on the small table and found some paper.

Rufus hadn't been a good father. He used the belt, sometimes starved Bee, and made her sleep on the floor. Aged four, she started cleaning Rolfen's courtyard of apprentice Reaper body parts, and she did this until her eighth year. He hadn't wanted a child, but the baby seller persuaded him he needed a vassal. She didn't have a name, and Rufus named her after his mother.

He saw her eyes turn black when she murdered two apprentices, and he knew what she was, though he'd never heard of a Guardian's eyes turning black. They only ever turned white. He took her in his arms, hiding Bee's face until her eyes returned to normal.

Nobody except Rufus saw it, and he convinced Fredrick Kendal, stating she showed promise of becoming an excellent Reaper if he could train her, and the Overlord agreed. It was the only way Rufus could keep Bee safe.

Bee learned meditation, how to fight, use of weapons, and to read and write. She was the only Reaper living with a parent at the castle, and Rufus gave Bee extra training. Sometimes he was a little too brutal, but other times, Bee curled up with him on his chair by the fire, and she'd fall asleep in his arms.

Rufus wrote one word on the paper. He didn't need to write anything else. The bird cooed as Rufus reached inside the cage, grabbing the greyish bird, head darting in all directions and he tied the message to her foot.

Rufus slipped the bird under his coat and headed back outside. He hurried across the courtyard, fires and torches burned, bringing an artificial light for the soldiers. The small tavern was already busy, bawdy laughter, women letting out joyful screams as the men most likely went a bit far.

Up the ramparts, he nodded to the soldiers, thick military coats and hats hid their faces as they tried to keep warm. Rufus looked out, in the opposite direction of Dai. A few lights dotted in the landscape showed signs of life below. He took out the pigeon, stroked her, whispered into her ear and let the bird go.

She flapped her wings and vanished into the night. Rufus headed back down the ramparts. He entered the tavern and ordered a beer, thinking he might as well enjoy himself while he had the freedom to do so.

The bird would take the message to the Overlord of Rolfen. The Butcher of the River was dead - had been for seven years - the new Overlord now was his son, Sagan Kendal.

Chapter Sixteen
Deman Circe Road, Kent

Bee watched the pub. It was a large whitewashed building, cracked walls, and sea-weathered. The old sign read, 'The Prince of Fortune,' and it creaked in the night's wind. Outside sat three riders, smoking and drinking, guarding the horses. Bee didn't like her chances, but if it meant rescuing Malick and Tristan, she'd have a go.

Sweat trickled down her neck. Bee had done nothing like this before alone, and her hands tremored. She'd taken many lives, but this was different. Bee didn't voice these thoughts to Somer. He didn't care if she lived or died.

Taking Malick and Tristan from Omega was not something she'd considered. She could face Omega, but she wasn't sure if she wanted Malick to witness her killing people. But if she didn't do this, Omega might kill Tristan, and she couldn't live with that. Getting them out and back to France was her only option.

She'd hidden their horses behind the pub, far enough away for them not to be heard. Bee checked the two belts she wore and pulled six revolvers out of the saddlebag, holstering two of them. She took two short double-barrelled shotguns and one machete. It was still in its sheath, and Bee slipped it down the cape of her coat. She was confident all her weapons were hidden from view.

The fingerless gloves went on and, with a flick, the pointed needles sprung out. Bee retracted them and Somer stepped away, muttering in disgust as Bee armed her body with daggers and throwing stars. It didn't matter if she used them or not; she wanted them, and then she filled her pockets with bullets.

'Can you do it?' Somer whispered, watching the two men and one woman.

'If I kill Omega, that's one less problem to deal with, and you won't have to smuggle people anymore.' Bee placed more bullets in her pocket. She didn't look at Somer and carried on checking her body for weapons. This action was second nature, but her heart raced, and Bee ripped three pieces out of her shirt, tuning out the heartache of seeing Malick.

'You can tie those three up and leave.' She pointed to the riders with the horses.

'How?'

'With this.' She handed Somer some rope, and placed her hands on the stock of the gun, fingers on the barrel. Bee walked over the rough road toward the pub.

Inside the pub, laughter sounded from behind the windows. The riders didn't see the figure lurking out of the darkness heading towards them. It was as if they were blind to Bee. The woman wearing a flimsy hat and black breeches only noticed when Bee was almost in front of them, and she went for her gun. Bee punched her and cocked the sawn-off shotgun, aiming it at the two men, who started for their weapons.

'Move.' She pointed with her gun for them to back away from the door and into the darkness. They followed her order, but Bee saw they weren't frightened.

'On your knees.' And each one of them dropped to the ground. Somer came from behind their horses. She ordered, 'Tie them up.'

'Somer Peron? Is that you?' one man turned. 'Somer, you can't let her do this.'

Bee knocked the rider around the head with the stock of the gun, and he fell into the dust. She ordered Somer to pull the man back onto his knees. He did, and Bee spotted Somer's handshake. She frightened him, but it was too late, there was no going back now.

He tied them up, saying nothing to the man, as Bee stuffed the pieces of cloth into each rider's mouth. The riders' eyes were glued to her.

'Go, Somer.' Her gun was trained on her three captives.

'What are you going to do, Bee?'

'I'm keeping my promise.'

Bee crouched before the man who'd spoken, grabbing hold of his hair. The man struggled, and the knife went into his right eye. He cried, anguished, with muffled screams, his body shaking from the shock. And Bee withdrew the knife, plunging it into his left eye.

Somer stepped in front of her. 'Not like this, Bedelia.'

'Well, I've not killed them, what did you think I was going to do, ask them politely if I can go inside and get my husband and son back?' she said sarcastically, pushing Somer fast, sending him flying backwards into the ground behind. 'I'm doing what you wanted.'

Somer hit the ground. Bee moved onto the woman, repeating the same fast, bloody action and then the third. The sucking sound lingered in the air as Bee put her foot to the thrashing man's shoulder, kicking him to the ground.

'If you care about these people, Somer, then why didn't you care about the people you stole?' she asked, heading toward the pub. Bee's heart pounded as she tilted her head, rolled her shoulders and counted to ten. Tristan and Malick were inside, and Bee's hand rested on the door. Malick was about to see the truth. To see what Bee had spent the last six years pretending she wasn't.

And then she opened the door.

Omega's riders sat around the dusty old pub. Bee closed the door, letting every single rider see her. The laughter stopped, and she calculated there were at least thirty or more riders scattered throughout the place. It reminded Bee of The Raven, but on a more significant and dirtier scale. Men and women were at the bar, and most sat at the tables, and the old barkeep stood, petrified. Bee scouted the pub, noting where everybody was, and in seconds this information would be useless, as she tried to work out where the first attack might come from.

In the corner Malick sat with Tristan. The boy smiled, grinned, seeing Bee in the pub, he pointed and Bee could hear him say 'Mamma' repeatedly to Malick. Tristan jumped from his chair, but Malick grabbed the boy back, wrestling with Tristan to stay in his arms, and Malick gritted his teeth, shaking his head at Bee.

Omega and Baptiste were next to Malick, they followed his stare. The woman sat up, and Bee, for the first time saw close-up what this Omega looked like. The shaven-headed woman chewed her lips, and Bee understood this was the sibling she'd felt in France. They studied each other and Omega nodded to her men.

The heel of Bee's boots tapped against the wooden floor, as she approached Omega's table. Bee didn't get too close, but she could hear Tristan squabbling with Malick, and him trying to hush Tristan, because all Tristan wanted to do was go to his mother.

'Are you here to give yourself up, Mrs Rose?' Omega grinned.

Bee saw a triumphant smile on Omega, and then called to Tristan, who'd started crying, and Bee spoke softly to her son, 'Tristan, do you remember the three wise monkeys?'

Malick wrapped his arms around Tristan, whispering into the boy's ear, and Tristan rubbed his tears away.

'I need you to be like the first two, baby, your father will cover your eyes, but you need to cover your ears, can you do that for me?' Bee watched as Tristan nodded, and then he wrapped himself into Malick's arms, holding his hands over his ears.

'You can surrender to these two.' Omega motioned for two men to approach.

Bee faced the two men, brought up the short-barrelled shotgun hidden under her coat and blasted one man in the stomach, and another blast followed to the second man. Blood, bone, innards blew in all directions, splatter hit Bee's face. Bee reloaded, the clicking of the chambers echoed through her body, as the men fell to the ground screaming. She shot the first and then the second in quick succession in the head. Their cries stopped, and there was a pause, as she looked at the many faces in the pub.

A third man went for his pistol as Bee raised her hand, released the sharp needles in her glove and plunged it into his neck. His blood sprayed over Bee as he gurgled and dropped to the floor.

She pulled out the machete from the back of her coat, as a shabbily dressed woman ran toward Bee wielding a knife. The woman swiped it across the air and Bee bent back as the blade flew over her face. The rider stopped lashing out, and Bee struck.

Bee swung her machete overarm, slamming it into the woman's head. The broad blade cracked the skull, slicing into the brain, blood flowed down the woman's face, and her dead surprised eyes stared at Bee. Bee lifted her leg, placed it against the chest of the woman and kicked her back. The body fell, slipping off the machete, and the riders stared.

A rider reacted, pulling his gun from his holster. Bee was quick. She grabbed his arm, twisting his hand and aimed the pistol toward his head. The man whimpered, realising what was about to happen. Bee gripped his hand, forcing him to pull the trigger of his own gun, blasting his head off. Blood hit Bee, and the rider dropped to the ground. She looked up as Malick kept Tristan covered with his coat, hiding the boy from the carnage.

Bee took hold of both belts, unleashing them and everybody watched as the silver metal solidified into two long swords. The riders hesitated, all eyes on the swords. Only one kind of person could open those swords - *'Reaper',* the men choked, all taking a step back. Bee watched each rider, steadying herself, waiting for someone to attack.

In the background, Omega rose from her stool, her eyes darkened. 'She's a Reaper!' she yelled. 'A killer of your women and children!'

Bee glanced quickly in Malick's direction. She'd frightened him, and then she stared Omega down, saying in an icy voice. 'That's right. I've killed women, children, men. I have no problem with killing. So, please step aside and let me take my husband and son.'

Omega bared her teeth. '*Mrs Rose,* that's not going to happen.'

The silence built, fingers twitched on triggers, more knives appeared, but nobody moved. Heat in the room rose and then Bee sliced through the closest man, and he went down. Two riders ran towards her, each holding swords. They attacked, and Bee fought. The clashing reverberated as the riders slashed. They forced Bee back, cutting into her flesh, her arms bled, and then she kicked one of them, twisting her body around, moving faster, slicing the rider's neck. Bullets flew as Bee spun her swords up and down, the bullets pinging off the blades as she edged closer to Omega.

Another woman struck, knocking Bee to the ground. She flipped her back and was on her feet. Both swords slipped back around her waist, and she took out a pistol, blasting a bullet into the attacker's face. The gunfire rang in Bee's ears, and the woman fell.

Then two riders attacked. One from the front and one from behind. They smashed Bee against the bar, and she dropped to the floor. One rider punched Bee, and the second rider slipped his arm around her neck, squeezing her throat. Bee grappled with his arm, her breathing harsh, forcing any life out of her. It was difficult to breathe, Bee flipped the man over to the ground, and she kicked the second attacker in his knees, and he went down as he tried to punch her. Bee blocked him, grabbing the sword from his belt and rammed it into his stomach. He fell by the wayside.

Another attacker grasped her coat collar, sending Bee sweeping across the floor towards Omega. She banged her head, looked up and met Malick's eyes, as he hid Tristan from everything.

Bee blinked, her heart skipped, twisting her legs fast, spinning around to get back up. She ripped off her black cuff bracelet, and held both ends, stretching them, revealing two thin pieces of wire. Bee kicked a rider, sending him to the dusty floor, and wrapped the wire tightly around his neck. She squeezed, and her heart pumped as the rider's faded. The two thin wires sliced effortlessly into his skin, and the blood poured out. She stepped off him, rising from the dust, the blood pooling under him, and Bee slipped her bracelet back on.

Eyes fixed on Omega, Bee threw a knife into the head of another man, and she wiped the blood from her face as eight more riders surrounded her. Bee stood ready, and then she kicked as the first man attacked.

Bee moved differently. She was faster, kicking high, punching them in the stomachs and they fell back, each time, getting back up, still needing to fight and protect Omega, but Bee carried on. She grabbed a butterfly knife, unbuckled it, flipping it around her hand, as one man attacked, and she plunged the knife into the man's hand. He screamed, backing away.

Bee inhaled, the blood and gunpowder became intoxicating, and she moved toward Omega, pulling out another short-barrelled gun, about to aim it at the woman as Tristan wriggled free of Malick and ran to Bee.

'Mamma,' Tristan screamed, holding out his arms.

Still holding the shotgun, Bee grabbed Tristan with her free hand. Picking him up as Malick ran after his son. She held Tristan against her, his head over her shoulder, and away from what she was about to do.

'Bedelia?' Malick whispered, stopping as he looked down the barrel.

She pointed the shotgun at Malick, pulled the trigger, and watched as her husband's body crashed into the wooden floorboards.

Chapter Seventeen
Deman Circe, Kent

The morning sun didn't bring any warmth to the Marsh, as Luther sat on his cavalry horse. The animal stood seventeen hands high, and its brown coat glimmered in the sunlight. He'd arrived outside Deman Circe in the early hours, taking the Marsh roads via Canteria and the sun was now beginning to warm The Channel.

The morning was usually a busy time for the villagers. They'd ready their boats, making sure they were seaworthy, even though they would have checked the night before. He'd been through many similar places, and there was always something happening. The small fishing vessels were pulled up onto the beach. It looked like nobody was planning on going to sea. The village was quiet. No voices, no sounds of children. All that Luther could see from the shoreline was a ship.

The Reaper wore the lightweight black uniform, with weapons secreted around his body. Luther's face was obscured by the helmet, only his eyes visible and he studied the ship. Taking out his spyglass, he read the name, '*The Angel*,' and there were a few people still on board, as it gently swayed with the currents underneath. The Barricade in the distance was broken, and Luther considered how long it might be before it finally fell.

Bedelia, he mused. It had been six years since he'd last seen her. Bee had lived with Lord Oren and his wife during her first pregnancy, and Luther visited Bee, almost every night as her belly swelled with the first baby. She'd excitedly let Luther rest his hand on her, and even his heart skipped a beat when the baby kicked.

Bee's room was dull, almost like her own dormitory, but her bed was soft, and they would lie together. He'd wrap his arms around his best friend, and she would hold his hand as they slept side by side, and each night they made the promise to kill each other if the time came.

They sent Bee back to the dorms after she'd given birth, and she was different. Luther knew being parted from the baby affected her, but she said nothing. Eldric sent them out on a triple warrant, and Bee completed the hangings as if she'd never had the baby. The woman never deviated, but she was quiet.

A month later, she returned to Lord Oren's apartments. Once she was pregnant again, Oren requested Luther to be his personal Reaper. Neither Luther nor Bee understood why, but it allowed them to carry on seeing each other.

He was out on a warrant, commissioned by the Lord Guardian when he'd learned Bee was dead. Luther mourned for Bee in private, and he guessed he bore some responsibility for her death. Whispers started that Claude Ramas had murdered her, and Luther continued his own life without Bee in it.

Waves rippled in and out as Luther watched the village. He knew what was behind him and what was in front. He didn't need to hear the sounds of the gulls chattering to know they were resting and watching the sea.

Luther rode up past the first tower, along by the human totems and crucifixes. He didn't hear any cries and assumed the convicts were dead.

The gentle breeze rustled the few trees, as the sea air blanketed the village. Luther stopped at the Temple and looked at the two severed bodies strung up on crosses. This was not the work of the villagers, this was Bee. She was sending a message, and it was for the people who sailed in from France.

The hooves crushed the shells into the road, and any faces at their windows backed away. Luther kept his face forward, but he could already sense the scurrying of feet. Villagers tended not to do this, they waited for Reapers to pass by before moving, with their eyes glued on the uniforms, praying a Reaper hadn't come for them. These were the sounds of the newcomers.

The village square was empty, with no sign of village life as Luther rode toward the pub. Outside, men and women sat, they talked with accents, and they clammed up once they realised a Reaper was approaching. He dismounted, watching the newcomers. They ignored him, but they were jittery. He removed his helmet and headed to the small table where the four newcomers sat.

'You,' Luther said, looking at the rider closest to him. 'State your business.' His voice was controlled and deep.

The Frenchman looked up. A rough-looking man with blotched skin, thin grey hair and hardly any teeth, said nothing. He took a gulp from his beaker of beer, wiped his mouth with his sleeve and burped. The others at the table laughed.

Luther grabbed the old man by the back of his neck and whacked his head against the table. The bang silenced the group and Luther un-holstered his revolver, pointing it at the old man's head.

'We're... we're looking for a woman!' the old man squealed, afraid.

'Her name?' Luther asked.

'Bedelia, Bedelia Rose, that's all I know.'

Luther said nothing. He breathed out. Bedelia had a surname, she'd never had one before. 'Where is the captain of your ship?'

The old man's eyes darted to his companions, Luther could tell he was debating what information he should share, and the others kept their eyes on the Reaper.

Another man stuttered, 'She's gone looking for the woman.'

Luther glared at the man. 'Why?'

'Because she murdered Philip, Omega wants this Bedelia,' the second man said.

'Why does this woman think this Bedelia Rose will surrender to her?'

'Because the captain has her husband and son, that's why.'

Luther paused. Bedelia was married and had a son. She'd escaped, carving out a life in a foreign land, something Reapers could only wish for and, for reasons unknown, she'd thrown it all away to come back to Britain.

'What does your captain propose to do with this Bedelia Rose?'

The group remained silent. They were hiding something. Taking the old man's collar, Luther pulled him from the table, sending the beakers of beer flying and spilling the beer. The man yelled, wanting help, but nobody came.

'Stop!' an English voice shouted. 'I know why they're here.'

Luther dropped the old man, forcing the man to remain in the muddy path, his boot on the man's throat, with his revolver aimed at the newcomer's head. The old man whimpered, grovelling and Luther waited for the Englishman to speak.

'My name's Feargal, they came looking for the English woman, but they now want Winnie, because they're Skin Traders.'

'Explain.'

Luther listened. His foot pressing more into the old man's throat as Feargal told the Reaper why they wanted Winnie. The man started struggling, clawing at Luther's leg. Luther pressed harder until he heard the cracking of the windpipe, and the arms dropped into the mud, and then he lifted his foot off the dead Frenchman.

'You three move,' Luther ordered, pointing toward the village green. The group did not move, then the two men got up, both went for their pistols, and Luther shot each man in the head. The woman didn't move, but Luther shot her anyway.

Collecting his horse, Luther grabbed Feargal by the arm, marching him through the village. A saddled horse, tethered, was stationed near a cottage, and Luther ordered Feargal to mount the animal.

'But it doesn't belong to –'

'Get on it,' Luther ordered, and Feargal did as he was told.

***

Captain Osbourne was in trouble.

The morning was bright. The sea was like a millpond, and nothing moved. It was, Osbourne thought, a contrast to the murderous thunderstorms two nights before. Their orders were to head to the village of Deman Circe. They'd reached Foulksten when the thunderstorms came, so they'd bedded down in the town's garrison for the night and watched the lightning. The men quickly lost interest in the storm and ventured into one of the bawdy houses, which lined the town's east end, surrounding the dock.

Private Burgess had gotten drunk on cheap gin, landing himself in the local gaol, accused of groping several whores. The marshal refused to free the young man until he paid the women.

They rode through Hath, a large town, a place where people liked to live out the last of their days. It was a quiet hilly town, with many pubs, a few Temples and a crypt full of old bones piled high.

The squad of twenty-two soldiers had only just reached an area the locals called Fisherman's beach and was about to rest at a shabby old pub, called 'The Prince of Fortune' when an old man came running out.

The barkeep, frantic, eyes wide and stinking of booze, slurred a story about French riders entering his pub, headed by a woman with black make-up and a shaved head. It took Osbourne a while to understand as the old man wittered on about an English woman coming into his pub, and killing at least ten of these foreign riders. She then shot a hostage and kidnapped a boy. And she was a Reaper, though she didn't wear the uniform. He repeated it fast, and spittle sprayed everywhere.

The old barkeep played with his silver beard, pointing to a mound nearby. The French woman had ordered her men to dig pits for the bodies and Osbourne noticed the ground had recently been overturned. His soldiers were now digging up the area. He didn't need to see the dead to know the old man spoke the truth.

'The English woman came back after the French had gone,' the barkeep whispered, looking at the grave.

'Why?' Osbourne asked.

'She had the boy and another man with her. They dug up the last man she shot. I think the man the Reaper shot was her husband.'

'Reapers aren't allowed to marry,' Osbourne stated.

'Well, the French woman called her Mrs Rose, and the boy called her Mamma.' The barkeep hiccupped.

Captain Osbourne groaned, fiddling with the collar of his blue uniform. He then straightened the lapels and the tails of his coat. Ten years, Osbourne had been in the service, and he'd never heard such an outlandish story. Osbourne had served in France before they erected The Barricade, and Lord Guardian Eldric had treated those people poorly, leaving them when they needed help. The French hated Eldric as much as many English did.

'Are you sure they were French?' he asked. 'Because they can't get through The Barricade.'

'I'm old, not fucking deaf!' the man snapped, wringing his hands. 'I know a French accent when I hear one.'

'Yes but –'

'Didn't you see the lightning?' the man carried on. 'Thunder so fucking loud, it could have woken the dead. Somebody came through that Barricade, somebody French!'

'Captain, we've uncovered the bodies,' a green-looking Private Burgess informed him.

'Good.'

'They've been shot or stabbed. Looks like they took quite a beating,' the Private remarked.

Osbourne walked over and looked down at the body as the Burgess rolled him over.

The Private pointed to four puncture wounds in the man's neck. 'This killed him, but I don't know how.'

The Captain closed his eyes. 'It's a Reaper. Give it a few years, Burgess, and you'll see it again.'

'But–'

'Get me the messenger.' Osbourne huffed, shaking his head and pulling the tie from his shirt, wanting air. This was supposed to be routine, a simple task, to check on a story about a young woman returning from the dead. Now, not only had he failed in discovering any more about this woman, but, somehow, a French ship had broken through The Barricade, landed, and ten of their men had ended up dead just outside The Prince of Fortune pub.

Chapter Eighteen
Deman Circe Road, Kent

Everything was wrong. There were voices, shouting, fighting and soil. The earthy smells got up Malick's nose, but he couldn't move.

'Bury him with the others,' a voice said. It sounded like Omega.

Malick couldn't speak or open his eyes. His body was carried and dumped as they threw him into something. A pit, a grave for the riders Bee had shot. He wanted to shout he wasn't dead, but his body refused to move, and the soil covered him. He felt Bee all over him, that secret something fusing into him, making him live.

He was at the top of a pile of bodies, and all he could do was inhale the deathly smells of those who surrounded him. Then images of Bee of flooded into him. She was alone, wheezing, sweat poured from her, and her heart raced. Malick's heart beat with hers as he saw Bee's torment because she was shielding him, taking away any pain he should have had.

And then it was as if Malick was with Bee as she hid behind a tree, and Tristan called, asking about her face, and that he wanted a hug. She kept gasping that she was fine, but he wasn't to come near. He sensed Bee sweating, afraid that Tristan might see her on her knees, doubled up in agony. Malick watched Bee rip her bloodied shirt and slump against the stump of a tree. She pulled a knife, hands shaking, and dug the tip of the blade into her belly, picking out the surface pellets, and blood trickled out of the wounds.

She couldn't remove them all with the knife. He knew that Bee didn't want to use her abilities, but there was little choice. She laid her hands over her wounds. Malick rushed into her that part of him which was always inside Bee, and swam through her. He experienced everything Bee was going through, as the shotgun pellets deep inside her belly moved. They dislodged themselves, being pulled like a magnet to the skin, and they popped out, creating new wounds, and Bee cried out, moaning as each pellet ripped through her body. It only lasted a few minutes, but Malick understood Bee had shot him because she wanted to protect him.

Then he only saw black.

'Quick, quick, quick!' He heard alarmed mutterings. It was Bee digging through the soil. Bee yelled at Somer to keep Tristan away. Malick was stiff. He wanted to push up his hand, grab hold of her, but his body refused the command.

'Tristan, stay behind that tree, don't come any closer.' He heard Bee's panicked voice.

Bee struggled, digging him up. She breathed in his ear, swearing, her hands on his face, wiping the soil away.

The warmth of the sun hit his face as another pair of hands grabbed him.

'Get him on that horse, Somer,' Bee commanded.

They pushed him, a dead weight up onto a horse. Somebody climbed up behind him, their arms wrapped around him. Tranquillity came over him, reminding Malick of standing at the water's edge, letting the tail end of the waves wash over his feet, drifting in and out. He felt safe as Bee held him.

And then Bee became a deluge inside him, infiltrating every single piece of him. The hypnotic thrust caught Malick off guard, and he jolted, hurting, because Bee wouldn't let go. She was lost, jumbled up, and drowning. The only thing Bee wanted to hold on to was Malick, making sure he was safe. She lost her grip and Malick was lost, but he could hear Tristan speaking to Bee.

'What's wrong with Papa?' Tristan asked, and there was worry in the boy's voice, as Somer told the boy to get on the horse.

And Bee said, 'He's asleep, baby. Papa needs to rest before he can see you.'

'But...but Uncle Philip was in the ground too, and he didn't wake up,' Tristan trembled.

Bee's arms tightened around Malick, and her voice was gentle as she spoke, 'Tristan, I promise that Papa isn't like Uncle Philip. He's sleeping because his body was hurt, but I won't let anything happen to him. I'm keeping him safe.' And Malick floated. He listened to the velvety softness inside every word Bee said to Tristan. The calm within Bee drifted toward Tristan, coating him in love, and the boy accepted his mother's words.

'Okay, Mamma,' Tristan said.

'You're a piece of work, Reaper.' Malick heard Somer whisper. He was close to the horse. 'You've killed ten people to get what you wanted.'

'I got them out, didn't I?'

Malick heard Somer huff. 'You probably let my sister die because you wanted Malick. Murdering Nadine, so you could be the next Mrs Rose.'

There was rapid movement, Bee's hand left Malick's stomach, dragging Somer closer to the horse. 'Choose your next words carefully, Somer,' she hissed venomously.

'Remember your promise to go, Reaper,' Somer whispered, but there was fear in his voice.

And then Malick heard nothing more. He was standing somewhere else, that same strange place he'd been only once before, with the red landscape and the burning tree trunks. Malick's heart pounded, and then three ghostly figures surrounded him, their faces blurry. One grabbed him, opened their mouth and a brilliant light burst out, and Malick cried, his body juddering, as the figure clasped their hands around him, and the light entered him.

He gasped, sitting. Malick coughed, remembering Bee aiming his own gun at him, and pulling the trigger. She'd shot him, and he should be dead. Instead, he was in the middle of some woods with a small campfire burning next to him.

Malick rubbed his eyes, and then checked his body. Nothing made sense. The last thing he remembered was the cracking sound of the gun, and an intense burning sensation in his stomach followed as the pellets entered him.

He blinked, everything was blurry. Bee squatted in the clearing, her face heavily bruised. She wrapped her arms around her knees, and her long leather coat trailed behind. Bee watched Tristan, sitting next to Somer on a tree stump.

'Uncle Somer, I want to go to Mamma,' he heard Tristan say.

Malick watched the scene. Tristan got up, but Somer pulled him back, forcing the boy to stay.

'No, wait till your father wakes up.' Somer shook his head.

Malick stumbled, getting up. There was no blood on his shirt. Somebody had changed his clothes, he was wearing a rider's top, and he checked his stomach. There was no hint Bee even pulled the trigger, and his head pounded. Wiping his forehead, Malick spotted mud on the back of his hand and over his clothes, and what he remembered scared him.

Malick approached the group. Stiffness radiated from Somer as he guarded Tristan, and the man looked at him, giving him a relieved smile, but Bee did not move.

Tristan's face lit up. 'Papa, Mamma said you'd sleep a long time.' He ran to his father, arms out, and Malick picked him up, kissing him on the cheeks.

Malick's heart thumped, he'd lost almost everything, but now he hoped Bee would give him the chance to apologise, to make her understand that he loved her. He stroked Tristan's face, pleased the boy was safe. He said, 'That's right son, but I need a word with your mother.' Bee was still crouched, and her intense stare moved to him.

Tristan giggled, as Malick set him down, and the boy ran to Bee. She got up, her hands stretching toward Tristan, smiling, excited to hold her son. Malick spotted the blood on her battered face. Grabbing the boy, he pulled Tristan back.

'Can you go with Uncle Somer, Tristan?' He pushed the boy toward Somer, as Tristan begged to go to his mother.

Somer threw the dregs of his coffee away. He stared at Bee, nodding. Taking hold of Tristan's hand, he said, 'You know, I think I saw a pond down there.'

Somer and Tristan walked away, hand in hand. They vanished behind the trees, only flashes of clothing seen. Malick stared at Bee, and she stared back. The forest became quiet. The birds didn't sing. Instead, they listened.

He stepped toward Bee, and she took a jumpy step back. Malick saw her harried expression. He didn't know if he scared Bee or if what she'd done frightened her. Malick didn't get any closer, worried Bee might run.

'You shot me?' he whispered.

Bee nodded.

'In front of Tristan, in front of *our* son?'

'He didn't see.'

'Don't you get it?'

She whispered, 'No, don't you get it? I'm not like you.'

Malick said calmly, 'I know that Bedelia, I saw the evidence at Deman Circe.' He held his hand, and she looked at it. 'Bee, I'm sorry I frightened you, I want you to come home.'

'Even after I shot you?' she asked.

He nodded, 'Yes, even after you shot me.'

Bee looked at Malick, then his hand, then back to him. She whispered, jittery, 'I learnt early that the physical body is nothing more than pieces held together by blood and skin. Once you understand that, you learn you are capable of anything.'

Malick frowned, hearing the coldness in Bee's voice. 'That's not an excuse for what you did to those bodies.'

'I'm a Reaper, Malick, that's all that I am,' Bee said.

'No,' he rejected her statement. 'You're more than that, you're my wife, you...you did something to me. You shot and protected me. I don't know what you did–'

'I shielded you,' she interrupted.

The horses neighed. As one shook its head, the bridle bit clanked in its teeth. Malick ran his fingers through his hair. Bee was being difficult, not revealing too much. 'Shielded me?' He didn't understand.

'I got you out. That's enough.' She moved sideways and Malick stepped in her way. 'I need to go,' she said.

He gripped her collar. 'Then why did you save me?' he asked as her coat opened, and Malick spotted the blood on Bee's shirt, in the same places he'd been shot.

A memory swamped him. Bee digging gun pellets out of her belly, Malick swayed, remembering the pain she'd inflicted on her own body. He grabbed the waist of her breeches, Bee tried to fend him off, but he was too quick, pulling the tucked in shirt out, and there he saw tiny stab wounds in her belly, all crusted with blood.

'It really happened.' He gazed at the marks, reaching out to touch her, but Bee tore the shirt out of his hands, backing away. 'How?' he asked.

'Because I'm a part of you,' she pushed him off, stepping back. 'That night we made love – had sex for the first time, I... I gave myself to you. Whatever I did, I shouldn't have done because I don't know what I've done.' She sounded confused. 'That's why I shot you because I could take the blast.'

He blinked, being taken back to that night. 'Doesn't that tell you anything?'

'It means you take *your* children and live. I should go.' She put her wide-brimmed hat on.

'Is killing your father going to make everything better?' he asked.

Bee didn't look at him. 'It's the only way I can be free of him. Be free of all this.'

'And that's worth destroying our family for?' he said. 'We were happy.'

Bee's body stiffened, her eyes narrowed, and she slipped past, scratching her scars. 'You saved me, and I saw an opportunity.' She stormed to her horse, checking the weapons were secured to the bags. Bee was about to mount the animal when Malick got in between her and the horse.

'You love me.' He took her arms. 'You burst into me when you gave birth to Viola. A sunshine so bright, I thought I'd go blind.'

She stepped back, faltering against the horse. 'That's... not true.'

'Sometimes you creep into me, but other times you explode, but you're always with me,' Malick's voice softened.

'How?' she whispered. Bee pulled the reins, pushing him out of her way, putting her foot in the stirrup and grabbing the horn of the saddle.

He forced Bee off and against the horse. 'Because... because since that night you've stayed. I can't escape you, Bedelia. I was wrong to think Reapers are the same because you've only wanted to protect our family.' Then

Malick pressed his body into hers, whispering into her ear. 'Bedelia, honestly... you scare the shit out of me, and I don't want to be scared, but what frightens me is losing you, is that so hard to understand?' He touched her face, pinning Bee against the horse. 'You're surging through me right now, and I don't want it to stop.'

'No,' Bee muttered.

'I heard what you said to Tristan,' he whispered gently. 'You are all I've ever wanted, Bedelia, and you know that.'

Bee stared as Malick's words in the air. She pushed him away, mounting the horse, and then she said, 'No, you were right, I am a heartless fucking Reaper.'

He gripped the horse's reins. It kicked, wanting to run. 'Don't do this, Bedelia.'

She rubbed her scars, locking her eyes with his. Bee put her boot to his chest, kicking him into the ground. 'I made a promise, I can't stay here. I can't stay with you.'

'Bedelia.'

'You saved my life, Mr Rose. Now I've saved yours, consider the debt paid.' Bee's voice trembled as she scratched her face. She jabbed the horse, making the animal run.

Malick lay there. Her words stung, but everything Bee said was a lie. She'd tried to block him from feeling her desperation to keep him safe, and Bee kept scratching those scars. This was her tell, her sign. She was lying, and then he remembered the promise she'd made to Somer.

Chapter Nineteen
The road of Bones, Kent

The horse galloped through the woods, hooves pounding the mud, as the green leaves swished past Bee. The woodland was dangerously muddy, and the low-hanging branches scratched her face. Bee wanted to ride, to get as far away from Malick and Tristan, and her lies.

Bee brought the horse to a stop, worrying she might break the animal's leg in the boggy ground. She threw the reins aside, slipping, stumbling off the horse, and fell hands and feet into mud, and then she screamed. Her cries echoed. Movement rustled the undergrowth, sparrows and blackbirds, spooked by Bee, took flight, shaking the trees.

These abilities took over. Bee couldn't block them, and they became uncontrollable, wiring their way into Malick, like she'd never known before. They refused to let go. Every twist welded Malick to her. Bee lay in the mud, breathing raspy, trying to free Malick, and she gazed into the treelines above. She couldn't fight it anymore, letting it overtake her.

The sensation subsided and Bee pulled herself out of the mud. Slinging the mud-covered coat over the saddle, she guided the horse to the edge of the woods, opening up to a green and muddy road. Bee took in the fresh air, glad to have the sun on her face.

Malick had been honest, pleading with her to come home, and Bee's heart burned with her untruths. Nobody would be safe if she went back to France. Reapers would come, and it didn't matter how many she killed, Eldric would keep sending them until one killed her.

Along the road, a grey-stoned building loomed. Old unreadable gravestones dotted its garden, and the dry stone wall encased the building. Bee stopped in front of the broken gate, tethering the horse.

The Guardian Temple had a tatty notice board by the gate and an invitation for the Purge of a one-year-old boy. The age had been four years when Bee left, now it was one year. They excluded vassals and children intended to become Reapers. Everybody in the community was to attend, as this was a way of asserting control over the people.

Bee had never set foot in the English Temples. She went to the French ones, so she could sit with Malick, and even that Bee found unsettling. The gate creaked, and the wood juddered against the old path as she stepped inside. Bee looked up at the bell and wondered if they rang it, asking for love from the Guardian.

Beside the gate grew a giant oak tree, over one-hundred and twenty feet tall, and the leaves were a healthy green, with a hangman's noose hanging from a branch. A reminder that people must obey the law. The graveyard was quiet, only the tweets and calls of birds hinted at any life.

The dead in the ground didn't belong to Eldric. They belonged to the other older religion, the one that existed before the Guardians. A belief that wasn't powerful enough to stop a new religion bulldozing its way across Britain, and then Europe.

Bee turned the door handle. Inside, the Temple looked like the ones in Bononia. Stained glass windows, uncomfortable wooden pews; she counted fifteen on either side. The walls inscribed with words said by Guardians of previous generations. That was a lie, she thought, now knowing Eldric was the first Guardian, only his body and name was different.

Five Clannen marble statues donned the walls of the Temple. Two males on one side and they represented the second and third Guardian, and two female dolls represented the women who had given him life. And, in the centre, where the priest stood, was supposedly the first Guardian, Alfred, and he served Earth. All the statues had a serene expression as if they were protecting the world.

Bullshit, Bee thought, staring at the dead eyes of each piece of stone. This was what the people were told to keep them faithful. Then a noise coming from behind a closed door caught her attention. A cry or a scream? Bee wasn't sure, but they sounded small and frightened.

The cries came from behind another door at the end of a wood-panelled corridor. Bee crept down, peering through the half-opened door. A tiny voice mumbled something, and she pulled her revolver out.

Pushing the door slowly, Bee stared into the Temple's office. A room full of books, papers, healthy and colourful plants dotted around, hanging from the walls, or stuffed into the shelves, and in the centre was a desk.

A man stood in front of the desk, Bee noticed the blond hair and priest's tunic. The pale skin shone, revealing the crack of his backside as he loosened his breeches. Bee's eyes widened. The man was bent over a boy, no older than ten, and his body spread across the table, with breeches pulled down around his legs.

'Please,' the boy whimpered.

'Now, Adam, if you struggle, the punishment will only be harder for you.' The priest bent over and licked the boy's cheek.

The position of the man forcing himself onto a small boy took Bee aback. She wasn't a woman anymore. She was eight years old, in the castle cellar fetching a bottle of wine for the Overlord.

The young Bee had been ordered into the lower parts of Rolfen Castle. A raggedy creature, her long auburn hair matted, dirty face, and she'd learned to carry a knife for protection.

Walking back through the poorly lit stone corridor, she'd heard a noise, somebody groaning, crying out in muffled pain. Somebody else laughed, and Bee stopped, wondering what the commotion was. A door was ajar, and Bee peered into a room full of boxes, watching two Reapers. One held down an apprentice, breeches around his legs, and he kept pushing himself into the bareback of the student. The other, a young woman, restrained the boy, forcing his hands on the table. Bee didn't know what the male Reaper was doing, but she saw tears rolling down the eyes of the apprentice.

The boy stared, and he locked his eyes with Bee. She stepped back into the gloom's safety, walking away, and then Bee stopped. She couldn't leave the boy, the terror in his eyes, and the agony in his face, told her he was scared. Bee knew that expression, she suspected, she'd looked like that when Rufus came hunting for her, though he'd never laid her across a table like that, because he'd beat her instead.

Bee placed the wine on the ground. Pulling out her dagger, she crept back to the door, taking the key, Bee slipped inside, locking all four of them inside. Quietly, she weaved through the boxes and chests. Crawling along the ground, and then only a box stood between her and the Apprentice.

The Reaper had black plimsolls on, and Bee knew she had to be quick. She only had one chance to slice through the back of his ankle, bringing him down. In silence, Bee moved, he didn't feel her lifting the leg of his uniform. He continued pushing himself harder into the crying boy and laughing.

Bee cut him deep. The blood poured, he screamed, falling to the ground. The Reaper's eyes widened as an eight-year-old girl rose and stabbed him in the forehead, and the blood seeped out, mixing into the dust.

The young woman ran. She rattled the locked door, banging on the wood. Her cries must have echoed down the stone corridor toward the housemaster because soon people were beating down the door, and she could hear Rufus's angry yells, but it was too late. Bee had already killed the second Reaper.

'Pull up your breeches,' Bee whispered. The hinges bulging as the door splintered. It wouldn't hold much longer. 'Give me your sword.' The boy handed it to her. It was lighter than she expected, raising it over the male Reaper's body and then chopping the head off.

'Thank you,' the boy said.

Bee smiled pathetically, knowing she would be executed, and she took hold of the severed head and held it toward the door. 'I'm Bedelia.'

'I'm Luther,' he told her.

'Don't tell them anything, Luther.'

Bee expected the door to burst open any minute, and then her eyes rolled back into her head. She was somewhere else. A different existence and Bee was now in its centre. The world was a place of red skies and red watery paths that spilt into ripples as she tiptoed through the strange unknown world. It was a place of dead trees, a void of emptiness. There were people, thousands of them, opaque and quiet, standing lifeless.

Something fed off them, draining them. Bee looked harder and saw they were all connected to each other. Things like branches grew out of these people, and all were fixed to one point.

At first, Bee couldn't make out what it was. She wasn't a part of this strange landscape, and she moved freely through the people toward the fixed point.

Nothing moved. The only sound was her footsteps in the puddles, as there was no wind, no rain, nothing. Creeping through the opaque life forms, Bee was afraid she'd be caught in this unknown place.

Her eyes widened as she saw the energies of these figures flow toward one place and into one man, and she could feel them flowing into her, strengthening Bee, making her powerful.

Bee realised she was like the man in the centre, but he was feeding off these people, and though her power grew, she didn't need them to make her more powerful. And then something moved in the corner of her eye.

There were three wraith-like figures, tall, black and smoky, they watched her, sizing her up. Bee's heart beat a little faster, as they descended upon her, and they whispered,

'You have come.'

The young Bee remembered the door smashing open and holding the decapitated head up to Rufus. He grabbed her as she dropped the head, holding her in his arms, hiding her face and pushing his way through the small crowd at the door. Bee saw Luther three months later. She'd been sentenced to train as a Reaper.

Closing the memories of her childhood, Bee clicked the pistol and placed the barrel of her revolver beside the priest's ear. 'I don't think the boy needs punishment, do you?' Bee asked icily.

The priest paused. He turned, and she saw a man, in his late thirties, cleanly shaven, with what Bee thought could be a trustworthy face, and she wondered how many parents left their children in his care.

The fear in his eyes was probably the same fear the boy had whenever this priest came near him, and the man stepped away from the table, buttoning up his breeches. Bee signalled to the boy, and he pulled up his clothing, stepping behind her.

'It's not... it's not what it looks like.' The priest held his hands up.

'No, Priest, it is,' she said.

Knocking books off the desk, she found some paper and wrote something on it. 'Move.' Bee motioned the priest toward the door, watching him sweat.

Bee grabbed his brown clerical tunic and threw the man into the ground. He cried out as she grabbed him by the collar, dragging him spluttering, crying out, and trying to fight her. He moved his hands along the stone floor as she dropped him at the first pew, and Bee smiled as his frightened eyes locked with hers. The boy followed, keeping close to Bee. She forced the priest to scramble up the aisle away from her with each step she took.

'Please, I wasn't –'

'You weren't what?'

Those abilities rushed through Bee. A heat rose. She holstered the gun and touched the pews on either side. A flame ignited, the varnish burst into orangey flames, each bench flaring into fire, as Bee walked toward the terrified man.

The priest gasped shakily, 'What are you?' He pedalled back toward the main door. His mouth opening and closing but nothing came out as the flames quickly took hold of the church.

'Boy, open the door, and then go find a hammer and some nails.'

The young boy looked puzzled and then did as instructed. Bee grabbed the priest's collar, picking him up and throwing him into the daylight and out to the graveyard, toward the oak tree.

The man tried to run. Bee kicked him in the back of the knee, and he flew into the old cobbled path. He cried in pain, turning onto his back, looking up at her.

'I've not done anything to you,' he sniffled, tears rolling down his cheeks.

'But you have to him, and probably other boys.' She untangled the noose from around the tree, lowering it onto the ground.

Widening the noose, Bee wrapped it around the priest's chest. He struggled, and Bee punched him. Bee was hot, she needed to calm down, but all Bee could think about was the boy, remembering Luther. The promise she'd made to Somer. And Bee's anger poured into the priest, seeing Malick's face when she'd lied. His hurt welled and mixed up inside her. Bee's blood pulsed around, and she tightened the rope, ignoring the priest as he cried in pain.

'What's your name?' she asked, as the boy returned with the hammer and nails. Bee dragged the priest to the tree. Behind her, the church crackled as the smoke bellowed up to the sky.

'Adam,' he said.

'Well, Adam, you need to go home, find your parents.' She picked up an old broken gravestone, and then found the axe she'd taken from the Marshal's home, and some rope.

'He's my father. It's only him and me.' The boy didn't look at his father.

The priest panted, and now smelled the sweat and urine. He cried, and Bee looked at the burning church. The orange flames were so bright, it was beautiful.

'Adam, I'm going to hurt your father,' Bee said coldly.

The young boy looked at the priest, and then Bee. 'Do it,' he whispered.

The man cried, begging Adam, and he repeated the boy's name several times. 'I promise I won't ever touch you again. Please, please don't let this crazy bitch hurt me!'

As Bee tied the man's hands together, the priest kept pleading, saying he wouldn't do it again, saying anything to stop Bee. She blocked him out, but different voices came back, filtering, echoing the same words this man cried. They had the same quiver to them as he had.

These were the voices of those she'd executed. Many accepted their deaths, but some sounded like the priest, begging hopelessly for their lives. Promising they'd vanish, they wouldn't do whatever crime they were guilty of, or that they had children. Bee never listened to the malefactors, and she didn't listen to the priest.

Bee wiped her brow. The fire intensified, flames reaching into the sky, black smoke belching out, asking the clear blue sky for forgiveness, but there was none to be given, as Bee shoved the priest, rolling him into the grass, forcing him to lie on his back. She pulled his tied hands above his head and laid them on the broken gravestone.

'Go stand by my horse, Adam,' Bee told the boy, 'go now.' She waited for the boy to do as he was told.

'Please,' the priest whimpered. Tears streamed down his cheeks. 'You… you don't have to do this.' He struggled, frantically trying to free himself, but Bee punched him in the chest, winding him.

'I'll let you live, but you won't do it again,' she whispered.

The man gasped, and Bee placed her foot on the priest's forearms, raising the axe. And then Bee did what she always did when she was about to execute a malefactor. She locked eyes with them for the briefest moment. Bee still saw something in those expressions. In the priest, the terror, his realisation of what he'd done to somebody else, and then she brought the axe swinging down, cutting swiftly into the wrists of the priest, severing both hands and the man screamed. Bee took the note she'd written, found the nails and then hammered it into the man's chest.

The screams splintered through the massive bellows of the flames. Bee didn't stop. She dragged the priest back to the tree, and threw the rope over the branch, hoisting him up. The man had passed out. He dangled, head drooping onto his chest, as the blood flowed out of his arms, and into his clothes.

And the sign read, *'Child Rapist'.*

'Can I come with you, Mistress?' Adam asked.

'If you come with me, you'll probably end up dead,' Bee explained.

Voices were coming. Bee turned and saw a few villagers heading up the muddy path. Men, women, and children, the women in long skirts and the men all wet from carrying pails of water. It sloshed over into the already muddy path, making it worse. Bee noted, any panic expressions they had, changed to anger as they stopped for a second, looking at her as the flames cremated the Temple.

'I know,' the boy said.

'Will you do something for me?' Bee asked.

'Yes, Mistress,' Adam looked at the group, panic in his eyes.

Bee held out her hand, Adam gripped it, and she pulled him onto her horse. 'I want you to look out for a man...' and they rode away from the burning building.

Chapter Twenty
Deman Circe Road, Kent

Malick clung to the saddle of the horse, his insides tightening. The animal shuffled as Malick collapsed into the grass and then Bee rushed through him. She was frightened and the hurt he'd caused ripped into him. Bee lied to keep him safe, and she battled to tear herself free of Malick, but she made it worse, fusing them more profoundly together, and he choked on Bee's despair.

He didn't know what he was doing, he'd always let Bee wash over him, never understanding the meaning within the union. Now Malick gripped hold of Bee, refusing to let go, but she wriggled free, and then was gone.

The intensity passed, Malick was light-headed, and nauseous. He remained on the ground until his head stopped spinning, and then he eased himself up and checked the weapons on the second horse. There were three revolvers, bullets and one shotgun. Not much protection, when Malick didn't know what he'd encounter, or where he was going. And, if he was honest, he didn't much like guns.

The distinctive laughter of Tristan travelled on the light breeze. Malick watched as Somer played with the boy. They pretended to trip each other up as Somer played the clown, keeping Tristan amused.

Malick finished his checks, making sure the girth was right, and the bit in the horse's mouth was comfortable. He patted the animal, and the horse made a satisfying noise as if it knew Malick was about to mount.

And he remembered the promise Bee said she'd made. She'd only left because of that; otherwise, Bee would still be here, and Malick guessed Somer had forced her to leave. Grabbing his coat from the ground, Malick shivered. Bee killing him still hadn't sunk in.

'Papa,' Tristan called, dashing through the trees. Malick wrapped his arms about his son, laughing, as the boy nearly knocked him over. Then Tristan asked for his mother.

Malick took Tristan's hand, leading him to a tree stump. He sat down, gathering Tristan onto his lap. He wiped Tristan's golden hair from his face and put on a smile. 'She's had to go.'

'Is she coming back...?' Tristan's bottom lip trembled.

Malick gave his son a tiny smile at the question he hadn't wanted to hear. 'Of course, she is. You, Viola and me are the most important things in Mamma's life, but...' he paused, 'I've got to get her back.'

'Is that wise?' Somer growled.

Malick stood, telling the boy to remain on the stump. 'I heard what you said about Nadine and what you made Bee promise. She wouldn't have left otherwise.'

'She killed Philip, remember? She put a gun to my head, and you saw what she did in Deman Circe.' Somer whispered, pulling Malick out of earshot of Tristan. 'She's the cause...the cause of this mess.'

'Tell me, Somer, when you started people smuggling, did you know what Omega was doing with those people?'

Somer bolstered himself up. 'Yes.'

'Then it wasn't Bee who put my family in danger, was it?' Malick retorted.

'She's blinded people,' Somer said in a hushed voice. 'That Reaper is dangerous.'

Malick considered Somer's words. The blinding sent a shiver through him, but he said, 'I always knew there was something dangerous about Bee, just never admitted it. You don't end up nearly dead on a beach with a Chelchith Smile if you haven't done something bad.'

'I watched her kill a man. Your so-called loving wife sat with him and then twisted his neck, just like Philip.' Somer repeated what he'd heard Bee and Tanner say before she killed him. 'Is that the kind of woman you want bringing up your children?' he asked.

Malick punched Somer, knocking him to the ground. 'Take Tristan back to that pub, keep him safe,' he ordered, throwing a small number of British coins to Somer. Coins he'd had left, from before The Barricade was built.

'Papa?' Tristan stood up, watching.

Somer shook his head. 'Nadine knew you were in love with Bee before even you did. You only married my sister because you felt obliged. You made that obvious by screwing any woman you fancied, and then you'd crawl back to Nadine. She was pregnant with Tristan, and you were more interested in Bedelia than you were in your own wife.'

Malick looked to Tristan, worried what the boy had heard. 'Don't bring Nadine into this.'

Somer got up, brushing himself down. 'Nadine died knowing that woman would take her place in your bed, and you'd love Bedelia like you never did her,' he barked.

'I didn't treat Nadine well, Somer, I know that and I'm sorry.'

Somer raged, 'You need to tell the boy the truth, you need to tell him that, that Reaper is not his mother.'

Tristan was behind Somer, his eyes wide. He'd heard every word. 'Papa?'

Malick's heart thumped. His son's face crumpled, there was confusion in Tristan's face, and he rushed to pick the boy up in his arms.

'Tristan,' he whispered into the boy's ear, 'when I married your Mamma, I already had you, and she loved me, but do you know what?'

The boy blinked not wanting to cry, shaking his head.

'She was in love with you. The day after your real mother, Nadine, passed away, I sat on the stairs, and you cried. I didn't know what to do. Mamma came up the stairs, took you out of your cot. I listened as she cradled you, and she sang English songs laced with love. Mamma said because your mother wasn't here anymore, she'd look after and love you and your mother could send her love to you. Mamma keeps alive your mother's love, and she wanted to tell you about your mother when you were old enough. She didn't want you to find out like this.'

'But –'

'And one night, I got into a fight. She rescued me, but her first thought was for you. Telling them sternly that her son was asleep and not to wake him. She put you first. Now I have to do that, I'm putting you first to get your Mamma back.'

The boy sat quietly listening.

Malick cuddled his son, saying, 'Once a week, you both go to the Temple graveyard, don't you?' And Tristan nodded. 'Mamma thinks I don't know, but Priest Felix told me, you put flowers on two plaques?' And, again, the boy nodded. 'One bunch is for an unknown man, but the others are placed before your Mother's plaque, because Mamma wants to remember her.'

'Mamma calls her a special lady,' Tristan muttered quietly. 'And, when I was old enough, she'd tell me about her.'

'That's right.' Malick stroked Tristan's hair.

'If Mamma isn't my mamma...' he asked, tearfully, 'is that why she left me?'

Malick wiped the tears from Tristan's face. 'She is your Mamma, never forget that. I did something stupid. I frightened Mamma so much that she ran away.'

'Uncle Somer called Mamma a Reaper, what's that?' Tristan said.

Malick's heart sank, and he answered, 'You know we have the militia back home, to keep control.' And the boy nodded. 'Well, Reapers are owned by Overlords and sometimes they kill to keep control.'

Tristan didn't understand. 'Do they kill puppies?' his small voice trembled.

Malick choked on the words, as he uttered, 'No, Tristan, they have to kill people.'

'Like Uncle Philip? And the people at the pub?' the boy asked.

Brushing Tristan's blond hair, Malick said, 'Mamma only did that because she was protecting Viola, all of us, from Omega, and she rescued us from the pub, didn't she?'

Tristan nodded.

'So, you see, Mamma thinks we're safe without her, but we're safer with her, as a family.' Malick kissed Tristan and then released him from his arms. 'Uncle Somer will take you to the pub, you'll wait there for us.'

'You'd choose a murdering Reaper over your family?' Somer sneered at Malick.

Malick stood his ground, making sure Tristan didn't hear. 'No, I'm choosing my murdering wife.'

***

Dai Castle, Dai, Kent

Claude looked over the ramparts of Dai Castle. People came and went through the Constable's Gate, as stallholders traded anything from bread to leather goods, and a busy buzz echoed around the castle walls. Farmers brought their cattle and sheep up toward the moat, to sell the livestock outside the walls. The shanty shops and homes situated near the castle opened, and the people sold their wares, all wanting to make money. Everything could be purchased from fish to flowers. The smells, at times, were delicious with vendors selling fresh bread or pies.

People pushed and shoved, making their way around the market and beer was traded from the homes. It was a noisy, chaotic place, and Claude usually mingled with the local population, but today he was apprehensive.

Laughter and swearing came from the stocks. He watched as children goaded the individuals locked inside the contraptions. Some threw rotting meat and eggs, while others threw worse, and even watching the scenes couldn't shift the darkening inside Claude.

The peasants, as Claude liked to think of them, were all dressed shabbily. The women in old long dresses; most were handmade or hand-me-downs, as they couldn't afford new clothing. Mud clung to the bottoms, as they made their daily trudge up to the castle in heavy boots, and big shawls, giving them no protection on a Dai windy day.

Outside the castle hung four gibbets. Two occupants yelled, begging for release; the second pair was dead. It was not unusual for the castle to display them as most were on the public highways leading into Dai or on the roads of the other major towns, but Gilbert liked to show he could mete out the justice when required.

Gilbert would use the gibbet for a number of perpetrators of heinous crimes,) from traitors, highwaymen, sheep stealers, to murderers. They'd been used for pirates until they erected The Barricade, and sometimes Gilbert used it against those who spoke out against the Guardian, but treasonous talk was rare.

Claude had drunk in the castle alehouse the previous evening. He'd heard the conversations about the thunder and lightning, many of them questioning what it meant and whether The Barricade was coming down. There was nervousness in the air. The lightning frightened people, tales of demons coming, and they talked the usual superstitious nonsense.

He'd also heard the whispers about people vanishing from the Kent shorelines, boats coming in and stealing people. This was the first time Claude had heard of such news, and he was confident they had not reported it back to Eldric. He'd have to find out what was being done about it.

Claude leaned over the stone, looking out toward The Barricade. The huge smoky black prison rose out of the channel, a colossus smouldering in all directions, reaching the sky, becoming lost in the clouds, and even Claude yearned to see what lay beyond.

He'd visited Dai Castle many times before Eldric built the wall. The Guardian feared the Red Plague would enter Britain, and he ordered the rulers of Iceland, Finland and the other upper countries to unite and create a Barricade, then nothing from Europe could get through.

Now though, as Claude stared out at the black void, it felt more like a prison than a place of safety. Eldric hadn't cared about his subjects in France as the plague entered the country, and he'd left them to the horrors of whatever it brought without even a second thought.

Claude was convinced the Plague had died out. Those on Eldric's council had also concluded the virus would have reached its peak and then receded, as all viruses do, but Eldric was used to being alone, and refused to bring the wall down. He preferred the isolation of his country.

Beyond that Barricade, Claude mused, he'd had a lover; a bouncy brunette French maiden, called Fleur. Claude had wanted to marry her, but he couldn't find her in time. After murdering Bedelia, he tried to find Fleur and her family, as she lived just outside of Bononia, but the house was empty, and Claude hoped, even now, that they had escaped the deadly virus.

After the loss of Fleur, and on his return to Britain, Claude found refuge in the arms of Gable. She'd grown bored quickly of Eldric as he would only come to her chambers, have sex and then leave. She was a young, beautiful woman, and Claude promptly learned she was adventurous. He enjoyed her company, as she was also intelligent, witty and cunning. Claude just hoped Eldric never found out; otherwise they'd both lose their heads.

Gable wanted her child to ascend the throne, and she convinced Claude to murder Bedelia's children. In the first few heady months of infatuation, Claude would have agreed to anything. He had initially refused, but Gable threatened him saying, she would tell Eldric, Claude had forced himself on her, and he preferred to keep his head.

Eldric and Oren had been away on one of their hunting weekends, when Claude set fire to the nursery with the children and nanny inside. Locking them in, making it look like the nanny had been drunk and knocked over a candle.

Now, as Claude stared out at The Barricade, he knew he should have never got involved with Gable. She was barren, and the Lord Guardian was becoming increasingly anxious that he'd never have a male heir, and Claude knew he'd made a mistake.

A messenger ran up the ramparts towards him. He bowed before Claude and handed him a small piece of paper. Taking the parchment, he read the note. It came from Gable, informing him of something Oren had gleefully told him, that Bedelia was alive. He screwed it up and tossed it aside.

That anxious gnawing inside him was getting stronger. By now Bedelia would know her children were dead and, though Claude guessed she would come for him because of what he'd done to her, he feared the agony she might inflict if she learned he'd murdered Hamish and Oliver. She was a Reaper and a Guardian, a combination, in which he did not fancy his chances.

Turning his back on Dai, Claude spotted Oren walking through the Keep's marketplace. Behind him was a young female Reaper, with the emblem of the castle sewn into her lightweight uniform. Oren had his own personal Reaper, a man called Luther, and he wasn't anywhere to be seen.

Claude carried on watching Oren, as he weaved and spoke with some market dwellers. This piqued Claude's interest, because Oren hadn't been relaxed in the coach on the way from London, and yet now he looked rather happy.

Then Gilbert approached, looking anxious, telling Oren something, and Oren kept nodding his head. Gilbert was getting agitated, and Oren tried to calm him, but nothing worked, and then Gilbert left.

Claude walked down the ramparts and into the mass. He weaved through the haggard people, most of them stepping out of his way because he was a higher class than them, and he stepped in front of Gilbert before the man vanished inside the Keep.

'Is there a problem I need to know about?' he asked.

Gilbert mused, stroking his potted face, and he played with his uniform before answering, 'We've had a report of a French ship anchoring just off Deman Circe. Apparently, there's another crack,' Gilbert huffed, 'also reports of a woman, chopping the hands of some poor priest and setting fire to his Temple.'

Bedelia, Claude thought, and a chill went through him. If she could do that to a priest, what was she going to do to him? He was going to have to be sure he killed her this time.

'Where is this Temple?'

'Outside Nova Clessia, it's a small hamlet on the Road of Bones,' Gilbert snapped, turning and walking away.

Pushing through the market, Claude headed towards the Armoury. The castle had placed the Tower's Reapers into a separate barrack away from the soldiers and their own Reapers. He passed through the soldiers as they went through their daily exercise.

The rifles fired, and Claude watched the expert marksmanship of the men and women. All dressed in their standard blue coat and white trousers and black boots. Smart and effective at keeping the peace.

Entering the barracks, he saw there were twelve beds in each room. Each dorm with white-washed walls and six bunks on either side. There was bedding for the visiting soldier or Reaper and an oven in the corner. It was a simple room for the military.

Claude walked down the dimly lit corridor, illuminated only by a couple of candles, and Claude found the Reapers, all of them sitting in their dorm, awaiting instructions. Reapers didn't mix with people, and Claude watched as some lay on their bed, while two meditated. He admired these killers because they accepted their role, although they rarely lived until after thirty-five.

The Reapers moved to stand in position as he entered, and Claude shook his head, telling them to remain as they were. Their uniform tucked away, hidden from view, but they always had weapons close by, if not on them. Claude said nothing, but looked for evidence Luther was there. He saw nothing.

'Karem,' he beckoned a young woman, small and pale with her hair cropped but Claude was aware of how vicious she could be. 'Where's Luther?' he asked as she approached him.

'He left us during the lightning,' she responded, her voice a monotonous sound.

Claude mused, 'Do you know where?'

'No, Lord Ramas.'

'There's been a report of a woman desecrating a Temple. In one hour ready my house, and bring two more reapers, as we need to find Luther.'

She nodded. 'Yes, Lord Ramas.'

***

Lunden Tower, Lunden

The Guardian's private crypt was a place Eldric didn't visit often. Inside each of the sarcophagi lay the bodies of each previous Lord Guardian. Every funerary box was magnificent in design. Large and distinctive, decorated with crowned skulls and winged angels, with women beautifully carved into the precious metals, and some boxes looked like carriages.

Eldric read the name of Alfred, the first Guardian, huffing. Ten Lord Guardians rested within the grand crypt and sixteen ladies, either in heart-shaped urns or their own magnificent caskets.

The Court, the Country, everybody believed that each Lord Guardian was the new male heir to the British Throne, and only three priests had known the truth. Each body was new but the same powerful Guardian resided in every new son.

Eldric lived because he could begin the transfer while the woman was pregnant. A slow process, but when the boy was old enough, the infant went to the Temple and the priests imbued the souls. Over two years, the boy's soul died, and the aged Guardian would appear to be going senile. Eldric would take his place, and the man's body he'd existed in then died. This was the way it had been for the last five hundred years.

He'd tried with Hamish. Eldric didn't need Bedelia to be anywhere near, but there was always something blocking him. Eldric didn't know if it was because he was trying to join with a grandchild or it was something else.

He guessed it was Bedelia.

Things were different now. Eldric gripped the handle of the box. He had no child to transfer to, and he was weakening every day. The body was decaying, and his power fading. It didn't matter that he forced every free child to go through The Purge, so they could fasten themselves to him, and he could feed off them for his power. He was still dying.

This weakening of his abilities hadn't started in this lifetime. It began when Eldric was Guardian Jandro, that's why he ordered the Purge. Eldric had created many Guardians during his first reign, allowing him to consume their powers, flowing between each other, no matter where they were in the world, and he was the only one who was reborn. The others would die, having created Guardians of their own, and Eldric would feed off their abilities.

Eldric was the source of all Guardians, and now most were dead. The Red Plague took them, leaving him weaker than ever before.

Breathing in the fresh, polished smell, Eldric touched the marble of Alfred. This body was whom Eldric belonged to, and Alfred was his correct name. He was named after some king who'd brokered deals with foreign invaders and his family created systems and laws which benefited the people.

Eldric remembered his young first self. Alfred would sit and pray in churches, waiting for Judgement Day and acceptance into the house of God. His young soul spent many hours praying, wanting the sign that never came.

And then he discovered mysteries hidden in the manmade caves of Chaslehurst. He'd been a young man, only twenty-five. He, like others before him, worked the mine every day, chipping out the chalk.

Eldric shivered. He'd not thought about this life in a long time, and he hadn't uttered his real name either. When Alfred had broken through the chalk wall, instead of there being more chalk, he'd discovered an underwater fountain, but this was different - it sparkled, many colours.

Alfred stepped inside, and the colours buzzed around him, interested in who he was. The five elements rose, Fire, wood, metal, water and Earth - they stood like magical beings before him, and the waters exploded. He screamed, ripped apart, mixed up and replaced, constructing the man around the abilities he desired.

These new abilities surged through Alfred. He knew he wasn't supposed to have these powers, but Alfred took them. He became a Living God, and Alfred placed his hands over the hole he created, bringing an avalanche of rocks down on the burrowed hole. He walked out of the caves and blockaded the entrance, killing three workers inside. Alfred built an army against the Rulers of Britain, bringing them down because their dead god could not defeat a Living one, and Alfred became the first Guardian of Britain. He wiped out the other religions, decreeing that a subject of Britain would only worship the true gods.

The Guardians.

Alfred learned too late that his mortal body wasn't immune to time. He could die like all gods and then Alfred remembered the Farscape, and he used that world to give his subjects an afterlife. The three men he'd killed in the caves were trapped there. They had transformed into shadowy spectres, but they couldn't reach him, and they watched, waiting, before they vanished. This was a bridge between the living and dead, where Alfred could transfer his soul into that of another living boy. But he had to be related to that body, and his need for male heirs was cemented.

Eldric never used Vassals or Reapers as they were tainted. He stood gazing at the bronze engraving; this was his mistake with Bedelia, because she was both.

He closed his eyes, speculating how he would deal with her. Bedelia never entered the Purge. She knew what he knew, that he wasn't really a God and that she could destroy him. She'd given him two male heirs, and he'd believed that was all he needed to keep his old soul alive, but the drunken nanny killed any chances of that.

Breathing out, Eldric wondered if Bedelia was the demon he'd been waiting for. Was she the one who was really going to cut him down? When he'd connected with the new Guardian, he'd felt something. The Spectres, they'd found her and attached themselves to the girl who had opened up The Barricade to let Bedelia come back.

'Lord Guardian,' a voice behind spoke.

Eldric turned and saw Torin standing at the entrance, with a nervous expression on his face.

'What is it, Torin?'

'We've received two messages, one about people being taken from Britain...and the other, well...'

'Spit it out, Torin,' Eldric snapped.

'The other says, a Temple was burnt down. It's in the same region, and reports suggest it might be your daughter.'

Eldric eyes widened. Bedelia had done the unthinkable. A blasphemous act against him and any Temple in Britain, and his heart raged. She was sending him a message that she was coming and Bedelia was going to kill him.

Chapter Twenty-One
Arena Porta, Kent

Marisol fumed. Ten men dead, three riders blinded, Malick dead, and Tristan back with his mother. Smoking a cigarillo, Marisol gulped whiskey from a bottle her men had taken from the pub. She stood in the early morning light, taking in the Barricade's view from the gun platform of the blockhouse at Arena Porta. Made from stone, brick and earth, the circular structures stood as memories of a time before the Guardians, and the one Marisol stood in was now a family home.

The small fishing community placed between Hath and Foulksten had a mixture of houses, some red brick, for those who could afford them, and surrounding them were modest one or two-storey buildings, thatched roofs, and most had small plots where the chickens and pigs lived. In the high woodland background, dwellings hid as the roof bellowed out smoke from the chimneys.

They'd taken the coastal route to Arena Porta, having piled the bodies into a mass grave in the Marshland near the pub. Marisol bit her fingernails. Those bodies all presented profit, and she'd had to bury them. They might have been men and women, who followed and worked for her, but they were still flesh and bone, and she could have made a lot of money out of them.

Baptiste knew the owner of the blockhouse, a Mr Edmond Harris. They'd been friends before The Barricade demolished any relations between the coastal towns of Britain and France, and the old man's face paled seeing Baptiste and a group of French and Spanish Netherlands riders at his stone fortress.

Marisol hadn't given the man time to reject them, pushing her way through the thick wooden doors, and Edmond blustered. She'd given him a look, and the old man quietened down and let them into his home.

Not that having so many riders and all with accents would be easy to hide. Marisol knew it wouldn't take long for somebody from the Arena Porta to send a message, but Marisol didn't care, because down in the Keep's goal was the young girl from Deman Circe.

When they'd arrived, she found a group of men, Flesh Finders, sitting comfortably inside the blockhouse. Marisol never asked for their names, as she bargained for the English Guardian. They'd suggested a price, and she'd suggested their payment was letting them live. The men had no choice to accept, unless they wanted to end up in the abattoir in Dulpenne.

The morning was crisp, and the fresh air felt good. Marisol listened to the sounds of the gulls as they squawked, announcing they'd found food, and she watched the early morning fishing boats being pulled down the pebble beach by three men, eager to start their day.

Marisol pulled out her pistol and cocked and un-cocked it several times. She should have known there was something different about Bedelia. Malick lied when he saw the bodies strung up at the Temple. Her gut told her he was lying, but Marisol had accepted Malick's words.

Below on the beach were several riders. They lazed in the morning breeze, but they were less confident than when they had landed. There had been an energy, a focus to bring back Bedelia Rose alive and milk her blood, that was until they witnessed the woman kill ten of their friends. The brave fighters stepped forward to protect her and slowly after each of them died, the riders stopped, and then they watched as Bee shot her own husband.

That callousness, the capability to murder somebody Bee loved, resonated with the riders because if she was prepared to do that, Bee would kill all of them and think nothing of it. The riders allowed Bee to leave the pub with the boy under her arms. Marisol shouted at them to go after her, but there was fear in their eyes. It was the first time they looked frightened of somebody else rather than her, and she'd roared in anger, but they still didn't go after Bee.

Marisol admired Bedelia, not that she'd admit it to anybody. To have the courage to kill Malick, and in front of their son, was something even she wouldn't consider, but then, Marisol mused, she wasn't a Reaper.

The platform door opened, Baptiste came up beside her and breathed in the fresh, salty air. He was once a handsome man, but the plague, loss of hair and the false teeth he'd jammed into his gums made him look fierce.

She threw the cigarillo butt over the wall. 'Baptiste, have two men go to the ship, tell them to return to France.

We need more men, have ships ready to sail back here, back through both Cracks. And has Lars returned with those bodies yet?'

Baptiste sat on the stone wall. 'Lars is back without the bodies because the army was at the pub. They know we're here; we won't get back to the ship.'

'Can we kill the soldiers?'

Baptiste hissed a laugh through his false teeth. 'Only if you want more to come. He said the bodies were dug up and laid out. He couldn't see Malick Rose. Overheard the barkeep saying Bedelia dug him up.'

Marisol pondered on this. 'Why would she do that?'

Baptiste muttered, 'You're the Guardian, thought you'd know.'

She moved toward the door, opening it Marisol beckoned Baptiste. 'Let's go talk with this Winnie girl.'

Walking down the stone steps, Marisol whistled. She hated being near Eldric, feeling him run through her. She had been free of him since she'd landed in The Spanish Netherlands, and now she couldn't get away from him, and he was getting closer.

They jumped down the spiral stone case, passing the opulent lounge, full of colourful carpets, reds and greens, and expensive furniture. Edmond sat at his writing desk with a rider sitting on a sofa, cleaning his gun.

Edmond turned and glared at Baptiste, who whistled to the man to get out, and Edmond smiled, giving him a nod. They continued through the stone hallway toward a smaller door. Baptiste took a candle, lit it, and the wooden door creaked as they stepped inside a narrow passageway, leading to the dungeon.

Through another door, the smell struck Marisol. The familiar smell of piss and shit, much like the holding pens in her abattoir. In the cell's corner, hiding in the darkness, she could make out a young woman. The woman was staring up, her fingers flexing, and she muttered to herself. Winnie had a twitch about her, and it sounded as if she was talking to somebody.

'So, you're Winnie?' Marisol lit a cigarillo and then wrapped her leather coat around her. The stone walls made the cell a cold place.

'I need to get out.' Winnie jumped to the bars. 'I did something. I brought something dangerous back. I need to close that Crack. She's going to kill him.'

'Explain yourself,' Marisol prompted.

Winnie twitched. 'The – the one from France, she's going to stop the Guardians, she isn't linked. I shouldn't have helped her come through. They lied to me.'

Marisol inhaled her smoke. 'Who lied?'

Winnie played with her silver hair matted into her head, and sunk to the floor. 'The Sinners.'

Marisol bent down, peering through the bars, coming face to face with her youngest sister. Winnie reminded Marisol so much of Verda that she was tempted to reach out and touch the young woman.

'Who are the Sinners?' Marisol asked.

Winnie licked her lips. She had a secret and was about to share. 'They've come back, they want Eldric.'

Marisol reached through the bars, banging Winnie's head against them. She almost felt the bump herself. 'Don't fuck with me, Winnie, otherwise I'll send for Feargal, and have him gutted in front of you.'

Winnie cried, struggling to rip her head out of Marisol's hand. She scurried back into the dank corner, sniffing, wiping her nose. 'They are where our abilities come from. Eldric stole the magic, used it to create us, and used it to rule. They don't belong here.'

These abilities Marisol rarely used as they had weakened over the years. She relied on mortal terror than anything magical. Being a Guardian hadn't helped Marisol escape Britain, nor had it helped build an Empire out of blood and bone. The only thing it had done was to assist in the killing of kidnapped Britons, selling tinctures and ointments to plague survivors who believed the blood had medicinal properties.

'What happens to the Guardians?' Marisol whispered.

'No magic, no abilities, no Guardians,' Winnie's voice became small, she giggled, 'and no Barricade. I shouldn't have opened it up.'

The girl, her sister, carried on giggling. Marisol rose, watching Winnie play with her hair, mumbling. She was sure Winnie hadn't been born this way, but because these abilities had burst into her. It had fractured her mind in a manner where she believed she heard voices.

There were no Sinners. They were just something Winnie had made up to protect herself. The Guardians would always rule. Winnie, Marisol thought, was useless, but she could milk the woman's blood, which would bring in a good profit. Marisol studied Winnie, thinking she wouldn't survive for long.

Marisol took a step up the stairs, and she heard Winnie whisper, 'They say the one from France has no God and will slaughter you.' Marisol curled her fingers, wanting to cut Winnie down. She breathed out, deciding that it was best to make a deal with Eldric. She would exchange Winnie because he needed more children, and she would have Bedelia's head.

***

The Prince of Fortune

Luther sat, back straight, at one of the unbroken tables in the pub of the 'Prince of Fortune'. He peered around the bar, noting the blood, broken tables and chairs, and shattered bottles.

The place smelled of cheap whiskey and coppery blood. The old man, Jamus Black, owner for more than forty years, was on his knees. He had a bucket of water next to him, sloshing it around with a dirty rag, trying to clean the floor.

Luther considered it a fruitless task. He thought the man should throw straw over the blood and let it dry in, but he said nothing, as the man jabbered on, surrounded by water, his breeches and shirt wet and becoming wetter all the time. He spoke about a group of Frenchmen who had entered his establishment, making a nuisance and frightening away his customers. A tough-looking woman, with black eyes and a shaved head, led this group, before a woman came in shooting several French riders.

The pub was in the middle of nowhere, on the road between Hath and Deman Circe. Behind it was woodlands and Marsh, and out front was the Channel. Luther rose and looked around the shabby décor; moth-eaten curtains, and grimy windows.

'I've already told those feckless soldiers all this,' Jamus grumbled. 'And the captain pissed off with some of his men, once he heard about the fire up the road. Those fuckwits outside who dug up those bodies don't have a brain between them.'

'What fire?' Luther asked.

'I don't know, didn't hear much – something about a Temple.'

'So, tell me about this woman,' Luther enquired.

'She shot her husband… he must have really pissed her off to make her shoot him.' Jamus sloshed more water onto the wooden floor, and water dripped through the boards. 'Strange thing is, she came back for his body.'

'Why?' Luther asked.

Jamus stopped scrubbing, and snapped, 'How do I know?'

Luther saw the old man cringe, realising the way he'd spoken to a Reaper. 'What about the boy?' he asked, and out of the corner of his eye he could see Feargal sitting there, a beaker of ale in his hand, nervous.

'Maybe six or seven years old – called her Mamma.' The old man wiped his wrinkled face. 'The woman called her Mrs Rose, though I didn't think Reapers were allowed to have children or marry.'

Luther ignored the question, asking, 'What made you think she was a Reaper?'

Jamus got up, arching his old back, and hobbled over to Luther. He glared at Feargal, sitting in the corner with his free ale. 'She wasn't dressed like you; I didn't know till I saw her with those swords. Two of them she had. And she killed about ten people to get to the boy. She must care for that boy… strange for a Reaper to care.'

Luther nodded, this sounded like the Bedelia he knew. She'd saved him from a vicious attack, and her punishment was to become a Reaper. Their friendship was deadly, knowing that at any time during their apprenticeship they might have to kill each other, as Overlord Kendal enjoyed pitting apprentices against each other.

The pub door creaked open. A tall, bulky man with brown hair entered. He held hands with a small boy, about seven and blond. They tweaked Luther's interest, and he watched.

The man, Luther observed, paled the moment he realised a Reaper was inside the pub, but he didn't turn and head back out. He gripped hold of the boy's hand, led him to a table and sat the boy down.

'You,' Luther acknowledged him, 'are you Mr Rose?' Luther spotted worry in the stranger's face. The man looked tired, angry almost, and his breeches and shirt were dirty as if he'd dug something up or had been buried himself. Luther stepped closer. 'I asked if –'

'It's not him. I've not seen him before, but that's the boy,' Jamus interrupted.

Luther took another step closer. The man didn't move, and Luther sensed he didn't know what to do. Every man always believed they could fight a Reaper, and Luther concluded this wasn't what the stranger was thinking. This man was thinking about how to protect the boy. Luther looked down at the boy, who smiled, and Luther then kneeled.

'Young man, what is your name?' he asked.

The boy stared at Luther. Then at the two revolvers in his gun belt, and finally the silver belt, and the boy recognised the sword. The boy peered up to the man he was with, who nodded.

'Tristan,' the boy said.

Luther paused. 'Is your mother Bedelia Rose?' And Tristan's face lit up, smiling, so Luther asked, 'and where is your mother now?' The man was about to speak, but Luther held his hand up, stopping him.

Tristan whispered, still looking at the sword. 'Do you know Mamma?'

'Your mother and I grew up together. You are lucky to have a mother like Bedelia, she must love you very much.' Every word was considered as Luther spoke.

'Papa frightened her. He's gone looking for her,' he said, crestfallen, and then he added, 'Mamma looks like you.'

'How do you mean, Tristan?' he asked.

Tristan stepped closer and he touched the sides of Luther's mouth, gently moving his fingers across Luther's face. 'She has scars like that.'

Luther remained in front of the boy. Bedelia had a Chelchith Smile, and he breathed a little deeper, realising Claude had tortured Bee before he murdered her. By now Claude would be aware Bee was alive and he'd go searching for her.

Luther stood, staring at the man. 'Who are you?' he asked.

Somer stuttered, telling Luther who he was and that he was the boy's uncle. Luther heard the tension in Somer's French accent. Something he'd heard often when people were forced to talk to Reapers. He asked questions, finding out Malick's name, why they were in Britain, and what drove Bee to leave as the boy looked up between them.

Luther half-listened, considering what he was going to do next, unsure whether he should send Somer and the boy to Lord Oren in the Barren Lands. He had been Oren's personal Reaper since Bee had gone to France. He'd watched and listened, learning about Oren, and then he decided.

The pub door opened. '–There's nothing else we can do. The Temple's burned, and they've cut down the priest–' Two farmhands entered, both young, clothes dirty, and both smelling of smoke.

They didn't notice Luther at first, but their faces dropped as they looked at the broken chairs and the blood on the floor. They paled seeing the Reaper and edged back to the door.

Luther approached; the men stayed quiet. 'Tell me about this fire,' he ordered.

One answered, 'Yeah, on the Road of Bones, the priest strung up, hands–' he noticed Tristan, lowering his voice, 'hands cut off, with a sign saying *child rapist*. Somehow he's alive.'

'Anything else?'

The man bit his lips. 'I heard somethin' about a woman – she took the priest's son.' He looked at his friend for help, but nothing came.

Luther nodded. The woman was Bee, and he didn't need to ask any more questions.

'Mr Peron, Feargal will take you and young Tristan somewhere safe.' Luther looked at the old man, raising an eyebrow as Jamus sat with Feargal, watching. 'Mr Black, do you have a horse?'

The old man screwed up his mouth, knowing better than to lie to a Reaper. 'She's out in the pasture. I want her back, though.'

'You two.' Luther motioned to the new patrons. 'Go with Mr Black and ready the horse.'

Jamus eased himself up from his chair, his clothes soaking. Luther watched as the three men practically ran out of the door, and the two farmhands started asking questions before Jamus was out of earshot of Luther.

'Feargal, take Mr Peron and young Tristan to Overlord Kendal at Rolfen Castle.'

Somer stepped forward, squaring up to Luther, and his voice shook. 'You can't send us to the Butcher of the–'

'Fredrick is dead,' Luther cut in. 'Sagan is now Overlord. He always liked Bedelia, he'll give you and her son sanctuary. Keep him safe.' Luther pulled a single silver coin out of his leathers and placed it into Somer's hand. 'Give Sagan this. He'll know I've sent you.'

'Not words from a Reaper I'd expect to hear,' Somer spat out.

Feargal took a sharp intake of air. Luther glared at Somer, and the man shrank, realising what he'd said.

Luther stepped closer, putting his hand on his gun. Somer stumbled back, knocking into a chair. 'You know Bee has saved your life. Under other circumstances...' He looked down at the boy. 'You would not be so fortunate.'

Somer nodded, apologising.

'What... what about Winnie?' Feargal asked, timidly.

Feargal had told Luther everything that had happened since Winnie woke up after breaking her neck. He'd ridden the road and did not pass anyone on the way to Deman Circe. Luther suspected Winnie was now in the hands of smugglers. They would sell her to this Spaniard, but there was nothing he could do.

Bedelia was his priority. He had to find her, and all he knew was that Bee was on The Road of Bones.

Chapter Twenty-Two
The Road of Bones, Kent

The burnt wood and stone choked Claude, making him nauseous. The whole temple was burnt to the ground. The last of the flames danced, wanting to consume whatever was left, but little remained of the entire building. Buckets lay discarded. There hadn't been enough buckets or people to stop the fire, and the only course of action had been to let the flames burn everything.

Claude dismounted, as Karem and three Reapers remained on their horses. There was a group of four soldiers muddling along, and a worn-out captain.

'Captain?' Claude extended his hand, explaining who he was.

The soldier accepted. 'Osbourne, Captain Osbourne.' He took off his hat, shaking his head. 'It's quite something when somebody burns down a Temple. Never thought I'd see the day...'

'You have any idea who did it?' Claude knew the answer, but he wanted to hear it.

Osbourne exhaled. 'They sent me looking for a girl at Deman Circe, and I've not even got there yet. There's a French boat anchored off its shore, but that's all I know.' He explained why they'd arrived at the Temple, having heard the news of the fire. He told Claude about the massacre at the pub, and the woman leaving the Temple with a boy. He thought the two were connected.

'And you say this woman is married?'

'The barkeep called her Mrs Rose,' Osbourne went on. 'And apparently a Reaper.' He shrugged his shoulders. 'How does a Reaper get married and have children?'

Claude smiled; the two were definitely connected. 'This woman is dangerous. I've four Reapers here, we'll arrest her, and you should follow your orders and look for this dead girl.'

'Yes but –'

'This woman *is* a Reaper,' Claude explained, getting excited. He'd have his opportunity once again to kill Bedelia. Then he noticed a man close by. The stranger was over six foot, dusty, dishevelled with dark hair, and green eyes. His long leather coat was covered in mud, and this piqued Claude's interest after what Osbourne had told him.

The stranger had ridden upon an old horse, dismounted and looked at the destroyed Temple. Claude pretended to listen to the Captain, but he concentrated on the stranger, hoping this man had something to do with Bedelia.

The barkeep said they'd called her Mrs Rose, and Claude wondered if this man was her husband. He did nothing and let the man wander back to his horse and ride off. Claude then called Karem over. He told her to follow the stranger, but not to get too close.

This man might lead him to Bedelia.

***

Rolfen Castle, Rolfen, Kent

Sagan drank his late evening coffee, sitting on the stone steps of his castle. The night's mist surrounded him, and Sagan watched his two girls play in the mud, knowing it was well past their bedtime. They should have been in bed hours ago, but the apprentice Reapers were engaged in night exercises, and this always kept the girls up. Sagan figured it was better to have them outside playing in the fresh air, and they could fall asleep in their own time. Their infectious giggles echoing around the stone walls, as his Reapers trained in the courtyard. The deafening sounds of guns and rifles being shot, or swords clashing rang through the mist. The trainers shouted, 'Again,' to their students, as the apprentices learned how to shoot in the dark.

There was no let-up for the eight apprentices; if they weren't training with weapons, they were learning to read and write. They had to learn meditation, because, as killers, they needed to ground themselves once they had been issued a warrant.

He'd received the message that morning. The pigeon came from Dai, and he recognised the hand-written scribble immediately. The name written down was a name he never thought he'd see again. Bedelia had returned, and he guessed she would head to Lunden to kill Eldric. Of all the people Sagan figured he'd never see again, she was one.

The girls squealed as Adeen, his eldest, tumbled onto her younger sister. Adeen was seven years old, with beautiful auburn hair, freckles, milk pale skin and a smile to melt any father's heart. Zoe, only five, adored her elder sister, and both kept each other amused for hours. Zoe had thick black hair with olive skin, and she looked more like her mother, Faith. Once they were older, they'd start asking questions, but, as he thought about the note, he wondered if those questions might come sooner.

Seven seasons past, Luther had arrived in the dead of night, cold, shivering and cradling a baby girl. He'd informed Sagan and Faith the baby didn't have a name, but to make sure the name 'Edith' was included.

The child, they were told, was Bedelia's.

Luther informed them, Bee would never know they had her daughter, and, unlike the twin boy, the little girl had no Guardian abilities. Luther stated the male foetus was stronger and absorbed any of her powers, making her useless to Eldric, so he'd discarded her.

Faith fell in love with Adeen, as they'd been trying for children, and she'd suffered several miscarriages, but then Zoe arrived unexpectedly, making the family complete. Sagan taught the girls they were to watch over each other, always. He'd decided, when they were old enough, he'd have Reapers teach them how to defend themselves, because, when he and Faith passed away, it would be down to them to protect the Medaway.

The message concerned him. He didn't want to get involved in whatever was happening in Dai, or to Eldric. The castle was quiet, only the sounds of his children playing and the Reapers training broke the silence. Sagan was a different man from his father. Fredrick was a butcher, but Sagan refused to behave in the same manner. Once Fredrick was dead, Sagan stopped the senseless killings of his subjects. It was better to have them alive, because the lands couldn't farm themselves and the rivers couldn't be fished without them.

A young man approached him. 'Please sir, do you know where Overlord Kendal is?'

Sagan looked up. The boy was nervous, peering over his shoulder at a boy and a man, standing near two worn-out looking horses.

'What is it, boy?'

The man clasped his hands together, and he coughed. 'Luther sent me.'

Sagan blinked; he'd only been thinking about Luther minutes ago. This wouldn't be good. 'And what did he say?'

'I need to speak with the Overlord, sir,' the young man whispered.

Sagan stood. 'That's me.'

Feargal explained, handing over the coin Luther had given him. He took Sagan over to the strangers and introduced Somer. 'And this is Bedelia's son, Tristan.'

Sagan stared at the boy. 'You'd best come inside.' And he called to Adeen and Zoe; they were to go inside the castle and make Tristan feel welcome.

***

The Road of Bones, Kent

Malick sat in the corner of the Crooked Billet. It was late, and the pub was quiet. A tavern, decorated with stuffed deer heads, large tables and a few patrons. The barkeep told him this was a road to Lunden, mainly used by smugglers because it was remote and unfinished.

The route was known locally as *'The Road of Bones'* due to the bodies left underneath. The vassals who built it were entombed beneath. Malick grunted here and there before taking his ale to a table. He hoped nobody guessed he was French, as he didn't want people asking questions. Hiding in the corner, he listened to the conversations from the other cubicles, and there were the usual grumblings followed by the rumours.

'...I hear she killed at least fifteen...'

'I heard twenty, and the husband as well.'

A slurp of beer. '–poor fucker, being shot by his own wife–'

There was laughter, then a shout to the barkeep for more beer. 'A Reaper turned up, took Jamus Black's horse.' And the voice lowered. 'I hear there was a French boy, about seven or eight...how the fuck did a French child get here? The Reaper sent him somewhere.'

Malick sat up. Tristan, it was Tristan they were talking about. His heart raced. Where was his son? Was Somer still with him? Silence shot through the pub as if ice had covered every piece of furniture. The locals stopped talking and looked at Malick. A man with four Reapers approached his table.

He didn't look at the man. Malick concentrated on the black uniforms of the three men and woman. These were the clothes of his father's killers, and the clothes Bee once wore and felt safe behind.

'Evening, Mr Rose.' The man spoke in a crisp English accent.

Malick's face darkened. 'I think you've got –'

'I am Lord Ramas, you may call me Claude.' Claude rolled his tongue over his lips, smiling, 'I'm the one who murdered your wife. Well, I thought I had. Anyway Mr Rose, does your wife have a beautiful smile?'

'I don't know where she is,' Malick said.

The well-groomed man slid along the bench into the small cubicle, removing his gloves. This was the man who had slit Bee's throat and given her the smile, and Malick curled his fists under the table.

'No, but she'll know where you are.' Claude sipped his beer. He pointed to a small boy. 'That boy's interested in you. I daresay he's the priest's son, you know the priest whose hands Bee cut off?'

Malick looked at the boy, sitting near the fire, sipping beer out of a beaker. The young boy was a couple of years older than Tristan, with blond hair and wore long trousers and a dirty shirt. He gave Malick a tiny smile before finishing his beer.

'Barkeep, two of your finest pies and two more ales,' Claude shouted at the grumpy-looking owner, who glared at him and then prepared the meals. He said nothing more until the food and drink turned up, and Claude paid.

'I don't know much about Bee, but I know Oren enjoyed boasting about having sex with a Reaper.' He grinned. 'He told us everything, panicking that she'd kill him and that he had to tell her what to do.'

Godless

Malick remained quiet.

'It was like having sex with a cadaver.' Claude grinned. 'That's what's he said, and he fucked Bee repeatedly.' Claude then congratulated Malick on not losing his cool. He laughed, pausing with a devilish smile. 'It was all for nothing, of course. Oren's wife, Leena, got jealous of those boys Bee produced. Gable was afraid of them too,' he paused again, peering down his nose at Malick, curling his lips. 'Gable has a way of getting you to do things. She and Leena had me kill them.'

Malick said nothing.

Claude gave Malick a sly look, saying, 'I had a little taste of Bee myself. I'd sliced her throat, she lay dying and I made sure my face was the last thing she'd see. And, you know what, Malick, Oren was right. It *was* like having sex with the dead.'

Malick was quick, punching Claude across the table. Claude flew into the dirt. Two pistols were pushed into Malick's face by Reapers and once again the pub hushed.

Claude rubbed his jaw, crying out. He scrambled up, moving his jaw, mumbling, 'Quite a punch you got.' He slipped back onto the bench. 'Sit back down, Mr Rose, I have four Reapers, there is nothing you can do.'

'Maybe this time, she'll kill you,' Malick whispered. He had no choice but to sit back at the table.

Claude beckoned the boy over, but the boy remained by the fire. A Reaper grabbed the boy, dragging him, yelping, to the table, and the boy looked terrified.

Claude gripped the boy's neck. 'Can you take a message to Bedelia?'

The boy looked at Malick as if questioning whether he should answer. There was fear in his face, and there was nothing Malick could do, so he nodded to the lad.

'Tell her, I have her husband, and if she wants to see him again to come here at noon, and give herself up. Otherwise, I'll slice Malick up very slowly and very painfully.' Claude smiled, and the Reaper released the boy who scuttled out of the pub, pushing drinkers, to get out of the place.

'And if she doesn't come?' Malick asked.

Claude raised his beaker of ale to Malick. 'Tomorrow you will find out whether your Reaper really loves you.'

***

Dai Castle, Dai, Kent

Sagan had been on the road for hours. Dawn was beginning to break, and he didn't know what the time was. Faith listened when he explained about the note. She accepted Somer and Tristan into the Keep, had chambers prepared and told Adeen and Zoe that they had a new guest.

They invited Somer to sit in the banquet hall. He warmed himself by the fire, ate the steaming hot stew brought up from the kitchen and glared at the Banners of the Overlords who'd once ruled his country. But he was friendly enough.

The words 'Shit Storm,' kept popping into Sagan's head. Bedelia being back was not good news, and he needed to keep Adeen safe. Not that he believed Bee would harm the girl, but the thought of Bee wanting her daughter back frightened him. Adeen was his and Faith's daughter, and the panic in Faith's eyes worried him.

Somer answered every question. Faith grilled him about Tristan and Viola until it satisfied her. Both were surprised to learn that Bee got married and, until she'd killed a man, nobody had any idea she was a Guardian and a Reaper. Sagan smiled. Bee was good at keeping secrets. Nobody in Rolfen Castle had a clue she was a Guardian until she revealed her abilities when she was at The Tower.

Faith stood at the gate as Sagan prepared to leave. She kissed him, whispering, 'Make sure that woman doesn't come anywhere near my daughter.' Sagan rode into the night, unsure how he was going to keep Adeen a secret from Bee.

He'd ridden hard and fast, and could just make out the outline of Dai castle. The early sun gave the dominating structure a silvery gleam, and, in the distance, clouds gathered, and rain poured out of them. But farther, along the coastline towards the west, the morning sky was clear.

Sagan continued on his horse, every hoof pounded the chalky path and he rode into the rain. What began as drizzle quickly turned into a downpour, soaking Sagan, his leather duster coat and wide hat gave no protection at all. He slowed his horse to a canter, as the road became treacherous, and the clouds remained as he headed toward the castle and into its open gate.

Bringing the horse to a stop, Sagan dismounted, taking the animal into the castle's stables. The livery smelled of horses and hay, and the usual whinnies sounded from the stables. Sagan dug around in his pocket and gave the groom a penny, asking that his horse be well cared for, and the young boy nodded gleefully, his eyes on the penny, rather than the horse.

Sagan stepped back out into the rain. The ground around his boots had turned muddy, and though he wanted to speak to Rufus, he headed to the Keep to make himself known to Gilbert.

Sagan stepped up the stone steps. Dai Castle was so much bigger and more dramatic than his own small fort, and he was glad he wasn't the Overlord of Dai and the South-East. Sagan handed his coat to the servant, delighted to be out of the wet, and headed to the Great Hall. He didn't know who he expected to find there, but Oren wasn't one of them.

'Lord Sagan?' Oren rose from the table, and Gilbert remained seated. Both were surprised to see him.

Sagan clasped Oren's hand, shaking it. Gilbert hugged Sagan and ordered more ale.

The massive fireplace was ablaze. Sagan looked up at Dai's banners, and the tapestries, featuring stories of significant battles, bows and arrows, people dying, soldiers surviving and women weeping. Sagan rubbed his hands and warmed them by the flames. He huffed, taking the goblet and gulping.

'What brings you here?' Gilbert gave Oren a confused look and then smiled awkwardly at Sagan.

Sagan took another slurp. 'Didn't you receive my message? Sent it a couple of days ago. I need my weapons maker back.'

Gilbert shook his head. 'Received nothing, but, a couple of nights ago, there was a great storm.'

'Maybe the pigeon got lost,' Sagan lied. Warmed by the flames, Sagan joined them at the table. Laid out was food in large dishes. He inhaled the breakfast stews, the garlic and beef filled his nose, and he spotted apples, figs and pears. He'd arrived in time for breakfast, and poured another beaker, dished himself a plate of food and sat down.

'There's a crack in The Barricade, Oren's come to fix it,' Gilbert explained, shovelling food into his mouth.

'A crack?' Sagan's eyes widened. 'I thought nothing could get through that.'

Gilbert laughed. 'Yes, apparently Bedelia came through.' And then his expression darkened, realising he'd let private information slip.

'The Reaper?' Sagan hoped he sounded surprised. 'Isn't she dead?' And silence filled the hall. 'How did she get back?'

Gilbert gobbled up his breakfast, giving Sagan all the details, explaining about the dead girl in Deman Circe and also another Guardian, while Oren sat listening.

'Two more Guardians?' Sagan raised his eyebrows, 'What does that mean?'

Oren picked at his food. 'It means we're in the shit, Sagan. Bedelia will be executed, and well...'

'What's Eldric planning?' Sagan licked his fingers after eating some figs.

Oren, startled by the question, blustered, 'The same as before in regards to his new daughter.'

Sagan nodded, understanding Oren's meaning. He paused as if trying to remember something, hoping his acting skills fooled both men. 'I remember something about Bee wanting to kill Eldric...' He frowned.

'Let's not think about that,' Oren whispered, looking into the bottom of his goblet.

Gilbert then asked, 'But wouldn't she have a claim to the throne?'

Oren smiled. 'Bee doesn't strike me as the kind of woman who wants the throne. She has one mission, that is to kill Eldric. After that, I don't think she's thought about it.'

Gilbert smirked. 'Leaves only you then, Oren.'

Oren laughed, and he settled back to his breakfast. 'Then I'd have to kill Bee, in order to sit on the Throne.'

Sagan mentioned no more about it, seeing Oren's fingers clench. He guessed there was an element of truth in Oren's words and he thought about Adeen. She was Oren's daughter, and he did not know she'd been brought by Luther to Rolfen Castle. Oren had visited Rolfen several times since her birth, and had never noticed Adeen. The girl might as well have been Faith's natural child, for most people appeared to have forgotten about her ever being born.

Oren left, explaining he needed to head to Krallar, and Sagan sat with Gilbert for a quarter of an hour discussing what might happen next. He then thanked Gilbert for the hospitality, explaining he needed to find Rufus and take him home.

***

Sagan walked out into the courtyard. Dogs barked, yelped and growled. In the corner, a small group of soldiers huddled close together, jeering, swearing and howling, placing bets on which dog might pull the other apart. The men banded together, pushing and shoving, vying for a better spot and Sagan ignored the noise. Even in the early morning, people could still be monsters.

The morning rain had cleared, leaving only puddles and mud, and the stalls were opening. Sagan knew about Omega and Winnie, but he chose not to share this with either Gilbert or Oren. Neither appeared too worried about either of the Guardians, both focused on Bedelia, rather than all three of them.

And everybody wanted to kill Bedelia.

Eldric, because he feared her. Omega wanted her dead to make money, and Oren because he wanted to be the Lord Guardian. Bedelia stood in his way because if she killed Eldric, she was the rightful heir to the throne of Britain.

Sagan doubted Bee would even consider sitting on the throne. The girl he remembered was nothing more than a vassal, and then a Reaper, and she probably did not understand what it took to run a country.

Bee sounded happy being married to Malick Rose, having a family and running a local tavern. If it hadn't been for the Skin Trader realising that she was a full-blooded Guardian, Sagan doubted Bee would ever have set foot back on English soil.

The Armoury was quiet and hot. Everywhere weapons were stored. Rifles in wooden boxes, bullets and carriages, boxed and shelved. Daggers, whips, swords - everything had a place - and Rufus kept it in order. This place looked like the armoury at Rolfen.

Behind a corner, back turned, Sagan called out Rufus's name, but the man was sharpening a sword, oblivious, and he shouted. Rufus turned and nodded, placing the sword down.

'Oren makes out he's not interested in being Lord Guardian.' Sagan clasped the man's arm in a handshake. 'He'll kill her before seeing a Reaper on the throne.'

'Oren would,' Rufus whispered, 'and Bee's always known that.'

'She's married, Rufus,' Sagan said, and he watched the weapons maker go back to his work. 'She has a son and a daughter.' He then repeated everything Somer had told him.

Rufus stopped. 'Has Bee brought the whole fucking family?'

Sagan grinned. 'Something to do with a Guardian Skin Trader, she brought the husband and boy.'

'Somer told an odd story about her shooting Malick, killing him, but somehow she saved him.'

Rufus whistled. He hunted around the workshop and found an old carpetbag hidden under some planks of wood. Opening it up, he put some tools inside. 'If that's true, I think the Guardians called it Imprinting. I thought they couldn't do it anymore. They certainly couldn't do it with a commoner.'

Sagan remembered the stories of his childhood, about how Guardians could strengthen themselves if they combined, imprinted themselves onto another Guardian. Still, they had been fairy tales, something to inspire awe and wonder in their living Gods, and, as Rufus pointed out, Eldric couldn't do it.

'What would this mean for this Malick?' he asked.

Rufus shrugged. 'Perhaps she can protect him... I don't know.'

Sagan was about to speak when there was a commotion outside. People shouted, horses neighed, there was running, scrambling about, and then trumpeting came. Both men peered out of the grimy window.

The Royal stagecoach drew to a stop. A servant scurried, almost slipping in the puddles to get to the door. They watched as Eldric opened the door himself and set foot in Dai Castle. The Lord Guardian looked around, dressed in a red and gold embroidered long-tailed coat, black breeches and boots, smartly dressed, but looking tired. He glared, expecting to see Gilbert, but he wasn't anywhere.

Eldric held his hand out, and a woman stepped out into the mud. Gable accepted his hand, yawning. She wore a simple dress, bodice long and flowing, not the clothing for a long ride. Sagan didn't recall hearing Gable having ever visited Dai, and her unimpressed gaze gave everything away. Behind her, stepped Leena.

'Oh shit,' Sagan muttered.

Rufus grumbled under his breath. 'I'll go find Bee.'

Chapter Twenty-Three
The Road of Bones, Kent

Breathing in the last of the morning air, Claude puffed up his chest, pleased with himself. Stepping out of the Crooked Billet, he'd slept well knowing that today he would capture Bedelia and it was all thanks to her husband. It was nearly midday, and Claude wondered if Bedelia would actually turn up.

Claude considered Malick to be a decent enough chap, just a little stupid not to recognise that his wife was a Reaper. Still, nobody, including Eldric, knew she was a Guardian until *she* revealed it, so he couldn't blame Malick for not seeing what Bee really was.

Claude hoped the boy had told Bee of his plan; otherwise, he was about to kill an innocent man. That didn't bother Claude, but Malick would die knowing Bee never loved him, and even Claude didn't like that.

Karem came out with Malick by her side. She looked impressive, a slight figure wearing the classic black Reaper uniform. Malick appeared tired, his clothes ruffled with traces of mud still smudged into his breeches. He probably hadn't slept much, Claude mused, after all, he wouldn't have slept either, knowing his wife might let him hang.

The tavern was quiet, and the few guests who'd spent the night were still in their rooms or had left. Claude spoke with the barkeep and learned hangings usually took place on the green opposite, as the old oak tree had probably stood there for over 500 years, making it a stable Dule tree.

The barkeep looked excited at the prospect of earning a bit of extra cash, because public executions always brought in more punters. Claude threatened the barkeep that if a crowd gathered, the Reapers would cut them all down. The noose had been prepared, but instead of it hanging from the tree itself, the Reapers had attached it to the saddle of a horse.

The September day had a chill, which Claude hadn't felt before. He pulled his long leather coat around him, and Malick kept quiet. At over six foot, much taller and leaner than Claude, his expression was one of acceptance that he might be dead shortly.

Claude grabbed Malick, pushing him toward the clump of trees. The Reaper followed, and Claude whistled, thinking of how beautiful the day was. Birds sang as Claude clapped his hands.

'The Road of Bones,' Claude laughed. 'Your bones will end up like those vassals, if Bee doesn't turn up.'

Malick said nothing.

Hooves clipped on the path. Claude smiled, seeing a horse and rider. The horse was slow with each step echoing, and Claude slapped Malick on the back.

'There, she loves you after all, Mr Rose. A Reaper prepared to die for somebody else, now that is unheard of.'

***

'She certainly is magnificent.' Claude whistled through his teeth. He stood on one side of Malick, with Karem on the other.

Malick watched the horse as the Reaper approached. The sleek black, durable uniform the rider wore clung to their body. Two swords crisscrossed their waist, with two gun-belts, each lined with bullets, daggers wrapped around the forearms, and behind the hilt of a machete stationed to their back, their boots laced to the knees.

The off-silver mask shone in the midday sun; it covered the face. The sunken eye holes were too dark to see the eyes, the cheekbones shallow and the lips slightly opened, with several metal crosses, like spikes allowing the wearer to breathe. Patterned across those lips were teeth and muscle carved into the metal, and that image took Malick back to the day Bee was found on the beach with her lips cut. Her head was covered by the stahlhelm, a distinctive metal helmet, and carved into the metal was the human skeleton.

This was Mrs Bedelia Rose.

This was the woman he'd married and loved. She sat in the saddle, back rigid, in black, her face covered, and Malick's heart quickened. The memory of his father's Reapers flashed, and even they were not as disturbing as Bee.

The attachment to Bee bolstered, seeing his wife dressed in the uniform which made her inhuman. He panicked, feeling naked because he could not protect Bee. It was as if Malick were on display, revealing his weaknesses that he was not coming to his wife's rescue.

Bee washed through him. She began as a tingle in his lips, and the warm caressing waves passed through

Malick, calming him. Bee joined herself to him, letting her husband rest inside her and his heart rate slowed, helping him put his fear aside, breaking down and dissembling him until there was nothing at all.

The void bleached everything, as Bee took him to the place, where she kept all her sorrows. Bee opened the door to her secret room, the place where she prepared to kill. The mantra Bee whispered as the calm spread throughout her body, warming and relaxing Malick, and he experienced the lack of any emotional empathy for the victim. This was Bee when she was about to execute somebody, but this time she was the victim.

Bee slipped off the horse, patting it, and she walked confidently into the clearing. She stood there, saying nothing.

'Bee, please–' Malick stepped forward, but the Reaper forced Malick to his knees. Karem pulled out her revolver, and the unmistakable sound of the trigger being cocked clicked in his ear.

'Bedelia,' Claude shouted, 'remove your weapons, mask and uniform.'

Bee unbuckled her guns, dropping them into the grass, followed by the swords, and then Bee removed her mask. She stood, short auburn hair, a dispassionate expression, the scars crossed her mouth, with her eyes fixed on Claude. Bee peeled the leather jacket off her shoulders, dropping it to the ground, standing there in a thin white top, with scars on show.

Claude laughed. 'Bedelia, you are quite the strumpet for a Reaper. Oren fucked you, I fucked you, and you – a Guardian – have let some shabby Frenchman fuck you.'

Bee stood motionless, still watching Claude.

Claude leaned over Malick's shoulder. He said, 'Nobody wants a Reaper as a wife, and you must have been desperate to marry that cunt. Tell me, Mr Rose, do you smell death when you fuck her?'

Malick shuffled, wanting to hit Claude, but the Reaper kept hold of him.

Claude turned his attention back to Bee. 'The Striking is fit for you, Bedelia. Do you have anything you want to say to your husband?'

Bee looked at Malick for the first time. 'I am not alone, as I walk out of the darkness with you by my side.'

Malick's brow furrowed. He didn't know what it meant, he couldn't remember where he'd heard those words, and then Somer sprang to mind. Those were the words she'd spoken to the Marshal.

He gave her a tiny smile, saying in his broad French accent. 'And I remain in the darkness, and wait for you until it is my time to die.' Malick saw Bee's eyes widen, and she managed a loving smile. She then turned, taking several steps back into the clearing. He didn't know what the Striking was, but it would end in Bee's death.

Three Reapers, each of them wearing masks, surrounded her. Bee turned and waited. Claude encouraged them to start and one by one, the three of them hit her, punching her in the stomach and the face repeatedly, and Bee did not defend herself.

Malick watched Bee sacrifice her life. The fists struck her chest, her breasts and face, and she stumbled back, but she did not fall. He saw a flash of something in their hands, small knives gleamed in the sun, and Bee's skin opened up into red, as they slashed at her skin, not deep, but enough for it to bleed. Malick closed his eyes, hearing his wife groan and whimper as she stumbled around, accepting the punishment, but she did not scream out.

Claude slapped Malick on the shoulder. 'She is quite something, Mr Rose.'

Blood seeped from a cut over Bee's cheek, and then another cut. Blood ran down her face into her blood-filled top and, eventually, she fell into the grass, and the black figures continued their torrent attack.

Two Reapers picked her up as one forced the noose over Bee's head. She struggled, trying to pull it off, and two Reapers kept attacking. The horse pulled away. The branch creaked, and Bee went with it. Her feet ran against the grass, as she held onto the noose and the horse took Bee up into the air.

Karem squeezed Malick's shoulder as he tried to move. He wanted to run, to fight these killers, but he was no match for them, and the horror of seeing his wife being dragged along the ground choked him. And, all the time, Bee rushed through him, comforting him, shielding him from the pain she was experiencing.

Bee hung, her body suspended by the rope in the air, fingers grappling with the noose. The body flared, her legs kicked out, and she twisted, but the knot got tighter.

Malick was inside Bee, and he couldn't breathe. She couldn't hide it; he felt everything. Her panicked state heightening becoming a frenzied need for air, and Bee lost the battle. Her arms dropped to her waist; her body limp.

A single gunshot shattered the silence. The nesting birds burst from the trees, chattering, signalling to each other there was danger below. The shot more precise, severing the rope, and Bee dropped into the grass. Malick's jaw dropped. He couldn't see her. And behind him, he could hear the sounds of hooves galloping toward them.

'Karem, kill that–' Claude didn't turn to the Reaper, and he screamed as the long sharp edge of Karem's sword plunged into his collarbone. He whimpered, seeing the silver bloodied tip pierce through his leather coat. Claude fell to his knees as Karem pushed the sword all the way through until the hilt was at his back and the Reaper stood behind him, holding him up.

Malick stumbled back, shaken, unsure of what was happening. A Reaper killing their master was unheard of, and as an unknown rider had shot Bee from the noose. The three Reapers stood, watching their victim on the ground, and Malick gasped as a blood-soaked Bee rose like a phantom from the grass. The horseman, an older man, potted face, grey hair, large and with a beard, crossed his arms, watching.

Bee kicked the closest Reaper, sending him to the ground. She strode over, taking something from him, a knife and she sunk it into his chest. Bee turned as a second Reaper attacked, she head-butted his helmet and he flew back as Bee jammed the blade into his throat, holding him until he took his last breath. Only the Reaper holding the horse was left. She didn't approach and turned her back on him, and Bee limped slowly toward Malick and Claude, with the dagger in her hand.

Bee stopped in front of Claude, focused on him. She nodded to the Reaper, and Malick cringed, as Karem put her foot to Claude's shoulder and pushed him to the ground, the blade slipping out of the wound, and the man cried. Karem plunged the sword into the ground next to

Claude, turned and dragged Malick away, keeping her hand tight around his arm.

'Bee don't–' Malick started.

'Be quiet, Mr Rose,' the man on the horse said.

'Hello Claude,' Bee whispered, 'you were the last face I saw before I nearly died, it's only fitting you see mine. You will have the death I should have had.'

'You… you… ' mumbled Claude.

She pushed him to the ground, straddling him. Taking the knife Bee sliced him across the neck. Claude screamed, letting out a hysterical sound, making Malick shudder.

Bedelia cut each corner of Claude's lips. She stood, killer and victim stared at each other, and then she kicked Claude between the legs, and he roared in pain.

The man's cheeks split, tearing away from the muscles, and the skull. Blood oozed from the wounds. Tears flowed as he tried speaking, but only gurgles came out. This was what Claude had inflicted on Bee, and Malick remembered.

The way the sand had collected in Bee's blood crusted wounds, the whimpering as they tried to move her. How he and Nadine stared horrified at her beaten and scarred body. The way Bee clasped his hand tightly, trembling. Her terrified eyes locked with Malick's, her breathing raspy, as Nadine sewed together the skin, but Bee never strayed from him.

That was the night Bee gave herself to Malick, not the night they first made love, but that night she'd lain in an unknown bed, surrounded by strangers. She fixed on Malick, saying nothing, but whispering everything, and in that moment, he was lost to Bedelia.

Malick woke from the memory as he heard Bee speak to Claude. 'I will tell you a secret, only the dead know.' And he watched as she sat back on Claude and whispered into his ear, and then Claude screamed.

Bee remained straddled over Claude's body, raised the dagger and plunged it into his chest. The man gave his last cry and then was still.

Malick stayed by the Reaper. A surreal energy filled Malick, his wife straddled a man she'd murdered, two Reapers lay dead, a rope dangled from the dule tree, and the bearded man sat on a horse, while the birds sang as if nothing had happened.

Bee staggered off Claude, dazed. Picking up the hilt of the sword, she wobbled. Raising it above her head, she swung it down, decapitating Claude. Heaving, Bee stood saturated in blood, and she stared at Malick.

'My daughter needs you, Mr Rose,' the man on the horse spoke gruffly.

Startled by the voice, Malick ran to Bee. The sword dropped out of her hand, and she waited, swaying. Bee's face swelled, and her right eye drooped.

'Please...' she whispered, 'Please let me in.' She fell backwards into the ground.

Malick caught Bee. He gathered her into his arms, wiping the blood from her face as blood bubbled from her lips. Bee gasped, wheezing, too tired to move.

Malick wrapped his arms around her. He opened himself up to Bee, caressing her face. Convulsing as her essence crept inside him, snaking around, clinging, and letting him breathe for her. Bee was slow, winding her way around, and that same fearsome seduction Malick had felt the first time they made love sailed through his blood as she cemented herself inside him. Malick choked as Bee became entwined. Her heartbeat slowed, and he heard echoes of, 'I'm sorry.' as Bee became encased inside him.

And then Bee opened up as he pulled her into him, disarming Malick, touching and tasting as she coiled around him, her touch so light, they skimmed each other, barely moving. The tenderness grew, a beguiling intimacy, leaving Malick breathless because Bee was no stranger. And he witnessed the vassal beatings she'd endured, and the murders Bee committed protecting a boy.

He saw every single person Bee had killed. Malick saw her with a Reaper, ordering her to murder two children, and she picked the children, killing them fast. He then saw the executions Bee completed, both alone and with another Reaper, and the name 'Luther' drifted protectively into him.

The memories rushed through Malick, and he was dizzy. Bee was empty and barren of emotion. And she spoke to Luther, only him, and the connection between them, powerful and bloody. A bond, killers have, and they'd whisper to each other, 'If I leave the darkness first, will you walk with me?'

And both would answer, 'Yes.'

A new image flashed as a man climbed over her, and she lay there, empty eyes staring up to the ceiling as Oren completed the Royal Decree, and then Bee had two boys. And he saw her plans to kill Eldric. Malick cried as Bee's abilities detonated, immersing herself within him, and he became the part of a fierce lightning pattern, far-reaching the ends of the earth.

Bee lay on a churned-up beach, her face all torn, eyes vacant, and the sound of grunting interspersed with chattering seabirds. And then Bee's lost eyes stared at Malick, forcing herself not to cry. He watched her life with him, the pleasure he brought Bee, the love for Tristan, and the happiness of Viola. Bee's secrets cascaded out, and Malick saw everything.

He whispered, 'Bee, don't leave me.'

A voice, softly spoken, said, 'Please, Mr Rose, let me take your wife.'

Malick jumped, the man next to him was not the rider on the horse. This was a different man, a Reaper, and Malick recognised the face, older now with scars, but this was the man who Bee had whispered with.

'Are you going to kill her?' he asked.

The man slipped his hands over Malick's, taking hold of Bee. 'No, I'm going to take her somewhere safe.'

Malick nodded, drained, and then he passed out.

Chapter Twenty-Four
Krallar, Kent

Oren stood in the abandoned village of Krallar. A place where ghosts walked, as the decayed cottages without windows or roofs all leaned progressively in the same direction, as the prevailing winds attempted to blow them down.

The cottages, little shops and Temple had turned into driftwood, ready for any incoming tide to take. The shingle drifted with the waters, laying pieces of seaweed at the pebbles as if making some kind of offering. Oren glared at the old Temple, a place destroyed by time and people. There wasn't much left of the grey stone building, a wall with an ancient bell hanging from its tower, moss-covered and bricks stolen, a devastated shell, and the coloured glass, smashed and likely lost to the sea.

He stood alone. The soldiers who rode with him, Oren sent to Almer, ensuring the Overlord would be ready for his arrival. Only one soldier stood guarding the horses, and as the waves slurped up and down the shingles, Oren stared out at The Barricade.

The ridged structure stood in the centre of The Channel, and the black mist shielded any sign of a crack. In the undergrowth, animals rustled, small and hidden from human eyes, and Oren knew then he did not have the strength to seal the Crack. Over the past six years, his abilities had weakened, and Oren had never worried about it until now.

The power he possessed pulsed through his body, allowing it to waken as it flowed, encasing itself around him. This power, this life-affirming capacity, which gave him strength over the people of Britain, was unsteady.

Bedelia was much stronger than he. He believed she'd masked her abilities, and the connection Bee made upon her return confirmed that. No Guardian should be able to disconnect from another. Rufus said it was because she had never gone through The Purge, but Oren thought it was more profound than that. He tasted the salt air, and his heart thumped. Bedelia was something to be afraid of.

Luther hadn't returned. No message came from his lodge to say he'd found her, and Oren guessed he'd been wrong to send Luther. The Reaper would betray his master for the woman he loved. Eldric had then arrived, bringing not only Gable but also Leena. Eldric allowed Oren an hour with Leena, referring to her as 'The Concubine,' and nothing else.

He found Leena in the chambers Gilbert was providing for him, and she was nervous, playing with her hair, moving things around the room, not wanting to stay still.

Gable, Leena informed him, had told her about the new Guardian, and Oren's heart sank. He'd wanted to tell her, perhaps after bedding the woman. Oren's mind flashed back to when he'd had sex with Bedelia. In the beginning, Leena waited outside the room, afraid Bedelia might hurt him, but eventually, Leena couldn't listen anymore and refused to be in their apartment.

'I know Bedelia's back,' Leena whispered.

Oren took a deep breath. 'We've nothing to worry about, Bedelia won't come for us.'

Leena said nothing, her face paled. Something was wrong, and Oren asked her several times before she confessed that she'd ordered Luther to inform Eldric about Bee's plans to assassinate him.

Oren held the bedpost to stop himself collapsing. He'd always assumed somebody else knew, never considering Leena would betray his trust.

'You'll be able to stop her?' Leena asked, fingers twitching, wringing her hands. 'You and Eldric?'

'I won't let her hurt you.' And he'd kissed her forehead before heading to Krallar.

The evening was drawing in, as the sun bowed out, turning the blue sky into fiery reds, and The Barricade looked more impressive than ever. Oren summoned up his abilities, and they breathed into life, sending his head spinning. Colours and energies formed, and he heard The Barricade rumbling, taunting him to seal it, and the red skies turned into darkness.

Oren threw up his arms, out toward the shield. Every piece of power he possessed flowed, the electrical charge splintering in all directions, hitting The Barricade which stood over ten miles away. Oren concentrated on sealing The Crack. Knitting it back together, making this piece of the divide safe from intruders again.

Summoning his strength, Oren bombarded the Crack which hid behind the black mist. He could feel it in there, but as much as he tried, Oren could not blow away the clouds which hid it.

Between his fingers, a static built up, making him grow in confidence as the fire sparked inside him. Unleashing it, the mass flew over the waves, nothing could stop it as it hit The Barricade, and the boom reverberated in all directions, making it hard to think, but as Oren stared at the monster before him, it did not budge, quiver or even fall.

Oren made no impact at all.

The waves lapped at his boots. Stepping back, Oren stumbled. Clambering back toward the guard, exhausted, this small explosion of power had burnt him out. He coughed, struggling for air and the soldier helped him back onto his horse.

It would be a slow ride back to Almer.

***

Rolfen Castle, Rolfen, Kent

Malick sat in an oversized upholstered chair by an open fire. The room was small, hidden away somewhere in the castle. It had little furniture, a drinks cabinet, with two chairs by the fire, and an oak table tucked away, by the large window, where the early evening darkness crept in, and the room was lit up with candles.

There were no banners on the walls signifying the castle in which he sat. Only after he'd woken, bouncing along in the back of an old cart, he'd learned they were heading toward Rolfen Castle, Bedelia's childhood home.

Malick had held Bee in his arms as the horses galloped across the land, and the day turned into dusk. She remained inside him, creeping about, exposing him to herself, refusing to let go. He'd wiped the blood from Bee's face, watching the forest turn into open green spaces, a few broken houses, more trees then more green spaces, until they ended up in the castle.

The bearded man and the Reaper did not introduce themselves. Instead, they concentrated on the road. Karem, who'd stabbed Claude, and a boy called Adam, rode in the back, along with the Reaper Bedelia had spared. Once inside the castle, Luther carried Bee up the stone steps and inside the fort.

Another man said his name was Sagan and took Malick inside, ordering a servant to clean him up. Malick demanded to see Bee, but Lord Sagan told him the healers would look after her, and the maid took him to a bed-chamber, stripped him, and ordered him to step inside a copper bath, then she washed him down.

Malick was uncomfortable having somebody else bathe him. Nadine had never washed him. This was something only Bee did for him, and he'd do the same for her. They'd spend time rediscovering each other, without the disruption of children.

And Malick missed Bee's touch.

The maid dressed him and placed hot food on the table. Once he'd eaten, the servant ushered him into this back room. A place for secret meetings Malick thought, and he studied the Reaper by the door. The man in the black uniform was tall, pale skinned, scarred with a short bowl hairstyle cut close to his head.

Luther stood rigid, eyes forward, silent. The man Bee had spent years in Britain with, and they'd existed in a world that Malick did not understand. Fleeting thoughts crossed Malick, of this man holding Bee in the quiet moments. He'd seen them sleep in the same bed, her body moulded into Luther's and his arm wrapped protectively around her. There were flashes of Luther smiling as Bee placed his hand onto her swollen belly, letting him feel the baby kick. Malick closed his eyes, not wanting to be jealous because Luther would never escape that world. Luther would never have children or a wife because if a Reaper did retire, they promised celibacy.

Bee had not kept that promise, and married him.

'Thank you, Mr Rose.'

Spooked by Luther, Malick stuttered, 'Thank you… for what?'

'Coming for Bee,' Luther answered.

Malick said nothing. He didn't have any words. He wanted to go find his wife, to check on Bee, but he sat in a room with the man whom Bee had killed with. Malick's skin prickled, thinking about it and he stood facing Luther.

'I was twelve when I met Bee. She was eight, and she appeared like a ghost to save me. She was a vassal, and she killed two Reapers. The punishment was to become a Reaper. We became each other's Unseen.'

Malick remembered Bee had used that word when he'd learned she was a Reaper, and Somer said the Marshal asked if she had one, but he didn't know what it meant. He approached Luther. They were almost the same height. Malick asked, 'What's an Unseen?'

Luther looked dispassionately at Malick. 'If we are fatally wounded during the issue of a warrant, we will kill each other.'

Malick couldn't speak, and his chest tightened. Bee had made a murder pact. 'I see,' he managed.

Outside the door, the sound of running footsteps, and little voices shouted. Squeals of laughter and the door burst open. A little girl, no older than seven, ran in. She stopped, realising she shouldn't be in the room, followed by Tristan, and then a younger girl. All three panted, and the two girls dressed in breeches looked nervously at the strangers in the room.

'Papa!' Tristan yelled, running to Malick.

Surprised to see his son, Malick gathered the boy in his arms, and gave him a kiss and cuddle, telling Tristan that he loved him. Malick took Tristan back to the chair by the fire, sat down and stood the boy opposite him. The two girls followed.

'Is Uncle Somer here?'

The boy nodded.

'Are you being looked after by these two lovely young ladies?' Malick gave the two girls a wink as Tristan blushed. 'And are you going to introduce me?'

Neither girl waited. 'My name is Adeen Edith Kendal, and this is my little sister –'

'Zoe Faith,' the young girl said proudly.

Malick looked at Adeen, and the name Edith struck a memory. This was the name Bee would have called her daughter had they had allowed her to keep the girl. Adeen had auburn hair and the same eyes, and Malick smiled at her.

'I'm Malick Rose, and I would like to thank you both for looking after my son,' he said, his French accent noticeable.

Both girls put their hands to their mouths, giggling, and Adeen said, 'You talk funny.'

'Do I?' Malick asked, smiling. 'That's because I don't live around here.' He considered it wiser not to say he was French, though he suspected Tristan would have already told them.

'Did you find Mamma?' Tristan asked quietly.

Malick gathered Tristan onto his knee. 'She's resting, so we can't see her. You'll be the first person she'll want to see when she wakes up.'

The boy smiled.

'Adeen, Zoe, Tristan,' a woman's voice called out from the hallway. She entered, saw the three children, Luther behind the door and Malick holding his son, and she flustered. 'I'm sorry, Mr Rose, you know how children are, like herding wild cats.'

Malick got up, seeing more of Zoe in Faith than Adeen. She had the same olive skin, dark hair and small face. Malick thanked her for looking after Tristan, explaining how happy Bee would be to know her son was safe. He spotted a flicker of worry crossed the woman's face at the mention of Bee's name.

Sagan and the man from the cart walked into the room. Surprise touched Sagan's features at seeing the children, and he ignored them, crossing the room to shake hands with Malick.

'Mr Rose, we need to talk, you want to see your son and Bedelia, but would it be acceptable that Faith looks after him a little longer? And she'll put him to bed with the girls?'

Malick didn't want to be parted from Tristan, but the boy grinned, and Malick suspected it was due to being allowed to stay up a little later than his usual bedtime. He nodded, gave Tristan a kiss, and wished all the children good night, as the girls giggled about his accent.

Luther closed the door on the children and Faith, and remained by the door. Sagan went over to the drinks cabinet, pulled out three glasses, filling them with brandy and handed them out.

'This is Bee's father, Rufus McKay.'

The man had a tight handshake. Malick noted, Rufus was gruff, mean-looking and roughly dressed, and he recalled the way Bee spoke about her father.

'I'm taking Bee home as soon as she's ready,' Malick stated.

'If Bee goes home now, you're all in danger. She has to kill Eldric, otherwise he'll keep sending Reapers until they kill her, and most likely your children,' Rufus stated bluntly.

Malick nodded, holding his brandy. 'And if she kills him, then what? Oren is on the throne?'

Sagan looked into his brandy glass, shifting from foot to foot. 'She has to kill him too.'

'Why?'

Rufus answered this time. 'Because she is a threat, if he sits on the throne.'

Malick looked between the men, already guessing the answer to his next question. 'And if she kills both Guardians?'

'She takes the throne,' Sagan answered.

Malick closed his eyes, already knowing what Bee would say. 'That's a rather simplistic outcome.'

'She has to take the –'

'That is not an option, find somebody else.'

'There is nobody else,' Sagan pointed out.

Malick slammed his glass on the large table. 'I said 'no'.'

Both men jumped, not expecting Malick's sharp outburst. Sagan's brows furrowed. 'As her Overlord, she'll do as I order.'

Malick gave him a half smile and stepped up to the Overlord. 'The moment Bee was dead on the beach she wasn't property.' He paused, and then said, 'Now I would like to see my wife.' He stepped toward the door.

'I don't think you under –' Sagan began.

'I understand very well, Lord Sagan.' Malick stepped back toward Sagan, neither Rufus or Luther stopped him. 'She's a vassal, a Reaper and, when it suited, a Guardian. She will not become your new Lord Guardian.' His accent got broader. 'Now take me to my wife.'

Rufus stepped in, grabbing Malick's arm. 'Mr Rose, my daughter has im –'

Malick shook his arm free. He glared at Rufus. 'Bedelia, now!'

***

The water was up to Bee's knees. The bathwater hot enough to warm her whole body, and the servant stood in the corner of the bed chambers. The room had a bed, a chest of drawers, mirrors and washbasin. Paintings were hanging from the stone walls, but Bee hadn't noticed what they were. The wood crackled in the fireplace, and Bee drifted from this world into another, imagining she was at home, with Malick, the children and Esther.

The healers had come in, dressed the wounds and cleaned her. Bee's face was swollen, as fresh bruises ballooned over the old ones, and the cuts had been sealed. There was a knock at the door, it creaked, and Bee recognised the low tones of Malick asking the servant to leave. Bee kept her head on her knees, listening, as Malick removed his boots. She did nothing, as he approached the vanity stand, and took the jug.

He rolled up his sleeves, kneeled down, and dipped the jug, gently pouring the water down her neck and over her back. His touch charged through Bee. She warmed as Malick swished the water over her hair, his hand touching her skin, moving over the contours of her body. She didn't want to be anywhere else, and he repeated this action over and over. Everything blurred, and Bee hummed. She didn't think she'd ever experienced this moment of emptiness, and Bee calmed, glad Malick had come for her.

'Is Tristan here? Is he safe?' she asked. 'I want to see him.'

Malick sloshed the water over Bee. 'You can see him in the morning.'

Bee kept her head on her knees. She whispered, 'The bullet wound on my shoulder, my father gave me. I was twelve, training in the courtyard just outside. He came up, ordered Luther to repeatedly hit me, and then father pulled his revolver, placed it into Luther's hand and ordered him to shoot me. Luther followed the order.'

Malick listened, swishing the water over her.

'Father told me, he did it because he didn't want the Overlord to see our friendship.'

'And why don't you use your abilities?' He poured another jug of water over her.

'These abilities don't belong here, they never have.'

'When you shot me, I was cold, and you sheltered me. You wrapped yourself inside me, and I saw... the pain you suffered, so that I didn't have to.'

Bee jerked; her body tensed. The water splashed.

Malick caressed her back. 'It's okay,' he soothed, 'it's okay.'

Bee shifted in the bath. She looked up at him, putting her fingers lightly to his lips, and she shakily tapped his face, whispering, 'I shouldn't have done it. I saw the message in your eyes... that same message all people who are about to die have, and I still pulled the trigger.'

He took her hand, kissed her palm. 'Claude told me what he did to you on the beach.'

Bee's face hardened. 'I was a prisoner, I may have been a Reaper, but people still did what they wanted... until I met you.'

'I knew I'd marry you. It didn't matter that I was married to Nadine, or that she was expecting Tristan. You were going to be my wife.'

'And if Nadine hadn't passed away?'

Malick hinted a smile. He found a sponge, soaked it, and bathed her skin. 'Then the scandal would have been far greater than marrying you only after two months of Nadine's passing.'

Bee's voice became small. 'You scared me. So unlike anybody I knew, unless I was to execute you. I don't get scared, but when I clasped your hand as Nadine sewed me up, something inside woke up. I tried losing myself, but I kept finding my way back to you.'

Malick listened as he washed her.

Bee laid her head back on her knees, watching Malick. 'Winnie calls them Sinners, but they've been with me since birth. I can't reach them, it's like I can see them through the glass, and I need Winnie to break it down. They showed Eldric, and all the previous Lord Guardians are the same being.

'Eldric wants male heirs, so he can infuse himself into the physical body of the baby, killing its soul, he's being reborn. That's why he forced Oren on me, so he could have male heirs, not so the bloodline might continue, but that he could carry on living. If I can kill him, we can go home,' she said dreamily, 'and I can hold Viola again, I miss my baby girl.'

Malick stopped soaking the sponge. 'That's the first time you've mentioned Viola.'

'She's happy, and I sense Esther is happy through Viola,' she whispered.

'I don't like the sound of that. One of Omega's men, a young man called Stephen is guarding her.' He rose from the wet floor. 'Come on, let's get you out of the water.'

Bee slipped her hands into his, he gently pulled her up as she stood in the bath, and the water dripped from her naked body. Seeing his green eyes, and those striking defined French features, she reached out, stroking his stubble. Soon Malick would have a beard, and she gave him a weak smile.

'When you go to sleep, when I hold you in our bed, do the dead come to you?' Malick asked, standing inches away from Bee.

She nodded. 'Yes, they come.'

'Do they forgive you?'

Bee stared. 'I don't ask. I know what I've done.'

'You know, Bee, those things you've done to those bodies, to that priest, is something truly frightening,' Malick whispered.

Bee's heart jumped and she defended herself. 'I'm not normal, Malick.'

'You never were, Bee.' He smiled, tenderly touching Bee's skin. Fingers rippled over the scars around her neck, the new rope burn, and then he touched the bullet wound scar. A lumpy mass of skin, he'd seen, touched and kissed many times, and Bee warmed, allowing him to relearn her body all over again.

He took a dressing gown and wrapped it around Bee. She was small, frightened, shivering, and Bee whispered, 'Those children, Hamish and Oliver, I feel numb, I don't know how to feel.'

Taking Bee towards the bed, Malick pulled the blankets back. Bee's hand tightened, she didn't want to let go, as he placed her under the covers. Reaching inside his pocket, he found what he was looking for, having taken it from his own clothes before the maid undressed him. He slipped fully clothed under the blanket with Bee, drawing it over them.

They lay eye to eye on the pillows, Bee warmed as he caressed her face. 'I've done terrible things, Malick.'

'I know,' he whispered.

'I'm a monster lurking just outside of your vision. Before this is over, I'm going to do more things, and I'm going to frighten you away.'

'Bedelia Rose, you are a vicious nightmare, but it has to be all of you. You can't hide, anymore,' he whispered, placing Bee's wedding ring back onto her finger, kissing her hand. And then Bee kissed Malick, never wanting to let go.

Chapter Twenty-Five
Rolfen Castle, Rolfen, Kent

Bee sat in the courtyard, with Tristan on her knees. It was early, and the yard was full of noises as the cattle and goats were waking, demanding their feed. The workers had already fed the animals, but they wanted more.

Voices shouted as the servants started their day, and delicious smells wafted out of the tiny windows. Somer sat with her and Malick at the table. He said nothing to Bee and carried on eating the breakfast he'd taken from the kitchen. It was a beautiful morning, better to sit outside, and Bee acknowledged him with a nod and nothing more. The smells were familiar to Bee, but as a child she'd never had the chance to eat any of it. If she had, she would have been whipped.

Bee held onto Tristan, afraid to let go. She'd spent the night in Malick's arms, and she was safe as he pulled the covers over both of them, kissing her. She listened in the quiet of the chamber, as the fire crackled, while Malick explained what had happened to Hamish and Oliver.

Claude had been sleeping with Gable, and he murdered those children because Gable and Leena wanted it. Bee kept quiet, and then she put that sorrow and hurt with the rest, locking it away.

Now she had to concentrate on Tristan.

Bee explained as gently as she could that she wasn't Tristan's natural mother. She'd been honest, telling him how Nadine passed away, and Nadine loved him because during her last days he was all she thought about. Tristan asked many questions, including why her face was so bruised, but the most important was whether Bee loved him.

'I loved you the moment your mother couldn't put you in her arms. I became her love, and through me she can still love you, do you understand?' Bee asked.

He nodded, but Bee wasn't convinced, and she took something out of her dress pocket. 'This is the silhouette of your mother.' Bee handed it to Tristan. 'I couldn't bring you with me, so I brought this. This image connects me to you, and I needed you.'

'Was she pretty like you, Mamma?'

Bee grinned, hugging him. 'Oh... she was much prettier, and a lady, not like me. When you were a baby, I'd hold this and tell her about you. She knows I love you.'

'You won't leave me, Viola, Esther, and Papa again?' he asked, as he sat on her knee.

She shook her head, kissing him. 'Never again.' And then she saw him. The only man who'd ever mattered to her before Malick.

Luther walked out of the barracks toward his horse.

Dressed in the black uniform, Luther had the same short bowl cut, and the same severe expression Bee remembered. He'd aged and new scars were evident on his face. Bee knew every inch of Luther. Both had fresh wounds, and neither could hide them from each other.

Luther didn't notice Bee sitting at the table as he kept his eyes forward, concentrating on his horse, already saddled by an apprentice earlier. He patted the horse, checked the girth, and took the reins. Two more Reapers walked out of the barracks, Karem and the Reaper called Thomas, whom Bee let go. And then Luther turned and saw Bee.

Bee's heart stopped. She whispered to Tristan to go to his father and turned to Malick. Bee saw his face muscles tighten and, as Tristan sat next to Malick, he gave Bee an awkward smile, nodding that she should go.

Rising from the table, Bee inhaled. Her legs wobbled. She hadn't seen this man in six years, and now she was somebody new. She'd wanted this for so long, but Bee didn't know what to do or say.

Her hands shook, clasping them together. She focused on Luther, and he remained by the horse, as the two Reapers mounted their horses, waiting. Bee approached, her long slim dress dragged, but she didn't care, she wanted to touch Luther, to see the man she'd left at the Tower.

Luther dropped the reins. He headed toward her, and Bee wanted to run, to throw her arms around him, and give him the biggest hug. To thank him for finding Tristan and saving her, but most of all, she wanted to hold him to know Luther was real. They stopped, inches apart, Luther's brown eyes bored into hers.

He touched Bee's face, gently feeling the scars across her cheeks. Luther whispered, 'Bedelia, you should have stayed dead.' He turned away.

Bee stood frozen in the muddy courtyard, watching Luther get on his horse. He looked down from his mount, anger etched into his face. Bee couldn't move, as her insides caved in. He'd crushed everything in one short sentence. Luther spurred the horse, making the animal move, and through the castle gate he went, leaving Bee alone, standing there.

Bee watched him disappear into the distance. The voices of the workers filtered through as shouts, laughter, and dogs barked. They were filling the void where Luther should have been in front of Bee, talking. Everything mixed up inside, as Luther's words cut deep. Should Bee have stayed away? She didn't understand as their friendship had been the only thing which had mattered since she was eight years old, and now it was nothing.

Malick slipped his hands into hers, clasping them. 'Perhaps he just needs a bit of time.'

She looked up, despondent, mouth moving, but words refused to come out. Bee nodded hastily, keeping her gaze fixed on Malick as he nodded back, holding her hands.

'Please, Mrs Rose, you and your husband are to go to the Grand Hall.' A young valet, no older than ten stood before them. 'Your son will be looked after by Lady Kendal.'

Bee turned; Tristan was already playing with two young girls. She didn't want to leave him, but Malick pulled her to go. Bee watched Tristan running around, his laughter sounded happy. The two girls ran around him, both giggling and playing in the mud.

Then she spotted it, the girl looked like Oren, and Bee's smile faded. Her legs gave way, and Malick caught her as the little girl with the auburn red hair danced around Tristan, tagging him and then her younger sister. Malick blocked Bee's view, shaking his head as she peered around, watching the girl she'd given birth to, play with Tristan.

***

Bee sat in the Grand Hall. This room she'd been in many times. The vibrant floral wall hangings, the tapestries and the paintings still hung in the same places. Nothing had changed since she'd left when she was twenty-two.

This was the room where Sagan's father, Fredrick Kendal, would issue his death warrants. Bee had stood here many times, accepting the declarations and then returning a few hours later with evidence they had been completed.

Sometimes it was nothing more than a signature on the paper, the offender acknowledging they were to die. Mostly, Fredrick wanted the head as evidence, and she would return with a bloody bag and hand it back to the Overlord. He would place it on a spike for all to see, just outside the castle walls. Fredrick prided himself on being merciful with his subjects, and that was how he showed them mercy.

Malick and Somer sat between Bee, and she made no contact with Somer, preferring the silence. On the other side sat Lord Sagan and her father, Rufus McKay, and Bee acknowledged both with a nod.

Bee played with the material of her dress, not looking at Rufus. He'd aged, his hair grey, and put on some weight around his belly, and Bee noted the twitch in his pitted face. The man was angry.

'Where's Feargal?' Bee kept her hands in her lap.

'The young man is under house arrest. I didn't want him going back to Deman Circe,' Sagan explained.

'And Adam?'

Sagan answered, 'I've put him into service.'

Bee's face darkened. Memories flooded, and she shivered thinking about when she was a vassal. 'No, the boy comes home with me.'

'Bee,' Malick murmured, touching her arm, shaking his head. 'We can't afford to feed another mouth.'

Rufus gave a gruff laugh, folding his arms, he said, 'Typical Bee, always picking up strays along the way.'

'And what does that mean, Father?' she turned toward Rufus, waiting for an answer.

Rufus stared straight at Bee. 'You picked up Luther when you should have let him die. You've saddled yourself with a widower and his son, and now you want to take another stray back with you.'

'Tell me, Father, what do you think I've been doing? Murdering my way around France?' Bee snapped.

'It would've been better than shackling yourself to a man who only married you because he needed a skivvy to bring up his son. Look at yourself, Bedelia, a scarred body and mangled face. No man wants to look at that... ' then Rufus raged, '...you should have been preparing for this.'

Bee's blood rose. 'Rufus, you are–'

Malick cut in. 'Mr McKay, don't pretend to know why I married your daughter. None of us are here out of choice. If that Crack hadn't appeared, we wouldn't be here. Bee is not one of your Reapers anymore, so don't think you can order her into doing what you want.'

'I spent years training Bee, and you think that because you've been fucking her for the past six years that gives you certain rights?' Rufus's face turned red. 'I made her into a weapon, Mr Rose, not a housewife.'

'Bedelia is not a weapon, Mr McKay.' Malick's French accent became broader. 'Don't forget that.'

'Mr Rose, for–' Rufus started.

Bee stood. 'Father, please, I've come back so let's get this finished and I can go home, and be away from you.'

Sagan interrupted, 'Rufus, Bee, this isn't helping. Apologies, Mr Rose, Bee please sit down.'

'I hope he makes you happy, Bee,' Rufus glared at Malick, 'because the man looks a little soft to me, and you're going to need him.'

'Malick's not a killer if that's what you mean,' Bee snapped.

Rufus, a large man, flew around the table, heading toward Bee. He pulled her chair back, facing him. 'I did everything for your own good, you're my daughter, and I kept you away from Eldric.'

Bee touched his pitted face. 'I was just a little girl. I wanted your love.'

Rufus nodded. 'The things you told me, the things you'd whispered in your half-dead state, everything I did was to ready you for now.'

Bee became a child again. Inside, her stomach churned, and the memories flushed around. She remembered the door to her home. A door she'd opened thousands of times and that door let the memories flood out.

The three rooms had a kitchen with two old chairs, two bedrooms, and a belt. Until Bee was eight, Rufus made her sleep on the floor in the kitchen with a rag, and she cleaned the courtyard after the apprentices had completed their day's training.

Once Bee became a student, Rufus gave her a room, but he'd still beat her. The belt appeared if Bee failed in weaponry, and Rufus forced her to stand for hours after he'd lashed her.

Rufus would occasionally whisper into her ear the same words. 'Concentrate and listen.' She'd believed Rufus meant about learning to be a Reaper, but then she understood. He wanted her to connect with her abilities and, in the quiet, she transferred into the other world, and The Spectres came for her.

She would sit in the twilight place between her and them. She couldn't touch them, but they spoke, and she learned of the dark places they existed in, and she became their light in the gloom.

Sagan clanked five beakers onto the table and brought Bee back. He poured out the brown hoppy liquid and placed it before each person. 'Well, now we've got the family greetings out of the way, can we carry on?' Everybody took a jug and looked into their drink.

Rufus asked after a minute. 'And how do you intend to kill Eldric?'

She answered honestly. 'As yet, I am unsure.'

Rufus barked, 'Bedelia, you start all this and don't even have a plan.'

'Father, it happened fast, all too fucking fast,' she whispered. 'I don't want to be here, and I've no *fucking* idea what I'm doing,' Bee said, and the room became tense.

Sagan cut in. 'Eldric is at Dai, he's brought Gable and Leena.'

Bee darkened, hearing the names of the two women responsible for the murder of Hamish and Oliver. She blinked, shifted in her chair, pausing, she said, 'I need to find Winnie Harper, the other Guardian. Omega, a Skin Trader, has her. Winnie's the one who can help me stop all of this.'

'You don't need this Winnie, Bedelia,' Rufus said.

She breathed out. 'Winnie and this...this Omega, they're my sisters. Perhaps I can convince Omega to help bring down that Barricade.'

Malick squeezed Bee's hand. 'Omega will never help.'

'Bee, you don't need either of them. You are not connected to Eldric.' Rufus's voice softened.

'But I think it's the only way.'

'When you meditated, you told me about The Spectres, do you remember?' Rufus asked.

'I remember you'd beat me if I didn't do it right,' she whispered.

'And that made you tough because you hid those abilities, even when I took the belt to your back. You don't feed off people. You are more powerful, and you don't need this Winnie girl to bring down that wall.'

Bee frowned. 'I wouldn't have made it through without her. I promised I'd find her.'

Rufus shook his head. 'Bedelia, you still don't understand, Winnie does not make you more powerful. Your husband does.' He looked at Malick.

'What–' Malick started.

'I had to protect you,' Rufus ignored Malick, '...and the only way to do that was to make you a Reaper. When you handed me that head, your eyes were that black void and I knew what you were, but a Guardian's eyes turn white. You were different.'

Bee listened, aware Malick and Somer were next to her, but she remained silent, wanting to hear Rufus speak honestly to her.

'I left you in that dungeon for three months, expecting Eldric to come. He didn't know you existed, and I convinced Lord Kendal to train you because I guessed you weren't connected.' Rufus turned and looked at Malick, his face wrinkling as he studied the man. 'Mr Rose, my daughter, has imprinted herself onto you, Guardians can't do that anymore, and certainly not with commoners. You make her more powerful, and that makes *you* dangerous.'

'Bee?' Malick looked quizzically at her.

She didn't look at him, her heart beat faster. 'I'm... I'm sorry, Malick... I... I –' and he squeezed her hand, rubbing her wedding ring finger.

Somer asked, breaking the unease. 'What's imprinting?'

'Guardians lost the ability to imprint on another Guardian about six generations ago. They would do this to become more powerful, transferring their abilities. They couldn't do it anymore, and the Lord Guardian, called...' He looked up, trying to remember the name. 'Guardian Jandro started The Purge, forcing his subjects to walk through the coals, it means the people feed the Guardians with their lives, they just don't know it.'

'What does that mean?' Somer carried on questioning.

Rufus huffed, blowing out air. 'It means your friend has some of the same abilities as Bee, and he can strengthen her.' He looked at Malick. 'You have to go with her to Dai.'

'What? No, I don't want him coming.' Bee rose from her chair, shaking her head. 'He's... Malick's not like me... he's not...'

'You did this, Bee,' Rufus breathed. 'You chose him. He can protect you.'

Malick took hold of Bee's hand. She paled as he whispered, 'It's okay, I'll come with you.'

'But...' she slumped back into her chair. 'I didn't want you to see me.'

'After what we've seen you do,' Somer interrupted, 'how can it get any worse?'

'Be quiet, Somer,' Malick retorted, keeping his eyes on Bee.

'Just don't get killed, Bee, and you, Malick, keep my daughter safe,' Rufus gruffly muttered.

'You'll have to kill both Eldric and Oren.' Sagan regained control of the table. 'I've a boat prepared to take Mr Peron and Tristan back through one gap, and they can take Adam.'

'Why do I need to kill Oren?' Bee frowned.

'Because no Guardian connected to Eldric through The Purge should become Lord Guardian.' Sagan chewed his lips after completing the sentence, and he turned from the table.

Silence filled the banquet room. The echoes of Sagan's last words hung within the stone walls, and Bee repeated them methodically to herself, and then she completely understood what Sagan was asking of her.

Sagan whispered, watching Bee. 'The people of Britain may not follow a Guardian who went through The Purge, but they might accept somebody of his bloodline.'

Bee looked up and stated harshly, 'And you expect them to follow the person who put a blade through his brain?'

'There is nobody else, Bedelia,' Sagan told her.

Bee rose from the chair, shaking her head. 'There is always somebody else, Lord Sagan. I'll kill Eldric and Oren if I have to, and take down The Barricade.' She shrugged her shoulders, looking down at Malick, giving him a tiny smile. 'After that, I'm going home.' Then she turned to Sagan. 'I'm not your leader, I'm your executioner.'

Chapter Twenty-Six
Almer Castle, Almer, Kent

To get to Almer from Dai, there was one of two ways along the coast, traipsing the shore at low tide, or navigating Dai's famous white cliffs. Overlord Norton Vickers learned that Eldric and his entourage were coming via the cliff paths.

He panicked when the message arrived that Lord Guardian Eldric would be there within the hour and the household turned to chaos. He shouted at the vassals, growled at soldiers, and screamed at women or children, who didn't appear to be working, that the Lord Guardian was coming.

Overlord Norton Vickers was a fat man in his forties who'd grown wealthy on the coal dug out of the ground and, unknown to Eldric, he'd also profited from smuggling people through the Barricade.

Once Eldric arrived, his men set their camp. Fifteen tents lined the green near the pebble beach, outside the walls of the castle. The concentric castle was insignificant, comprising of six inner and outer bastions and the Keep, built on the flats of Almer, and it didn't dominate the skyline. The castle was built to defend the English Channel from a long-forgotten invader.

The Lord Guardian had ridden with four Reapers and ten soldiers through the gate and into Norton Vickers's courtyard. The grooms quickly took charge of the horses, as the servants and vassals all stopped their work, lined up, waiting for their living God. Norton spotted something disturbing at the end of the procession.

A gibbet fastened to a cart came through the gates. Flames sprang out of the iron casing, and inside, Norton saw the body of an old man. The man was being slowly burned, and Norton shivered as the demonic howls came from the man's mouth, and the sweet roasting smell of flesh wafted around the courtyard. Norton stared at the ghoulish spectacle, becoming light-headed at witnessing the horror.

The Overlord managed to recompose himself, waddled up to Eldric's horse, and got down on one knee, keeping his head to the ground. 'Lord Guardian, the town of Almer welcomes you.'

'Get up, Norton, you look like a fat turd waiting to be stood on,' Eldric grunted, dismounting the horse and throwing the reins at a young valet.

Norton struggled to get off his knee, he didn't brush himself down, worried, he might not be able to keep up as Eldric headed toward the keep.

'My soldiers' camp is outside, and I assume my chambers are ready?' Eldric questioned.

Norton tried not to look at the man on fire, but the terrifying display stumped him, and he nodded. 'Yes, of course, everything is prepared. Oren is at Krallar, he's looking at The Crack.'

Eldric stepped closer to Norton. 'Why did it take a year to find this crack?'

Norton's heart raced. 'We...our boats rarely sail that close to The Barricade, Lord Guardian.' He pulled a handkerchief from his inside pocket, mopping his brow.

'My subjects disappear along these shorelines, and you don't notice?' Eldric sneered.

Norton closed his eyes. 'Townsfolk are a superstitious lot, they're afraid, thinking it was something supernatural taking them.'

Eldric grabbed Norton by the throat. Norton gasped, his hands pulling at the Guardian's, gagging for air, and Eldric tightened his grip as he picked the man up and walked with him, slamming him against the stone wall of the Keep.

'Then you should have informed me,' he shouted, letting the man go.

Norton fell to his knees, choking. 'Yes...yes, Lord Guardian.' He pulled the collar of his shirt, slowing his breathing down.

'If I find out you've anything to do with The Crack, you'll end up like poor Rupert here.' Eldric pointed to the gibbet. 'He lied to me and, for the next year, he'll die every day.' And he stormed past Norton, pushing him into the ground as he entered the Keep.

Norton stared at the fiery gibbet. Rupert, he couldn't recall the man at first, and then his heart almost gave way, as he realised Rupert was Eldric's personal valet and had been for many years. The Overlord shivered, wondering what crime the valet had committed to earn this punishment.

Pulling himself up from the mud, Norton smartened himself up, tidying his collar. He noticed some of his serfs watching him, and he growled, 'Get back to your work, otherwise I'll have you all whipped!'

***

Rolfen Castle, Rolfen, Kent

Bee stroked the horse. Three horses were saddled and waiting. Malick was coming with her, but Bee's heart sank seeing Somer walking out with Malick. He had new clothes, a different coat, and it looked like he was coming with them.

She wore the black Reaper uniform. Both belts crisscrossed her waist, and the stable boy had fastened several weapons to her horse. Bee watched the activity of the workers, lots of them walking about, carrying baskets with food, or pieces of meat. Men dressed in breeches, and the woman in long dresses, all keeping the castle running.

'What are you doing here, Somer?' she asked coldly.

'Bee, I never knew about the things you did for Tristan, for Nadine. She knew Malick was in love with you and she was surprised you never noticed....' Somer stuttered. 'I'm trying to say 'sorry', and I'm coming with you.'

She glared. 'I'd prefer it that you didn't.'

Malick cut in, 'Bee, Somer is trying to apologise.'

Bee shook her head. She stepped up to Somer, having to look up as he was tall. 'Those people with Omega, are they friends? Because I will kill them if I don't get Winnie.

Can you live knowing that I will leave children orphans?' Her voice frosty.

'Look–' he started.

'Stay away from me, Somer,' Bee snapped.

Malick grabbed Bee's arm, squeezing it as he dragged her away. 'You need to forgive Somer.' His face inches away from Bee, and he pointed his finger at her. 'I'll say this only once, and I promise I'll never say it again, but you shot me, Bee. I could've accepted what you said in the woods, but I didn't because I love you and I'm prepared to see whatever horrors you bring. You've put Somer through a lot of shit, so accept his apology.'

Bee kept her eye on Malick's finger, as he jabbed it, and Bee felt like Tristan, being told off for misbehaving. Malick was right, that she should accept his apology but a piece of Bee didn't want to.

She approached Somer, Bee muttered, 'I'm sorry.'

Malick stood next to Bee, slipping his arm around her waist, he pinched her. 'Say it properly, Bedelia.'

'I'm sorry for everything I've put you through, Somer,' Bee said clearly, but she didn't smile. 'And that I threatened to kill you.'

Somer nodded. 'That's okay, and I'm sorry too.'

'Mrs Rose,' a woman called.

Bee turned, seeing Faith, walking with Tristan and her two girls across the courtyard. Tristan ran to Bee, wanting a cuddle, and he insisted on introducing Adeen and Zoe to her as Faith stood over all three children, watching.

'It's a pleasure to meet you both. Tristan has told me a lot about you.' Bee smiled at both girls, but she kept an eye on Adeen, watching the way the child swayed as she listened. Bee looked to Faith, and the woman nodded.

Bee, in her Reaper uniform, got to her knees and extended her hand to Zoe, telling her how lucky Tristan was to find two lovely girls to play with. She felt Malick's presence behind her, and Bee extended her hand to Adeen.

'I understand you are called Adeen Edith, that's a beautiful name.' Bee let the girl slip her hand into hers and Bee shook it, her heart pounding against her chest. This girl was her daughter, Bee never dreamed she'd see her, and now that she was inches away, all she wanted to do was look at the child. The auburn hair was the same as Bee's, and she noticed the same bone structure and brown eyes Oren had.

'If you're a Reaper, how come you're a mummy?' Adeen asked.

Bee looked at her uniform, then to Faith, and she smiled at Adeen. 'Because I was able to leave, that allowed me to have Tristan and his sister, Viola.'

'How did you get your scars?' Zoe piped up.

'I got them because I wasn't always lucky,' she whispered.

'They don't hurt anymore do they, Mamma?' Tristan wanted to be a part of the conversation, and Bee shook her head.

'Can I touch them?' Adeen asked.

Bee froze. She looked at Faith as Adeen reached out with her little hand, touching the scars. Bee closed her eyes, allowing the girl, her daughter, to caress her face. Bee tingled, thrilled to have this moment because this would be the only time she would be close to her child.

Adeen traced her fingers around Bee's scarred smile, and Bee burst with happiness. Her heart sang. Bee had to do everything in her power to stop grabbing hold of Adeen and wrapping her arms around the girl and giving her a kiss. The gentle touch seemed to last forever. Bee took the touch, memorised it, and stored it with everything she cherished about Tristan and Viola. This memory would be the only thing she would have of her daughter.

'Bee, I think we should go,' Malick said, still standing behind her.

'Come along girls, let Tristan give his Mamma a kiss and I'll get you all some chocolate,' Faith suggested, and the girls squealed at the thought of chocolate.

Tristan hugged Bee. 'I love you, Mamma.'

Bee kept hold, feeling his hands all over her, and she kissed him on the cheeks. 'Now I don't want to hear you've been naughty for Lady Faith when we come back.'

Tristan nodded, hugging Malick before running off with the two girls, and Bee watched all three of them running excitely toward the Keep steps. Bee stood up and looked at Faith.

'Thank you,' Bee whispered.

Faith pursed her lips, wringing her hands. 'You need to go, Bedelia.'

Bee took Faith's hand, she felt the woman tense, and Bee said, 'Lady Faith, I'm glad you're Adeen's mother.'

'And your son loves you very much, Bee.' Faith clasped Bee's hand and smiled.

***

Almer Castle, Almer, Kent

Eldric ate a large lunch, full of different hams, quail and goose eggs, along with various slices of bread and many sweet cakes, all at Norton's expense. Eldric laughed, smiled, and licked his fingers as he ate the multiple dishes, all the time watching Norton as the man mopped his brow, nervous, and Eldric made the Overlord sit through every single meal.

He then ordered the kitchen to make up a Royal hamper for a late supper, because after he'd sealed The Crack, he'd need something to eat. Eldric ordered Norton to have a platoon of thirty men readied in one hour. They would accompany him to Krallar to meet Oren and, to his surprise, the Overlord prepared them in thirty minutes.

He'd had enough of Norton the moment the man opened his mouth. The Overlord was lying, Eldric didn't need his abilities to tell him that. The panic in the man's face said enough, and he wondered how long Norton had been sending people through the gap, and into the hands of whoever wanted them on the other side.

Norton had grown wealthy out of smuggling, and Eldric would make an example of him. He would send a proclamation out that anybody involved in sending people across the Channel would hang.

It was late afternoon when Eldric and the soldiers rode into Krallar. The empty village was small, a few collapsed cottages, many with no roofs, and others were fighting a battle against the ever-encroaching tide. This lifeless hamlet hidden at the bottom of the cliff was the right place for smugglers. The kidnapped could be brought there without being seen and rowed out into the waiting ships, and Eldric's anger grew.

Wild cats hissed at the hooves of the horses, startled by the heavy sounds on the chalk paths, and feral dogs barked, protecting their territory, afraid these newcomers were here to stay.

Ordering the soldiers to rest, Eldric dismounted, looking up at the dilapidated Temple. The beautiful windows gone, brickwork missing, and only the bell remained on the single wall. The heavy oak door had gone, either stolen or blown away, and Eldric likened himself to that building. He felt the same, old and afraid he might crumble.

Leaving his horse in the hands of a soldier, Eldric marched down the beach towards the figures standing at the shoreline. Oren turned, his face paled, and Eldric tried not to smile. He knew Oren hated him, but Oren was adept at not revealing it. Today, it showed.

'Lord Guardian,' Oren frowned. 'Why are you here?'

'You've not sealed the gap yet?' Eldric played with his clothing, smartening himself up.

'Yesterday I attempted, I'm not strong enough. Only just now am I beginning to regain the abilities strength, and that's taken me most of the day.'

Eldric slapped his nephew on the back. 'You always were a weak piece of shit, Oren.' He shouted at his valet to bring him a drink. He shouldn't be here, having to seal the break.

'Bedelia's back,' Oren whispered.

Eldric sucked in some air. 'I know the bitch is here. All of Verda's brats have returned.' Eldric spoke of Marisol, not telling much, but enough for Oren to understand what he'd done to Bedelia's mother.

'Why didn't you have sex with this Marisol?'

Eldric gave a sly smile, licking his lips, thinking about the girl. 'I would have done, but she was a late bloomer, hadn't started her periods. Then she escaped, probably with Rupert's help.' Eldric took a step closer to the shoreline.

'Rupert?' Oren frowned.

Eldric said nothing more, ordering Oren to stand next to him. 'I've not done this in a long time. I've only used The Purge to sustain my abilities, I've not needed to draw this much power so quickly. Pick five soldiers and have them take our horses to outside the village. They are to remain there.' Eldric looked at the debris of the rotting village. 'Or what's left of it.'

Oren left, and Eldric kicked over the shingle. He was an old man now, and he could feel his force weakening. He needed Winnie; he needed a male child to blend into. Staring out at the serene view of the sea, Eldric considered that for many it was a place of solitude. A life that for many of his subjects was hard but simple, and he smiled thinking about it. His thoughts darkened, and he realised he didn't have any comforting thoughts of the nullification of those people. Instead he would bring only death.

'I will take what I need from you,' Eldric uttered as his nephew returned.

Oren nodded.

Eldric took off his boots, placing his feet in the shallows. The ripples soothed the Lord Guardian, and he stood there, quietly enjoying the pure pleasure of water against the skin.

And then he roared.

Opening his arms out, the different energies spurred out of him, feeling like a thousand cuts slicing into his skin and bursting out. A brilliant light exploded out of Eldric and flew into The Barricade, crashing into the wall, again and again.

The wind blew, and the thunderous noise echoed back, and Eldric hit out again. Blood rushed around his body as his skin cracked. Eldric's heart swelled as he took the powers from his subjects, from those who had gone through The Purge. They connected to him, and Eldric gripped hold of them, making everybody a part of this.

Eldric gasped as he peered into the red Farscape. The people belonged to him, and he drew from them, blasting the dangerous white lightning into the giant structure. And the only answer he received was a deafening boom, travelling up and down the wall.

Falling to his knees, the beautiful day vanished. The winds howled, moving in all directions, and the waters raged, soaking his clothes. His breathing was raspy, sweat poured down his head. Never had Eldric experienced this weakening in him, and it was frightening.

'Eldric!'

There was pulling at his clothes. Oren gripped hold of him, and he screamed as they touched, unable to let go, as Eldric dug into Oren, transferring his nephew's abilities into and through him.

The power erupted, travelling through the sea currents, waves exploding and clawing at The Barricade, each crushing wave sending terrible sounds as if trying to seal the wall back together, but nothing happened.

Eldric's eyes lit up, pure white. The power he was taking was not enough. Energies that didn't belong to him or Oren came from the soldiers. He sensed each soldier inside him. They were dotted around the village and coastline, all now standing to attention and looking toward The Barricade.

One by one, they all came to Eldric. All connecting themselves freely to the God they believed in, and he sucked all their energy, harnessing it, and sent it out into the seas and into the wall.

Their voices came to him, screaming as they died. There was no escape now, and each soldier withered, their skins dried, making them look like dried fruit, and their souls burned as their bodies collapsed on the shingle.

Twenty-five souls burned in the red Farscape, the plane, a mass of fires scattered the blood-red wilderness. A place where Eldric came and took their essence, consuming it, and making it his. But with every bolt he threw at The Barricade, nothing worked, and he returned to this between world, needing more of the chosen ones to assist in the task.

And then he saw her.

Bedelia stood there, dressed in the black Reaper leather uniform, two sword belts wrapped around her waist and her lips scarred. Her eyes blackened, and she stood amongst the burning bodies, watching.

He moved, and she moved with him, her footsteps rippling the blood-red lake. And behind her, he saw three Spectres, so faint, but they were there. He gasped. Those things shouldn't be there. He'd locked them away, but they were standing, waiting behind his daughter, and it took all of Eldric's strength to remain where he stood.

The girl, his second daughter, came to him and he heard the name, Winnie, whispered in the wind, and she was the one he needed. She'd somehow woken these Spectres, and Winnie would be the one to quell them. Within the ever-changing Farscape, Eldric saw the girl. She was cold, frightened, trapped in a dark place; a prison cell. Outside he could hear the sea crashing and French voices. The name Edmond Harris, and the tiny fishing village, Arena Porta, flashed before him. He knew where Winnie was being kept.

And then Bedelia was gone. And Eldric collapsed into the shallows. 'I know where the girl is,' he gasped, needing air, and the last thing he remembered was Oren dragging him out of the waters.

***

The road to Arena Porta

The cloth covering Bee's face kept the flying insects out of her mouth, but not her eyes. The roads were dusty, but the wind was favourable as the three riders galloped back toward The Fortune pub. She didn't know where else to start. Winnie wouldn't be in Deman Circe, and Bee connected with her, but not long enough to learn where she was. All she knew was that Winnie was afraid. Her mind was a jumble of everything which had happened; the girl was beginning to lose control, panicking.

Bee remained in front, determined they would find Winnie before Eldric did. Bee concentrated so hard that nothing got through to her. No bird sounds, no people on the roads, everything was a fleeting moment in her vision and then it was gone.

They rode hard for several hours. Bee hoped to protect Winnie, knowing that whatever happened would most likely turn out to be her fault, and Bee didn't have a good feeling about what might come next.

Slowing her horse down, Bee let Malick and Somer catch up. The horse panted, and the animal shook its mane, happy to have stopped running. There was nothing but trees, wildland and pastures. They'd passed cottages, most of them tumbled down, and they stopped when possible to allow the horses to rest and drink water.

The horses trotted, as Bee kept quiet. She listened to the surrounding sounds, the birds in the air, the flies, and the wheat rustling against the wind. The smells in the atmosphere changed from the earthy manures spread over the pastures into the salty aftertastes of the distant coastline. They were nearing the sea, but were still not close enough.

Something was wrong, but it wasn't coming from the landscape. Bee felt heavy, as another horse rode up next to her. Malick pulled off his own mask. He was speaking, but Bee couldn't hear. His expression was confused, and Bee felt drunk as if she'd spent the afternoon at The Raven. Everything was woozy, and Bee tried to speak as her body tremored and her eyesight blurred. She was sliding off the saddle, as Malick struggled to keep her on the horse. Then Bee was somewhere else.

The landscape was what she remembered as a child. A red, watery place with sparse outlines with dead trees dotting the strange place, and a chill ran through Bee's body. People peppered this world. Men, women and children stood, freely giving over their energies. All had a smile of wonder on their faces as something connected with them, and this force moved toward one man. Yet this power, this force, Eldric was taking wasn't enough, and the images of these people faded.

There were soldiers, men and women, smartly dressed, all with their eyes closed. Caught in a half-life. Then, one burst into flames. And then another, followed by another. Bee backed away, afraid something might happen to her. Twenty-five soldiers looked like human candles, burning bright as they lit up the Farscape. And then she saw him.

Eldric stood there, stealing their lives, strengthening himself, attempting to close something. Bee convulsed. He was trying to seal The Crack, but even with the power he'd taken from the souls of these soldiers, he was not strong enough.

He saw Bee. Eldric froze, frightened by something in her face. Bee didn't know what, but she felt her abilities rising, moving up through her body and into her face. A black mass surrounded her as she watched Eldric kill people for more power. And then she felt The Spectres. They stood behind her, saying nothing, just waiting, and Bee saw Winnie.

Bee gasped, sitting up. She looked around, not recognising where she was. There was a fire, a chair, and a table, in a small one-room cottage. Malick and Somer sat at the table, while an old couple stood near the fire. Both looked terrified. She lay under a tiny window in the room's corner, in a single crib. It smelled old, woody and of damp dog. The dog, an old grey mutt, the size of a small child, looked at her quizzically, because she had taken its bed.

'Malick, what happened?' Bee croaked.

Malick checked her over, taking an interest in her eyes before giving her a beaker of water. The old couple stayed near the fireplace. The fear in their eyes, she'd seen many times, and it didn't help that her face was bruised and cut. Nobody liked Reapers, and nobody wanted one in their home. Clambering out of the crib, Malick caught Bee as her legs faltered, but after a second she could stand by herself.

'Please,' the old man whispered, looking at his wife, and then to Bee. 'We don't want any trouble.'

Bee placed her hands on one of the chairs. 'Don't worry,' she wheezed, 'I won't hurt you.' They did not believe her.

The old woman ruffled her shawl, her skin wrinkled. 'The Frenchman...Mr Rose... said he's your husband?' Her husband prodded her, shaking his head, encouraging her with his eyes, don't question a Reaper.

Bee nodded, and the couple took another step back. 'Yes, yes, that's correct.' She sipped from the beaker Malick had given her. 'Thank you for letting me into your home.'

'How does a Reaper get married and to a French–' the old woman started, but the old man poked her. Instead, the woman said, 'We didn't have much choice. They burst in with you.' Again, the old man poked her, telling her to shut up.

'I'm sorry for the intrusion.' Bee plonked into the chair, still weak.

'We're not far from the coast. I rode out this morning, I saw Hath in the distance,' Somer said, about to sip his hot tea. He looked at the steaming mug and slid it over to Bee.

Malick put his hand on Bee's shoulder, and she touched it, giving him a warm, loving smile. 'I saw Winnie, I know where she is. She's being kept somewhere in Arena

Porta.' And she described the place where she'd seen Winnifred being held.

The old couple had a nervous look, seeing the way Malick and Bee interacted with each other, understanding the Frenchman hadn't been lying, and they spotted the wedding ring on Bee's finger, and the old man nodded to his wife.

'We... I know the place you're talking about, it's the blockhouse there, owned by Edmond Harris.' The old woman told them.

'Is it guarded?' Malick asked. Both his and Somer's French accents were noticeable.

'It's a home now, no guards, but the Marshal uses the dungeon from time to time,' the old man said.

'Apart from the front door, is there another way in?' Bee asked.

The old man frowned. 'The only other way would be the sewers.'

'Omega has Winnie, there were French voices,' Bee explained, 'and Eldric knows too.'

'Then we'd better get her fast.' Malick rubbed his chin, sighing. 'Can you do it, Bee?'

Bee looked at everybody in the room, the old couple, Somer and then Malick, and inside she quivered. She wasn't sure if she could really get Winnifred out, but Bee had made a promise to the Harpers, saying she would bring their daughter home, and that was what Bee intended to do.

Finally, Bee nodded her head. 'Yes, I can do it.'

Chapter Twenty-Seven
Arena Porta, Kent

There were days Captain Osbourne wished he wasn't in the army, and today was one of those days. His small platoon of soldiers had reburied the French riders found at The Fortune pub, then had to cut down a priest found strung up in some Temple on the Road of Bones. Now they were in Arena Porta, a tiny fishing village with a pebbled beach, a pub called The Anchor, and a small Temple. And they were being shot at.

The circular blockhouse dominated the village, it looked out toward The Channel. Inside the Greystone fortress were the French who'd travelled through a crack, he'd since discovered had been created in Deman Circe.

They were in the middle of a gunfight, and Osbourne didn't have enough men. He'd observed several strangers as they entered the tiny village, all of them watching, and then without any provocation, they opened fire. And now Osbourne and the few soldiers were shooting their way to anywhere safe. The villagers hid in their homes, closing their shutters, probably hiding in their cellars. Nobody was going to come and rescue Osbourne, and he considered that perhaps he was going to die in this little unknown place.

The gunfire came from all directions, the blasts sometimes collided with objects and the pinging sounds echoed. Riders took shots from the rig of the blockhouse, and Osbourne saw there was a woman there, with a shaved hair and wild mane down the centre of her head, directing these men. She was determined that his soldiers would not enter the great stone fortress. And then three Reapers entered the village. And as much as Osbourne hated Reapers, he was glad they were here.

All of them wore their death masks, and every so often there was a shot coming from their horses, as they picked off the French riders hidden from the soldiers' views, yet these Reapers could see them.

He watched, as they dismounted, and moved like ghosts through the place, fading, masking themselves and killing people without any remorse.

Their movements were fast, much faster than the riders', and they kept shooting. They did not stop. One of them broke necks, the other brought out their sword, and it was frightening and thrilling to watch these killers at work.

The three Reapers moved in line, each of them spotting a threat and eliminating it, and every so often, a cry came, as their victims last dying gasps penetrated the gunfire. It sent shivers down Osbourne's spine, but he was grateful it wasn't him dead in the street.

***

Marisol watched her men die. Unsure how this gunfight had started, she shouted for the soldiers to be killed on sight. The day had started off quiet. She'd enjoyed a morning coffee on the rooftop of the small Keep and watched Edmond Harris twitch, concerned that she and the riders were still on his property.

She'd overtaken the blockhouse and was comfortable with its serene surroundings. Marisol had decided she would send a message to Lord Guardian Eldric saying Winnie Harper was her hostage when the soldiers rode in, and the shooting started.

Now three Reapers arrived, killing her men, and they were nearly at the front door of Arena Porta's tiny fort. Marisol wiped the sweat from her forehead. It wasn't hot, but she was nervous. She'd taken shots, reloaded and fired repeatedly. Marisol was glad she had her sword with her, in case she had no more bullets left, but she'd be able to kill a few more soldiers before they finally subdued or killed her.

Gunfire surrounded the blockhouse. The villagers retreated into their homes, closing the shutters. Soldiers hid behind carts, heads popped up, a shot would be fired, and the head vanished behind the cart. Horses panicked, some galloped off, kicking up the scallop shells, heading fast out of the village.

Marisol watched as the three Reapers walked down the centre of the village. Each one took shots, never missing, and her riders started dying. Reapers, she'd forgotten about them while living in the Spanish Netherlands. They had not been something she'd worried about, and now as they blasted their way toward her, Marisol panicked.

Groans, blood, gunfire, smoke, and the dying wails of men begging for somebody to help echoed in Marisol's ears. Others called for their mothers as a bloody hand rose as if death had come to collect.

'The Reapers are nearly at the door,' Baptiste shouted, shooting somebody from over the wall. 'You need to do something.' He took another shot.

Marisol ducked as a bullet flew past. 'I don't kn –'

'You're a fucking Guardian, Omega, kill them!' He fired again.

The Reapers slipped past and shot most of the riders outside the blockhouse. Marisol looked at the carnage, the anger came, and her abilities rose up inside, and then the Reapers vanished.

Marisol had always traded on the fact that she was a Guardian. She had created a reputation, but in the years since she left Britain, Marisol had never needed to use her abilities. The fear of what she was, made people do what she wanted.

The feeling flowed. Marisol summoned what she could. She reached out, touching and taking the energies of the men. She stole the dying embers of the riders who died because of her want of Bedelia Rose.

Marisol protected the few remaining riders she had with her. Colours changed, and the power flowed, it buzzed inside as if she'd swallowed a bumblebee. Little pinpricks inside burst all over and Marisol's heart raced, as it grew.

It built slowly, like a thousand angry ants crawling over her body, and Marisol was about to let it explode when there was a deafening blast. She turned, confused, toward the centre courtyard.

Some riders were hurt. Wood from the heavy doors lay in all directions and pieces impaled some of the men. The smoke wasn't settling, and she heard their cries for help.

Reapers, she thought at first, and then she saw Eldric.

The Lord Guardian appeared in the clearing smoke. Memories, of a young version of the man who stood in the haze, flashed before Marisol. This same older man was now in command of the situation.

Marisol jumped down the stone steps, demanding Baptiste follow. And the riders started shooting, protecting her, as she ran through the house, and down into the dungeon.

Eldric was here for Winnie. This girl was her only bargaining tool for her and the men to escape. Almost slipping on the old stone, Marisol shouted at the guard to open up the cell.

'That's not the French lady, it's him.' Winnie was hiding in the corner. She rose from the dirt, expecting to be let out.

'You're going to get me out of here.' Marisol pushed Winnie up the stone steps and through the house. She took her revolver, cocked it, pushing Winnie out of the keep, down the steps and towards the centre of the courtyard. The smoke was settling and, in the centre, stood Eldric, with Oren behind.

'Marisol,' Eldric smiled.

She kept her gun on Winnie, Marisol's heart pounding as she moved gingerly into the courtyard. Winnie whimpered, stumbling over her feet, trying to back away. Marisol sensed Winnie's fear, seeing the girl twist her hair.

'I want the girl, Marisol, that's all,' Eldric shouted.

She paused. Winnie would end up like her mother, she'd be imprisoned, and most likely Eldric would perform the act himself. Marisol remembered her mother's screams, and then the acceptance that Eldric would pay her a visit.

'I want Bedelia Rose,' Marisol shouted, keeping a tight grip on Winnie.

There was silence. Eventually, Eldric responded, 'I don't know where she is.'

'You will only get Winnie in exchange for that bitch,' she shouted.

Somebody took a shot, but it wasn't at Marisol, they were shooting somebody behind. She turned and saw Bedelia standing there.

***

Bee, Malick and Somer waded through the sewers. The stench was unbearable. Human faeces drifted along a running stream of water, mixed with urine and blood. Dead rats and other vermin scattered the tunnel, while the live rats scurried out of the way of the newcomers. The animals congregated, squeaking and trampling over each other, as Malick and Somer held torches, and water seeped out of crevices, while moss and insects infested the walls.

Somer moaned about the stagnant water, and this was the only way they would gain access to the blockhouse without being discovered. The plan had been to sneak in, kill the guard and grab Winnie with nobody seeing. A big explosion came, the tunnel rumbled. Eldric was here, and once again Bee was without a plan.

The wall squelched as Bee rested against it. She looked at the greasy entrails on her hand, wiping it down her uniform. This was not how she envisaged rescuing Winnifred.

They came to an end where the system started within the walls of the Keep. It was small and deep, making Bee cough, choking on the odours which felt like they were burning her eyes.

'Couldn't you have picked a better way?' Somer grumbled, coughing.

Bee said as the stream got a little deeper, 'We would've sneaked in and out if Eldric hadn't turned up.'

'Fucking hell,' Somer muttered under his breath, as the waters rose to his knees.

The tunnel opened out. Bee looked through the grated bars and saw the pigpen. The animals huddled together, hiding away from the noise, frightened and sniffing the air. This was where the vassals swept the old straw, faeces, and small dead animals. Sending swills of water down and, when it rained, most of it would wash away.

Bee gripped hold of the bars, pulling the grating. It gave way quickly, and she slid under the open gap. Staying hidden, she pulled her revolver out, and Malick handed her a shotgun. She had the swords, but nothing else. They couldn't carry anything else unless they wanted to ruin it.

The smoky courtyard was settling as Eldric stood there. He and Omega were in conversation, and Omega held Winnie. The young woman looked terrified.

'Both stay here,' Bee ordered, crouching as she moved through the pigpen and the pigs squealed, announcing the intruder, but nobody listened.

Bee stayed in the shadows. She cocked the shotgun, took aim and was about to shoot, when somebody on the outer wall shot at her. They missed, and Bee shot them. The rider fell over the wall into the ground, creating a tiny dust cloud around their body.

Omega turned and fired at Bee, still holding Winnie. The girl screamed, struggling, and Bee saw how tightly the woman held Winnie.

'You can have Bedelia, just give me Winnie,' Eldric shouted, and then he exploded, sending a powerful jolt through the courtyard. Everybody jerked, some fell to the ground, and Bee felt his essence blast into her, making her dizzy.

And she heard through all the noise, Winnie's voice cut through, shouting that she was sorry, that she shouldn't have brought the Sinners. She begged Eldric for his forgiveness, proclaiming her love for the Lord Guardian.

Bee turned to Eldric, he was the one she wanted dead, and everything swelled up inside. The agony of having children, then having them taken from her, and Bee spotted Oren behind Eldric. He was as much to blame for Bee's misery as Eldric.

And the anger became a sea of black.

Dropping her shotgun, she clenched her fists together. It was all happening too fast, and Bee blasted fire towards them. The thermal energies she generated burst out of her body and aimed purely at those two men.

Her eyes turned black, she became a dark force, but Eldric created a field, hiding himself and Oren behind it and he pushed back. Bee slid in the straw as the anger flowed out.

Omega shot at Bee, but missed. Bee turned fast, hearing the click of the gun and held out her hand. The weapon flew out of Omega's hand, and Bee sent it smashing into the fort wall. And with this unseen power, she gripped hold of Omega's neck and squeezed, taking the woman up into the air, suspending her there.

A boom rang out. It came from Bee, and the castle shook, sending everybody flying, except Omega, Winnie, Eldric and Oren. Bee became more potent as the presence of the Spectres surrounded her. They were making Bee more powerful than she'd ever been before. Bee shuddered as Omega used all her abilities to hold Bee off breaking her neck, and Bee dropped Omega to the ground.

Eldric shouted at Omega, 'Give me Winnie and I'll give you safe passage!' He stepped further into the courtyard. 'You know you're not strong enough to defeat Bedelia.'

'I've her daughter.' Omega held on tightly to Winnie.

Bee stood there, motionless. The things she'd kept secret were rising, and they were about to explode. And that primeval darkness grew, waiting to come out.

'He won't give you safe passage, Omega. He'll kill you.' Bee's voice was different. This was the voice of a Reaper.

Bee experienced Eldric, as he fastened himself into Omega. Omega fell to her knees, clasping Winnie. The woman cried in agony, gasping, spitting, as Eldric drained her of her abilities. Omega paled, eyes bloodshot, heaving, fighting to keep hold of her powers but she couldn't resist.

Omega pushed Winnie into the dirt. Struggling to stand, she sneered at Eldric as he consumed her powers. Marisol shook as she fought with him, and Bee could see Omega's anger rising. Omega grappled with her sword, pulled it out, and swiftly cut off Winnie's head.

Bee watched eyes wide open. Winnie's decapitated head rolled to one side, facing her. Eyes opened, saying to Bee, *'You didn't save me.'* Blood poured into the dirt and Bee raged inside. This wasn't supposed to happen, she was meant to come and rescue Winnie, not take a body back to her parents. She'd broken her promise.

A powerful energy charged through Bee, crushing her. The Spectres, the Sinners as Winnie called them, bombarded her, and Bee fell to her knees screaming.

She couldn't take the pain they inflicted, and each rush came like a thunderbolt hitting her body, corrupting her soul. Bee contorted her back, as the pain shot up through her bones. They fractured, spilling out from the marrowbone and into her blood. Everything rushed around, and Bee burned.

And then she ruptured. A wave flared out from Bee. She screamed as the power hit every corner of the blockhouse. Anybody not shielded by a wall was hit, and they fell to the ground. Even Eldric, Omega and Oren were hit by the strange unknown sound, and outside beyond the blockhouse walls, the peculiar sound travelled at such a fast speed that it hit The Barricade, and that boomed a thunderous noise, spreading out in all directions.

And Bee carried on screaming.

Two shots came from the ramparts. Bee did not move, her body craned back, and somebody ran to protect her. They were fast and took the bullets which exploded from the rifles high above. Somer slid over as the impact hit his body.

Malick pulled at Bee as Eldric struggled to fight the noise. Malick held out his hand to stop the Lord Guardian, as Bee flowed through him, and the Spectres followed. Bee witnessed these beings wrapped themselves inside him, clamping themselves onto Malick.

The darkness that surrounded Bee burst out through him, and Malick's eyes changed from green into black. He cried as the power erupted through him, sending Eldric flying back, knocking him out, and then Malick stopped.

'Bee,' Malick breathed. Smoke, silence, only the frightened cries of the animals broke the otherwise quiet courtyard.

Bee woke up. Malick's voice brought her back, and she looked at the courtyard. Bodies fell everywhere and Bee didn't know if they were alive or dead. Malick dragged her up from the ground, and then she spotted Somer.

He lay there in a pool of blood. His eyes darted around, unsure. Bee slid over to him, she didn't know where the blood was coming from, and Bee grabbed him.

Chapter Twenty-Eight
Arena Porta, Kent

Bee and Malick threw Somer onto the pub table. Blood poured out of Somer's arm and the side of his chest. Bee shouted at the barkeep of The Anchor Inn to bring over some whiskey. Somer thrashed, arms, legs kicking out, screaming as Bee tried to look.

'Hold him down, Malick,' she shouted through Somer's cries.

The pub was small, old and smelled of stale smoke. The fire had been lit earlier in the day, and Bee poked the flames, throwing on more wood. She left the poker inside the fire to heat it up. The barkeep vanished through a door behind the bar, only to reappear, hands shaking with whiskey, bandages, instruments and water. He'd been through this several times before.

There were pellets in the side of Bee's face, as Somer had taken most of the blasts. The burning in her flesh eased off and Bee couldn't think of anything else, except helping Somer.

He'd protected her from the blast, and the left side of Somer's arm took most of the shot. Bee ripped off the blood-soaked shirt, and inspected the pellets, and saw a bigger hole in his shoulder.

'Look at me, Somer,' she said, and he did. 'I'll sort you out, Malick will assist, do you understand?' Malick held Somer's hand, and Somer became confused.

'He's going into shock.' The barkeep pushed past Malick, looking at the bloody wounds, and he said, 'I can get them out.'

Bee knew that feeling. The burning would rip into Somer, giving him a nightmare, and mixing with the most terrible pleasure. Only to give way to complete annihilation of the senses, as they exploded into the fantasy of nothing.

Bee first experienced this when she was twelve, when Luther shot her, and the final time when Claude slit her throat and cut her lips. There were times Bee hadn't wanted to wake from the nothing. It was a feeling she envied because she couldn't remain there.

Bee doused the cloth in water and cleaned the blood from Somer's arm and part of his chest. The barkeep ordered Malick to hold Somer, and then he moved around the table, pushing Bee next to Malick, inspecting the wounds.

'He's lucky, these are only flesh wounds. However, this bullet's gone through.' The barkeep pointed to the large gash on Somer's shoulder.

'Are you sure?' Bee asked.

The old man prodded the wound, and Somer groaned. 'Bullets are like magic, they can travel anywhere in the body, but this one has gone straight through. He's a lucky man.'

'What about the pellets?' Malick asked.

The barkeep inspected Somer's side, wiping away the weeping blood. 'I just said –'

'I mean on my wife?' Malick pointed to Bee.

The barkeep looked at Bee, at the uniform. Confused, he stuttered, 'Your wife?'

The pub door burst open. Bee and Malick looked up as Luther came through the pub, followed by Karem and Thomas. The barkeep paled, at having more Reapers in his pub. He backed away as Luther stormed toward Bee, grabbing her by the neck, and her feet tripped as he thumped Bee against the pub wall.

'What sort of cluster fuck was that, Bedelia?'

Bee started going red, struggling, her fingers at his hands.

'You almost got yourself killed.'

Malick placed his hand on Luther's arm. He said calmly, 'Now's not the time, Luther. Speak to Bee once we've dealt with Somer.'

Luther looked down at Malick's hand. He nodded. 'I'm sorry, Mr Rose.' Luther glared at Bee, slamming her again at the wall, dropping her. Malick grabbed Bee before she crashed to the floor, coughing, and the barkeep's mouth dropped.

'Are you okay?' Malick stroked her face, and Bee nodded, still coughing. 'Right, let's sort out Somer.'

'Give the man some whiskey and then hold his shoulders,' the barkeep directed Malick, who did as he was instructed. 'And can the Reaper hold him down?' he addressed his question to Bee.

'Luther, hold Somer,' Bee snapped, still coughing.

'You don't need–'

'The man's never been shot before.' She stood by the table and clicked her fingers, pointing to the side opposite. 'Please hold him down.'

Luther straightened his leather uniform and approached, taking hold of Somer's arm, who'd had passed out, and Malick placed his hands on Somer's shoulders. Bee held onto Somer, as the barkeep prodded the flames with the poker. Taking the metal object, he carefully moved toward Somer. He nodded, showing what he was about to do, and then he placed the hot rod onto the open wound.

Somer sprang up, screaming as Luther and Bee held him down. His legs flew in all directions. He glared at the old man, swearing in French, and Malick struggled to hold him down. The old man doused the cauterised wound in a small amount of whiskey and Somer cried. The barkeep ordered Somer to have more whiskey and then he turned over, and heated the rod for a second time. Malick held Somer again, as the old man repeated the same procedure, and Somer passed out. The barkeep's hands shook, and he dropped the poker, stepping away. He watched everybody in the pub, as they watched each other.

'Get him onto his back, and I'll take the pellets out,' the barkeep eventually ordered.

Luther stepped back. He waited by the wall as Bee cleaned up the table. She helped turn Somer over, and the barkeep began his work. They'd given him enough whiskey to sleep through the pain.

Bee ignored Luther. She took a cloth and tweezers from the tray the barkeep had brought in, and behind the bar, she found a glass, filling it with whiskey. She went to the table at the back of the bar and sat down. The heat from the initial blast was gone, but they numbed the inside of her face.

Malick pulled up a seat next to her. He washed his hands in the alcohol, and wiped her face with both water and whiskey. Gently Malick caressed her face, and she let him feel out the rises in her cheeks as he hunted for any pellets. Finding one just above her cheekbone, Malick turned Bee to face the incoming sun and sterilised the tweezers in the alcohol. Without speaking, he felt her face again and gently prodded the pellet to raise it to the surface. It wasn't in too deep, but Bee winced as it moved inside her.

'Pulling pellets out of my wife's face is not something I thought I'd ever be doing,' he said light-heartedly, pulling one out and placing it onto the table. He then dabbed her face with more whiskey and looked for another.

'And seeing your eyes and you blast Eldric is something I never thought I'd see, Malick. What happened?' she asked, as he removed a second one.

He carried on his work, gently searching and finding the pellets. He didn't speak for a long time; instead, he pulled one out after another, wiping away the blood as it came to the surface.

'That is the result of the first time we made love,' he finally said. 'I told you, I always feel you.' Malick carried on searching Bee's face. 'I wasn't lying in the woods when I said I never want it to stop. You are one of the most pleasurable things I have.' He rubbed her leg. 'When I hurt you, and you got a little scary, even then I couldn't let go.'

'Thank you, for not letting go,' and then Bee said, 'I feel different.'

'Different how?'

'I feel more powerful than I ever have done in my whole life, but I failed Winnie,' she whispered. 'I failed her parents.'

'You didn't know Omega would kill her.'

'But she released something, and I think... I think I have it now.'

'Can you kill Eldric?' he whispered.

She nodded.

Luther didn't wait any longer. He walked to the table. 'Bedelia, I'd like a word?'

Bee scowled. 'You can be a right wanker at times, Luther.'

'And you –'

Malick stood up, getting in between Luther and Bee. 'Now is not the time.'

'Mr Rose, I understand she is your wife, but –'

'Luther,' Bee cut in, she remained sitting down. 'Malick is right. I need to rest, we'll speak later.' Bee didn't turn to look at him. She didn't want to look at Luther at all.

***

Dai Castle, Dai, Kent

Eldric had been told it was Bedelia who'd overpowered him at Arena Porta, but Eldric knew it was the man, the man who rushed to Bedelia. This man had been the one who'd given him the final hit which had sent him flying across the yard.

His body hurt everywhere, and he had rested for an hour since being brought back to Dai Castle. The chambers set up, Gable had sat with him until she grew bored and went looking for Leena.

Gable, he would have to use her abilities as well to stop Bee. He drained much of Oren's power trying to seal the Crack, and the man had proved useless at the fort.

Sitting just outside the dungeon, Eldric contemplated what was going to happen next. He'd rested enough and wanted to speak with Omega. She would have the answers he needed.

The soldiers had dragged him and Oren out of the courtyard. He didn't know what had happened to the Reapers, but Omega was arrested. Eldric wanted to execute her for killing Winnie, but he decided to treat Omega like he had her mother, because he needed a child, and he was running out of time.

Eldric ordered the guard to open up the dungeon door. It creaked, and different odours escaped up into the fresh air. The Guardian coughed, but he did not shy away from going down the steps and into the prison block. The cell was small, and Omega lay on the floor like she didn't have a care in the world.

'I understand you are the one, who's been taking my subjects,' Eldric uttered.

Omega lifted her head, not moving. 'When people are desperate, they'll believe anything, and the blood of a Guardian is the greatest panacea I can give them.'

'You murdered my people?'

Omega sat up, laughing. She said, 'That's not all I did. I cut them up, made them into tinctures and potions. The survivors believe the blood of a Guardian is some kind of holy relic which might save them, so I give them what they need.'

'Does that make you happy, Marisol?'

'It makes me rich, Eldric.'

'Tell me about this man.' He changed topics. 'Is he Bee's husband?'

'His name is Malick Rose, and he married Bee about six years ago. They have children, a boy and girl.'

'Interesting.' Eldric rubbed his cheeks.

'The boy is somewhere here in England.'

Eldric's eyes widened. 'The boy is here?'

'Are you going to let me go?' Omega asked.

'Marisol, my beautiful Marisol, of course, I'm not letting you go. You killed my daughter, so you can now be her replacement.' He smiled at her through the bars.

Chapter Twenty-Nine
Arena Porta, Kent

Bee sat opposite Luther.

The Anchor pub was empty. The barrelled chairs and round tables were lined in an orderly fashion, and the barkeep lit the gas lamps bringing light into the small place. The inn smelled of old beer and stale smoke, and the ever-present odour of rotting fish and saltwater saturated the building.

Hanging over the walls were old tangled fishing lines and, in the corner, fish pods stood. The fishermen usually collected them in the morning, if they'd had too many ales the night before. Nobody was venturing out of their homes, not after the bloodshed in Arena Porta.

Bee sat opposite Luther in the corner. A candle by the window allowed her to see his face, though he didn't look at her. The two Reapers, who worked with Luther, sat in another corner, while Somer dozed in a scruffy old armchair that the barkeep kept near the bar. Bee sensed Malick within her peripheral vision. He didn't bother, sitting casually at the bar. He sat, watching only his wife.

Bee was grateful for the kindness the old man showed them, allowing her and Malick to wash in his home behind the inn, cleaning as much of the stench of the sewers out of them, but it was still there.

The barkeep looked at the strange group, two Frenchmen, and four Reapers, all in their leathers. The only people drinking were the Frenchmen, and the old man started refilling the shelves, keeping busy.

Bee sat, back straight, against the back of the seat and stared at Luther. Remembering the words that he'd uttered at Rolfen, and she clasped her hands in her lap.

'I missed you, Luther,' she whispered. She did not reach out to touch him, though she wanted to.

'You look like shit, Bedelia,' Luther looked at her. 'And you cut your hair.'

Bee played with her hair. 'I cut it off once I was able.'

He glanced over to Malick, then back to Bee. 'Is he good to you?'

Bee smiled. 'Yes, he's a good man.' She paused as Luther shifted in his chair. He wasn't comfortable. She could always tell when something was wrong because Luther refused to meet her gaze. 'Are you going to look at me?' she asked.

He did, but there was no smile.

'Why did you say I should have stayed in France?'

Luther leaned over the table. He answered in a generic tone. 'You escaped. You didn't need to come back.' He stared again at Malick and then back to Bee.

'Why...why didn't you come with me, as you were supposed to?'

'The Lord Guardian ordered that I remain in Britain.'

Bee recalled the Argent, the Scribe who issued an Overlord's warrants. He'd instructed her, that Luther would be her second and they'd sanctioned him to execute any individual who attacked.

Bee whispered, 'The Argent authorised you as my chaperone, but Eldric declared you unsuitable.'

Luther muttered, 'I'm sorry, Bee.'

And then she understood, he'd reported her to Eldric. 'You…' she whispered, 'I only ever told Rufus. How did you know?'

'Lord Oren overheard you with Rufus. After you killed those priests, he told Lady Leena, but he didn't say who you were talking to, which is why Rufus is still alive. Lady Leena ordered me to inform Eldric. I followed her order.' He looked down at the wooden table.

Bee sat quietly. He was the reason she'd ended up in France alone and her heart quickened. 'You screwed me over, Luther,' she hissed. 'I thought I knew every inch of you, we made promises.'

He leaned closer, snapping, 'You kept it from me.'

'I was protecting you.' Her voice rose, 'There's no kindness in our world, and if I'd told you… I thought… you are my Unseen, I depended on you. I'd have waited in the darkness if I'd died in France.' Bee hands trembled, as the words got stuck.

'I've regretted it every day, but you were giving Eldric male heirs. I thought–' Luther whispered.

Bee uttered, 'That bastard forced his nephew to fuck me repeatedly because he needed children. Tell me, what kind of a man does that to his own daughter? I'd stare at the ceiling pretending to be dead, as Oren crawled all over me, pawing my body, grunting like a pig into my ear.

'And after Oren came inside me, I waited, unable to clean myself up. Two Reapers held me as a maid split my legs apart, inspecting me,' Bee choked. 'And if I bled, I spent two days in the hole to think about why I wasn't pregnant. So, tell me, Luther, what *did* you think he'd do?'

Luther's face paled. 'You never told me.'

'I've never told anybody, not even Malick.' She looked toward the bar, seeing Malick, as he kept his eyes on her, hearing every word she uttered. 'The only thing he knows is that I was forced to have sex to have children. I'm ashamed of what that *motherfucking* Guardian did to me.' Bee hammered her finger onto the table, as the barkeep dropped a bottle of wine on the floor, shocked at hearing a woman swear.

'I didn't think he'd send Claude to kill you,' Luther said.

Bee let out a distressed laugh, and then her voice turned icy, 'I was exhausted, alone. Claude killed that chaperone, cut my throat, and ripped my cheeks. He thought I was dead and climbed onto me like Oren did. I couldn't fight him and, after what he did, I needed you to...' she stammered, '...I wanted you to kill me.'

Luther peered down at Bee. 'Bedelia, if I had been there you wouldn't have survived, met your husband, had your children, you wouldn't have lived.'

'Fuck you, Luther, because none of that would have happened.' Bee banged her hand on the table, letting out a breath, 'Fuck you,' she repeated, broken. 'I would have been dead, and that's all that mattered.'

'Bee, please understand –'

She spoke fast, 'I was frightened, Luther. Their lives are alien, their rules so different, even now I get confused, and I hid, afraid people would discover what I was.'

'But you got married?' Luther frowned.

Bee carried on. 'With no real understanding of what marriage actually was. I was so scared that on my wedding night I almost broke Malick's arm. I thought... I thought he was like Oren or Claude that he would force himself on me, and then he tried to kiss me...' she closed her eyes, thinking about that night. '...but I was wrong, he loved me.'

Luther asked, 'How did you know?'

Bee looked nowhere else but at Malick, and said, 'I'm a Reaper camouflaged as a wife, and I mourned the death I didn't have. He took me into this strange fragment of the world. Malick wove me into it, taking the ends of each thread, tying them to people, places and to him.

'Every question asked, every request made, every French lesson given, was all because Malick wanted me to feel safe. I was in love with him before I married him, I just didn't know it, and I wanted to be his wife.'

'But you still kept your secrets?'

Bee closed her eyes, saying, 'Luther, we aren't scared of death's secrets because there aren't any. I can take care of myself, but his priority was that I was safe, and his safety became mine. Keeping my secret was an act of love which strangled me because I didn't want to lose Malick.'

Luther kept quiet, and nobody in the pub spoke. Even the barkeep had stopped restocking and listened to the conversation.

Luther didn't speak for a minute. 'You don't scare easily, Bedelia.'

'No, Luther, I don't, but perhaps what scares me the most is realising I made a mistake.' She leaned her head back against the board behind her.

'What mistake was that?' Luther asked.

Icily, Bee answered, 'That I didn't let those Reapers kill you.' And the hurt in his eyes hit Bee, and she regretted her words.

'You're lying, Bee,' Luther's eyes narrowed. 'For nearly fifteen years, it's only been us, and *we* love each other. Our relationship is violent and it will always be, but we don't abandon one another. We're twisted together in a way that you will never be with him. Leena ordered me to report you, I did, and you would have done the same.'

Bee said nothing. The foundation of her British existence had collapsed. Anger swelled up inside, but Luther was correct, she would have reported him. 'Reapers are always loyal to the Lord Guardian,' she whispered. This wasn't the conversation Bee wanted, but learning he'd been the one who'd reported her cut deep and Bee needed to hurt Luther, and then she rose from the table.

Bee leaned down toward him, taking his hand, and she kissed him on the cheek and whispered in his ear. Bee pulled away, and they held each other's gaze. The shadows found them, and Bee and Luther were back in the one world, where they loved each other and would die for each other. She placed her hand on his cheek.

'Yes,' he whispered.

Bee walked towards the door. She couldn't bring herself to look at Malick. Keeping her head down, Bee sped out of the pub.

***

Bee slammed the pub door, and Malick followed. He couldn't see Bee as she'd vanished onto the beach. He heard footsteps as she ran, and he felt the hurt building inside. And she was going to let it out.

Malick ran his fingers through his hair. There had been a strange coldness rush over him when Bee spoke to Luther. The secrets they had, the years they'd spent together, was a darkness Malick never wanted to visit.

Hearing Bee speak of wanting to die on the beach of Bononia almost broke Malick, but it was the way she spoke of her love for him that astonished him. Bee had never spoken so truthfully because she'd always kept things secret.

He thought about his life, the kind of man he'd been before he met Bee. He married out of duty, and Nadine knew it. He had been as lonely as Nadine in their marriage, and while he took comfort in the arms of other women, she was left accepting his affections only when he chose it. Nadine died knowing Malick would marry the English stranger, and that he'd love her in a way that he never loved Nadine.

Malick whispered, 'I'm sorry, Nadine.'

Bee stood in the shallows, staring out to sea. The clear night glistened on the calm waves as they lapped around his wife. Malick came up behind her, and she pulsed through him.

Bee said, 'I need you, Malick.' And she held out her hand.

Malick slipped her hand into his, squeezing it. Anger and hurt whirled up, and Bee's pain ripped into Malick, almost exploding out of him.

'Bedelia,' he whispered.

The wind blew, Bee turned and faced him. Malick stared at the face. Bee was different. Her brown eyes transformed into the black void he'd seen when she passed out on the horse, and it sent a chill through him.

'It's time,' her voice was monotone.

Malick stayed close as Bee stepped further into the shallows, staring out to the channel. He allowed her to crawl around inside him, gathering her strength as Bee fastened a part of her soul to him.

It was a scary, experiencing the heartache Bee had endured all her life. The pain she'd suffered crossed into him. The hidden isolation powered up, as Bee reached deep inside the dark to seek what she needed. Everything was there, the shadows, the hurt, the domination, and sorrow rushed through Malick, exploding from a tiny light into something dangerous.

'The Spectres will protect the shorelines,' Bee muttered.

Malick's blood rushed. There was a stirring, something he remembered but couldn't quite place. A piece of the puzzle he'd always looked for but could never find, and it exploded inside him, blowing dazzling colours through him, and it was beautiful.

That darkness travelled, it liquefied, and Malick joined Bee as he channelled the power back into his wife. She consumed it, as they shared the abilities, and Bee took what she'd imprinted into him and spun it out across The Channel.

Malick lost balance, falling to his knees in the water. He needed air, and Bee kept hold of his hand. Bee shot her other hand forward, roaring as the power inside her exploded toward The Barricade. The waters that clung to the wall rose, bashing against the structure as the thunderous energy shook The Barricade.

Bee spread her hand out, and a powerful boom came from The Barricade itself. Everything that could fly, did. Trees bustled with activity as the birds burst into life. Animals, dogs barked, as the cattle and horses made panicky sounds, many kicking their stable doors, to escape whatever was coming. Pollock, cod, dogfish, usually hidden below in the currents, splashed above the waves, jumped and sprang, trying to outswim what was happening.

Bee exploded. And the fires blew up.

The Barricade was so high that the clouds consumed it. The night turned into flaming reds, mushrooming into hot oranges and blistering out in all directions, bringing light to the sky.

Bee held her stance.

She was still inside Malick, using him to protect herself from these abilities. Bee channelled the flames into The Barricade. The first crack came, splintering, as the fire consumed the giant monster which separated Britain and France.

The Barricade crackled, like a hog being turned over hot flames. The fires spat out into The Channel as the sea raged, angered by Bee's energies. The waters heaved, screaming in a fury, choking on the blaze as it burned the solidified wall.

Regurgitating deep hidden waters thrashed up toward the shoreline. Malick watched as the outraged sea flew back towards the beach. But as Bee predicted, it never hit the beach, it never washed away the village, as if something unseen and powerful was stopping the destruction that would otherwise occur.

Villagers left the safety of their homes, gathering on the pebbles, all wrapped up in shawls and heavy coats, carrying tiny lamps as they followed the thunderous noise to its source. They watched and screamed, terrified, that The Barricade might wash them away.

The fires took hold, blasting along the wall, leaving nothing untouched. The orange flames snarled as the air gripped it, and the night sky boomed. Rapid explosives charged as super-heated gases blasted along the wall, setting off fires in every direction.

Malick didn't move as the fracturing Barricade creaked. The flames crackled, as the black smoky mass which had stood for more than six years, broke, crumbling into the waters below. The fiery embers sent giant pieces bombing into the waves. And The Barricade started to break.

Villagers cried out, watching the wall fall. Many backed away, frightened to see what might lie beyond. Some moved closer, desperate to know there was still life in France, but all they saw were the smouldering black plumes of smoke as the thunderous outcries of the flames reverberated east to west. Extending its fiery arms and absorbing everything in its path. Bee weakened. The wall was coming down, and she stepped backwards, wide-eyed, surprised at what she'd done.

'I always wanted The Barricade to stay up.' Bee still held Malick's hand. 'All the time it was up, I didn't have to tell anyone.'

'I made a promise to keep you safe, and I broke that promise. I'm sorry, Bedelia.' Malick stood up, gasping.

Bee kissed his hand and burst into tears. Malick caught Bee as her legs gave way, and he held her in the shallows, the lapping water soaking them as Bee sobbed.

And for the first time in the six years they'd been married, Malick heard his wife cry.

Chapter Thirty
Dai Castle, Dai, Kent

Eldric peered over the Keep's high walls. The view of Dai was dramatic on the best days when the skies were blue and clear. This was the key to Britain, and during his younger days, Eldric had spent many summers here. He'd travel the magnificent white cliffs many times and always found them awe-inspiring.

Today Eldric was seeing a different Dai. The town below was quiet. The bustle he associated with the busy fishing town appeared to have remained dormant. He, like the townsfolk below, was seeing Britain for the first time, without its defence of The Barricade.

Oren, Leena and Gable stood with him. He'd forced them up the spiral steps and out onto the platform during the night to witness the fires rip through The Barricade. They'd watched in silence as pieces broke off, crashing into the sea and vanishing forever into the depths below. All saw the morning sunrise and, as the smoke dissipated, they saw the shoreline of France.

Leena cried, begging Oren that she wanted to return to their chambers, that she didn't want to watch anymore. Eldric, enraged by her whining, slapped her, ordering that she was not to move from the platform until he decided. Leena quietened down, and he wanted all to see the devastation that Bedelia had caused.

In every corner, two soldiers were stationed, and four Reapers remained near the door. Nobody had left since Eldric hit Leena. The fires heated everything, as the smoke was carried on the winds and pieces of ash fell from the skies, and when great chunks crashed into the sea, it never created a tidal wave that could destroy the town.

Gilbert puffed as he made his way up the last of the spiral staircase and stood on the platform behind Eldric. The man was twitchy, playing with his coat, wringing his hands, wanting to speak but keeping quiet.

'What is it, Gilbert?' Oren asked, putting the man out of his misery.

The man said, 'Reports suggest there is nothing left of The Barricade, it's come down everywhere.'

'Impossible!' Eldric roared. Turning, he struck Gilbert across the face, sending the man flying. 'One Guardian can't do that!'

'I'm sorry, Lord Guardian, but –'

'She's getting help somewhere,' he carried on.

Gilbert and Oren looked at each other. After a long silence, Oren said, 'The day you arrived, Sagan was here, he'd come –'

'Who's Sagan?' Eldric interrupted.

'Overlord Kendal of Rolfen. He collected Rufus McKay, Bedelia's father,' Oren explained, and then he added, 'I'd sent out Luther, the Reaper, to look for her. He'd partner with Bee, and he hasn't returned.'

Eldric glared at his nephew in silence, eyes blazing. 'And you're only just telling me this now?'

'Sagan said he'd sent –' Gilbert began.

'What's the nearest castle to Rolfen?' Eldric asked.

'Hutes Castle is a few miles away,' Gilbert muttered.

'Do you have birds from this castle? If so, send a Royal Command, send Reapers to that bloody castle, I want it searched, and anybody connected to that bitch brought here,' Eldric raged. 'Fuck it, burn that fucking castle down. Make sure everybody knows if they help Bedelia, they'll end up dead.'

'Uncle, I think –'

'Bring me, Marisol. I want to know about this Frenchman.' He vanished back down the spiral steps. Eldric's anger rushed inside him, but inside he was weakening. He was losing his grip on these abilities. Oren and Gilbert followed behind, their boots stomping the stone steps, keeping up with Eldric.

Once out in the courtyard, he waited. Gilbert shouted at his soldiers. There was a scurry, a flow of activity, people buzzed and then Marisol was brought out in hand chains. The soldiers forced her to kneel on the ground. She squinted, looking up into the sun as Eldric blocked most of it.

'Tell me more about this Malick Rose?'

Marisol sneered, rattling her chains. 'She shot him dead. I buried him, and now he's up and about.'

'How do you think that is possible?'

'How the fuck should I know?' And Marisol's answer was met with a punch from the guard.

'Is he a commoner?' Eldric asked.

'A boat owner and runs a tavern,' Omega said, keeping an eye on both guards.

Eldric grimaced at the thought of a Guardian, his daughter, being married to nothing more than a boorish low breed. 'Did he know she was a Guardian?'

Omega shook her head. 'Bee killed one of my guardsmen, that's when he learned she was a Guardian.'

Eldric remained silent. The man had no indication of what Bee was. That meant he had no Guardian blood running through him. He was nothing.

'Are you certain he was dead when you buried him?' Eldric questioned. He walked a little, looking at Oren, who remained silent.

'The man bled out on the pub floor, he wasn't breathing,' she snapped.

Eldric nodded and then ordered the guards to take Omega back to the dungeons. She swore, kicking as they dragged her. He watched, almost smiling, he would enjoy taking her to bed. She was a fighter, not like her mother.

'Bedelia has imprinted herself onto this Malick Rose,' he mused. 'I don't know how she's managed it with a non-guardian, but she has.'

'What does it mean?' Oren asked.

Eldric shivered, realising how powerful his daughter actually was. 'We can't imprint anymore, but she has made another guardian. Bee's more powerful than us, with or without him. She can hide pieces of herself in him, and channel them. That is very dangerous.'

'What do you want to do?'

'She's coming for me. The only way I can protect myself is to start the absolution.' Eldric didn't look at his nephew, walking away.

'Uncle, you can't.' Oren stopped Eldric, pushing him back. 'You'll kill –'

Eldric shoved him aside. 'And summon more Reapers. We'll kill her one way or another.'

***

Arena Porta, Kent

The silence in the pub gave Bee comfort, but she wasn't alone. Inside her, something scratched around, burrowing, looking for the piece she kept hidden. These Spectres, or as Winnie called them, Sinners, were seeking it out, and she was determined they wouldn't find it. Not yet.

Bee slept for a few hours. She had been drained from bringing down The Barricade, and her dreams consisted of repeatedly seeing the wall come down, and within the dream came a mist. She didn't know if the fog was real or part of her vision, but inside the smoky haze came voices, some from the living, and others from the dead.

The soldiers who'd arrived with Eldric didn't look for Bee. Instead, they arrested any of Omega's riders who weren't dead or hadn't managed to escape. Omega, Bee learned, Eldric had taken but she didn't know what had happened to Baptiste. Nobody was sure who'd got out, but Arena Porta was free of Omega's people.

Somer had rested. He eased his way around the pub, learning to move with his injuries, and he'd headed outside into the sun. Malick was already outside preparing the horses.

Bee kneeled, facing the wall of the inn. She focused, staring past the old flaky wallpaper, and beyond, to something else. She'd been sitting there for three hours, meditating, and she focused only on what she was about to do, unfazed by any movement.

The Spectres buzzed around her. They could not kill Eldric themselves. They needed a physical entity to cut the Lord Guardian down, and then they would take him, destroy the man, and leave the shell to rot in the dust, and all the power he'd stolen would be returned to The Spectres.

The world would return to a place where there were no Guardians, and no religion to strangle the people. Bee didn't know what would happen once she killed Eldric, but knowing she would destroy the world he'd created, made her feel better.

Bee never really understood why she'd always had this urge to destroy Eldric, putting it down to having been born a Guardian but brought up as a vassal. She knew the stories told by the priests were lies, but as The Spectres drew near, Bee understood their influence on her.

Standing up, Bee brushed herself down. She caught onto the overpowering smell of the fishing tackle and, touching the rope, she hoped she'd have the strength to finish this.

Leaving the pub, the sun blinded Bee. She covered her eyes and walked down to the beach. If there had been a mist, the sun had cleared it away. Stepping on the pebbles, they crunched under her boots and, for the first time, Bee saw how beautiful The Channel was without The Barricade, as the rippling waves glistened like a thousand pennies in the sun.

Seagulls sailed on the wind, extending their wings, gliding, and then perched on the new rock formations which jutted out of the waters. They would eventually crumble into the sea below but, for now, they gave the birds somewhere new to sit. The calm waters twinkled, and beyond that, Bee saw France.

She breathed in, seeing her home. It was still far away, but Bee was one step closer to returning. A young couple walked along the beach, Bee smiled, but they hurried by, afraid of the woman in the Reaper uniform.

Bee returned to the pub as Malick finished saddling the last horse. She pulled him close and kissed him, wanting to feel him next to her. And the young couple watched, aghast, as a Reaper kissed a man.

'Things will happen, Malick, things out of my control, but whatever happens, I need you to know that I love you because that might be all that I've got to cling to... if I get lost,' she whispered.

'I won't let you go, Bedelia.' He kissed her back, as Somer came around the corner out of the pub. Bee and Malick separated, conscious they'd been caught.

'Have I interrupted something?' he asked.

Both shook their heads.

'Malick, I'm giving you this.' Bee went to her own horse and pulled out the three-bladed dagger.

'I don't think I can... I don't think...' Malick started as Bee placed it into the palms of his hands.

'It's the best blade I have, simple and effective. Plunge it into the body or head, twist it, and you'll likely kill whoever's attacking you,' she explained, matter-of-factly.

He paled, giving her a small smile. 'You might need to brush up on how to romance your husband.'

'I'm serious, Malick,' Bee snapped, hearing Somer snort a laugh from behind a horse. 'Just take it, and if all else fails...' She squeezed his fingers around the hilt. '...it might save your life.'

Malick huffed, snatching the dagger out of her hand. He didn't look comfortable, but Bee said nothing, and then Malick helped Somer onto the horse.

'Somer, you can stay here,' Bee reminded him, and he shook his head.

They headed out of Arena Porta, and the horses' hooves crunched the shells on the road, flattening them into the mud, each hoof evening out the path. They wouldn't take the route through Foulksten, they would ride around it and into Dai, and Rufus had told her what pub to meet in.

Somer would remain at the pub, with her father. She'd wanted Somer to return to Deman Circe, but with Omega's men still being in the village, she couldn't risk his safety. Bee rode, thinking about Tristan. She wanted to see him playing with his little sister again, and she wanted to listen to the pair of them laugh. Bee closed her eyes as they rode, locking those feelings away in her private sanctuary. She wouldn't think of either of them until this was all over.

Chapter Thirty-One
Hutes Castle, Rolfen, Kent

All that was left of Hutes Castle was the Constable's gates. Two imposing turrets made from grey stone and an old wooden gate. Behind the stone structures were large brick buildings. The family home of Ivan La Cote was a two-storey steeply pitched roof that varied in height, made of brick and decorated with timber.

Birds nested in any open space found and, at certain times of the year, Ivan shared his living area with a wasp's nest. The rest of his land was filled with barns, living quarters and animal pens, all made from wood. The castle had vanished, and most of the stone was in the tumbled houses of the surrounding hamlet.

A messenger pigeon had arrived at Hutes Castle, and Overlord Ivan La Cote read the message. He understood the order, but frowned. There was a small indentation on the paper, meaning it was a Royal Command and Ivan would have to complete it. Otherwise, he would end up in the same position as his good friend, Sagan.

Standing in pig shit, he looked around the pen as the animals squealed, waiting for food. The young farmhand waited outside the fences, expecting an answer. He didn't get one, and Ivan told the boy to leave.

Ivan, a tall blond haired man, who worked the farm every day, was young, married, with children, like Sagan. They'd been friends since childhood, and he had lived with the Kendals for a period, before returning home to take over from his dying father. Now both men were in their thirties with lives of their own, and they would meet up for family gatherings or hunting weekends.

The message read the Kendals were to be arrested, along with a French boy. The household was to be executed and the castle burned to the ground. Again, Ivan read the declaration, and he muttered.

As he wiped mud down his shirt and breeches, the typical animal smells got up Ivan's nose. He almost slipped, getting out of the pen, and headed towards the Reaper quarters. The day was turning into a glorious clear blue sky, and that normally lifted his spirits, but what Ivan was about to order his only two Reapers to do, darkened his thoughts.

The Reapers were not the finest, which was why he had them. They were young and inexperienced. Two men in their early twenties with eight executions between them, and they'd never arrested an Overlord's family before. Sagan had far better Reapers. This would not end well.

Ivan muttered greetings to his farmhands as he headed toward the Reapers' quarters, which was nothing more than a shack at the back of the barn.

The men were already up. They'd had breakfast which the cook had provided and were cleaning their swords. Both were smartly dressed, but neither was in their uniform. It was law that Reapers were always supposed to be on duty, but in Hutes, where rarely much happened, Ivan grew lazy with rules, allowing the assassins to dress how they wished.

'Dominic, Fisher, you've a Royal Warrant to execute,' he said, striding up to the pair of them.

Both looked up from their cleaning, surprised. They stood to attention and waited for more information.

'I'll draw up the papers, be ready in fifteen minutes.' Ivan walked back around the corner and toward the house.

Back inside, Ivan's wife's footsteps were somewhere above, thumping through the floorboards. He sat in his cramped study, an old musky room, full of books, papers and half-burned candles and gas lamps. Pulling out the parchment, he wrote the appropriate wording, signed, dated it and then heated some wax, sealing the warrant with the Royal Seal, something only used when Eldric issued a direct order to an Overlord.

Ivan was back outside the front of his house as the two Reapers rode up on their horses. Both dressed in their uniforms, neither had their masks on, and Ivan handed Fisher the warrant.

'You are to go to Rolfen Castle, arrest the Kendals, and a French boy. Execute the vassals, and burn the castle down.' Nausea rose inside Ivan, but he did not shake, speaking each sentence clearly.

'Yes, Lord Ivan,' Fisher nodded his head. He took the warrant, placed it inside his uniform, and both Reapers steered their horses out of the old castle gates.

Ivan watched them. The trotting turned into a canter which quickly changed to a gallop. It excited the young men, as this kind of order did not happen to the Reapers from Hutes Castle.

***

Dai Castle, Kent

Eldric stood in the Roman lighthouse of Dai Castle. He should have been in the Temple, where he could have gazed upon the Clannen Dolls, sit in a pew, and listen to the silence. Instead, he chose the Roman lighthouse, a crumbling old tower, with nothing inside it, except dust, and mice, and he listened as the wind funnelled through the slot windows and through the non-existent doorway.

He remembered this place when he'd come to Dai for the first time. This was when he was Alfred, and not much had changed over the last five hundred years. This building was a testament to people who'd expanded across Europe, landed in Britain and eventually colonised a country which they believed to be full of ghosts and monsters, and they took this land and made it their own.

The Romans had built a vast Empire. Eldric had done the same as his powers had once run deep into Europe, up to the northern lands. The Red Plague and The Barricade meant he'd lost most of that Empire, and he could lose it all, if he did not kill Bedelia.

Claude hadn't returned, he assumed Bee had killed him, and that enraged Eldric. He lashed out at Gilbert Evans after he failed to send more soldiers to Arena Porta, and when they did go, the soldiers returned with reports of a great mist covering the village. This mist was black and grey with shadowy figures forming, standing guard whenever a soldier tried to enter. There were sounds, like something caught between the living and the dead, voices whistling, calling out, and it frightened the soldiers. They refused to enter, and if one was brave enough to try, the shadowy figures cut them down.

Eldric didn't know how Bee had done this, but it was enough to scare the soldiers, and they'd returned to Dai, terrified. Bee was strong, much stronger than he'd given her credit for. Witnessing The Spectres entering her, made him understand, it was those souls imprisoned all those years ago within Chaslehurst Caves that were coming back for him.

There had to be some way to get through to Bedelia, that she was being used by these Spectres. He might convince her to spare his life and normality could return. Eldric would be in power, but he'd have to give Bee something back. Perhaps he would have to let her live in France with her low-breed husband. Wishful thinking, Bee would not let him live.

Outside stood two Reapers, both came with him wherever he went, even in the castle. Eldric would have to use the people. He would have to take their connection to him, and through the people, Eldric would become more powerful, maybe powerful enough to stop Bee.

He walked out of the lighthouse, the Reapers following behind. People stopped, gawping at their Lord Guardian. Men bowed, as ladies fell to their knees, and Eldric ignored them. The courtyard was busy, a pig turned on the spit, crackling sounds intermingling with the noise of geese and ducks. People shouted, and then stopped, watching Eldric take the steps up the ramparts.

Eldric would take the power of his subjects and consume it. This was the only way he could survive. He would start with the peasants, who lived just a little farther out of Dai, that way nobody would notice, not till it was too late. After that, it would be the townsfolk, followed by the soldiers.

Eldric considered the Guardians before he'd put up The Barricade. They were connected to him, but the ones in France and beyond had been lost. With the wall being down he still didn't sense them, guessing most of them had probably died. Everybody was susceptible to the plague, Guardian or not.

Those Guardians had always been the key to his power. They kept his colonies under control. The Guardians fed unknowingly off the people, giving them their abilities and he had fed off them. All that was gone. This had been Eldric's mistake, perhaps he should never have put up the Barricade.

Eldric stood seething. He was about to start the Absolution, and a little guilt whispered inside him, but Eldric brushed it away. Better he lived, and they died. He looked to France as the view was spectacular, but if Eldric didn't start the Absolution, he'd lose everything. Closing his eyes, he began.

The people on the outskirts of Dai crept toward him. He stood in the Farscape, in the world of vibrant red skylines and watery pathways.

The last time, he'd called only the soldiers at Krallar, and they came, wanting to be close to him, only for him to drain them of their connection, of their lives. Now he called to the people, and many people stood there waiting.

Men, women, children, the few who tended the land outside of Dai, men wearing breeches, and women in long thick skirts, all opaque in features, thin and faint, but there they stood, and slowly he drew from these people.

Eldric's fingers tingled. The children moved first, like ghosts through the uncharted landscape, and all of them approached him. Energies flowed, and Eldric became more potent as they ebbed toward him, and then they cascaded like a rush of water all going in one direction, and into him. Eldric opened himself up, colours changed, the landscape glimmered, as the reds in the world mutated into beautiful golds and blues, each colour merging into the other, softening the world.

And then the first child dropped. A little girl, no older than five, gave him everything. Her obligation to the Lord Guardian was over, and she died in the Farscape, just as she did out in the physical world.

And then the second child came, followed by a third, followed by the adults. These spirits, these people who gave themselves to Lord Eldric, all died, as he feasted on their power. He didn't take everybody, but Eldric would, if he needed to. He took their own vitality and made it his, and he became drenched in the lives of his subjects.

***

Karem had ridden through the night, and she did not look back. After Bee and Luther had spoken in the pub, Luther ordered Karem to ride to Rolfen Castle to evacuate Lord Sagan, his family, and everybody from the Castle. Bee told him she wanted them safe, and Eldric would most likely arrest or kill them. Karem had asked what he intended to do, and Luther mounted his horse and left Arena Porta without giving her an answer.

She left the town just as Bee had opened up and started bringing down the Barricade. Whatever was happening behind brought a violent wind, and every tree shook as the horse battled, pushing forward until the weather calmed, as the late morning sun rose.

The ride was hard and fast. Not stopping as Karem rode into the castle. She spotted two Reapers standing in front of the Kendals in the courtyard. One Reaper had his pistol aimed at Sagan.

Karem scanned the courtyard. A few vassals stood watching, all in scraggy clothing, and frightened. Five Reapers were behind Sagan's family; they did not intervene. Tristan was with the family and two sisters.

Karem slid off her horse. Neither Reaper wore his mask, and she slipped a knife into her hand, approaching. The Reaper with the pistol was about to speak, when Karem gripped hold of the man's neck, plunging the knife into his throat. The man gurgled, blood spurted from the neck, and he fell to his knees. Karem dropped the Reaper gently to the ground.

Faith screamed, shielding her girls and Tristan. The second Reaper scrambled for his revolver, but he was too slow, and Karem pulled her gun, shooting the man in the head, and the Reaper dropped into the mud.

Faith dragged the children away, tears, and screams echoed throughout the courtyard, as Karem stood in silence, watching Faith shove the children back up the stone steps and into the Keep.

Sagan shouted, 'You'd better have a good explanation for killing those Reapers in front of my children.'

Karem checked the first Reaper, then the second and pulled the document out of his uniform. 'The warrant, Lord Sagan.'

Sagan's eyes widened, seeing the Royal Seal and he ripped the paper open, and read the words. 'Bloody hell.'

'Bee brought The Barricade down last night, Luther ordered me to come. We didn't think Eldric would have acted so fast,' Karem spoke in an orderly manner.

Faith came running out of the Keep, screaming at Karem, frightening the livestock, making the animals bray. Demanding to know what was going on. Karem did nothing as Faith raised her hand about to slap the Reaper, but Sagan reached out, stopping Faith.

'She's stopped us from getting arrested.' Sagan pushed Faith away, and he reread the document. 'They were to execute the household and burn down the castle.'

Faith gasped, 'You brought this on us, Sagan, by bringing that bloody woman here.'

'I suggest you all leave now,' Karem said.

'And where are we supposed to go?' Faith shouted sarcastically.

Karem ignored her and said to Sagan. 'Send your Reapers to Hutes, let them stay there till this is over, and I'll take Tristan to Bee.'

Faith shook her head. 'No, the boy stays with me, where he's safe. She wants her son back, we'll all go.'

'Faith, I don't think –' Sagan started.

'I've a friend who lives outside Dai, we'll go there, that way we can be close to Bedelia and give her Tristan back.'

She didn't wait for an answer, storming back toward the house.

'You need to hide, Lord Sagan, Bedelia will finish this,' Karem stated.

Sagan smirked unhappily. 'At what cost? And even when this is all over, we don't know what's coming next.'

'You need to get ready, Lord Sagan, I'll deal with the people,' Karem said. 'And she said something about Adam and Feargal.'

Sagan nodded, shouting at his Reapers to go to Hutes Castle, and await instructions. Karem watched Sagan head toward the castle. She saw the unhappiness. The pain at having to leave the only home he'd ever known.

The Reaper looked around the castle walls. To her, they were bricks and shelter. She'd never had possessions, always ordered to go to places. Karem would only escape this life through surviving until she was thirty-five, and then given a situation in a small village, like that of Deman Circe. Karem prayed Bedelia would kill Eldric, because no child should be made into a Reaper.

Karem ransacked the armoury, taking anything which might be of use. She placed them inside a bag while shouting at the servants and vassals that the Castle was to be burnt.

Cattle ran as she opened the pens, shooing them out. Pigs scampered, then the dogs started barking, and within seconds it was havoc. People ran around screaming, trying to get out, and taking anything of value with them.

Children cried as people ran in every direction. The geese and ducks squawked, as confused as the people. Sagan carried a few belongings, putting them into a wagon and then ran back inside. The two little girls came running out, Adeen held her sister's hand and also her teddy.

Faith followed with Tristan and another boy. Both boys looked confused as Faith placed all the children into the wagon. Several times, Faith and Sagan ran inside, and after a few minutes, a young dishevelled and bewildered-looking young man came out. Sagan saddled a horse and told the man to leave.

Sagan jumped up onto the cart, cracked the whip and it sped out of the castle. Karem stood watching as Faith turned and looked at her home one last time, and then Karem lit the first stack of hay.

She moved around the courtyard, keeping only to the combustibles, lighting all of it. Kareem did not set fire to the Keep. She didn't know if the family could ever return, but if the Keep was still structurally sound, they might. Once alight the flames could go anywhere, but Karem hoped the whole place wouldn't burn down.

She stripped one dead Reaper of his uniform. The smoke was building, bellowing up, hiding the crisp blue sky, and Karem coughed, as the flames jumped. There might be serfs left inside, but it was too late as Karem pulled the large wooden gates closed. The fire would be self-contained within the walls, and now it was up to the flames where it travelled.

Pinning the Warrant onto the Rolfen public board outside the walls, Karem made sure it was visible for all to read. The notice included that nobody was to put out the flames and to let the fire burn everything inside. If anybody read the message, they knew better than to try to put the fire out.

Better to let it all burn.

⋯⋯◄◇►⋯⋯

Chapter Thirty-Two
Road to Dai

The ride toward Dai had been smooth and, as they made it through Kearsnei, a thin mist started coming in. The mist coated the ruins of the old manor house, floating around the brickwork that jutted out of the grey. The old abbey, as it was known, ran alongside the River Dai, and the trickling of waters from the gardens opposite mingled with the eerie fog.

Bee, Malick and Somer rode through Annata Valley, missing the town of Foulksten, toward Mansum Valley, with its high hills, pastures and low roads. Bee stopped several times, concerned the ride was too much for Somer. She expected a few complaints, but the man rode on, and though she'd heard a few groans, he never told her to stop. In the end, Bee lied, explaining she was tired and needed to rest. Both men knew she was lying, but neither challenged her.

Kearsnei was a small hamlet, hidden by thick trees and bushes, with a muddy holloway travellers used if they wanted to get to Dai. The horses clipped along the well-trodden path, and Bee listened as the birds in the trees became quiet, only chirping a signal to their mates that they were nearby. Otherwise, there was no noise, except for the noise of the horses.

Stationing the animal, Bee turned it to face the few houses and she closed her eyes. The mist washed over her. It crept into her bones, and this was down to Eldric. He had started the Absolution, cleansing the souls of his people, and he started with the residents outside of Dai. It began with those who were indentured to this area, or who had completed The Purge here. He would move closer to Dai if he didn't get enough strength from these sacrifices.

Bee saw the thin outline of a young boy. The child was about seven, wearing long raggedy trousers, a dirty white shirt, and was shoeless. Their eyes locked, Bee and the boy stared at one another as he walked by.

'What is it?' Malick asked, as both he and Somer rode up next to her. Bee sat there, her expression vacant, and Malick repeated his question.

'Eldric's starting the Absolution,' she whispered.

'What's that?' he asked.

'It means he's killing everyone.'

And behind them, an ear-splitting scream came from the mist. Both Malick and Somer turned, but Bee didn't move. The unseen voice called, crying, for her husband, panicked, as the hidden woman cried out, wanting help.

'We should go,' Bee whispered.

'They might need help.' Somer turned his horse in the direction of the woman.

Bee refused, 'Not from us.'

Somer raised his eyebrows to Malick, as a woman, almost tripping over her long drab skirt rushed out of the mist, holding a boy, about Tristan's age.

'Please,' she blubbered, 'he won't wake up.' Tears rolled down the woman's cheeks. She held the boy up to Malick, and he reached down from his horse. He was about to dismount when Bee reached out, stopping him.

'Stay on your horse, we can't do anything,' Bee said.

'I... I can't find Jack... I can't find my husband... I need him... Robbie won't wake up,' the woman whimpered, still looking at Malick. 'The children...they've collapsed... they've all collapsed.'

'We'll go look for him,' Malick said.

Bee kept a grip on his leather coat. 'I said 'no'.'

Malick's eyes widened. 'Bee?'

The woman ran around to show Bee her son. The boy's arms flopped as she held the child up. 'Please...' the woman whispered, 'he's still breathing.'

'Your son is dying.' Bee remained on her horse. 'Take him home.'

A man, the woman's husband, rushed out of the mist. 'Sarah?' he whispered, seeing his wife, holding their boy. He gathered up the child, cradling him in his arms. 'Come back, love, stay away from the Reaper.' And he disappeared back into the mist.

The woman screamed, yanking at Bee, begging for help. Bee leaned forward, placing her hand on the woman's shoulder. 'You need to be with your son.'

The woman sobbed, slapping Bee, and then she spat in Bee's face, saying viciously, 'You murdering whore. I hope those you've killed tear your soul apart.'

Bee's face hardened and the woman shook, her jaw jittery, realising what she'd said. The woman paled, faltering on her feet, understanding the Reaper was about to execute her, but she couldn't move.

Bee placed her hand on the grip of her revolver, but she didn't release the weapon from the holster. 'Leave now.' Bee watched the woman blink, eyes on the gun, knowing what the woman was thinking. She looked surprised Bee hadn't jumped off her horse, thrown her to the ground and put a bullet in her head. The woman gasped, turned and ran back into the mist, away from the Reaper.

The three sat in silence, and the mist gathered them. Bee suppressed her anger, wiping the spit away. She steered her horse, and the clopping of the horse's hooves faded into the mist.

Malick rode up next to her. He reached out, touching the leather sleeve. 'Bee?' he whispered.

Bee said nothing, as they plodded along in the mist. A single bird chirped, and then a baby wail came out of the fog. Somer rode up next to them, as the cries got louder.

'Can you hear that?' he asked.

'No, Somer, we carry on,' Bee directed him.

The cries pierced through the mist. A shrill, echoing throughout the thick smoky atmosphere, and there was movement, scurrying in the undergrowth, as unseen animals moved through the grass and the bushes. Bee let the screams reverberate up and down her body and she ignored them. Nobody would come for the baby; they were most likely dead.

The cries got louder as they rode closer. Bee's heart beat faster, ignoring the cries. She didn't want to think that she'd willingly passed by the agonising wails of a helpless infant wanting their mother, and did nothing.

Bee heaved, trying to keep her emotions under control. She looked ahead, and only the horse's shoes on stone cut through the world the three of them existed in. And out of the mist a considerable manor house loomed.

The fog moved around the building, sometimes revealing parts of it, and then the mist sucked it back up again. Another scream came. A terrified bone-breaking cry, that sent the birds and animals into a panic. The forest came alive with bird shrieks coming from all directions.

'Oh, for fuck's sake,' Bee muttered. The cries clawed at Bee, like a demon scratching her skin. She steered the horse sharply toward the house, toward the sound of the baby. And both men followed.

A magnificent palace, Bee thought as she gazed at the fourteen large windows, seven on the first floor and seven huge windows on the bottom. The house had a large porch, with a grand conservatory at the end, full of greenery.

It was silent except for the baby's cries.

Bee dismounted and took a shotgun out of the saddle. 'You both stay here. If it goes wrong, get to the pub, find Rufus.' she whispered.

'No, we're coming with you.' Malick followed her action, pulling his shotgun, as did Somer, with some difficulty.

Bee readied her weapon, looking all around, and only the sounds of the ducks quacking interrupted her thoughts. Something was wrong, and it wasn't just the dead bodies lying inside the manor house. Gingerly, she opened the grand doors. Pointing the barrel of the gun, she skulked inside, checking either side of her.

The hallway was beautiful, filled with paintings, chairs, tables, and flowers of all colours in every part of the space. Its beauty overwhelmed Bee. Reds and golds flashed, and the floral, winey scents of the buds hit her.

Bee stepped over the bodies of the servants. Three of them lay near the staircase, their trays, and the morning breakfast strewn all over the polished floor. She'd seen nothing like it. Even Oren's apartments were bare compared to this stately home.

Quietly, Bee stepped up the staircase. She swung her body around, as she tiptoed up, listening to sounds, listening for anything. Behind her, Malick and Somer creeped up the stairs, and she ignored their weighted breathing, both nervous, both scared.

At the top of the stairs, Bee motioned for them to stay close. She'd have preferred to do this alone, because she'd have to protect them as well as herself should anything happen.

The baby screamed again.

Bee's survival instincts set in. The bright yellow corridor loomed - tables, plants on both sides - and the bodies of two well-dressed people, a man and woman lay on the carpets. Bee guessed they were the owners, and at the other end was a white door. There were rooms on either side and, quickly but carefully, she stood by the first door, opened it, aimed her shotgun inside, checked it was empty and moved on.

Bee did this methodically with each room, and behind, Somer and Malick kept an eye on her back, checking nobody was coming out. She came to the final door at the end of the corridor. She pointed for the men to stand on either side. Bee stood next to Malick, his breathing heavier than hers and quietly turned the handle.

Inside the room, she saw Reapers. Bee was about to fire when she heard the click of a gun behind her. Two Reapers stood there, aiming their weapons in Malick and Somer's faces.

She blinked, unsure how they got there and then saw the secret panel. They'd hidden inside, waiting. The nursery door opened fully, and ten Reapers stood in the large nursery. A gentle breeze came through the large open bay window, and in the centre stood a tall Reaper. A man dressed in black, holding what looked like a rag doll.

Her heart banged. She was alone, with no one to help, and she'd messed up because of a crying baby. The Reapers pushed them all inside the room. They stood in front and kept their eyes firmly on Malick and Somer. Two more Reapers forced the men to their knees, placing iron bracelets on each man.

The Reaper holding the doll, smiled, 'Hello, Bedelia, I'd heard you were back.'

Bee nodded, 'That's right, Jacob.' Memories flashed back to the Tower. She'd seen him in the barracks, but avoided him. A sturdy brown-haired brute, who took pleasure in torturing the malefactors, rather than getting the job done. She'd gone out on one warrant with him and hated every single minute.

The room stayed quiet. Bee remained motionless as she spotted it wasn't a doll in Jacob's hand, it was the baby. The body floppy and arm broken, and then the baby made a pitiful meowing sound.

'I like your bruises, Bee,' the Reaper grinned. 'They go with that lovely smile.'

Bee kept quiet.

'I hear you married a Frenchman and have two children?' Jacob looked over Bee's shoulder at Malick and Somer. 'We are to bring you in, dead or alive.'

Bee nodded, keeping an eye on Jacob as he approached Malick. Jacob placed his hand on Malick's shoulder and grinned.

'Your wife is an efficient killer.' He crouched next to Malick. 'They ordered me to make an example of a Malefactor.' Jacob raised his eyebrows. 'Eldric ordered two of their eight children to be executed, and I had to observe. Bee picked a boy of seven, and a little girl of four. She didn't hesitate, putting a bullet right between the eyes of my brother and sister.'

Bee breathed slowly. She remained impassive, but the painful memory of killing those two children squashed everything and Jacob moved back into the centre of the nursery, as Bee turned her back on Malick.

He brought the baby up to his face, Jacob said, 'Each Reaper will have a go. Whoever brings you down, will enjoy freedom. They can have the life you've had for the past six years.' Smiling, Jacob threw the baby out of the window. The baby screamed as it flew out, and then there was a thud, and nothing else.

Bee stood. She did not move or flinch, but she'd heard the frightened mutters behind, and Malick and Somer's fear began creeping toward her as if it were prowling around, ready to pounce.

'No guns and no swords.' He looked down at the weapons around her waist and Bee unstrapped them, leaving them on the carpet. He said, 'No ability bollocks, Bee, otherwise it's an unfair death.'

All she had were two machetes, a baton, an array of blades and her hands. Bee's stomach churned, taking a prolonged drawn intake of air, as one Reaper stood in front of her.

A young man, no older than twenty, cricked his neck and flung out his hand, Bee heard the familiar clicking sound and the baton extended into life and the man was ready, but Bee had already extended the pins in her gloves and was plunging them into the young Reaper's neck before the final locking of the baton. Bee's hand was around his neck, his eyes wide, astonished he'd been attacked. Surprised he'd been murdered so fast and Bee dropped him to the ground.

A second Reaper kicked her fast. She stumbled backwards, deflecting the repeated kicks. He jumped, legs flayed back, and he flew at Bee punching her in the face, quick to the ribs, and then another kick and Bee fell onto her backside. She got up fast, and the Reaper high kicked her.

Bee punched him in the stomach, then quickly and repeatedly in the ribs, sending the Reaper back. The killer high kicked, and Bee gripped the man's leg. She brought a dagger down, smashed it into his leg, ripping the blade fast along his femur, through his leathers, skin and muscle, and the blood poured. The man roared. The screams punctured the white floral walls of the nursery. She threw him to the ground, lifted her leg high, and stomped her boot down into his head.

The man stayed down.

The other Reapers came at Bee. One kicked, one punched. In all directions, the fight happened. Bee breathed, watching, and guessing every single next move.

She pulled out a machete as a Reaper came at her with his. Bee dropped to her knees, sailing just under the blade as it passed over her head, and Bee turned, stabbing him in the back. Sometimes she escaped the clash only through falling. Other times, she'd beat a Reaper, picking them up, smashing them against a wall or piece of furniture. Someone jabbed her body, she bled, stumbling.

One Reaper flipped her over, and Bee twisted her body, snaking it around his, as she broke his neck. Another dragged her and flung her against the wall. Bee screamed, rushes of blood attacked her insides, and she gasped, falling to the ground, but she kicked, and the Reaper flew back.

She'd killed five Reapers.

A gunshot blasted from outside the door, killing a Reaper. Luther ran, sliding on the polished floor, aiming his gun, pulling the trigger again and again. Blood, bone and shots rebounded off the walls. Some attempted to grab their weapons, but Luther shot them, and the last bullet he fired was in Jacob's face. Blood soaked into the white carpets, a crimson beauty spreading out.

The room became silent.

Bee breathed out, bent over, gasping and she stared at Luther. The man placed the shotgun on the carpet and stood to his full height in his black leathers and he waited. She ran into him, clasping him tightly.

Luther's arms wrapped around Bee and she clung to him, looking up, she tightened her hold. Everything was the same and that clean leather smell she associated with her best friend rushed through Bee, and she relaxed, not wanting to let go.

He stood, holding Bee, with his chin on her head. 'I'm sorry, Bee, I wasn't there for you in France.'

She patted his leathers, giving him a tiny smile. 'I'm not,' she said.

***

Dai, Kent

Malick insisted on burying the baby with the people he assumed were the parents. Bee and Luther stood behind Malick and Somer as they said a few words. Bee warmed, loving Malick a little bit more as he uttered words for a family he didn't know. This was the man she'd married, and fallen in love with.

Luther had not considered the burial necessary, explaining the dead were to be left, and Bee agreed with Luther, but kept those thoughts quiet. Instead, she gently suggested to Luther that Malick and Somer should bury the family.

Nobody talked as they headed to Dai. Bee rode next to Malick. She'd tried speaking to him, but he remained quiet, hands tight around the reins, and Bee experienced something she'd never felt before, as Malick became tangled inside himself, and he attempted to shut Bee out.

Dai was quiet. The bodies lay in the narrow streets, and hadn't yet started the decomposing process. Most had only been dead a few hours. The faecal smells mixed with the salty air, but they weren't strong enough to affect Bee.

Chimneys still bellowed out smoke, as they rode from the leafy wooded area and into the urban landscape. Most houses were old and tumbledown, one-storey and not much more. The structures creaked, a sound rarely heard because of the noise of the town. Other houses were grander, brick made, with thatched roofs. Many were two-stories, but there was no bustle in the town, no voices, just animals braying, wanting attention and none were forthcoming.

The group stopped, and Bee looked up to the Castle. There were no guards on the towers. It was quiet. She sat between Malick and Somer, with Luther behind, as the horses rested. They stared at the market square, looking at the piles of bodies.

'I remember Bononia, the first time you and Nadine took me to the Temple. I know what you all did; during the worst of the Plague, you helped with the dead. The bodies are fresh here, but I'm still sorry you have to see this.' And she carried on into the town.

The wind blew up the streets, sometimes carrying a voice or a baby crying. Not everybody was dead. Few scurried about, men and women, those who hadn't gone through The Purge. They hid at the sound of the horses as the group rode through, seeing a Reaper heading through the streets.

Dogs barked as cats ran along the back alleyways, and in every street lay bodies. The mist had long since vanished, revealing what Eldric had done. People lay together, others in the middle of the road, in the muddy paths. The bodies were all at different stages of death.

Bee concluded The Purge had started over twelve hours ago and was still going on. A few of the dead had passed through rigour mortis, their muscles loosened, while others were in full rigour, eyes opened, and the ones who'd dropped only a few hours ago had the reddish-purple discolouration formed near the skin closest to the ground.

The smell would come later, and already the rats were gnawing the faces, with the opportunity to gorge on free food. They squeaked, talking to each other, that there was an abundance of food.

Bee was careful as they rode through the streets. They turned in one direction and followed the road, as a woman stood there, dazed. Another survivor rocked his son in his arms, and the tears rolled down his cheeks.

People ambled, many with bundles, afraid that whatever had hit the town might now come for them, and they moved in different directions, and always out of the way of the Reapers.

Bee stopped outside a pub called 'The Rose,' and all four dismounted. Bee stared up at the castle in the distance, standing guard over Dai and she shivered, dreading what was going to happen once inside. A man lay across the pub's doorway, and Bee dragged him aside. Pulling out a revolver, she opened the door. Luther stood on the other side.

'In here, Bee,' Rufus called out.

Bee stepped over the bodies, ushering everyone inside, and Luther remained by the door. The place was old, dusty, half-drunk beakers, and the customers were dead. Their eyes were vacant and questioning, as if wondering how and why this had happened.

Malick remained with Somer, neither wanting to get too close to any of the bodies, as Rufus propped up the bar, drinking ale. He stepped around behind the bar, asking if anybody wanted a drink, as he dragged the dead barkeep out of the way, bringing up some beakers.

Bee nodded her head and turned to Malick and Somer. Both had a green appearance around their faces. 'Only for me, Father.'

He poured the ale. 'I've had a look around the castle, Eldric's left the doors open. He's waiting for you. I didn't go in, but spoke with a few survivors. It was market day, busy, and the soldiers are dead. Gilbert Evans and his family are dead. Eldric's taken most of the town, and he has sixty Reapers up there.'

Bee choked on her ale. 'How come there are so many Reapers?'

Rufus shrugged. 'He ordered them here.'

'If he's harnessed all these people, I don't know if I can beat him,' Bee whispered, drinking. She then asked, 'Are Leena and Gable still there?'

Rufus slurped his beer. 'And Oren, he'll use Oren and Gable's power, you need to be prepared, Bee.' Then he looked at Malick. 'You as well.' Rufus smirked, seeing Malick spring to attention, as he'd been gazing at the dead.

'Omega?' Bee whispered.

Rufus finished his beer and poured another. 'Somewhere in the dungeons.'

Bee tapped her fingers on the bar, finishing her drink. Inside, her heart raced. This had been her only focus when she lived in Britain, and now it was here, Bee hoped she could complete it.

As an apprentice Reaper, Bee would lie in her cot, imagining different scenarios and different ways to kill Eldric, and now all of them appeared easy and stupid. Yet, now the Lord Guardian kept the gates opened at Dai Castle, inviting her in.

'Bee, there's something I want to say.' Rufus sipped his beer.

'What's that?' She wasn't listening, more interested in watching both Malick and Somer, the way they stared at the bodies. Both had seen their fair share during the plague, but neither looked comfortable.

'I was a terrible father, Bee.' He rubbed his cracked face, adding, 'I'm sorry I wasn't better.'

Surprised, Bee focused on him, saying, 'You were a shit father, Rufus.'

He nodded, coming around to stand on her side of the bar. 'But I'm pleased you got married, as he obviously loves you very much.'

Bee blinked; she wavered a little. Rufus had never spoken so kindly before, but she accepted what he said. 'Thank you, Father,' she whispered, taking his hand and squeezing it.

The pub door opened, and in walked Karem and Thomas. Karem placed a bag on the bar, and a Reaper uniform, she then spoke to Luther. Somer stepped away from the Reapers, not wanting to be close as Malick stood by the window.

'Bee, Karem got these.' Luther pulled six pistols out of the sack.

She looked at them. All of them were different from the revolvers she'd used. Picking one up, she found it was lightweight and sleek. Bee liked the feel in her hand.

'It's a semi-automatic, introduced just after you went to France. You need to take it outside and practise. It is self-loading and holds eighteen bullets,' Luther said, showing her how to load the weapon. She followed, taking a single clip, and loading it as if she'd done it before.

'Outside, Bee,' Luther said, exiting the pub into the bright sunlight, and he explained how to use the pistol. She followed his instructions, aimed and fired the weapon, only once. She leaned into him, as he showed that she could repeatedly fire.

'Use the dead,' he ordered.

Bee aimed the weapon at the body of a young man. Pulling the trigger, she blasted the bullets into the head, the chest and the legs. She reloaded the weapon, and this time, shot at a tree, then a wall, and back to the body, emptying the clip. Bee gave Luther a huge grin, and he laughed at her. She felt lighter, being able to smile with Luther, and Luther gripped her arm, pulling her close.

'Thank you, Luther.' She slipped her arms around him, and they held each other. He had always been there, the only person she'd loved, until she met Malick.

Luther released Bee. Turning to head back inside, she caught Malick at the window, arms folded and eyes narrowed. Something was wrong. She'd never felt it from him before, it was new, a little dark, and angry, but it wasn't directed at Bee, it was directed inward, because he was angry for feeling it, and Bee realised it was jealousy. She headed back into the pub, not looking at Malick, sensing him watching her, and she noticed Rufus talking quietly to Karem.

Luther touched the uniform. He glanced back at Malick, and Bee sighed. 'Malick, you should wear this.' Grabbing the outfit, she pressed it into his hands.

'I'm not wearing that,' Malick snapped.

Bee knew why. 'Please, it might save your life.'

'It didn't make a difference to the Reaper.'

'But–'

'No.'

'Get him dressed, Karem,' Luther ordered, and the Reaper approached Malick, as he stepped back.

'I'm not wearing it.' He shook his head, and Karem did not move again.

'Bee, make your husband wear it,' Luther ordered.

'I can't force him,' she argued.

Luther turned toward Malick. 'Then, I will.'

Bee squared up to Luther, getting in his way. 'You touch Malick, and I'll put a bullet in you.'

Luther muttered, 'Yes, you would.'

'Now, Bee, something happened–' Rufus interrupted.

'What?' Bee demanded, noticing him twitch. 'And don't lie to me, Father, I've just threatened to shoot Luther, and I'll do the same to you.'

Rufus mouth dropped, and he looked to Luther, who shrugged. 'Tristan and the Kendals are safe. They are at the home of one of Faith's friends in Dai. The family they went to are dead.'

'Go find them, Father, and keep them hidden,' Bee snapped, guessing that Rufus would have lied, to make sure she went up to the castle. 'And Somer's going with you.' Somer didn't protest, and she gave him a small smile, seeing the relief in his face.

She turned to Malick, asking coldly, 'Are you ready?' knowing what was bothering him, but for now it could wait.

And Malick nodded.

Chapter Thirty-Three
Dai Castle, Dai, Kent

The late afternoon shone as bodies lay strewn along the path toward Dai Castle. Malick's heart pumped. He rode behind Bee, and between the three Reapers, feeling like he couldn't take care of himself, that he wasn't capable of defending himself, and though Malick drew his pistols when he had to, he'd never pulled the trigger. Now Malick wondered, could he actually do it, could he kill somebody?

Dai Castle was impressive. He'd seen it before The Barricade went up, through his spyglass from the deck of the Juna, but now as he gazed up at the Caen stone walls, his jaw dropped at the fortress, built for nothing else except to defend Britain.

He watched Bee as they plodded forward. He guessed she was checking the great curtain walls for any would be assassin as she kept staring up. He worried somebody might take aim and shoot them but nobody did, and Malick turned his attention to the dead. Crows settled on the faces of the dead, picking at their eyes. The eyes were always the first to go, the softest bit of a human to devour. They cackled amongst themselves and, as the horses moved carefully through the dead, the birds did not take flight.

The horses all stopped as Bee slowed her horse, all four of them hidden within a line of trees. Only the wind blew. It wasn't a howl, but they could hear the sounds of chattering as if something was whispering, and Malick tried to block out the sounds.

'Leave the horses here,' Bee said, dismounting. 'Malick, you will stay with Thomas.' She looked at the scarred man. 'You've the most important job of all and that's to keep Malick safe. I don't know what shit show this is going to turn into, it's too quiet, and I don't want my husband's head blown off because some fucker is using a murder hole. *Don't,* Thomas, cock it up.'

'Yes Bedelia,' the blond Reaper nodded.

Malick paled, hearing the blunt words Bee used about his possible death, and he watched the four Reapers check their weapons. They went through their guns, knives, and things Malick couldn't name, but looked sharp and dangerous. The way Bee spoke to her own kind differed from the way she behaved at home.

In Bononia she ignored the insults. Even after six years, people still called Bee names, and she took the abuse because she hadn't wanted Malick to find out she was a Reaper. She'd never tell him what they said and it was only when Gerald or Mr Allard told him, that he found out. Malick confronted the gossipers and they left Bee alone, but then it would start again. She wouldn't take the abuse when Bee returned home, and once people learned she was a Reaper, they'd be too afraid to say anything.

Watching Bee and Luther, as they synced together, saying nothing, but carefully checking each other's uniform, and that they had enough bullets. She checked his hands, and Luther pulled up the back on Bee's uniform, slipping a weapon into the back of her breeches. The attachment between them was unbreakable, as they scrutinised every inch of each other.

Malick's stomach tightened, watching them. He couldn't help it, it gnawed into him that Bee had loved somebody before him, and now Luther was here, helping, about to do things that Malick couldn't dream of doing. The bond between the two Reapers was intense, and the devotion was something Malick would never understand.

Bee came over, she was close but not enough, and she then stated, 'Since I was eight, it's only ever been Luther and me. He's the first person I loved and still do.'

'I know I shouldn't be jeal–'

'On our wedding night, I thought Somer and Teppo would hold me down, that's what I thought people did. I wanted to give myself to you freely because you saw a person. When we kissed, it released something growing inside me, and I shot that robber because I didn't want to lose you for the sake of a few pennies.'

'Bee–'

'Falling in love with you is the most dangerous thing I've done,' Bee whispered breathlessly, inching toward him. 'You're my madness, and the only man that's ever made me feel this.' She inched closer.

He pulled her close, and Malick whispered in his French accent. 'I can't protect or keep you safe the way he can, so please allow me my jealousy.'

She touched his stubble, and Bee turned serious. 'Remember that afternoon you said you'd always keep me safe? I knew then you always would.'

'But–'

Bee cut in again. 'It's about you loving me without knowing all of me, protecting me from the gossips, and accepting I didn't fit in. I don't need somebody who can shoot, that's why I'm in love with you, because a gentle man can keep somebody safe.'

Brushing Bee's hair, he said, 'I love you.' He kissed her, and then Malick whispered. 'You need to go to Luther.' He released Bee from his clasp, and she walked away. Malick breathed out, he wanted to protect Bee from whatever might come, but he was glad Luther would be by her side.

Luther glanced back toward Malick, nodding at him as he handed Bee her helmet. She put it on, and the mask came to life as the teeth around Bee's lips appeared, along with the skeleton across the skull of her helmet.

Malick watched Bee straighten her back, take the rifle Luther handed to her, place the stock in her right hand, the barrel in the left, and heard the distinctive click sound. Malick breathed out as the sweat trickled down his back. The pistol in his hand didn't feel real, and Malick gripped it, muttering to himself.

The group crept up the well-trodden muddy path toward the gatehouse and across the bridge. The moat had long since gone, leaving only a significant dip where water should be, and grass had taken its place. Thomas stayed next to Malick, as Bee and Luther entered the Constable's gates. They stopped. Bee kept her focus on the murder holes cut out of the stone above, Luther surveyed the rest of the stone gateway as Karem inspected the back. Thomas grabbed Malick, dragging him through, before pushing him against the stone near the exit. Malick jittered, he closed his eyes, and prayed. He looked down as his hands trembled and he realised he was praying that Bedelia would keep him safe.

***

Bee peered through the holes in her mask, and she looked out to the courtyard as dusk turned into night. Soldiers and traders lay silently on the ground. None of these bodies had any signs of violence. No bullet wounds, no knife injuries. All dead, because of Eldric.

They passed through the first courtyard, making their way toward the second set of high walls. Bee looked back, Malick stayed close to Thomas, and then she refocused.

Bee didn't know where the attack might come from, but none came. Bodies lay around the stalls, and the smell of cooking had long since turned into burned flesh. Silence filled the space between the outer and the inner bailey. The quiet fed on Bee, sweat trickled down her back, and she wanted to turn back.

Each footstep became a little harder, and Bee tightened her grip on the gun. Her heart pounded; palms wet, as they ventured further into the silence. The group was exposed; there was too much land between them and The Guardian's Gate, the second gateway. While the crows called out as if mocking Bee, telling her to prepare for her own death.

Shaking these thoughts off, she watched Luther stride with confidence, and though Bee walked and held herself in the same manner, inside something was churning up. It had been over ten years since she'd been in a situation like this, but here they would be outnumbered by Reapers, not villagers, and that was a different prospect altogether.

Dogs sniffed the few bodies laid across the final gate as they entered the inner bailey. The animals barked, some whimpered, pushing their noses into the crevices of the fallen people, hoping their master might rise from the dead.

There was nowhere for the group to hide and they walked toward the Guardian's Gate and on the other side stood the Keep. This would be where the Reapers would attack. She again checked for any unseen assailant and whistled for the rest of the group to join her. Bee monitored Thomas, and he proved his worth, keeping Malick close.

They hid inside the safety of the gateway. The darkness shielded the group, and though The Great Tower was only a short distance away, there was not much cover between them and the building. There were a few stalls they could use for protection, and Bee stared at the women and children dead on the muddy grass.

Bee and Luther peered out, and a shot fired down on them. It hit the wall, and pieces of stone flew into the air as the sounds of horses came from behind. The animal's hooves sounded angry as they pounded the path, and Bee turned. Two Reapers rode up fast, entering the small space, and Thomas grabbed Malick, pushing him protectively into the stone.

Karem fired her shotgun into the horse, as Luther did the same. The gate was too small to aim at the moving Reapers, taking out the animals made it easier to attack. The horses went down, wounded, neighing, as legs buckled on the cobbled stones. Then Karem and Luther pulled the trigger of their shotguns a second time into the heads of the fallen Reapers, and blood seeped into the stone paths.

Movement from inside the stalls came. Bee signalled to Luther, pointing to her eyes and then in the direction of the sound. Somebody was moving toward them. Luther and Karem scurried out, running behind the stall, and the gunfire splintered the quiet.

'Malick, next to me.' Bee pointed to the wall beside her, and he slid up there, followed by Thomas. She stood out and fired up into the tower and hid again behind the stone wall.

A shot fired back, and then Luther shot from his hidden position. Bee repeated firing and hiding, as the shooter shot back. Luther's weapon exploded, and seconds later, there was a thud.

Within seconds they heard another shot. Somebody had taken over the first marksman as Bee and Luther repeated the same action another two times, and the sounds of two more thuds came.

Bee reloaded her shotgun fast. She breathed profusely, and it was the only sound she heard. Sweating, Bee's heart pounded. She looked briefly at Malick, nodded, and gave out a frightened breath as if she was blowing away her fear.

'We go now, stay between Thomas and me.' And she moved out of the gate and into the open. Standing straight, she aimed the rifle, shot, reloaded, shot and continued as they hurried toward the tower.

Bee had announced she was here.

Thomas fired behind her. He gripped hold of Malick, pushing past Bee as she continued firing at the Tower. The sound was deafening, and Bee ran to the steps of the tower, where Malick and Thomas hid.

'Are you okay?' she asked Malick through her helmet. He didn't answer, just nodded, but his face was pale.

Bullets hailed from another direction. They came from the ramparts, and Bee instinctively pulled Malick close to her, hiding his face, as Thomas started firing. From the few stalls, Karem and Luther fired in the same direction. Bee took the opportunity and grabbed Malick's hand, wrenching him up. He felt heavy, not wanting to move, but he ran as Bee pushed him up the steps.

The Overlord's banner swayed in the wind over the great doors, and Bee spotted something horrible, a gibbet hanging between the banners, and inside a body burned and then it screamed, echoing around the ramparts. Behind them, the bullets kept coming, but she was inside with Malick. And one step closer to her target. She turned to see Thomas was now on the steps, still firing, and then he stopped. Thomas crumpled and fell back down the stone stairs toward the grass, and Bee realised there was nothing she could do to save him.

Bee gripped hold of Malick. Ripping off her helmet, she let out some air, wiping her forehead. She gasped a smile at Malick and loosened her leathers.

'Are you hurt?' she asked, seeing the panic in his eyes. 'Have you been shot?'

Malick shook his head.

'Good.'

The gunfire carried on. Out of the corner of her eye, Bee saw the boots of Karem and Luther. Then she heard a cry, and she stopped. Her eyes widened, and she ran back towards the tower's doors.

'Luther,' she screamed. He lay at the bottom of the steps.

Malick gripped hold of Bee. She struggled, taking Malick with her as she headed back out into the exposed firing line.

'Luther,' she cried out again, throwing down her guns, almost at the steps, as Malick wrenched her back inside the entrance.

'Bee,' he yelled, wrapping his arms around her body, pulling her back. 'You can't help him; you have to finish this.'

Bee growled, Luther couldn't be dead, as she grappled with Malick. Seeing her only friend drop made Bee's heart stop, she wanted him with her, needing him by her side. Bee ran backwards, slamming Malick against the wall. He cried out, winded, letting go, and Bee started back down. Luther lay in the mud as Karem came running up.

'Stop her,' Malick shouted.

Karem collided with Bee, and both fell hard onto the stone steps. Bee wheezed with pain as Karem dragged her up by the collar of her uniform. She threw Bee onto the cold floor, glaring.

Bee lay in the quiet of the entrance, bones hurting, and she let out a pathetic cry, knowing she had to leave Luther alone in the mud. Bee knew Luther would tell her to *'Get up and move'* but Bee didn't want to, she wanted to close her eyes and pretend none of this was happening.

Coughing, Bee gingerly got up and picked up the rifle. She arched her back, letting the bones crack and stared at Luther, and then she turned, ignoring Malick, Bee ran up the stairs toward the next level.

A few bodies lay on the spiral steps, and she jumped over them, all the time hearing Malick and Karem run to keep up. Bee heaved as she came to the second floor, and three Reapers, without their helmets, waited.

Bee stepped forward, shooting one. Another she threw a star at, hitting him in the chest, and he went down, struggling to pull it out. The third held his sword, and Bee released both swords, attacking.

The Reaper was bigger than her and, as the swords clashed, he pushed Bee back. She dropped one sword, taking a knife, stabbed him in the waist. He fell to the ground, and Bee pulled out the automatic pistol, shooting him in the face. The blood poured into the stone, forming a small lake around his head.

The Reaper she'd stabbed, struggled to get up, and Bee stood beside him, aimed the gun and released several bullets into his chest, and finally the head. Then from the corner of her eye, Bee saw movement, a flash of blue and the person moved fast.

It was Leena.

Bee marched toward Leena as Malick and Karem followed. The woman closed a door on Bee. She opened it, then slammed it behind her, locking the door. A Reaper took aim and shot, Bee cried as the bullet grazed her arm, and she fell back against the door. Behind the door, Malick and Karem hammered their fists, wanting to get in, and the Reaper loomed over Bee, pointing his gun. She kicked him in the groin, and he staggered back.

Bee jumped on him. They wrestled, and in the background, the woman screamed. The Reaper kicked Bee off, and she rolled as he plunged his knife into what should have been her head. Bee straddled herself over him, trying to twist his neck. He kicked Bee off, sending her flying over his head, crashing onto the floor. The Reaper picked her up and smashed her against the door. Bee cried, bones cracking, and the man dragged her up off the floor, strangling her.

The door rattled, but Malick and Karem couldn't get through, and then the shooting started outside the room, in the corridor. Bee choked, spittle flying everywhere, her feet were off the ground, and she tried to free herself. She gripped hold of his face, hands on either side and squeezed, forcing her thumbs into his eyes.

Leena appeared, running toward the door.

Bee kept pushing, and the man screamed. She withdrew her blood-covered fingers from the soft mush of the eyeballs. Taking off her bracelet, she pulled it free, exposing the two metal wires, and laced them around his neck and she pulled it fast, putting the man out of his pain, and he slumped backward, taking Bee with him.

Bee clambered off the body. A tidal wave surged through her, starting in her stomach and hitting every single nerve of her body at the same time. Bee had given the Spectres the final piece and they consumed her. Her breathing became raspy, her fingers stretched out. They took over, and she let them. Bee's eyes became the black voids.

Leena unlocked the door, flinging it open, and ran out. She tripped over a dead Reaper, screaming as she fell. Bee walked up behind her, grabbed her ankle and dragged Leena back inside, slamming the door. Bee turned the lock with her thoughts alone, but she didn't hear the key turn.

Malick banged on the door. There was a small window, and Bee ignored his cries, as she turned over Leena, who screamed, kicked, and punched trying to free herself from Bee's clutches.

'I'm... I'm sorry, Bedelia,' Leena whispered.

Bee's black void stared down at Leena. She experienced Leena's terror, and then she whispered. 'I know what you did.' And Bee took out her sword.

Chapter Thirty-Four
Dai Castle, Dai, Kent

The power inside Malick became a flood, almost knocking him to his knees. Whatever this power was, it was pulsing through him, and it hammered through Bee.

Karem killed the Reapers who'd attacked once Bee entered the room. He'd been lucky with a couple of shots, shooting one in the back. The chamber's door opened, both he and Karem watched a woman run across the small landing toward the spiral stairs, only for her to trip.

Neither moved as Bee strode out of the room, grabbed the woman's legs and dragged her back inside. She screamed, clawing at the carpet, foaming at the mouth, begging Bee. Malick was about to intervene, when Karem pulled him back into the shadows, shaking her head.

'Don't,' she whispered.

The door shut. Malick's heart raced, and he banged on the door, crying out for Bee to stop. She rushed through him, her anger, the pain, enveloped him, and then she slowed everything inside herself down. The calm swept over Malick. Bee, instead of being breathless and scared, became tranquil. Her heart rate slowed, and Malick felt the black void wash over Bee and into him. It almost knocked him down, and he could see somewhere in the distance of his inner self, she stood there, alone, and she welcomed this strange existence. The power inside Bee erupted, and Malick tried the door again, but he didn't have the strength to force it open.

'Out of my way,' a man shouted from behind.

Malick saw a finely dressed man, and Karem pulled him aside as the man discharged an unseen force to the door, and the wood exploded, as the man ran inside.

'Bedelia, stop!'

Malick could see Bee standing over the fleeing woman with her sword ready to cut her head off. The man blasted his power into Bee, and she flew back across the chambers, flying into the furniture, breaking it as she crashed back into the wall.

Bee stood as the woman scrambled toward the man. She was different. Her body moved out of time with the rest of the world. The black uniform smouldered. When Bee moved, black smoke followed her. She stood in both in this world and another. Bee dropped the sword, clasped her hands together, and slowly pulled them apart.

'Bee, please don't do this. I'm sorry for what I did, I'm sorry I raped you, and I'm sorry our children are dead,' the man cried.

'You can blame Leena for their deaths, Oren. She planned it, along with Gable. Claude was the one... he started the fire,' Bee snarled.

'What?' the man gasped, 'that's a lie.'

'Ask her,' Bee roared.

There was silence, then mumbling. Malick heard hushed questions, and then the man cried, screaming at the woman at his legs.

Bee rippled through Malick. Oren, the name flashed inside him, and she would not stop. Malick grabbed Karem, hiding back in the shadows. The waves lapped over him, becoming more potent and dangerous, as Bee prepared, and then she let go.

The blast was extraordinary, and Malick thought he might pass out. Bee threw the black sphere she'd created toward Oren and Leena. They flew back, the whole level shook as the force of the blast lifted them off the ground, into the walls behind, and as the tower walls exploded, bricks soared out, their bodies mixing up with the debris as the night air entered the second floor. And Bedelia screamed.

Malick ran inside, sliding toward her. 'Bee?' he whispered.

Nothing in her face said she recognised him. The black void became deadly, and he peered closer, seeing a deep, dangerous swirl inside them, and the wind from the gaping hole she had created in the tower blew gently as seagulls squawked in the distance.

Bee said nothing more, and she leapt up. Malick watched her run toward the gaping hole and jump out.

***

Bee landed, crouching in the courtyard. The impact created a crater around her. Her eyes were still black, but as Bee stood, she saw Dai castle was a wreck as bodies, fallen stones, debris in the air, and dust danced in the night's air. Any animal had vanished, seeking refuge, and the wind had stopped. It felt like the place had taken its last breath.

Bee turned, and there stood more Reapers than she'd ever seen. Row upon row, all wearing helmets. They stood motionless, waiting for the order to shoot. Behind the Reapers stood Eldric and his wife, Gable.

Eldric glimmered, his abilities were so much more forceful than she'd seen when she lived in Lunden Tower. Bee spotted Leena's body sprawled across the rubble, and Oren lay nearby gasping, coughing up blood. She stomped over to Oren, pulling the automatic pistol Luther had placed in the back of her uniform and aimed it at his head.

'Bee...' Blood spluttered out of Oren's mouth.

Bee shot him in the head and turned the gun on Eldric. 'Hello, Alfred,' she said, and behind her words, echoed three more voices.

Bee's energies pulsated as The Spectres roared inside her, and Bee vibrated. She felt everything, as Eldric slivered through her. He glistened in strength, and though he'd killed everybody in Dai and the surrounding villages, he still wouldn't be strong enough.

'Shoot her,' Eldric roared at the Reapers.

Everything slowed down. Bee listened to the distinctive click of the shotgun's trigger, as if each Reaper was preparing individually. Click one, click two, and down the rows it went, but they were all being cocked at the same time.

Bee inhaled, and she stayed firmly where she was. The power stormed inside her. Looking down at her hands, they tremored as she counted, waiting for it to swell.

And then it hit her.

Raising both her arms, the click of the guns not yet finished, Bee waved her hands out in both directions. She lifted the Reapers up, suspending them in the air, and then flung them across the courtyard. Bodies flew so fast, the first Reapers crashed into the stone walls, and the rest followed. Bones cracked as their bodies thudded to the ground. They piled up like old rags.

'Reapers,' Bee shouted, the echoes continued behind. 'Stay down if you want to live.'

Eldric roared angrily, 'Kill that fucking bitch, and I'll give you freedom and lands.'

The surviving Reapers stood, grabbing their weapons. They prepared to fire and then Bee took over. Closing her eyes, she linked to them, breathing slowly. Her hands twitched as Bee fought to control them, and they stood like statues, guns aimed at her. Bee sensed each one. They fought, but she was too strong, and her abilities connected through each of them until she overtook them.

And they turned their weapons on Eldric.

'Fire,' she echoed.

The first crack shattered the silence. Eldric and Gable moved fast, hiding within the castle, the bullets missing them, and then Eldric fought back. He gathered his energy. Bee let it pulse through her, feeling it building as he prepared to attack. He blasted her with such a violent force that Bee flew back into the stone wall, fracturing it. Bee coughed, spitting out mud as rubble fell around her. Dust particles choked Bee and she wiped her forehead, seeing blood on her sleeve.

The Spectres inside her were swelling. They grew in mass, swamping Bee, making her angry, making her a part of them. She wanted them out of her body, but they dominated every inch of her until she drowned in their black lake as if she were being soaked in the thick oil they called life.

Bee slipped, getting up out of the mud. Bullets hailed in her direction. Bee let the black mass coat her, and she held up her hands, crying, stopping the shots in mid-air before they hit her body. Heaving, the bullets remained suspended in the air. So many of them ready to kill her. She summoned the strength, released it and shot the rounds back in the direction they came.

The bullets moved much faster, and the velocity was greater, speeding towards the Reapers. The bullets hit arms, legs, and heads, entering their bodies with such force it sent Reapers flying backwards. Their leather uniform didn't protect them as the bullets they'd shot returned to their own bodies.

Eldric stepped forward, protecting his wife, as Bee ran toward him. He built up a shield, and Bee's darkness crashed into it, and he pushed her back, two powers colliding. Bee accelerated toward her Father, and Eldric compelled her back, Bee skidded backwards in the mud as she drew in the surrounding air, trying to overpower him. Bee couldn't make it through. Instead, she went under.

Still pushing against the shield, Bee allowed the energies to burrow underneath, and black swords sprang up out of the grass. Each one trying to cut and stab at Eldric and Gable, and one went into Gable's heart. Eldric saw what was happening, dropped the shield and rushed to Gable, and he held his dead wife in his arms.

Bee approached, hearing Eldric mutter, begging Gable to stay alive. She leaned over, whispering into his ear. 'You know that barren bitch murdered your grandchildren. All the time she's been married to you, she was fucking Claude. She and Leena murdered them, and Claude set fire to their nursery.'

'No.' He shook his head, looking at Gable as blood trickled out of her dead lips.

'She killed the only opportunities you had.' Bee patted Eldric on the shoulder. 'Don't worry, Father, I killed Claude. I cut off his head, so he won't come back. Not like me.'

'Bee...' he growled, 'you know those things are using you. Why do you hate me so much? You're my daughter, and I should have loved you. Bee... Bedelia, we... we can start again. You... can bring your family with you.'

Bee darkened, remembering Tristan and Viola.

And then Eldric struck.

He summoned his powers, attacking Bee. Bombing her with great fires of energies, and there was nothing to do except retreat. The flames consumed everything from the Reapers to the stalls, and Bee was thrown into the inner bailey's wall. Her body cracked the stone walls, walls which had stood for more than eight centuries.

She turned inward, looking for Malick, and she found him, dazed, dishevelled and wandering in the rubble, alone. He was searching for her, but she'd found him and then Bee plunged inside him, racing through him, making him cry out in pain, as their abilities combined. Bee submerged herself in his blood, and then clawed into his bones, tangling themselves together as one, and he erupted full of fire and pain. Crashing Malick to his knees as Bee took back what she'd hidden inside him. And then like she had done at Arena Porta, Bee detonated.

Every part of her body and soul fractured, as Malick and the Spectres exploded like fire through her. Bee screamed, and it echoed throughout the castle, as the skies above thundered, and she gripped onto Malick galvanising him. Bee became a black drumfire blasting out toward her father, not stopping, and Dai Castle's great Caen stone walls splintered under the heat. But Eldric held his strength. The energy she'd created blew up a wind, and everything became dust, mud, and stone, striking into Dai's inner walls, and Bee broke them down.

Eldric ran toward the dust and debris, the wind surrounding Bee became like a whirlwind, but he got through it. Bee stood there, her eyes black, and she watched him come for her. She didn't know why he wasn't dead, and she weakened from the explosion she'd made.

Eldric grabbed her collar. He pulled her close, a film of dust coated his face, and he sneered. 'See, Bedelia, you will never beat me, because I am a god. I am your God.'

Bee spotted movement with the dust clouds. Closing her eyes, Bee experienced the fear coming from the person within the dust, and she let them inside her, entwining herself to her husband, soothing him as he silently crept toward them.

Bee coughed, spitting blood into Eldric's face. She slipped her hands over Eldric's, gripping them tightly. 'No, Father, don't you understand...' she coughed again. 'There is no God.'

She saw Eldric's eyes darken, confused, and behind him, a dagger rose. The three-bladed knife, her knife, came into view and Malick smashed it into the back of Eldric's head. Blood splattered into her eyes, mouth and face. Eldric gasped, he squeezed Bee's collar, as Malick twisted the blade.

Eldric exploded. Brilliant white light burst out from his body, blowing Bee in one direction and Malick into another. Both lay somewhere in the walls of the inner bailey as the dust settled.

***

Malick's bones hurt. He been thrown into the Keep's wall and the shooting pain around his body were like nothing Malick had ever felt before, and he wanted to lie there forever, preferring to stay still, than to risk discovering he'd broken something. Around him, it was still cloudy, but he could make out bodies, broken stalls, bits of the castle and its wall. Grimacing, he pulled himself up and limped forward. He didn't know where he was going, but Malick wanted to find Bee. The dust was settling, and the fires burned, lighting up the night's sky. Malick inhaled the toxic fumes of bodies crackling under the intense heat. The fatty stench of burning flesh mixed with the sulphur residue of gunfire and burned woodpiles, and he desperately cried out Bedelia's name. His voice shook with each shout and Malick's heart pounded, as tears rolled down his cheeks. He could see nothing in the thick black haze.

There was no answer to his cries.

He stumbled around in the debris, coughing and tripping over the charcoaled bodies shouting, but Bee didn't answer, and then he found her. She stood hunched over, back to him. He scrambled through the dust, pulling her around to face him. Bee's blood-covered face was crusted in white, and her eyes the same black void he'd seen earlier.

'Bee?' he whispered, stroking her face. 'Bee, can you hear me?'

She stared forward.

'Look at me, Bedelia,' he demanded.

'Bee, isn't here.' Three voices came out of Bee's mouth, each one saying the same thing, only a few seconds after the first voice.

Malick stammered, 'What…who…who are you?' he asked, wiping his face. He got hotter, heart racing, as he looked at the woman who was his wife.

'An echo,' the voices answered.

'No…no, no, no, where's my wife?' He gripped hold of her arms, shaking her. 'Where is she?' he repeated, shaking Bee.

The black-eyed Bee placed her hands around Malick's cheeks. 'Don't be afraid,' and then she pulled him close, kissing him passionately.

Malick cried out as Bee rushed through him. He saw a red, watery world, where the trees were dry and barren, and inside each tree fire grew, whirling around, but never burning the bark outside. There were so many trees alight, it brightened the strange half-world. The place was a haze in which he could hardly see, and Bee was there. She was pulling at him, tangling herself inside him, creating that sensual warmth of seduction and fearsome love, like she always did, and she waited.

He saw her, standing on the edge of a precipice. Here she looked different, there was no blood, no dust and no scars around her lips. She was beautiful, as the wind blew around her.

'Bedelia?' He edged closer, heart pounding.

Bee smiled and held out her hand. 'Malick Rose, I will always love you; will you love me?'

'Always,' he whispered, edging closer to Bee, slipping his hand into hers. She pulled him close, wrapping her arms around his body.

'I said you'd keep me safe,' she whispered. 'I don't think I can come home; I think I belong here because I'm a Guardian.'

Malick gripped hold of Bee, he touched her face, the palms of his hands tingling as he smiled at his wife. He shook his head, saying, 'No, you belong to me.' And then he pulled her into the precipice, and they fell into darkness.

Chapter Thirty-Five
Dai Castle, Dai, Kent

Bee coughed.

Dai Castle's inner bailey walls were little more than dust and rubble. Bee's eyes widened, choking on the air. She held tightly onto Malick as she rested her head on his chest. Staring up the red morning glow broke through clouds, and she swam through him, comforting Malick. Bee closed her eyes, enjoying the sensation.

'Thank you,' she whispered into his ear.

He held onto her. 'For what?'

Bee smiled, 'For coming for me.'

She sat up, looking around at the courtyard at the devastation she'd caused. The bodies, the broken castle, the blown-up walls, as the smoke and dust lingered in the air. Standing, Bee held onto Malick, and they stumbled toward The Guardian's gate.

Luther, she remembered Luther. The pain burst. Looking around, pulling away from Malick, Bee screamed his name. Her voice echoed in the silent courtyard, and

Bee cried out again, running toward the Keep. There had been movement, she'd seen his legs move, and reaching the mess of rocks at the bottom of the keep, Luther wasn't there.

'Bee?' Malick followed.

'Luther.' She stared at Malick, and a tear rolled down her cheek. 'I can't find Luther.' And she hollered out his name, stumbling over the rubble, tripping up.

Together they searched, Bee becoming more frantic, pulling over the bodies of Reapers, praying one of them was him. Malick called out his name, but nothing. Bee choked, scrabbling over the rocks, moving anything which lay in her way.

And then she found Luther, propped up against the north wall, with Karem next to him. She ran over, skidding as she came to a stop. Bee shuddered, he'd been shot twice, once in the stomach and also in the back, but somehow, he was still breathing. Karem had bandaged him up, but the blood came through. He would not live much longer.

'Luther?' She got down on all fours, her face close to his, whispering his name.

Bleary-eyed, Luther looked up. He smiled, and a little blood encased his teeth. 'My Bedelia,' he whispered, 'I never forgot you.' A tear rolled down his cheek.

'I never forgot you either, Luther.'

Karem got up and stood next to Malick, and both watched as the man lay dying.

'And... and I'm going to take you home. I'll take you home, where you can get better,' Bee gushed, wiping the tear from his eye.

'I… I think I might just stay here a while,' he whispered. 'I'm dying, Bee.'

'No, I love you, Luther, you can't die.' She wiped her own face, smudging the blood with her tears, as they trickled down her face. 'You… you just need to rest.'

Luther closed his eyes. He breathed slowly and then looked at Bee. 'Thank you… for rescuing me that day.'

Bee touched his face, attentively, each fingertip stretching out on his cheeks. 'I'm going to take you home,' she whimpered.

'I was… was never allowed to tell you I love you,' he wheezed.

Bee heaved a smile, wiping tears from her cheek. 'You told me every day. When you shot me, when you risked everything to hold me, and when you rested your hand on my belly, and in the way you smiled when Hamish kicked inside me. I love you and always have.' She sniffed, wiping her nose on her sleeve.

He put his hand up to her face. 'I'm glad you came home. I got to see my Bedelia, one last time.'

Bee blabbed out a snotty laugh. 'I'm your ghost. I left you, and I'll never do it again.' She blubbered, squeezing his hand as she brushed the hair out of Luther's eyes. 'We didn't have the life together we should have had.'

Luther touched her blood encrusted face. 'I wanted to give you the life you have with Malick.'

Bee whispered, 'And I wanted that with you, Luther.'

'I remember that triumphant look on your face when you held up that Reaper's head to Rufus,' he laughed, wheezing as he held Bedelia's face. 'I knew then, you would be my Unseen. I'm…glad, I spent… my life with you.'

'I wouldn't have spent it with anybody else. I love you, Luther,' she carried on babbling.

'Please, Bee, do it,' he gasped.

'I don't want to.' She pressed her forehead to his. 'Please, please don't make me,' she begged.

'We promised,' Luther smiled, blood leaking through the gums in his mouth, and he coughed, choking. 'I am not alone as I walk out of the darkness with you by my side.'

'No, Luther,' Bee sobbed.

'You have to.'

'No, I can make it better. I can–' she pressed her hands against his chest, willing her abilities into Luther, but nothing came. Bee's powers were exhausted, and she cried, wanting help.

He struggled for air. 'Please, Bee.'

'I...I don't want to; I've only just found you.'

'We will always be together, Bedelia Rose.' He squeezed her hand. 'I am not...alone as I walk out of the darkness with you by my side,' he choked.

Bee wiped the tears from her face, inside her heart shattered. 'And I remain in the darkness and wait for you until it is my time to die.' Bee cupped her bloodied hands around his face, and she kissed him and kept kissing him. Luther touched her cheek, and they were together, as one, like they'd always been. Bee pulled out her small dagger and plunged it into his neck. Luther's body convulsed for a second and was still.

Bee stared at the slumped body of her best and only friend. Sitting back on her knees, she let out a cry which rapidly turned into a nightmarish scream.

And, in the distance, what Bee didn't see was the beginning of a fire inside Dai Castle's Temple. The pain of losing Luther was too much, and she howled. Bee's anger and sadness spread to all the Guardian Temples in Dai and beyond. She was burning all the traces of the Guardians out of the land.

Bee lay next to Luther, like she had done when she'd been pregnant, took his hand in hers, resting her head on his shoulder and she cried.

***

Malick didn't know how long he'd stood watching over his wife. The temple fire took hold, but as everything else in the castle was still in flames, it made little difference to Malick, as he watched Bee cry into the shoulder of the one person she loved, and then killed. There would be nothing he could say to make it right. He ignored the voices coming up from behind, and then Tristan was at Malick's side, tugging on his sleeve.

'Papa,' the boy called.

Malick looked down, surprised to see Tristan and he kneeled, cuddling his son, and he kissed the boy. Behind, in the Guardian's gate, were Rufus, Somer and Sagan. All three stood in the morning sunlight, horses behind them, waiting.

'Tristan.' He stroked the young boy's face, smiling. 'I think Mamma wants to see you.' Taking the boy's hand, Malick led him to Bee.

Tristan looked up, confused at seeing his mother next to another man. 'Why is she crying?' he asked.

'Because Luther's the man she loved before me. She still loves him.'

The boy frowned. 'Mamma,' he said in a tiny voice, 'Mamma, can we go home now?'

Bee's eyes sprang open. Malick saw bewilderment as she stared at Tristan. Her eyes widened, and she pulled herself away from Luther, hurrying on all fours towards her son.

Tristan stepped back, his face crumpling. He hid behind Malick, keeping hold of his father's hand.

'Mamma doesn't look right,' he said timidly.

Bee pulled Tristan into her arms, kissing him, holding him as she cried. Malick crouched down, slipping his arms around both of them. 'We'll take Luther home,' he whispered, pulling Bee up and taking Tristan into his arms.

The men approached with the horses. Sounds came back to the castle, as the animals whinnied; ruffling their necks and the hooves clopped into the mud and stone. Somer took hold of Tristan while Malick held Bee up.

Bee stopped in front of Rufus, looking at the man who brought her up. The man who lashed her severely if she'd got things wrong. He taught her to read and write, forcing her to become a better Reaper, and made her listen to the voices inside her head and learn from them. Bee stared at the man who made her what she was.

'Thank you, Father,' she whispered.

Rufus gazed at Bee, and he wrapped his arms around his daughter, taking her away from Malick as she fell into him crying. Bee clung to him as he rocked her, like he did on the few occasions Rufus had showed her affection as a child.

'You can go home now, Bee,' he whispered to her, kissing her forehead as she rested on his chest and Bee gurgled a tiny laugh.

Bee freed herself of Rufus, she rubbed her face with the sleeve of her uniform, wiping her tears, and then she looked at Sagan. 'You have what you want, you can start again now.'

'We need you, Bedelia,' Sagan reminded her. 'The people will follow you.'

Bee looked up at the Keep. The gibbet wasn't on fire anymore. 'I don't know what kind of a leader Adeen will make, but perhaps with your guidance, Lord Sagan, she'll be better than her grandfather.' And Bee watched Sagan's face pale because a seven-year-old girl was about to take the throne of Britain.

Chapter Thirty-Six
Bononia-Sur-Mur, Northern France

Today was the day Bee was going to leave the house for the first time in three months. Snow lay outside, unusual for December as it usually came late in January or early February.

Tristan and Adam let out riotous laughs, as snowballs hit the side of the house. The kitchen fire roared, warming the place as Bee sat with Viola crawling all over her. Not caring that Bee's belly had swollen as she was now four months pregnant. Everything Bee had smashed up when she'd murdered Philip was replaced, and now it really felt like home.

She'd told Malick she was pregnant after they'd returned from Britain. Bee hadn't known for sure, but when Malick threw her off the precipice, she'd seen the protection the Spectres had given her. The way they'd warmed her, shielded her, and loved Bee for what she had done.

These Spectres had long since gone. They returned to their Farscape, taking the abilities with them, and the world returned to a place where nobody could use them to have power over other people. The Guardians were dead.

All except for Bedelia.

She still possessed traces of her abilities. They weren't as strong, but she could feel them every day pulsing through her. She didn't know why these spectres hadn't taken them, but it still warmed her to know she had a little of them somewhere inside. Malick was also left with traces, the connection they had was still there, and as strong as it ever had been. These abilities they shared brought them closer to one another, and they fell in love all over again.

Malick was furious when she told him she was pregnant and how far gone she was. He'd seen everything Bee's body had gone through and worried she'd hurt the baby, but Bee assured him The Spectres protected the child. He scolded Bee but beamed proudly and didn't stay angry for long.

'Let me take her.' Stephen picked Viola up, ignoring the 'Mamma' wails as he placed her on the ground, giving her some blocks to play with.

'Thank you, Stephen,' Bee smiled. The young man, who once worked for Omega, now lived with them. He and Esther formed an attachment during the time he was guarding her. Stephen stayed after Bee and Malick returned from Britain, and that was the first scandal because neither of them wanted to marry.

Watching Stephen as he helped Esther hang the new curtains, she thought about Omega, wondering where she was, where she was hiding. Bee and Rufus searched the dungeons and grounds of Dai Castle, turning over the bodies. They'd found either empty or dead bodies in the cells, and there was no sign of Omega or any of her riders. She'd escaped before Bee could kill her.

Bee hadn't stayed in Britain too long after Malick murdered Eldric. She took Winnie's body back to Virgil and Nell, explaining everything, and how their daughter had helped stop Eldric.

No words or apologies made up for the loss of a child, as Nell slapped, and thrashed her fists into Bee's chest, blaming Bee because she was a Guardian and worse than that, she was a Reaper. Nell collapsed at Bee's feet, begging for Winnifred and Bee did nothing except watch a mother crumple with grief. Bee paid her respects to the sister she never knew, and watched the coffin being cremated.

Lord Sagan Kendal rode to The Tower and proclaimed his eldest daughter, Adeen, the new Regent of Britain. The council weren't happy, but accepted Adeen being the only surviving relative of Eldric, and next in line for the throne. They were relieved to learn that the girl possessed no Guardian abilities, and Sagan explained, Eldric reported that her twin brother, Oliver, had consumed all of Adeen's abilities when she'd been growing inside Bedelia's womb. Sagan then lied to the council saying Bedelia had died at Dai Castle.

Sagan would be the new Regent's advisor until she was eighteen, and the seven-year-old began her education in how to rule a country. Faith decided Zoe would have the same education because then Adeen would always have somebody she trusted, close. The council and Sagan started to work on new charters, dismantling the Reaper system, and bringing in new laws which would reshape Britain, and the country offered assistance to France and Europe to help rebuild.

Karem stayed with Adeen, appointing herself the new Regent's bodyguard. Bee told her she didn't have to do it, that she was free to do whatever she wanted, but the Reaper replied, *'It is what Luther would have done.'*

Faith, Bee was told, took in Oren's children. She explained their parents had died in an accident at Dai Castle, and they would now live in the Royal Palace with Adeen and Zoe, rather than the apartments.

Bee sailed back on the Juna with Tristan and Malick by her side. She asked Adam if he wanted to join their family, and Tristan's face shone at the thought of having an older brother. Bee breathed more easily, at never having to set foot on British soil again. Teppo had looked for a signal, saying he didn't know what it would be, but when The Barricade came down, he figured that was a good enough reason to sail back. He hugged Somer when he saw his younger brother and scolded him for getting shot.

Rufus came with them, telling Malick that he wanted to spend time with his daughter, get to know his son-in-law, and all his grandchildren. The way Rufus said it, it was not a suggestion, and he was coming whether or not Malick liked it.

When Bee opened the door to her home for the first time, she ran, picking up Viola, cradling, crying and kissing her baby daughter. She hadn't wanted to be anywhere else, as Viola grumbled, and she hugged Esther, and Bee didn't want to let go.

Bee rested for a week, and then she and Rufus rode down to Dulpenne. She'd suggested Malick remain with the children, and they argued over the pregnancy. Bee compromised, and they took the carriage. The factoria was deserted except for the Britons.

They freed them, and Rufus and Bee burned everything. The prisoners were taken to Bononia, and Malick sailed them back to Britain.

Rufus started travelling around the region, and would come back every few days. He and Bee would have discussions, and Malick would ask what they were talking about. Rufus would smile, saying he was taking in the new country, learning about the people.

Bee sometimes found Malick sitting in the bedroom, staring out of the window. She'd watched him from the door, noticing the way his shoulders hunched. Bee lay on the bed with him, letting him hold her. She'd never experienced the guilt of killing another person, but watching Malick in his quiet torment tore into Bee because she didn't know what to do. Bee asked if he wanted her to take away the pain, that she would hide it away with her own heartache, but Malick always said 'No', saying it was his guilt, and he needed to settle it.

Bee only told Rufus that it was Malick who killed Eldric. There were still many Guardian believers in Bononia, and Bee took the blame. She was hard enough to deal with their comments, and they were afraid of her because they thought she might kill them.

Bedelia Rose, being a Guardian and a Reaper became the next piece of gossip, to sweep through Bononia, and it made Esther's and Stephen's living arrangements old and unimportant news.

Before the destruction of The Barricade, people rarely spoke to Bee, as they considered her odd, and blamed her for the partition. Most called her names because she'd married Malick so quickly after Nadine's death, but now people wanted to talk to her.

People wanted to take afternoon tea at the Roses'. They'd knock at the door, and it was Stephen and Esther who sent them politely away. They didn't really want to talk to Bee. They wanted to look at the scarred face of a Reaper, drink tea with one, and gossip with their friends that they'd spent time at the Rose household and survived.

The only people Bee allowed into their home were Aimee and Gerald from the tavern. Aimee had always been protective of Bee before the Barricade came down, and even when she learned about Bee's background, she simply shrugged her shoulders, saying, *'Well that makes sense.'* Aimee had called that morning, she'd made Bee a beautiful dress, and Bee was going to wear it out.

Teppo and Somer spent more time at the house. They'd bought another boat, and went into partnership with Malick, allowing Malick to spend more time with Bee, and she loved it.

Bee was no longer half a person. Malick had seen the things she'd done in Britain, witnessed the brutality, and he experienced her loving, warm side. He'd seen his wife in full, and though she was frightening, Malick never backed away.

'I'll be outside,' Bee said to Esther, lacing up her heavy boots, putting on her thick coat, hat, gloves, and she took a small bunch of wildflowers, she'd managed to find growing at the front of the house.

'Do you want me to walk with you?' Stephen asked, opening the door, letting the cold in, and he shouted at the boys. 'Your Mother's coming past, don't go throwing snowballs.'

Bee smiled, hearing groans from Tristan and Adam. 'No, thank you.'

She made her way past the vegetable patch, and the shed, up to the old tree, and a quiet bit of the garden. And Bee stood before the grave.

Malick had ordered the stone mason from another town to make a headstone. Bee refused to have Luther cremated, and she refused to have a Guardian ceremony because even though there were no more guardians, the people still wanted something to believe in. While new religions were creeping up from east and west, some people still held onto their old beliefs. Priest Felix had come around asking if Bee wanted him to perform the ceremony, and she politely shooed him away. Bee didn't believe in anything. Having spent so much time around death, growing up with it, she and Luther only ever knew living and dead, and nothing would change that.

Placing a small bunch of flowers on the headstone, all it said was 'Luther' nothing more. Malick brought him home. Bee always liked the headstones she'd seen in the Temples, they'd belonged to a dead religion, and she was content to have one for Luther, and Bee kept him in the back garden, where he could be close.

'Is that a new dress?' Malick asked, he came up behind her, slipping his arms around Bee, and kissing her on the neck.

Bee held onto Malick. 'Aimee made it for me. Your favourite doesn't fit me at the moment, so she made me this.'

He smiled. 'Green suits you, really shows off your scars.'

Bee laughed. Her face was different now. The pellet wounds had healed, leaving her face potted, but she still had that dangerous smile.

The backdoor opened, Rufus shouted, 'Bee, the buggy's ready. Let's get you down to that bloody pub before you change your fucking mind.'

Malick stiffened around Bee as Rufus shouted, and the boys giggled. Bee smiled, Malick learnt to say nothing if she swore, it was the way Rufus and Bee spoke to each other. The way they told each other they loved one another, and somehow, they muddled along.

Kissing the children 'goodbye', Bee's heart skipped a beat as she stepped out of the front door and got into the buggy. Rufus held the reins as Malick helped her up. All three of them sat wrapped up, making it a tight squeeze.

The small town was quiet, as the snow kept most people inside. This was why Bee had chosen tonight, knowing the weather would keep most customers away. Rufus stationed the vehicle outside The Raven, and Malick alighted, helping Bee down.

Bee shook a little. She wanted to step back, turn and go home. People inside would look at her, their eyes would see the scars on her face and, eventually, they'd ask questions.

'Shall we? And remember, you only work for an hour, and then I'll carry on,' Malick whispered, taking her hand, guiding Bee toward the door.

Nothing had changed, the same people stood at the bar, and it had the same smoky smells. People muttered, watching Bedelia as Aimee gave her a kiss, allowing her to walk behind the bar as Rufus came in and asked for a beer. Malick took a seat at the end of the bar.

Bee filled the tankard, handing it to him. She spotted Helena approaching, the scraggy woman looked even worse, her skin decayed, and Helena had a sweet sickly scent, which made Bee want to gag. If she hadn't been pregnant, she wouldn't have noticed the deathly smell.

Helena coughed, worried. 'Hello, Mrs Rose,' she said politely, slipping a coin across the table. 'I see your trip to Britain has made you even prettier than you were before.'

Bee studied Helena, pouring the beer. She said, 'Yes, Helena, almost as pretty as you.'

Chapter Thirty-Seven
Dulpenne, Spanish Netherlands

Marisol rode through Dulpenne, the place she'd once called home. This had been her kingdom. The moonlight shone down, and the muddy streets were quiet. She'd heard what had happened once Bedelia Rose and her father came through.

They'd set everything alight.

The townsfolk had not stopped them. They'd heard the whispers that Bee was a Reaper, and that while the Guardians were dead, she still had some of her abilities. Marisol didn't know if that was true, but nobody dared find out.

It had been just under a year since Marisol had been back in this part of the Spanish Netherlands. She'd listened to the whispers that Bee had given birth to another daughter, who was about two months old now, and Marisol considered it safe to return to Dulpenne and collect her money.

Everything she'd earned from the factoria was hidden in a secret place. She'd buried it deep, and Marisol prayed the fire hadn't consumed her money. The horse plodded through the quiet town.

No torches were burning, and only the tavern was busy. Stopping the horse, she dismounted and went inside. Marisol kept her mask on, and she'd grown her hair, hoping nobody would recognise her. She paid for a beer and got a room for the night, not wanting to spend too long in the town.

Taking the beer through to a small snug, she sipped it and thought about how Bee really was a hard bitch. The woman had been pregnant when she'd entered the bar in Britain and killed all those riders without even a second thought, and though Bee was powerful enough to protect her husband when she shot him, she still shot him. Only a cold-bloodied killer would do something like that.

And yet, Marisol admired Bedelia Rose, wondering if things had been different, what would they have been like as sisters. She remembered seeing the baby being taken away, and Marisol had cried for the death of her little sister, because she'd believed her mother when she was told the baby had died.

Foolish, Marisol thought, and she finished her beer. Taking the key from the barkeep, Marisol followed the candle-lit corridor and placed the key in the door. The room smelled stale, musky, and of old smoke. She could just make out a vanity table next to the bed. She wanted a nap, and then she'd go get her money. Marisol decided it was better to wait until it was after midnight before she went looking. She didn't light a candle, instead, threw her bag onto the bed and lay down.

Marisol woke. She didn't know how long she'd slept, but it was still dark outside, and the moon shone through glittering light into her room. Marisol sat up, staring at it, it looked quite pretty.

Something moved in the room's corner. Marisol shivered; somebody was behind her.

'You really are a cold-hearted bitch,' Marisol said. 'I thought because you'd had a new baby, you'd forget about me. Carry on with your life, but I guess once a Reaper...'

Bee moved out of the shadows. She stood before her, dressed in the black Reaper uniform, her auburn hair short. 'That's correct, Marisol.'

Marisol gave a mirthful laugh.

'You wasted your time coming here,' Bee whispered, and Marisol gave her a bewildered look. 'Rufus and me, we found your money, we sent it back to Britain, it ain't much, but it might help those families of the people you killed.'

Marisol remained on the bed. 'I'm not going to beg for my life.' She spotted the revolver in Bee's hand.

Bee stared down at her. 'I don't expect you to. I'm killing you because you killed Winnie, and because you made Tristan watch Philip being dug up.'

'And what will your husband, your children, think of this? Malick will learn of my murder, he'll know it was you.'

'He'll think - it's over,' Bee said. She cocked the revolver, aimed it at Marisol's head, and pulled the trigger until the chamber was empty. Omega lay dead on the bed, her crimson blood soaking into the old blanket and sheets.

And then Bedelia was gone.

Milton Keynes UK
Ingram Content Group UK Ltd.
UKHW020658290124
436892UK00018B/613

9 781915 164087